THE TRAI

Three days later t
the entire operatic
and had been wrun
of information. He
was painstaking, t ... relieved when at last Major Lawrenson said, 'I think it's time for you to leave here.' He stood up, a strange expression on his face, and pressed the bell-push on the table.

The door opened, and Lawrenson gestured towards it. He refused to meet the other's eye.

The man walked into the corridor, then stopped as if he'd been smashed in the face. Waiting for him were two soldiers of the uniformed branch of the Czech State Security service. They were carrying M14 automatic rifles. There was another man, in plain clothes, who gave what passed for a smile, revealing six stainless-steel teeth.

'Hello, Vaclav,' he said in heavily accented Czech. 'You didn't really think you'd slipped away from us?'

THE TRAITOR MACHINE

MAX MARQUIS

THE TRAITOR MACHINE

ISBN 0 600 32989 5
A Hamlyn Original

First published in Great Britain 1980
by Hamlyn Paperbacks

Hamlyn Paperbacks are published by
The Hamlyn Publishing Group Ltd,
Astronaut House,
Feltham,
Middlesex, England
(Paperbacks Division: Banda House,
Cambridge Grove, Hammersmith,
London W6 0LE)

Made and printed in Great Britain by
Hunt Barnard Printing Ltd, Aylesbury, Bucks

PROLOGUE

The car's engine faltered again, and the driver swore viciously. The words were forced out of him by panic, not anger, for his heart was labouring as painfully as the engine. If he didn't get to the rendezvous, he was dead. In a few hours they'd find that the files were missing, and that he had disappeared with them. There'd be no second chance to get away.

God knew when the Moscovitch car had last been serviced. Poor-quality petrol, and a set of points that should have been changed months ago, were nearly enough to strangle the last sparks of life out of the engine. Not that he could have driven much faster, even if the car was capable of it. Rain lashed the windscreen, and turned a bad road into an almost impossible one. The wiper blades should have been replaced two winters ago, but getting spares for a Russian car wasn't all that easy. One headlight was little more than a token yellow glow. The car pitched and rocked, barely under his control, and all the time the engine was as irregular as a dying heart. Water dripped through the battered vehicle at a dozen places, and even ran down the inside of the windscreen. He could be a yard from a brick wall, or the edge of a cliff, and not know it. From time to time he caught glimpses of hedges on either side, just often enough for him to orientate himself and keep the car on the road.

And all the time he was aware of time racing by. If he arrived ten minutes late at the rendezvous his contact would be gone, and he'd be left alone to die – by his own hand if he was lucky, or his captors' when they inevitably caught up with him.

When the voice on the telephone had given him the details, it all seemed straightforward enough. That was before he'd seen the car he'd have to use, and before the weather broke so pitilessly. Now five minutes of his precious margin of safety had gone, and he was still half an hour's normal run from the meeting point.

He became aware that he was gripping the juddering steering-wheel so hard that his hands had gone numb. He wasn't sure if he still had the power to unclench his fingers. He made a profound effort to relax a little.

He was hunched up, leaning forward as if he was physically urging the car on, so he forced himself to sit upright, his arms straight out in front of him to hold the wheel. He took a few deep breaths.

Next he decided to lift his right index finger from the wheel. He glanced down to see if the unfeeling hand had obeyed the message from his brain. The finger was raised, away from the wheel. This small triumph of control briefly helped ease the tension that was making his heart hammer loudly enough, it seemed to him, to be heard above the wild racket of the night.

Without warning another spasm of fear gripped him, making his bowels go icily slack.

He'd missed the turn-off.

He *must* have missed it. It was six kilometres past the stone bridge, on the right, just past a barn and a pylon – that's what the voice on the phone had said.

He looked at the odometer, but it indicated he'd gone only five kilometres since the bridge. That couldn't be right. He checked it against his watch.

Just over seven minutes? But it had seemed like an age, like a journey to the end of the earth and beyond.

A flash of lightning demonstrated its unbelievable power by suddenly painting the landscape a shadowless white to the very horizon, a dazzling white so intense that it seared the eye. The massive, lowering clouds were incongruously turned to silver, and the dark, punishing rain was transformed for a microsecond into motionless glittering jewels that remained imprinted on the retina long after the light had gone.

The driver saw none of it. Two hundred metres or so ahead were a barn and a pylon, with the entrance to a turn-off plain to see. His heart leapt, but this time with hope. He took the lightning for a sign. For the first time in a long while he really believed that he would succeed.

He took the turn-off, towards the even darker blackness of a wood. He kept his eye on the odometer and, exactly where he had been told, the road widened for a few metres. The car slithered to a stop. A few yards ahead was a medium-sized truck. Just perceptible in the light of the car's headlights was the TIR sign on the back. That meant the truck was sealed by the customs of the country of departure, and the contents wouldn't be examined by the customs of intervening countries until it arrived at the country of destination.

He picked up the briefcase from the seat beside him and walked awkwardly towards the truck, trying to ease the stiffness out of his neck and shoulders.

He forgot to switch off the headlights.

A man dressed in a leather jacket and dark trousers climbed down from the cab and took a few steps towards him. His flat Slavic face was expressionless, his eyes unblinking despite the rain. 'Are you Mich – ?' the man from the car started to say, but the truck driver cut him short.

'No names.' He paused. 'You look awful. You can stop worrying now. Drink some of this.' He held out a flask.

The fugitive took it, and drank deeply, then coughed as the spirit burned his throat. The cheap cognac left an unpleasant, slightly sulphurous taste in his mouth, but that could have been the cigarettes he'd been smoking.

The truck driver turned, beckoning him to follow. Passing the TIR boards, he remembered that the customs seals on these trucks were difficult to fake. He wondered how the driver was going to hide him.

The truck driver climbed into the cab first, leaving the door open, and moved the passenger seat from its position. He pressed against the partition, and a small opening appeared, just big enough for a man to slide through. The man from the car squeezed through it painfully, and was surprised to find himself in a comfortable and relatively spacious concealed compartment. There was even a faint light from a tiny bulb.

Less than five minutes after the truck began to move away, the man from the car was deep in the sleep of mental and physical exhaustion. He woke briefly when the truck stopped, and he could hear men moving round the vehicle, examining the seal, looking underneath it. There were muffled voices, the engine started up again, and the truck rolled forward. He felt a wild surge of exultation when it was obvious that the truck had crossed the border, then unaccountably he felt drowsy again. His last coherent thought was that the cognac had been drugged. *Like a bloody lapdog being smuggled through English Customs to avoid quarantine,* he thought. *Well, at least I haven't got rabies.* He had a momentary lunatic desire to bark, but was asleep again almost before the thought was formed.

'My name is Major Lawrenson,' the tall man in the plain grey suit told him next morning. 'I hope they made you comfortable.'

The man nodded. Rested, bathed, shaved, dressed in new clothes – *and* on the other side of the border – he felt a new man.

'It's a bit primitive here, I'm afraid,' Lawrenson went on. 'A former transit camp. Still, you'll only be here a couple of days, then you'll go on to Vienna while we arrange your new documents and all that. I'm afraid we've got to give you a debriefing here – details of everything you did once you decided to . . . ' He avoided the awkward word 'defect' and added ' . . . while it's all still clear in your memory.'

It'll always *be clear in my memory – for the rest of my life,* he thought, but didn't say anything.

'Terrible bore, but there it is. At least you speak good English, so we won't need an interpreter. They always slow things down.' Lawrenson led the way into a small, bare room with only a table and two chairs in it. 'Shall we begin?' he said politely.

Three days later the man had gone over the entire operation half a dozen times, from the moment of his first contact to his delivery across the border, and had been wrung dry of the last drop of information. He was as patient as he was painstaking, but he was relieved when at last Major Lawrenson said, 'I think it's time for you to leave here.' He stood up, a strange expression on his face, and pressed the bell-push on the table.

The door opened, and Lawrenson gestured towards it. He refused to meet the other's eye.

The man walked into the corridor, then stopped as if he'd been smashed in the face. Waiting for him were two soldiers of the uniformed branch of the STB – *Statni Tajna Bezpecnost*, the Czech State Secret Security service. They were carrying M14 automatic rifles. There was another man, in plain clothes – an old-fashioned suit with baggy trousers. He gave what passed for a smile, revealing six stainless-steel teeth. They were not the hardest-looking part of him.

'Hello, Vaclav,' the plain-clothes man said in heavily accented Czech. 'You didn't really think you'd slipped away from us?' He gave a chuckle even more terrifying than the smile.

For a long moment Vaclav was paralysed, shattered to realise how easily he'd been tricked into believing he'd crossed the border from Czechoslovakia into Austria. Much worse: how he'd betrayed every single person who'd helped him in his flight.

Last of all, he contemplated what would happen to him now. He set off at a despairing run he knew was useless, but he had to try. As he took the first couple of paces towards the window at the far end of the corridor, he actually hoped they'd shoot him.

At least that'll be better than –

The corridor suddenly exploded and he felt himself falling, grateful to escape them this way. But soon he was aware that he hadn't been shot. He was lying on the floor, his head spinning, warm blood from a broken nose trickling back into his throat and making him choke for breath. One of the soldiers had caught him full in the face with the butt of his M14.

'Do be careful,' the man in the baggy trousers said with mock reproof to the soldier. 'Don't mark his face.' He stretched out a hand to help Vaclav to his feet. 'Come along,' he said. 'You're going to be a film star.' He gave that awful chuckle.

All the fears that Vaclav had known in the past few days and the past few minutes were as nothing compared to his icy terror when full realisation of what that meant flooded over him.

1

'God, what a marvellous view,' she said. 'It's so beautiful . . . and romantic. If I lived here I'd do nothing but look out of the window all day long.'

They were on the top floor of Dolphin Square, the large block of flats on Chelsea Embankment facing the river. Richard Carr wasn't all that sold on the view. The Thames at night could look attractive enough; but a large stretch of weed-covered wasteland, a GPO van park, Nine Elms, the New Covent Garden Market and the Power Station on the other side of the river didn't bring stars to his eyes. Still, it was true that if you stood tiptoe on the end of the divan and leaned out of the window, you could just see the tops of the tallest trees in a corner of Battersea Park.

He was much more impressed by the back view of the girl at the window. Her name was Elizabeth Hughes, but he called her Peg-the-Legs because she was Welsh and had legs like Mistinguett's, *interminables.* Her figure was lithe and boyish, and as she turned to walk towards him, it was obvious why. She had the toes-turned-out walk that professional footballers call 'quack-footed', and that instantly betrays the ballet dancer.

The taped music from the hi-fi segued into *An American in Paris*, and Peg-the-Legs did a few steps of modern dance. It was quite spectacular, high kicks and all, because she was stark naked, like Carr himself.

They had met three months previously at a Buckingham Palace Garden Party, which she thought was an excellent character reference, but Carr knew that you could get even Garden Party tickets from the leading ticket touts, at a price. He'd given her a lift home to her flat in Putney, and taken her out to supper the next night. Predictably she had the appetite of a python, even if her manners were rather better.

Now it was a little after midnight, and for the past four hours they'd been drinking champagne and making love, on and off.

'That turned you on,' she said, lying beside him. It was manifestly impossible to deny it. Not that he wanted to.

Ballet dancers, contrary to popular belief, don't get all that much sex. Their biggest problem is that they frighten the hell out of most men. Fragile and doe-eyed they may look from a distance, floating about the stage with their feet hardly touching the floor, but get them undressed and lying next to you . . .

Intertwined with Carr's legs, those long shapely limbs that seemed so smooth and graceful when Peg was at the window were now obviously as hard as a wrestler's, the muscles clearly defined and powerful. Her diaphragm was ridged and unyielding as a washboard. Even her small, but perfectly formed, breasts were as firm as polystyrene.

A woman who can run up three flights of stairs without losing her breath and then squeeze the life out of the average male with her thighs engenders all sorts of feelings of inadequacy in most men. She appeals only to a man whose own physical condition is exceptional – or whose sexual tastes are ambivalent. Carr, however, was thoroughly enjoying himself with Peg-the-Legs. He was very fit, and he never indulged in feelings of inadequacy: they could prove to be literally fatal. Besides, she wasn't hard *all* over. Among other things, her mouth was soft and seductive, her hands gentle and expert. Added to that, she could get into some extraordinary positions without the slightest strain. Finally, she had enormous stamina, so she could join in the love-making with a great deal of activity on her own account. It all added up to a rich experience.

At last Carr rolled to one side and poured a couple of glasses of Moët et Chandon – hardly the finest champagne, of course, but it seemed to go best with the Rémy Martin cognac he generously added to it for both of them. Curiously, the mixture never gave him a hangover.

He sipped his drink, dragged himself to his feet and slowly walked to the shower. He stood for a long while under the rapidly pulsing jets of alternating very hot and very cold water. The champagne-brandy mixture and the expensive Swedish shower were two of his few judicious indulgences.

The phone rang, its high-pitched warbling note clearly audible even from the shower.

'Let the bloody thing ring,' the girl said. 'It's probably a wrong number, and if it isn't, it ought to be. Ignore it.'

Carr walked into the living-room, leaving a trail of dark wet footsteps on the carpet. He picked up the phone. 'Hello,' he said in a voice without expression.

'Hello, Richard,' a man replied. 'This is Godfrey.' Then, after a pause. 'Are you alone?'

'Yes, there's nobody here,' Carr said, winking at the naked girl near his feet. 'You can talk all right.'

The man who said his name was Godfrey, which it wasn't, knew at once that Carr meant that there *was* someone with him. It was a convention that had honourable beginnings, a code that the Resistance used in the war,

When you rang a member of the Resistance you could never be sure that he didn't have the Gestapo standing beside him, poking a gun into his ribs. So you asked *Are you alone?* and the answer was always the opposite of the truth. *Yes, there's nobody with me; it's perfectly all right to come over* meant *The bastards are here: stay away!*

By now Peg-the-Legs had scrambled to her feet and was pressing her ear to the phone in Carr's hand. She wasn't jealous, only curious, she told herself, which made her as big a liar as 'Godfrey' and Carr.

'I'm afraid I have to tell you that Aunt Alice has taken a turn for the worse, and I really think you should come to see her. She's been asking for you.'

Alice was top priority. *Aunt Bertha* or *Uncle Bill* was next in importance, followed by *Aunt Celia* or *Uncle Charles.* The name wasn't important, only the initial letter: A, B or C.

'I've taken the liberty of sending a minicab to collect you. I hope that's all right?'

'Yes, of course,' Carr said formally. 'I'm sorry she's ill. Tell her I'm on my way.' He hung up and shrugged apologetically at Peg.

'How long will you be?' she asked.

'No idea.'

A thought struck her. 'Is she rich, your aunt?' Peg-the-Legs wasn't Welsh for nothing.

'Filthy. And she's left me all her 1914 Imperial Russian War Loan stock in her will.' While she worked it out he went into the bedroom to dress, calling out over his shoulder, 'Stay here if you like. I'll be as quick as I can, but if you have to go before I get back, give me a ring some time.'

It was perfectly safe to leave her. There was nothing in the apartment for her or anyone else to find. In the most unlikely possibility of her planting a bug, the most any eavesdropper would hear, between now and the next electronic sweep of the flat, would be heavy breathing.

The minicab was waiting outside for him, although Carr thought the Princess saloon deserved a better title. He recognised the chauffeur, a man named Donald Something or Something Donald. He was ex-Flying Squad, whose drivers have a deserved reputation for skilful driving, knowledge of London, and tight mouths. The car belonged to the firm run by the headquarters of British Intelligence at Waterloo. The minicab firm was in the phone-book and did a lot of legitimate business with an unsuspecting public. It was an ideal arrangement, because that made it difficult for anyone interested to know precisely which cars to follow and when. The firm also actually made a small profit. Not a profit in the class of some CIA operations like airlines and publishing houses – and, once, part share of a brothel – but better than a permanent hole in the budget.

Carr sat in the back, his face half hidden as the car moved along Chelsea Embankment, Grosvenor Road and Millbank. Donald kept the car to what he considered a reasonable speed, which meant that it was in no immediate danger of actually taking off. He crossed the river at Lambeth Bridge, thus avoiding the one-way system on the north side of Westminster Bridge.

British Intelligence headquarters in the Waterloo Station area is not difficult to spot. It is a twenty-storey glass and concrete building of the Modern Shoebox school of architecture, surrounded by scaffolding festooned with wire netting, which seems to have been there since the place was built. The windows of the lower floors are screened with heavy net curtains or venetian blinds, or both. Because of the wire netting it is known as 'the Birdcage' – though also as 'the Waterloo Hilton'.

It is simplicity itself for anyone to walk through the front door, but getting any further is a problem. The ground floor has an internal protective barrier of steel latticework, and the glass of the reception-desk area is suspiciously thick. All this is plainly visible from the outside, which makes the entire complex highly conspicuous. In the forecourt is a petrol station, as effective a disguise as a crepe ginger moustache on a Brazilian.

It would be most naïve to think that the front door is the only way in, and more so to believe that the other entrances are labelled British Intelligence HQ, or, for that matter, that they even look like entrances.

The conference was in a windowless basement room. Four people were already there when Carr arrived. Checking the arrivals was 'Godfrey', a tall young man so smooth and impeccable that the Old Etonian tie he wore didn't seem good enough for him. His name was Peter Harris, which was a bit of a let-down, and he was working on ways of getting people to call him Piers. He was personal assistant to William Parker, a senior officer in SIS, who hadn't yet turned up.

'Any trouble in getting away from your guest?' Harris asked Carr.

'I managed to get uncoupled,' Carr told him.

'Good,' Harris replied automatically. He hadn't been issued with a sense of humour.

Carr nodded to Guy Adams, an MI6 man with a profile straight off an ancient Greek coin. He'd earned a reputation as a very hard man in the field. Maybe it was because of his father. Frank Adams survived three years of war in the OSS, and was shot a day after VE Day by a Russian NCO who thought he might be a German black-marketeer, but didn't care very much anyway. Adams had a desk now, but Carr couldn't quite remember which one it was.

Already sitting at the table was Eric Kirby, from the DSI – the overt Directorate of Service Intelligence which operates from the Ministry of Defence in Whitehall. Kirby, now a senior officer in the Directorate, had worked his way up through the ranks, as his accent sometimes betrayed. He raised his hand in greeting.

The fourth man in the room was unknown to Carr. He was about fifty, tall and slim, and looked like a television actor used to playing senior surgeons and QCs.

'I don't think you two know each other,' Harris said, like a superior hostess. 'Major Patterson, MI5 – Richard Carr.' They muttered how-do-you-dos. 'From where, exactly?' Patterson asked Carr in a muted parade-ground bray.

'Commercial and Technical Information.'

'Really?' Patterson raised an eyebrow, turning his best side to an invisible camera. 'I shouldn't have thought that was quite the sort of briefing for a department that, er . . . ' He let it die. Carr gave him a look that would have made a more intelligent man embarrassed.

'Oh? What sort of briefing is it?' Carr asked. Patterson

coughed. Adams and Kirby, who knew something of Carr's work – something, but not much – grinned quietly.

Perhaps Patterson was deceived by Carr's appearance. He was good-looking, but with a face that would be hard to remember and describe five minutes after he turned his back. His suit was well-cut, but unremarkable in style and colour. He looked like a civil servant, which he was, in a way.

'Do you know what this is all about?' Carr asked Adams. He shook his head.

'It's my day off. I was called in from home.'

The situation was resolved by the entry of Clifford Forbes, of Foreign Office Intelligence, and William Parker, who comfortably outranked them all. Harris practically genuflected, and Kirby stood up abruptly as if someone had switched him on.

Parker had eyes that seemed to bore straight through to the wall behind the person he was looking at. They were unnaturally pale and deep-set, beneath formidable eyebrows. Not untidy, sprouty ones, but two heavy black bars as neat and precise as if they had been stencilled on his forehead. He dressed like an undertaker to Transylvanian royal families. In the penumbra of Parker's personality, Forbes could have indecently exposed himself, and no one would have noticed.

Parker signalled for them all to sit down.

'No need for minutes,' he told Harris, who instantly tried to look as if his notebook and ballpoint had been forced into his hand against his will.

'Something's gone very wrong in Czechoslovakia,' Parker continued brusquely. 'The STB and their "Uncles" have . . .' He broke off as Patterson shifted uneasily in his seat. 'The KGB. The Czech Intelligence people call the KGB "The Uncles",' he explained. Patterson nodded importantly.

'As far as we can make out they made a simultaneous mass round-up of all our people in the Comenius group – all of them – at dawn this morning. Yesterday morning,' he amended glancing at his watch.

Adams looked ashen. Carr remembered now that he ran the Czechoslovakian section.

'How do we know?' asked Carr. Adams was too shattered to speak yet. There was an awkward pause. 'If it was a simultaneous round-up of all of them, how do we know?'

Parker stared at Carr without concealing his dislike. The antipathy was not for Carr himself, whom Parker liked and respected, but the department he worked for. Although it came under SIS for pay, allowances and admin – theoretically – it had a certain autonomy in its operations, and Parker suspected that he didn't know everything the department got up to. It was as well for his peace of mind that he didn't. Nor did he see why Carr's department – however much he might like Carr personally – had to be brought in on a matter of this kind. It seemed to be against all 'need to know' principles. But it was on the list, and Parker was a by-the-book man.

'We had an urgent message from one of our people that was probably meant to be a warning, but it was broken off in mid-transmission, and there's strong confirmatory evidence from the F.O. Intelligence people at the Prague Embassy. There's very little room for doubt, I'm afraid. We haven't been able to raise anybody at all.'

There was a heavy silence. Adams looked ghastly. Harris was deeply intent on tracing designs on the table top with his finger.

'The comprehensiveness of the STB operation can mean only one thing: a leak. Either in the group, or' – he looked at Patterson – 'at this end.' The MI5 man gave his impressively important nod. It was the best thing he did, and it had taken him a long way.

'We're working on an assessment of the probable damage now. If we get anything, you'll be informed. In the meantime . . . ' Parker stood up to show the briefing was over.

Carr stopped in the main hall to make a call from a public phone. He had trouble getting money into the box.

'Richard,' he announced. 'Are you alone?' Waiting while the telephone squawked into his ear had put the man at the other end into a bad temper. 'No, I'm having an orgy with the Luton Girls' Choir.'

'I'm at Waterloo Hilton. There's some bad news,' Carr said.

'I've just heard,' said the other man, whose name was Streeter.

'Shall I come over now?'

'No point. I'll see you at the office tomorrow.'

'But – '

'What the hell could we do tonight?' There was a click as the phone was hung up. Carr replaced the receiver thoughtfully. Streeter was right, of course. There was nothing could be done. He picked up the phone again and dialled the number of his own flat.

'Hello?' said Peg the Legs.

'So you're still there. I'm coming back.'

'Here, I've been thinking. Those Imperial Russian War Loan things –they're not worth anything.'

'Good God, are you sure? Aunt Alice must have been stringing me along all this time.'

'How is she?'

'Sleeping. The doctor said I'm to go back in the morning. Pour me a drink and I'll be home before you can do a couple of entrechats.'

As he left the building, Carr remembered what Streeter had said: there was nothing they could do tonight. In fact there was nothing they could do ever.

The Commercial and Technical Information Service of the Board of Trade is a small department located in a handsome Victorian four-storey house in one of the elegant roads running down from the Kensington Road area. It is a corner house, which means it has a side entrance and a small garden with a garage. On the other side of the building is a similar-looking house converted into flats. The entrance hall of this house, with a thick, dark carpet and a massive staircase concealing a creaking lift, recalls the days of the Empire. On the brightest day only a little light manages to insinuate itself into the hall, and that with great difficulty. Between the two houses is a total soundproof and electronic screen, built into the fabric of the CTI premises.

At one minute to nine Carr walked up to the front door of the Information Service building. The door opened before he needed to ring, rather like the door at No. 10 Downing Street – suggesting that someone inside was keeping an eye on the street.

No one showed an identity card or a pass to enter the building, but you were only admitted if you were known. A casual caller who rang the doorbell, would be told after a long wait, if he hadn't got fed up and gone away, that all enquiries should be directed to the Board of Trade, thank you and good day. Then the door would be closed in his face.

Every foreign Intelligence service knew that Commercial and Technical Information was an organisation involved in industrial and technical espionage – and that Carr was an industrial and technical spy. Sometimes he wryly admitted that it was rather depressing to be so well known.

In fact the CTI processed 'raw information' – everything from published material to reports from overt and clandestine agents – into finished intelligence. Carr had very little to do with it: just enough for a believable cover.

He took the lift to the second floor. The lift went only as far as the third floor, and none of the floor-indicators over the doors worked.

Carr went straight to his own office to see if there were any routine messages to deal with. There weren't, which was usual, because he wasn't really a desk man. He took the stairs to the third floor, and came to a small reception area on the landing. It was occupied by an alert young man who looked out of place behind the desk. He nodded at Carr, who passed him and continued up the last flight of steps to the top floor. He walked along a corridor of closed office doors, then turned a corner into another short passage that ended with a door. Carr made sure that no one was coming along behind him, then swiftly unlocked the door by slipping into an unobtrusive slot what to all appearances was an ordinary bank card, but which had a special magnetic key imprinted into it. He went in.

The small storeroom, with shelves and cupboards, had artificial lighting because there was a partition between the door and the window. Seen from the room side, the partition was simply a wooden wall running from floor to ceiling, about three feet in from the window. Seen from the window side it was a cunningly planned and constructed three-dimensional *trompe-l'oeuil.* The distorted perspective of the construction made it look as if there were fitted cupboards and shelves running right back into the full depth of the room. It was a technique used in film studios where a street is constructed in the back lot. The street is life-size at one end, then it rapidly diminishes to half-size or less at the far end, giving the impression that the street is at least twice as long as it really is. From ten feet outside the window, no one could possibly guess that he wasn't seeing the entire room. It may have seemed an elaborate subterfuge, but permanently closed curtains or shutters finally arouse suspicions. Anyone keeping the building under observation would have seen only a storeroom.

Feeling faintly ridiculous, as he always did, Carr walked over to a cupboard, opened it, pushed against the back . . . and walked through into the top-floor flat of the building next-door.

2

Carr was in the headquarters of the SID, the Support Intelligence Department, a title and acronym close enough to a number of other Intelligence departments to be confused with them if the name slipped out. It was one of the smallest Intelligence HQ groups in the business.

The orthodox entrance to the flat, in the private house next to the offices, was conventional enough. Behind the deceptively solid front door, with its two Bramah locks, was a small hall leading to a living-room. From time to time the registered owner of the flat, a retired Treasury official who spent most of his time in the country, put in an appearance and stayed for a while. His electricity, gas and telephone bills were all paid by cash through Giro.

Beyond the one living-room the rest of the flat was bricked off, leaving the other six rooms for the SID. The ex-Treasury man was well paid for roughing it for a few days in the single room at his disposal.

SID was formed shortly after World War II, and occupied a couple of rooms in the famous Queen Anne's Gate building. One of its jobs was to function within Intelligence rather like A10 Department functioned within Scotland Yard. When a traitor in an Intelligence set-up is discovered, he or she is dealt with in one of three ways. The first and most usual is arrest and trial. Sometimes, though, the spy manages to get out in time and take up residence near his Swiss bank account. If disclosure of the fact that a traitor had been operating for years in a sensitive post would be bad for public morale – and, more important, make a lot of very senior people look stupid – the spy is quietly ignored and allowed to enjoy an early, wealthy retirement. That is the second method.

The third method is what the CIA call 'extreme measures', and the KGB call 'the highest form of punishment'. Among the KGB's assassination methods, which include a cyanide gun that gives the victim a 'heart attack', is the injection of a fatal poison for which there is no known cure – at least, no cure known by the West. The KGB and its satellites started eliminating people this way in the early sixties; the poisoning of the Bulgarian defector Georgi Markov in a London street was, unhappily, nothing new. (There is only one case on record of someone recovering from such an assassination attempt. After heroic medical treatment by American physicians the man recovered. It was subsequently discovered that he'd been injected with thallium which had been made radioactive. The Bulgarian Yolkov who was apparently attacked in Paris does not seem to have received a fatal dose of poison into the system, or even any poison at all.)

Later the SID got rid of its job of what was known as 'house-cleaning'. It moved to Kensington and began to branch into mounting operations of its own, largely at the initiative of a brilliant and quite potty academic who came into Intelligence almost by mistake. The expansion of the SID's activities was made possible only with the passive acquiescence of a succession of government ministers whose thickwittedness and lack of perception was remarkable even among politicians.

The SID soon became well established and acquired some powerful, silent protectors. Improbable as it may seem, among the most significant of these was in the Treasury, which operates the tightest, most effective Old Boy Mafia in Western Europe. The backing from inside the Treasury was crucial. At the same time, the SID was highly effective, often simply because of its unorthodoxy and position outside the wider Intelligence set-up. Like Lawrence's Arabs, the Long Range Desert Group, and Wingate's Chindits, it produced results out of proportion to its size because of that unorthodoxy.

One of the most important factors in the SID's early survival, though, was curiously British. It couldn't be wound down because nobody knew how to wind down an organization with no official status. There were no forms or precedents.

Carr walked into the main room, one of four that had the windows blocked off. The two smaller rooms had voile curtains on the windows; these faced a blank wall and couldn't be seen from outside, except by pigeons.

Henry Streeter, head of SID, sat behind his large desk. It had three press-button telephones, two on the Federal exchange, 01-333 – a manual exchange not shown in the London telephone directory. The SID extension numbers on this exchange, which serves the senior members of Government and the Executive, were listed at a rarely-used office in a distant building.

In one corner was a computer terminal. It was linked to the main Intelligence computer bank, which was steadily taking over from some sections of Central Registry. It was also linked to certain other computers which would alarm a great number of people if they were made aware of this. Streeter had become very skilled in its use, Carr knew, and managed to get some surprising information from the computer.

Not that everyone had access to the information. To extract data from the different computer banks, the correct codewords and numbers had to be fed into the machine. Streeter and Carr knew all the codes to tie their computer into the various other computers. At least, Carr thought he knew all of them.

There was another safeguard built into the programmes, although it had about it a touch of bolting the stable door after the horse had gone. Every time the computer was activated it recorded the enquirer's personal number, the date and time of the enquiry, and the information extracted.

Along one side of the room were a line of custom-built, specially reinforced steel filing cabinets fitted with both key and combination locks.

Streeter was a man of about fifty, with thick wavy grey hair, carefully dressed, and a long face like a Modigliani painting. His close-set eyes sometimes appeared to squint when he was worried or angry, making them look even closer together. He sucked cheerlessly on an expensive cigar. Streeter was also Carr's brother-in-law, but in name only. Carr was married to Streeter's sister Judy; they no longer lived together, but the ruptured family tie didn't affect the professional relationship between the two men.

'How is it I got the call to the Birdcage last night?' Carr asked. 'The Birdcage' – so-called because of all the steel lattice-work and wire netting – was another name for the 'Waterloo Hilton'. 'I've only been back four days.'

'I was out. You're next on the list.'

'Where were you?'

'Out,' Streeter said in a tone that put an end to that topic. Carr remembered, though, that Streeter had already heard of the Comenius group's disaster five minutes after the briefing.

'It's not just the Comenius lot,' Streeter continued. 'I . . . We had a man operating in the area as well. Codename Mercury, real name . . . ' He hesitated. 'Real name Michal Ondrach.'

'How long have you had him?'

'Three or four years. He's been really active only for the last two.'

'Thanks for your stirring confidence in telling me about him quite so soon,' Carr said sarcastically. 'Do they know about Ondrach at Waterloo?'

'No, he's mine – ours . . . exclusively. He's the best border man in Eastern Europe. I wasn't going to let them get their hands on him.' He hesitated. 'But we haven't heard from him for more than a week. He *could* be all right, just keeping his head down with all this stuff flying around . . . '

His squint became more marked.

He picked up his direct-line telephone and quickly dialled the code for Bratislava, 010-42-7, following it with Ondrach's number, and then the figure 2. He switched to the phone's loudspeaker attachment, for Carr's benefit. There was the usual hum, then a click as the connection was made, but there was no sound of the ringing tone.

'Ondrach has put in an improved Infinity Bug,' Streeter said.

Concealed in a telephone, an Infinity Bug makes it possible for conversation on that telephone to be monitored from anywhere in the world as long as it's possible to dial to it direct. The call doesn't cost anything, because it doesn't register on the meters in the exchange. Carr knew of two directors of a merchant bank who had the bugs installed in special phones in their offices in London and New York, so they could have long, free transatlantic calls.

With the modified version of the bug, Streeter could pick up all the sounds in Ondrach's flat through the phone, even though it was still on the hook. The expensive electronics were all for nothing: there were no sounds of activity in the place. Streeter replaced the receiver, then called a Vienna number, beginning 010-43-222. Again there was the unmistakable silence of emptiness.

Streeter hung up again. He thought hard for a moment, then came up with a considered observation. He said, 'Oh, shit,' then walked over to the filing cabinets with double locks and tugged irritably at the drawer handles. 'It's not just Ondrach,' he said at last. 'He was bringing over Doctor Zvalen.'

Carr was startled. Dr Vaclav Zvalen, one of the Communist Bloc's very few recent Nobel Prize winners, was well known in the West for his frequent criticism of Soviet domination of Czech affairs. But he was basically a patriot, Carr thought. He hardly seemed likely to defect.

'He's finally got fed up with all the difficulties the Russians have been making for him. It's only his Nobel Prize that's kept him out of jail up to now, and he has the feeling they're going to pull him in at any moment. Probably to send him to the Serbsky Institute.'

'They could fix him so he couldn't add two and two any more.'

As Carr well knew, the Serbsky Institute of Forensic Psychiatry in Moscow was where a number of leading dissidents had been sent for diagnosis of 'mental disorders'.

'You know what he was working on?' Streeter said. 'Lasers.' He paused, and looked even gloomier. 'The most important bloody defector since Sherchenko quit the U.N. in New York, and he has to go and disappear, along with all the Comenius group.'

He went and sat at his desk, and crushed his half-smoked cigar in the ashtray. It had been a complete waste of money; he could have got as much satisfaction from a Woodbine.

Carr had never seen him quite so jumpy. Streeter got up again and drummed a noisy tattoo on the cover of the computer terminal. For all his restlessness, not a hair was out of place, and his beautifully cut suit was as uncrumpled as if he was still in a Hawkes fitting room. Streeter's unfailing elegance sometimes made people forget he'd been an agent in the field, and a very good one indeed. Although he now sat behind a desk, giving orders, he knew what it was to be out there in the cold and dark.

Without warning, Streeter walked over to a door and opened it. Its other side was heavily padded for soundproofing.

The air in the next room – the SID communications/operations room – practically crackled with static electricity from the advanced equipment there. Or maybe it was from Streeter himself. 'Still nothing from Ondrach?' he said.

A man of about thirty stood up from the small desk. His name was Roger Chapman, and he was a smaller edition of Peter Harris at the Birdcage – smooth, unruffled, with a quiet arrogance and no sense of humour.

'No, sir. But he doesn't make contact through here.' He indicated the electronic hardware behind him.

'How do we contact him?' Carr asked. Chapman looked to Streeter for approval before answering. 'Prearranged calls to phone-boxes, advertisements in personal columns of foreign papers and the *Morning Star.*' He smiled thinly. 'In some countries it's the only English paper you can get.'

'Well, at least they get the football results right,' Carr said.

'When's our next call to a phone-box scheduled?' asked Streeter.

Chapman consulted a list. 'Today – in thirty-five minutes. Ten o'clock our time. It's to a box in Bratislava Railway Station.'

Both Streeter and Carr, who'd lived through it scores of times, clearly visualized the scene at the other end. The solitary man entering one of a row of phone-boxes, occupying it five or ten minutes before the rendezvous time and carrying on a simulated conversation, one eye on his watch so he can depress the receiver ten seconds before the deadline. After all that, it sometimes doesn't ring anyway. At first the pulse quickens and the hand holding the phone grows moist. After two carefully-timed minutes that seem two hours, the man leaves, half disappointed, half relieved. Oh, they both knew the scene all right.

'We'll try once more. Then you'd better go and find out what's happened.' Streeter looked at Carr.

Twenty-five seconds before the hour, Chapman started dialling on a loudspeaker phone. The clicks and hums of the routing mechanism seemed inordinately long to the three waiting men. Almost to the second the single-pulse ringing tone began. Miles away, in a depressing, echoing railway station the phone in an unpainted box began ringing.

It rang three times, which should have been more than enough. After the fourth ring Chapman stretched out his hand to switch off. The phone at the other end was picked up.

'Hello, who's there?' said a surprised young woman in Slovak.

Chapman cut the connection and said a very rude word. It was curiously out of character, and it made Carr wonder why he'd said it.

'Try again in five minutes, sir?' Chapman asked.

Streeter shook his head. 'He'd have been in the box long beforehand if he was going to be there at all.' Then he continued, angrily, 'For Christ's sake, you'd think the bloody man could have risked one very quick direct phone-call from *somewhere*, even if he was on the run.' He turned towards his own office. 'It's no good kidding ourselves. He's been taken.'

'He could be in hospital with a broken leg, or smallpox, or something,' Carr said, closing the door of the communications room behind him.

'Trust you to be optimistic.' Streeter wasn't being sarcastic. 'I want to know how it happened, where the leak is. Start in Vienna.'

'The whole area'll be crawling with people from Waterloo. They're much more likely to find out something than I would on my own.'

'Ondrach had nothing to do with their Comenius group. I told you – they don't know he exists.'

'If they do, that could be the link. Maybe Waterloo have been running him too. They could be holding out on you.'

'It's not possible.'

'You're not telling me it's just a coincidence he's disappeared at the same time Waterloo's lot got lifted?'

Streeter shrugged. 'So find out.'

'How? Walk up to the Czech Embassy and ask if they know where he is? Where do I start? Do you have any other contacts there?'

Streeter avoided his look. 'Have a try on your own first. If you run into a blank wall, well, we'll see.' He added, with the faintest trace of embarrassment, 'There's still a chance that Zvalen is holed up somewhere near the Czech border and trying to cross. Maybe *you* could get him over.'

'I see,' said Carr acidly. 'So that's the fine print at the bottom. One small question. How do *I* get over in the first place, to bring him back?'

'I've been thinking about that,' Streeter said.

'I bet you have.' Carr took a deep breath. 'Let me see if I've got this right. You want me to find out what happened to Ondrach, next find Zvalen – which presumably half the STB can't do if he's still free – then dream up a way of bringing him back under the noses of the other half of the STB.'

'That's about it,' Streeter said, unabashed.

They subsequently agreed that it would be better for Carr not to travel under his own name. He was on the opposition's list of people in Intelligence, though only on the industrial fringe of espionage as far as they were concerned. At least, Carr hoped that was what they still thought. But the break-up of the Comenius group would inevitably provoke a great flurry of Intelligence activity on both sides. Flights to Vienna and Prague would be monitored as a matter of course. Carr didn't want any involvement with that sort of operation, however tenuous. His arrival in Vienna wouldn't be simply written off as coincidental. Intelligence people don't believe in coincidences, not even real ones.

The organisation of his run was fairly straightforward, as these things go. He would fly to Vienna for a package holiday on a charter aircraft, taking the place of someone who'd dropped out. 'Don't worry,' Streeter said blandly. 'It was quite voluntary. We didn't do anything.'

Once in Vienna, Carr would go straight to another hotel and book in as Samuel Connell, an Englishman of Irish descent. 'Connell' would eventually go to Czechoslavakia, ostensibly as a tourist, but really to buy arms for the IRA. This would explain any odd behaviour. Officially the Czechs were against illegal arms deals, but they were not too nosy if the arms would be used to embarrass the West.

'There's a real Connell, and we've got a file on him,' Streeter said. 'It's odds on that the opposition have as well.'

'Supposing I meet someone who knows the real Connell by sight?'

'Very unlikely. He's never been east of Paris.'

'And what about Connell himself?'

'He won't pop up to make things awkward for you.' Streeter rubbed the side of his nose. 'He had a sort of accident. All you have to do is learn something of his background. Have a look at his file on the computer here, before you go.'

Norman Hillier on the third floor of the Kensington office, was the man who provided passports.

'Make sure they're ones the computer won't throw out,' Carr said rather grumpily, knowing major airports have a list of 'suspect' passport names and numbers, and that a forged passport can be shown up in a matter of seconds by access to computerised-records. He wasn't looking forward to the trip at all.

'How are you travelling?' Hillier asked.

'Holiday group on a charter flight.'

'Who's going to do a computer check on a passport of a charter-flight passenger? Who the hell ever heard of a hijacker in a holiday group?'

'I did. The Mogadishu hijacking.'

'That was from Majorca. I'm talking about a major airport, not a cowpatch with one policeman, one boy and a dog. But don't worry. The passports will be good ones,' Hillier promised. Carr never doubted it. It was a ritual they always went through, and it cheered him up a little.

Carr went back to his own office. There was a cryptic memorandum on his desk which meant Streeter wanted to see him.

'You'd better have a look at Ondrach's operational file,' Streeter said. As he opened a filing cabinet he kept his body between Carr and the locks, so he couldn't see the combination.

Carr took the file and headed for the door. 'No,' Streeter said. 'Read it here.' Carr looked at him in some surprise. 'Sorry, no exceptions. Even I don't take these files out of the office.'

The file was made out partly in Streeter's own handwriting, partly in rather poor typing, which Carr guessed had been done by Streeter as well. Routine matters that didn't include real or operational names were typed professionally.

Ondrach's record made impressive reading. 'I can see why you don't want to lose a man like this,' Carr said eventually.

'It's not only Ondrach. If he could get Zvalen out, we could have him to ourselves for a while before handing him over to the Waterloo Hilton.'

'They'd crucify you on Traitors' Gate with rusty nails for that.'

'They should be grateful to get him at all.'

Carr grunted noncommittally. 'I'd like to see Ondrach's personal file.'

Streeter carefully secured the operational file back in the cabinet, then took a microfiche from a locked box inside another drawer. He slid the card into a projector, set up the correct number on the selector, then switched on, projecting the information on to a screen the size of a medium television set.

At the top was Ondrach's photograph. It wasn't particularly good: a slightly blurred shot taken in a street that could be anywhere in Eastern Europe. Ondrach was putting a cigarette into his mouth, and half his face was in shadow.

'It's the only one we could get. It's probably the only one there is,' Streeter said.

Carr read through the personal details. Ondrach was thirty-five. Born in Austria of Czech parents. Married a Czech woman, since dead. No children. Compulsory military service in the Austrian tank corps. Three years in Geneva as representative of an Austrian chemical manufacturer where he learned French and Italian. Six months in Milan for the same company. Now an exporter-importer on his own account. Fluent English, French, German, Czech. Some Italian and Russian.

It took Hillier two days to produce the passports. He handed over the first, in the name of Geoffrey Chatfield. 'Sign the passport, and this,' Hillier said. 'This' was a back-dated application form for a passport in the name of Chatfield. 'Just in case somebody manages to photocopy one signature and compare it with the other.'

Pinned to the application was a photograph of Carr. The certification that the man in the photo was Geoffrey Chatfield was signed by a Dr Armstrong, who declared he had known 'Chatfield' for ten years and this was a true likeness. Carr wondered who Dr Armstrong was.

Hillier read this thoughts. 'He died last year. Now the Connell passport. And this application form. The details on this application are the same as on the original one, of course.'

'Of course. What else?' said Carr. He closely scrutinised the passport. It contained a visa for Czechoslovakia and an entry stamp for the Austrian frontier. Both would pass anything except microscopic examination.

'You entered Austria from Switzerland by train,' Hillier said. 'That way no one can back-check the airline passenger lists.' Carr found Hillier's thoroughness comforting.

The travel man was Boyd Gatward, manager of a travel agency not far from Barker's in Kensington High Street. It was another firm that performed a useful function for the SID, helping to hide its travel arrangements in the mass of legitimate business and making a modest profit at the same time.

Gatward had dark brown, sad eyes, and a head that had been bald since he was less than thirty. Maybe that's why his eyes were so sad. His great passion was timetables. As musicians look at a score and hear the music, Gatward travelled the world on an international railway timetable. He also took odd trips by air in aged aircraft of unknown airlines – in his mind, of course – but these took second place to his exotic trips in outlandish trains. He loved looking up footnotes that gave unexpected information such as 'Dining-car on Tuesdays between Daltonganj and Kharagpur, March 13 to August 19', and arranging his mental expeditions to take advantage of it. Gatward's dream was to have a modern-day Phileas Fogg come in and ask for a round-the-world itinerary using only local and suburban trains. As it was, he had to content himself with a quarterly season ticket to Westcliff-on-Sea.

'What's the name of the passenger?' Gatward didn't commit the solecism of asking, 'What name are you using this time?'

'Chatfield. Geoffrey Chatfield.'

Gatward made out the ticket and the rest of the documents himself. 'It's for ten days at a decent three-star hotel, room and continental breakfast, with conducted coach-tours included. You also get dinner on the first and last nights. Here's the brochure.'

'What happens if I don't go on the trips? Do I get fined, or just lose my good-conduct badge?'

'Participation in the organised tours is optional,' Gatward said primly.

'I only asked because someone else may be arranging some alternative entertainment for me.'

3

Carr went back to the Commercial and Technical Information Office in Kensington, and got straight into the lift. After the windowless outer door closed, he pressed the buttons for the ground floor and third floor simultaneously. The lift silently went down to the basement, which wasn't indicated on the lift panel or anywhere else. The original cellar had been enlarged when the house had been converted into offices, and now ran under the garden.

A small rectangle of light showed in the outer lift door. A pair of thick glasses with a moon face behind them appeared, blocking off the light momentarily. A heavy bolt was drawn, and the outer door rolled open. It was made of heavy-duty steel, and the small window in it was bullet-proof glass. The door couldn't be opened from inside the lift without a key, and there was only one of them. The moonfaced man had it.

His name was David Nurse, and he was the SID armourer. If there was anything he didn't know about hand-guns, either it didn't exist, or wasn't worth knowing anyway. Nurse was scandalously henpecked by a vinegar-bottle of a wife who had no idea of what he really did for a living.

'What sort of weapon do you need?' he asked politely.

'Unobtrusive and handy,' Carr said.

'Well, then,' said Nurse, pretending to consider the problem, although they both knew he had the answer already. 'About .32, I suppose.' He opened a drawer in a cabinet rather like the ones common in chemists' shops half a century ago. 'Beretta 1931 model. Well-made, reliable, accurate, won't let you down. But' – he clucked his tongue as he picked it up – 'the safety-catch isn't what *I'd* call safe.

Not at all. And look at that nasty projection under the hammer. As for that finger-rest sticking out of the magazine like a fishhook! If you weren't careful you could rip your pocket or holster quite badly.'

'Or still be struggling to get it out while somebody shot you twice with a muzzle-loading flintlock.'

Nurse opened another drawer disapprovingly. He felt that an armoury – his armoury – was no place for pleasantries.

'Walther PPK. Not bad.' PPK meant Police Pistol Kriminal, that is, a pistol to be worn concealed in ordinary clothing – a modification and improvement of the Walther PP model, which is a gun for uniformed police. He balanced it in his hand. 'Not bad at all. This one is pre-war manufacture, of course. I wouldn't have one made during the war in the place. Not even as a paperweight. Yes, very nice,' he conceded, but put the gun away.

'It was PPK that jammed when Princess Anne's bodyguard tried to shoot back, wasn't it?' Carr said innocently.

Nurse looked like an angry rabbit. '*My* guns never jam. I examine each gun and each round of ammunition personally.'

'I know. I was only joking. I trust your stuff implicitly.' Which was true.

Nurse was mollified. He opened a third drawer as if it contained precious jade. 'If I may, I suggest this gun.' He took out a smooth, streamlined automatic and placed it before Carr. 'Mauser HSc. Completely reliable, perfectly designed and balanced for quick drawing and fast, accurate shooting. Beautiful gun. Beautiful.' Carr had been issued with this gun five times, and had used it three, but he said nothing.

'Not all that powerful with the .32 ACP cartridge, of course,' Nurse went on, 'but for close-range work in experienced hands . . . ' He closed his eyes and mentally shot his wife eight times between the eyes with a one-inch grouping.

'Close-range will do,' Carr said. 'I'm not expecting any OK Corral situations. I'll take two spare magazines.'

The light over the wallphone flashed. It was Streeter, for Carr. 'Come up and have a word. I'm in my flat.'

The flat was immediately underneath the SID headquarters, in the house next to the offices. It was comfortable and well furnished, but the agreeable surroundings weren't doing much for Streeter. He was morosely introspective, which at least made him physically reposed compared with his normal state of jagged activity. 'You'll need these,' he said, handing over the sets of keys for Ondrach's flats in Vienna and Bratislava. 'Everything else fixed?'

'More or less. I've arranged communications with Chapman.'

'There is one other thing,' Streeter said. 'You'll need to know the locations of Ondrach's dead-letter drops.'

Carr stared at him in astonishment. 'Dead-letter drops? But Austria isn't a hostile country.' Streeter looked at him sideways. 'Well, not actively, anyway,' Carr admitted, 'even if their government are weak-kneed with terrorists, and can be pretty frigid with refugees sometimes.'

'The Jews would put it a bit stronger than that,' Streeter said. 'The point is, there are people Ondrach doesn't want walking up to his front door and ringing the bell. And there are occasions when he goes to ground somewhere. Some days you can see more KGB men in Rathaus Park than in Red Square on May Day. So, he needs back-up communications. Drink?'

'Scotch. Malt – not that cheap Black Label stuff you give the visitors.'

Streeter poured one for Carr, and a second one for himself, a stiff one. Or maybe it was a third. Carr hadn't known Streeter to drink like that, except to celebrate, which he certainly wasn't doing now.

'I hope you find Ondrach,' Streeter said gloomily, 'but frankly, I've written him off as a *mokrie dela* case.' The Russian words meant 'wet affair' – what the KGB call blood-spilling activities like assassinations; operations carried out by the V Section of the First Chief Directorate of the KGB. 'I expect the best you can do is discover how he got taken.'

'As long as I don't do it the hard way, like King Wenceslas's page. Following in his footsteps,' Carr added. 'Oh, never mind.'

'You sound depressed,' Streeter said.

'For a very good reason. I *am* depressed.'

'What's wrong?'

Carr paused a long while before he replied. For a number of reasons he wasn't sure whether he should tell Streeter. Eventually he said, 'I'm tired of being outside all the time – '

'Not all the time.'

'No,' Carr admitted, 'but I'm tired of being in the field. I've had it.'

'At your age?'

'I'm a thousand years old. I've seen empires fall.'

'Just this run, and then we'll see. I'm breaking in a new man to replace you.'

Paradoxically this irritated Carr. Although he desperately wanted to come inside from the field, he resented Streeter suggesting that he wasn't indispensable and someone else would eventually replace him.

'Well, let him do this one.'

'He's not quite ready. Besides, there's Zvalen . . . ' Streeter let it die, then he poured himself another drink. 'Richard, there's something weird going on. Bloody weird. I can smell it. All the Western Powers are bickering, like poor relations at a rich uncle's funeral, talking about family spirit and hating everybody else's guts at the same time. And it's getting worse.'

'International relations have always been as uncertain as the English climate.'

'It's not the same,' Streeter said doggedly. 'It's like a plague that starts slowly. One case here, one case there and, before you know, it's everywhere and there's no place to run. I mean, you only have to read the papers. People – important level-headed people – are acting out of character and behaving like . . . ' He gestured vaguely, and thought for a while. 'Respectable politicians, if that's not a contradiction in terms, getting themselves into the brown stuff right up to their necks, bloody UNO putting a senior KGB man in charge of a vital department, a hard-headed heiress getting hooked by the KGB . . .'

'It's a good thing the KGB are so accident-prone – although people don't believe it if you try to tell them.' This was true. The KGB is the biggest Intelligence service in the world, but overmanned and often bureaucratically inefficient. It gets its results by sheer weight of men and money.

Streeter's gloom lightened for a moment. 'They don't understand capitalism. They thought all she had to do was sign a chit and they'd have all those oil-wells. I bet the dust hasn't settled in Moscow Centre yet,' Streeter said cheerfully.

'And what about that Russian bank going into the red for four hundred million, or whatever it was? No pun intended.'

Streeter's eyes came closer together again. 'But the fact remains – there's something bloody weird going on, and it's frightening the hell out of me.'

Carr had just finished a lunch of home-made pâté, lamb chops and out-of-season *fraises du bois* from the deep-freeze. His favourite fifty-fifty mixture of continental and mocha coffee was beginning to percolate when the phone rang.

'Hello, Richard. It's Eli. Are you busy?'

'Not really.'

'See you at your office?'

'I don't want to go back there. Usual place in the park?'

'Thirty minutes?'

'Right.'

To save any parking problems Carr rang the Waterloo minicab firm for a car to take him to Queen's Gate at Hyde Park. He slowly drank his coffee while he waited for it to arrive.

Eli Yelkov was already sitting on the fourth bench along the north side of the Carriage Road in the park, when Carr arrived. Yelkov, a massive, ageless man with a great domed bald head, looked like a Rodin statue of a retired wrestler carved from ironstone. Somebody once said of him he had a face that would break rocks, and frequently had.

He was turned away from Carr, facing the modern monstrosity of Knightsbridge Barracks, but said, 'Hello, Richard,' when Carr was still ten yards directly behind him.

Although Yelkov was nominally on the staff of the Israeli military attaché, he was really a senior officer of the Mossad, the Israeli Intelligence agency. Almost certainly it was the most efficient – man for man – and the most deadly, in the world; and operated mainly outside Israel. Most Western Intelligence organisations were well disposed towards the Mossad, and there was a great deal of unofficial passing of intelligence. It was a two-way traffic: the Israelis seemed to infiltrate into unexpected high places where Western agents failed to tread, and had important information to offer their friends.

Yelkov's involvement in intelligence went back to the days of the *Shai*, which operated in Palestine to the authorities' great discomfort during the British Mandate. Yelkov joined the Palestine Police and fed the *Shai* with a steady stream of secret intelligence, and was able to warn Israeli agents when the police were getting too close to them. All that had been forgiven long since, even though the information was still in a British Intelligence 'Foreign Agent' dossier on Yelkov. The only mystery about Yelkov at the moment was what a man of his abilities was doing in England, which was not hostile to Israel.

'Pity you couldn't make it at your office,' Yelkov said. 'You've got the sexiest secretaries in London.'

There was an element of truth in the exaggeration. Streeter's department always picked young and attractive female staff, and kept them only as long as they stayed that way. Streeter was more ruthless than the most dictatorial Playboy Mother at the first signs of drooping and sagging. The reason was simple: women who are lonely, plain, frustrated or middle-aged, or any combination of them, are particularly vulnerable to the advances made by practised, professional seducers – and the KGB has a special training course for seducers of both sexes. Streeter was taking no chances of his section being got at through susceptible women. All his secretarial staff had two or three ardent boy friends, and no hormonal difficulties.

'I'm the clean outdoor type,' Carr said; then, not unfriendlily, 'What do you want this time?'

'Want? I ask a friend to sit in the park in the sunshine and relax for a while –'

'It's cloudy, and cold.'

'So I'm an expert on the weather?' Yelkov, a Ph.D. of the Sorbonne, often spoke like a stage Jewish tailor. ' "What do you want this time?" he says. Such a way to greet a friend. Why should I want something?'

'Because you always do.'

Yelkov grinned. He passed over a slip of paper with three names on it. 'Three names, one man. Erhardt Roeder was a "doctor" in Blestau concentration camp during the war. We're fairly sure he took the identity of a Dr Lauritz Paulus, who was a prisoner there, and was killed in a bombing raid near the camp towards the end of the war. According to most reports, Roeder-Paulus died in eastern Germany, near the Polish border. Just recently, though, we've had reason to believe he changed his name again, this time to Ernst Honecker, or something like it.'

'Why should we have anything on him?'

'Your troops helped . . . clean up the place. And your Intelligence people were in there quickly. There was somebody you wanted, I think. Could you run a check on him in your computer files?'

'I expect so,' Carr said after an unnecessary pause. He added, 'You, chasing Nazi war criminals, this late in life? Isn't there enough going on in the Middle East to keep you busy?'

Yelkov looked away. When he turned back his eyes were expressionless, his voice flat. 'First things first.'

'Why don't you just go through channels?' Carr said. 'You wouldn't have any difficulty if you asked Waterloo direct.'

'I've been in the business more than thirty years. I can't

do *anything* the simple way. Besides, it means pieces of paper, and waiting.'

Carr stood up. 'Come to my place this evening, about seven. I should have it by then.'

Extracting information from the records was simple enough. First he punched up Erhardt Roeder. Apart from biographical data that could be found in any German medical register of the period and a brief reference to the fact he worked in Blestau, there wasn't much on him. The entry concluded with the terse note that Roeder was believed to have taken the identity of a Dr Lauritz Paulus. Just that, and nothing more about what had happened to Paulus.

Carr put Paulus's name into the computer, but it merely gave a cross-reference back to the Roeder file.

Carr finally tried Ernst Honecker, then added the code for 'Or analagous name' to the computer instruction. Four similar-looking names with brief details and reference numbers flashed up. Three of them were obviously irrelevant, but the fourth was Yelkov's man all right. Carr put the reference into the computer.

Dr Erich Hoenigger. Believed to be Dr Erhardt Roeder, born 9.7.1915 Chemnitz (now Karl-Marx-Stadt). Roeder was assistant to Dr Lobenz (executed 14.7.1946, q.v.) *for crimes at Blestau concentration camp* (q.v.).

Roeder believed to have taken identity of Dr Lauritz Paulus, killed in air raid on Blestau town 10.4.1945. Roeder/?Paulus believed to have gone to Czechoslovakia in 1950 as Paulus, and probably again changed name to Erich Hoenigger. Although Hoenigger reported dead about 1969, possibly some confusion with Dr Ernst Hencker, no record, who died 30.11.1969. Present location and activity unknown.

The files on Dr Lobenz and on Blestau concentration camp had no reference to the names Roeder, Paulus or Hoenigger.

The strange lack of co-ordination between the separate

records puzzled Carr. Particularly odd was that the first file on Roeder had no reference to Hoenigger, even though the Hoenigger file definitely mentioned the original Roeder entry. That was far from all. Even an eye less experienced than Carr's would see that there were unusual gaps in the information. Carr quickly ran through the records again. All but one of them were last updated in 1968, and then only with the note 'No further information'. The odd one out, the Hoenigger file – the one with the information in it – had been compiled in 1976.

Carr considered the implications of this briefly, came to no simple conclusion, then stopped wasting mental energy. It wasn't his problem.

Eli Yelkov called a little early, when Carr was finishing packing his case, carefully stowing away the Mauser and the spare magazines. The doorbell rang as Carr put down the case with its gaudy labels: *Spellbinder Tours, Vienna-Wien.*

Carr gave Yelkov his usual-sized whisky, big enough to stagger a Scotsman, and the notes he'd made from the files. 'Something cock-eyed about this case,' Carr said, explaining what he'd found.

As ever, Yelkov was as unsurprised as a hippo. 'Just bad record-keeping. You can't get the help these days.' He looked at the notes for a long moment, and Carr wondered what he was finding so interesting in them. 'Thank you, Richard,' he said quietly. 'They're a great help.'

Carr shrugged. 'I can't imagine how.'

They spoke inconsequentially for a while, then unexpectedly, Yelkov said, 'Do you know anything about PSI?'

'I know what it is. Parapsychology – the lot. Telepathy, psychokinesis, clairvoyance, hypnotism and anything else you can think of. Why?'

'The Russians and Americans are suddenly taking a big interest again. The Russians especially. They're spending an enormous amount of time and money on it.'

'Nice to know they're wasting their roubles.'

'Anything but.'

Carr looked at him in astonishment. 'You don't believe in it as a practical proposition, do you?'

'Not in its present stage of development, but the potentialities are enormous.'

'You're joking,' Carr said.

'They're running PSI research stations in Moscow, Leningrad, at least another half a dozen cities, and in Siberia. Fact. The KGB are controlling the whole thing, of course. They've even been doing experiments on telepathy from submarines,' he added. 'Fact.'

'And that *works*?'

'During the war our people sometimes got information out of concentration camps by telepathy and clairvoyance. Also fact.' Yelkov held out his glass, and Carr poured him another massive whisky. 'Apart from the Russians, there's a lot of research going on in Bulgaria, Poland, Rumania and Czechoslovakia right now. Fact. Fortunately our contacts there are pretty good because Jews did most of the preliminary work on PSI. We're particularly gifted at ESP.'

'Ah, Uri Geller,' Carr said without thinking.

Yelkov gave him a look that could have bent a fork. It was obvious he wasn't greatly impressed by Mr Geller's public performances. 'Think of it for a moment,' he said. 'Supposing you had men who could "tune in" to any of the world's political and military leaders. Not to what they were saying, but what they were actually *thinking* . . . A lot of people believe that it'll be possible, eventually.'

Carr stirred. He felt faintly embarrassed at Yelkov's apparent naïvety. Or was he merely dissimulating for some purpose of his own?

'It doesn't stop there, Richard. Some years ago the Russians began a project to find ways of indoctrinating people from a distance. "Re-educate antisocial elements" they called it.' Yelkov smiled wryly. 'Remember the world chess championship? Korchnoi wasn't having an attack of Russian paranoia when he said KGB agents were trying to hypnotize him at a distance and upset his concentration. He knew what he was saying.' Yelkov stared into his glass.

'The Russians don't dismiss anything out of hand: telepathy, psychokinesis – they've got one of the best in the world at it – hypnotism, Kirlian photography, astrology . . . '

'Astrology, for Christ's sake!' said Carr disbelievingly.

'Listen. Ever since the formation of the state of Israel in 1948, we've been running an astrological analysis chart. Yes, a sort of national horoscope. Just for a start, the predictions in the Six-Day and the Yom Kippur wars were stupefying, they were so accurate. Then not long ago, a big operation was planned. The people running the chart predicted a successful event connected with aviation.' He paused for effect. 'The operation was Entebbe.'

Carr poured himself a whisky as big as Yelkov's.

'After the indoctrination experiments the comrades took it further. In controlled conditions certain powerful natural telepaths intercepted and *modified* mental telepathic messages passing between two other people. Apart from the indoctrination-from-a-distance experiments, they also managed to affect non-telepaths' actual thought processes. They deformed certain attitudes and made their subjects significantly more susceptible to error.'

'Eli, there's a limit – ' Carr began, but Yelkov's sudden glance shocked him into silence. 'Stop trying to make my flesh creep,' Carr said eventually. 'You've been reading too many science-fiction horror stories.'

'Too true I have. *Everything* I've told you is a matter of serious scientific record. The trouble is you Western nations don't take it nearly seriously enough. We do, because – ' He checked himself and left it at that.

'Why are you telling me all this?'

'I owe you a favour.' For a moment Yelkov reassumed his stage Jew persona. 'And there's only one thing better than owing a friend a favour. It's owing a friend several favours. It means you've been getting the best of the bargains.' He became deadly serious again. 'Listen, there are all sorts of signs that the Russians have made a significant breakthrough in applied PSI; that they're somehow getting at people's minds and thoughts. They're breaking down security and turning good men into traitors. As yet it's on a limited scale, but . . .'

Yelkov, the solid rock of a man, looked at Carr with troubled eyes. 'I tell you, Richard, it's frightening me to death.'

It was the second time someone Carr admired had said that. He suddenly felt very cold.

4

Carr hated flying. It wasn't fear or air-sickness, but boredom and too much time to think too much. He often tried to read, but the physical surroundings were all wrong.

He stared sourly through the window of the Spellbinder Tours' Trident 2 charter flight, at the French coast. Perversely it seemed to be keeping its distance despite the fact that the aircraft was flying at 500 mph, or whatever it was. He was even more bloody-minded than usual because he'd failed to get his favourite seat, rear-facing next to the emergency exit in Row 12. Apart from being one of the safest places, it also has more leg-room, as long as you can tacitly agree with the passenger sitting opposite which side you're going to put your legs, and change over together. Instead, Carr was cramped in a seat that was scientifically designed to be slightly too small for anyone, irrespective of size, who sat in it. The passenger in front of him had put his or her seat back in the reclining position, and Carr was forced to do the same in self-defence. In turn the passenger behind Carr let out a grunt of annoyance and put his seat back, too.

Carr believed it was something about the bright-lit but claustrophobic interiors of aircraft that so thoroughly depressed him. It was almost chemical in its effectiveness. Maybe it was aircrafts' lack of character. A French train felt and smelt different from a German one, which looked and sounded quite unlike an Italian one. Rattling over the Andes from Mendoza to Valparaiso was like no other train journey in the world. But no matter what part of the world aircraft were flying over, they all made you feel you were permanently hovering over Seattle. Only the uniforms of the impersonal hostesses were different; the plastic-flavoured food was the same over the equator and the pole.

Travelling in aircraft always – *always* – made Carr go through the same pointless self-examination of what he was doing in Intelligence, and what good it all was. It was as familiar and frightening in its inescapability as a recurring dream, and as frustrating in its inevitable lack of conclusion.

There was no logic in it. The suggestion that there is a secret desire in all of us to be a spy didn't explain it. He wasn't as well paid as a company accountant, and his life expectancy wasn't anything like as good as an airline pilot's or a shepherd's. He had a broken marriage without a marvellous adulterous affair to blame for it, his home was little more than an address with furniture, and he had two teeth that needed filling.

'Bugger the sodding lot of them,' he said.

He became aware of something pressing against his thigh and upper arm. The woman in the seat next to him was leaning across him, trying to see through the small window. The gentle pressure was from her knee and left breast.

'Sorry,' she said with a smile that declared that the contact with him was deliberate.

Carr hadn't noticed her when she sat down beside him: he'd been staring out of the window, watching spectators on top of the airport building waving to friends arriving or leaving, wandering around with short-wave radios held to their ears, eavesdropping on the ritual conversations between pilots and the tower, or simply breathing in the fumes of aircraft fuel. Now he looked at her properly.

She was about thirty, maybe a year or two less, mid-blonde with grey-blue eyes and a bee-sting lower lip that gave her an anxious-for-bed look. It went well with her unsubtle figure. In a couple of years she'd be talking about seriously going on a diet, and another two or three years after that she'd abandon the idea for good and settle for being 'jolly'.

'Change places with me,' Carr offered.

'If you're sure you don't mind,' she said. She stood up and moved into the aisle, taking a superfluous deep breath that made some of the passengers regret they'd brought their wives with them. When she sat in the window seat her skirt rode up above her knees but she didn't seem to notice.

'Are you on your own?' she asked, turning her back on the window she was so keen on a minute before. He admitted that he was. 'So am I. My friend Lesley was supposed to be coming with me but her husband broke his leg playing football and she's had to stay at home with him,' she said without pausing for breath. 'So we're the odd ones out.'

'There's nothing odd about me,' Carr said. The girl giggled and her skirt moved up another couple of inches apparently by psychokinesis.

Her name was Daphne Brook, and she was single. 'I was engaged three times, but I broke it off,' she told Carr.

'That must have been painful,' he said gravely, and Daphne giggled again. A stewardess, utter indifference showing through her professional smile, plonked down two plastic trays of food-resembling matter in front of them and moved on, passing out other trays with the skill of a blackjack dealer.

Before they had finished their cold beef and ham, warm lettuce and a tasselated gherkin, and started on their pineapple rings, Carr had learned that Daphne was twenty-nine, lived near Kingston, worked as a radio despatcher for a taxi firm, and was on the pill. 'It saves so much messing about,' she explained ingenuously.

Once again Carr was astonished by the way some English women left their sexual inhibitions at outward Customs. In fact, so did most single women from Western countries once they got overseas, now he came to think about it. Casual sex seemed to be considered as integral a part of a holiday as Mediterranean sunshine and cheap Spanish plonk. He made no moral judgements: he was just glad he was on the receiving end this time.

Daphne stifled a yawn. 'Oops, sorry. I didn't get much sleep last night. I was on late turn, and then I had all my packing to do. I'll be glad to get to bed,' she said, this time not underlining the double entendre. But he barely heard her as two thoughts struck him in quick succession. The first was that he would be staying at the hotel with the rest of the tour party only that evening before assuming his second identity, so he had little time to make the most of the situation.

The second thought was chilling. Had Daphne been ordered by the opposition to pick him up and keep surveillance on him? Find out what she could – maybe to try to get him into a blackmail situation? Carr rapidly considered the odds. Was it possible for them to have found out that he was on this flight, and still have enough time to get Daphne on it? Difficult, but far from impossible. For her to grab the seat next to him would be no problem at all. But it was such an obvious pick-up; she was so obviously available and inviting. An experienced agent would be more subtle – or maybe the brashness was a double bluff.

No, no. For the opposition to have sicked someone on to him, they'd have to know he was much more important than his accepted job in commercial and technical espionage. If they'd found out that much, he was in serious trouble anyway.

For Christ's sake, how paranoid can you get? Even supposing she is *the opposition, you can find it out and get rid of her as soon as you have to. Forget it, she's what she seems to be. God, how I hate this grimy job. It's got me to the point that if it starts raining I think it's a bloody KGB plot.*

'I said, have you got a single room, or are you sharing?'

He pulled himself together. 'Single.'

'That's good. I mean, you never know, do you?' she said with pointed vagueness.

'Not that I'll be using it all that much,' Carr told her. 'I'll be staying with friends. Noblesse oblige, and all that. I came on this package holiday because even with the hotel thrown in it's cheaper than the normal fare.' Better explain – she was the sort of woman who'd cause a fuss and start phoning the police if he disappeared without warning.

Daphne looked disappointed. As far as he could tell, it was genuine. 'Still, that doesn't mean we won't be seeing each other, does it?'

'Of course not,' he assured her, with all the sincerity of a bomb-site car salesman.

It was evening by the time they arrived in Vienna, where it was an hour later than London anyway. Their courier, Miss Newman, shepherded them all through Customs without delay, smoothly helping people to get their own bags, and trolleys to put them on. She made the other tours' couriers look rather bumbling.

She was earnest, and of obvious Mittel-Europ origins. She wore glasses like twin carriage-lamps and a screwed-on permanent smile which Carr found faintly unnerving. He was ready to believe she did twenty-five press-ups every morning before putting on her bra, which appeared to be made of Lego.

Daphne stayed close to Carr as if she was afraid of the dark from the moment they left the aircraft, through the boring coach journey, until they got to their hotel just off the Liechtensteinstrasse, near the Franz-Josefs railway station.

When Carr signed the registration card the reception clerk said, 'Oh, Mr Chatfield, there's a message for you. Mr Sidney telephoned and said will you please contact Herr Axelman when it's convenient.'

'Mr Sidney' was Streeter – the SID of the section's title made it an obvious choice of a name for him. 'Axelman' began with an 'A', which meant it was urgent.

'I'll see you later,' Carr told Daphne. 'I'll have to go out as soon as I've unpacked.' Her face fell. 'I'll be as quick as I can,' he said, aware he seemed to be making a habit of saying that to women.

He half unpacked his case. There was no point in taking out everything; he'd be moving on tomorrow, trying to make contact with a man who was probably dead in an unmarked grave.

Carr hoped he could come up with something positive here in Vienna. The thought of going to Bratislava gave him a griping feeling in the gut, for a number of reasons.

He changed his mind and unpacked the rest of his things, just in case someone checked on him. Finally he took out from its hiding-place a chamois-leather shoulder-holster, and put it on. The Mauser fitted it perfectly, and made no bulges in his jacket. He put one spare magazine into his left-hand trouser-pocket, and hid the other one in the cardboard tube of the toilet-roll. When he returned – if he hadn't used it – he would hide the second one by taping it behind the U-bend of the lavatory pan. Not in a plastic bag in the tank: ten-year-olds with Spy Club badges from cereal packets knew enough to look there.

As he went through the entrance hall Miss Newman, the courier, was standing near the reception clerk. She spotted him and called out like an old-style nanny, 'Mr Chatfield! Dinner in half an hour!'

'*Bon appetit,*' he said, and walked into the street. How anyone would want to eat after the assault on the appetite by the aircraft meal, he couldn't imagine. He wondered for a moment about Miss Newman knowing his name – out of all the forty or so members of the party. But he put it down to her ghastly efficiency and the fact that she was nearby when the reception clerk had told him of the message.

Carr walked briskly, then slowly and briskly again, then doubling back on his tracks, an automatic reaction to make sure he wasn't followed, to the Franz-Josefs Bahnhof. He went to the telephone counter and gave the operator a London number. The man indicated a cabin.

In London a telephone listed at an Earls Court address rang four times in an empty room, then went silent as the call switched automatically to Streeter's phone.

'Hello, Herr Axelman,' Carr said. 'I got a message from Mr Sidney.'

'Can you speak?' asked Streeter.

'Of course I can't. I'm in a phone-box in Vienna and the

Southall branch of the Enoch Powell Fan Club is in here with me.'

'Czech radio has put out a story announcing the arrest of five "imperialist" spies. They've given the names.'

'And?'

'No.'

So Ondrach wasn't one of them. 'Anyone at our friend's home?' Carr asked. He knew Streeter would have listened to the Infinity Bug in Ondrach's apartment.

'No. You've got the key. The sooner the better.'

'Thanks,' said Carr bitterly, and hung up.

Carr took a taxi to within a few yards of the corner of Ondrach's street. It was in the Schönbrunn district; a nice, quiet, upper-class area full of independent or high-salaried, tax-paying families, all respectably married. The flat itself was in one of those converted turn-of-the-century houses to be found in big cities all over the Western world. Only one side of the street was built on; a small park was on the other. Ondrach had picked the flat carefully: concealed observation couldn't be kept on it from a house opposite.

Carr walked past the house to the end of the street, apparently looking straight in front of him, but although his head was steady, his eyes were busy checking the passersby and the cars lining the kerb. Only one, on the park side of the road, was occupied. Two thickset men were sitting in a black Taunus saloon with a whip aerial. A hatchet-faced woman with bulging calves was walking a dog along the pavement. It showed no interest in any trees or lamp posts.

Carr continued on until he came to a taxi rank, with a single taxi there. He ignored it, and found a roving one. He told the driver to go along the Grünbergstrasse, and he'd give him further instructions. The Taunus with the two men was still there, and so was the woman with the dog. *'Westbahnhof, bitte,'* Carr said to the driver.

He ate a sandwich, then waited an hour before taking a taxi outside the station.

The Taunus was still there, and so was the hatchet-faced woman with the miserable-looking dog, which must have been empty as a drum. Twice more, at about hourly intervals, Carr took taxis along the street. On the first of the journeys the hatchet-faced woman had been replaced by a man in baggy trousers. *You'd think they'd have learned about trousers by now,* he thought. *It's unbelievable.*

On the second trip, the dog-walker had gone, and so had the Taunus. In its place was a Volkswagen Passat, with two different thickset men sitting in it. *I bet they've got baggy trousers,* Carr told himself, but there was no one to take the bet.

He proceeded to the Vienna West Station and took another taxi back through the empty streets to the hotel, mentally tabulating the facts and calculating the probabilities.

One thing was certain: Ondrach's flat was under permanent surveillance, and obviously it wasn't by the Austrian police.

It followed then that the opposition knew about Ondrach. Leading on from that were three possibilities. The first was that Ondrach was dead and the KGB were on a stake-out to see who turned up to check the flat. That was the most likely case, bordering on a certainty. The second possibility was that Ondrach was still alive, and on the run; and the heavies were hanging around in case he came back to his flat. That was the least likely – especially that Ondrach would go back to the flat if the comrades were after him. The KGB would surely realise this. Or perhaps not.

The third possibility was that Ondrach was blown, but didn't know it, and they were waiting for him to turn up so they could snatch him. Quite possible.

'One thing's for sure,' he murmured. '*I'm* not bloody going there.'

At the hotel there was a note on his bed.

I'm in Room 117.
I'll leave the door unlocked.
D.

After a shower and a drink he pussyfooted along to Room 117. He tapped on the door and quietly went in.

There was a single bedside lamp burning. It had a pink chiffon scarf over it, giving the scene a faintly raffish air. Daphne was half sitting up in bed. She was fast asleep, softly snoring and bubbling. She was wearing a thoroughly inappropriate baby-doll nightdress from which her impressive right breast had completely escaped and the left one was doing its best to break out. Unfortunately Daphne also had three metal curlers in the front of her hair, and half her face was cold-creamed. On the bed was a packet of tissues, on the bedside table were two or three greasy tissues in an ashtray. The long day had been too much for her. It would be unfair to wake her, looking like that.

Regretfully Carr closed the door carefully behind him and sneaked back to his own room.

'I could do with a good night's sleep anyway,' he lied to himself.

Next morning Carr quit the hotel. He left suitable notes for Daphne and the formidable Miss Newman to say he was going to stay with friends for a while and didn't know when or if he'd be returning to the hotel.

An hour later, after taking routine precautions to make sure he wasn't being followed, Carr checked in as Connell at a hotel near the Mariahilferstrasse, Vienna's main shopping street. It was conveniently near to Ondrach's flat in the Schönbrunn area.

Again he hid the spare magazines for the Mauser in the toilet-roll holder and behind the U-bend of the lavatory pan. The bathroom of both hotels seemed to have been designed and equipped by the same company. He had a busy day ahead of him, travelling round the dead-letter drops and signal points.

He left coded messages to set up a meeting at any of the regular prearranged times and rendezvous points. One drop was behind a stanchion of a railway bridge; another a scribbled note on a certain page of the directory in a phone-box, another stuck to the side support of a cinema seat; yet another behind the extreme right-hand mirror of the men's lavatory in the air terminal in Invaliderstrasse. Ondrach had left no message at any of the points.

After this Carr went round leaving signals that there was a message to be picked up at the most convenient drop. He stuck a small black map pin in the bottom of the lavatory door at the Café de Paris; a piece of plastic-coated wire twisted on to the bottom of a wire rubbish basket in the Botanischer Garten; he left unobtrusive crayon marks on tram-stop signs and on particular bricks in walls.

It was all wrong, leaving so many signs and messages at once all over the place. Wrong and pointless, Carr thought. Ondrach must *know* London would be wanting to contact him; he didn't need to be told. But the whole situation was cock-eyed anyway. What else could he do, to start with?

Carr decided to give it four days. He turned up at the rendezvous points specified in the messages at the dead-letter drops: he sat on park benches, visited public lavatories – 'I've been in more loos than a bloody queer with a weak bladder,' he finally told himself – drank coffee in certain cafés, stood on railway platforms, and went to a small cinema showing old classic films. He saw two Serbo-Croat black-and-white movies with bad German subtitles. They didn't do a great deal for him.

He also managed to drive past Ondrach's flat every day. The goons were still watching it.

On the evening of the fourth day he returned to the hotel feeling fed-up and useless. He was having a shower to take some of the stiffness from his limbs when he thought he heard a slight noise outside the bathroom. He left the water running, wrapped a towel round himself, and moved silently to the main room. He cursed himself for letting the tedium of the past few days make him careless; he'd left his Mauser on the bedside table.

He put his head round the door.

A neatly-dressed man of about thirty-five sat in the room's one easy chair. He seemed vaguely familiar. He was completely at ease, and nodded cheerfully as Carr appeared. At the same time he made a cautionary gesture of putting a finger to his lips.

Carr glanced quickly at the bedside table. His gun was still there in its holster, exactly where he'd left it.

The man rose from the chair and switched on the radio. Then he loosely rolled a newspaper and put it to his lips. Carr understood at once. He put his ear to the other end of the newspaper tube. It was a simple but fairly effective procedure when a room might be bugged.

The man said something quite ludicrous. 'Excuse me, sir, do you know the way to the Reisenrad?' he whispered.

Carr took the newspaper and put it to the man's ear.

'I'm sorry, I'm a stranger and I've lost my map.'

'Then I shall go to the police station and ask.' It was the last recognition signal that Ondrach had been given.

Carr was suddenly fully alert again, and not until a long time afterwards did he see anything ridiculous in grown men, one of them wearing only a towel, whispering passwords to each other like this.

'I'm Ondrach.'

Carr took the newspaper. 'How did you know it was me? How did you get in?'

'When we knew you were coming I watched a couple of times at a rendezvous and then followed you. I wasn't going to risk you being a KGB plant. And how did I get in here? My dear man, any second-class thief can get into a hotel bedroom.' Carr knew that this was true. 'Now, get dressed. I've got a car outside. There's somebody I want you to meet.'

Carr raised his eyebrows in a question.

'Vaclav Zvalen. Oh, yes, I got him out all right, eventually.'

Carr tried to speak, but Ondrach cut him off. 'I'll tell you all about it later.'

Carr dressed quickly. Before he picked up his jacket he put on the holster with the Mauser. He looked at Ondrach as he did so. Ondrach shrugged, uninterested.

They were halfway down the corridor towards the service stairs – Ondrach wouldn't take a lift – when Carr grabbed his left wrist. 'Damn. I've left my watch in the bathroom.' He turned back.

'I'll come with you. I don't want to hang around on my own,' Ondrach said quietly. His English was almost accentless.

Carr opened the door of his room and went straight to the bathroom, leaving the door half open. Ondrach waited in the main room. 'Won't be a minute,' Carr called out. 'I've had this stomach trouble ever since I came here.' He was careful not to refer to Ondrach by name. If the place was bugged, the listeners wouldn't hear anything more significant than a lavatory being flushed.

The car, a Volkswagen, was parked in an alleyway near the hotel. Its rear windows were encrusted with mud, which was as effective as curtains, and far less attention-attracting. A thick-necked man, wearing a black leather jacket, was at the wheel.

'Anything?' Ondrach asked in German. The man shook his head.

Ondrach opened the near-side rear door, the right one on a continental car, inviting Carr to get in, but Carr stood back to let Ondrach in first. Ondrach climbed into the car without hesitation. Experienced people who carry guns and may have to use them always sit in the right-hand back seat of a car when they travel with people they don't know. In the left-hand back seat a right-handed man is at a serious disadvantage if he wants to draw a gun and use it on the man sitting beside him. Ondrach had cheerfully conceded the right-hand seat to Carr, which was reassuring.

'This is Berti,' Ondrach said as the car drew away without conspicuous noise.

'Hello,' said Carr. 'Now, what's all this about Zvalen? Where is he?'

'In a safe house, hiding.'

'Why hasn't he asked for political asylum?'

'He's scared shitless. It was a pretty rough trip across the border. The worst I've had.'

'He's safe now?'

Ondrach nodded. 'But with all these people getting arrested and the whole place swarming with the opposition, he won't risk giving himself up here, in case the Russians put pressure on the authorities to send him back. He doesn't trust the Austrian government.'

'I can't say I blame him.'

'He wants a genuine English agent, or an American one, to get him out. Right out.'

'How do I convince him I'm English and an agent? Show him my badge and sing the rude version of the Eton Boating Song?'

'I've thought about that. There's a phone in the safe house where we're going. Zvalen can dial the Federal exchange in London for himself, then you'll ask for the extension and speak to someone you know while he listens in.'

'Ingenious,' Carr said. 'Now, what the hell's been going on over here?'

'There's been a bad leak somewhere. They rolled up the entire Comenius network in Czechoslovakia. You heard about it on the radio?' Carr nodded. 'I only escaped by the skin of my teeth,' Ondrach went on. 'It was pure blind luck. I was in Bratislava, on my way back to the flat there from a meeting, when I had a puncture, and then damp got into the ignition. I was two and a half hours late getting home. As I drove up to my place two carloads of KGB pulled up at the front door and rushed in. I simply kept going. Three days later I got across the border with Zvalen. I wasn't going to risk going to the flat here in Vienna. We went to a safe house I've got. Just as well. Berti's driven past the flat a couple of times. The comrades are waiting there for me.'

'I've seen them.'

'I expect they plan to grab me and take me back to the monastery, if they can. Kill me if they can't.'

Carr knew he meant the famous Monastery of the Knights of the Cross in Prague, on the Vltava River, now the headquarters of the STB, the Czech Secret Police.

The Volkswagen rattled north and east along the one-way system of Schellinggasse, Stubenbastei and Dominikanerbastei to the Franz-Josef-Kai by the Danube Canal, and on to the Schweden Bridge. From there Berti took the Praterstrasse.

The windows of the car were too grimy for Carr to see the Johann-Strauss-Haus in the Praterstrasse, where Strauss composed the *Blue Danube* waltz, even if he wanted to, which he didn't particularly.

At the end of the street is the seven-road junction, the Praterstern. Nearby is the famous ferris wheel, the Reisenrad, where Orson Welles uttered his much quoted and quite inaccurate line about Switzerland and the cuckoo-clock. Carr didn't bother to try to see that either.

They continued straight on, past the Vienna North Station, along Lasallestrasse, which meets the River Danube by the mighty Reichsbrücke or 'Empire Bridge'. At least, where the bridge used to be. It fell down all on its own in 1976 because of lack of maintenance. Carr hoped the Reisenrad was better cared for.

'You didn't have any links with the Comenius people, so how did the opposition get on to you? Who blew you?' Carr asked at last. He saw Ondrach's face harden.

'It was one of your Waterloo lot – there's no doubt about that in my mind. You'd better start turning over stones when you get back there.'

Carr remained silent again for a while. 'You've put on weight,' he said idly.

Ondrach looked at him with surprise. 'We haven't met before.'

'I saw your photograph in the file.'

'I didn't know there was one of me.'

'It's not very good.' Carr peered through the windows, still without seeing much. 'At least you get about in this job. Last week I was in Amsterdam, the week before that in Geneva. Been back there recently?'

Ondrach shook his head.

'Quand est-ce que tu as quitté Genéve définitivement?' Carr asked. *'Soixante-seize?'* (When did you leave Geneva for good? Seventy-six?)

'Non. Soixante-quinze.' (No. Seventy-five.)

Carr nodded, satisfied. 'Something's just occurred to me. It's all very well you handing Zvalen over to me, but supposing *I'm* the leak at Waterloo?'

'I've thought about that, too,' Ondrach said flatly. He didn't elaborate.

5

It came on to rain. It washed some of the concealing mud from the Volkswagen's windows, and against the night sky Carr could plainly see the outline of the great TV tower in Danube Park and the three new semicircular skyscrapers of the 'United Nations City' on the other side of the river. They outraged the classical Viennese skyline, Carr thought. Remembering the City of London and the glass and concrete slabs surrounding St Pauls, though, he felt he was in no position to throw stones.

Soon they were crossing the Floridsdorfer Bridge; at the Am Platz they turned right into Donaufelderstrasse, and then left again. By now it was clear where they were headed: the far north-east suburbs of Vienna, part of the 21st District, which is anything but a tourist attraction. Eventually they came to a mean, narrow street.

They stopped outside a house with a leprous façade and dark greasy windows. It looked as if a demolition gang had knocked off for a tea-break and would be back soon to give it the *coup de grâce.*

Berti, who hadn't said a word since they had left the hotel, took a key from his pocket and opened the door. The hall was quite dark, and Carr stumbled. Ondrach held his arm to steady him. As soon as the front door closed behind them, Berti switched on the light, a single fly-specked, yellowing bulb. The place smelt of ancient damp, cats and fried cabbage. And, bizarrely, of hospitals.

Berti led the way along a corridor of creaking floorboards to a door at the far end. He switched on another light, barely more attractive than the first.

The room's one window was blacked out with a blanket held by a wooden frame. There was little furniture: a table, a chest of drawers, a couple of chairs, and three narrow iron beds – two of them neat, one with a pile of dirty blankets like a dog's nest. On the chest, standing out like a bloodstain, was a stainless steel surgical dish, a piece of cotton wool, and a small bottle of alcohol. A smaller piece of cotton wool with a bloodstain lay on the floor.

The whole atmosphere had suddenly changed. There was an electric, bristling hostility in this sordid place. Carr moved further into the room away from the others. Near the covered window he turned to face them. His Mauser was in his hand, cocked and with the safety catch off.

'You're not Ondrach,' he said. There was a pause.

'What makes you say that?'

'For a start, the Swiss don't use the comic French system of counting, with "sixty-sixteen", "four-twenties, ten-seven" and all that. Anyone who'd learnt his French in Switzerland wouldn't say "*soixante-quinze*": he'd say "*septante-cinq*". And Ondrach doesn't know about the Comenius people.'

'You're quite right,' the other admitted blandly. 'I'm not Ondrach. But it took you a long time to realise it.'

'No. I knew at once.'

'Then why wait until you got here?'

'There was a slim chance that you really did have Zvalen.'

'Ondrach' shook his head, amused. 'He's served his purpose by now. You know, he may have been clever, but he was awfully naïve. He fell for the oldest trick in the world. He thought he'd crossed the border, and when he was debriefed by a British officer, he gave the names, addresses, recognition signals, the lot, of the people who'd passed him on. Oh, by the way, my name is Capek.'

'And Ondrach? What's happened to him?'

'He's dead. He was quite helpful: he told us everything he knew, as well. He was rather upset about it, and to show our gratitude, we put him out of his agony.' His smile was terrifying.

Not quite everything. He didn't tell you he wasn't run from Waterloo.

The false Ondrach gestured towards Carr's gun. 'You can put that away,' he said. 'I unloaded it while you were in the shower. He put his left hand into his jacket pocket, then threw eight .32 cartridges on to the table.

Berti, quite unhurried, took a heavy automatic from a shoulder-holster, and Capek himself produced a revolver. They had Carr thoroughly in the bag. Nevertheless, Carr wasn't too impressed with Capek. He'd talked too much, even though Carr was as good as finished. And both Capek and Berti were holding their guns rather casually. It was all pretty unprofessional.

'Now what?' he asked.

'Berti will give you an injection to keep you quiet for twenty-four hours. We'll all wait here until tomorrow night, and when everything's ready we'll take you across the border.' He turned to Berti, and said in Russian, 'Give him the injection now.'

'Wait!' Carr said sharply. 'I'll say it once. Put your guns on the table, slowly, then your hands on your heads, both of you. Otherwise you get it first.' He pointed the Mauser at Capek's head.

'Please don't be stupid,' Capek said. 'It's empty.'

Carr shot him twice in the middle of the forehead. Capek was dead before he had time to look surprised. Carr swung round towards Berti. He wished Berti had been closer to Capek to narrow the angle, but there it was.

Even the most self-possessed and alert man can be shocked into immobility sometimes; the measure of his ability and training is how long it takes him to recover. Berti was good. His gun was already beginning to move up to point at Carr.

Carr was tense. His first shot nearly missed altogether. It hit Berti about half an inch above the left-hand corner of his mouth, smashing two teeth and sending splinters of bone and amalgam fillings to the back of his throat. The teeth deflected the bullet out of the side of his face, just below the ear, missing the spinal column and the carotid artery. The second bullet hit him in the temple as his head was wrenched round by the force of the first shot. The third bullet went in a couple of inches below it. The exit wound on the other side of his head was ghastly.

There was a fourth, heavier explosion. Berti's gun fired, hitting the floor near his feet as his unfeeling fingers responded to the last message sent by the brain before it had exploded in a pink shower. Carr knew he'd been right to go for the head shot. There was no telling what Berti might have managed if he'd been hit in the chest.

Carr went over and kicked away Capek's revolver, a short-barrelled .38 Smith and Wesson Model 10. He moved quickly to Berti and picked up his heavy automatic. Carr never took chances: he always thought of what he called the Rasputin syndrome. When Prince Youssopoff and his friends tried to kill him, the Russian monk ate enough cyanide to kill a dozen horses, was shot in the heart, and then he suddenly rose up and tried to strangle his assassin. He didn't fall until he was shot in the temple, and even then moved once more. So no matter how dead they looked, he never left a gun within reach of anyone who wasn't actually buried.

He looked at Berti's automatic. It was an Austrian-manufacture 9mm Steyr, one of the most powerful automatics made. Carr slipped it into the waistband of his trousers.

He quickly emptied both men's pockets, not bothering to look at the papers in their wallets, but stuffing everything into his own pocket to examine later. He kept Berti's car keys separate. Lastly, Carr thoroughly frisked the bodies, to the extent of examining their shoes for hollow heels, and prodding the shoulder-pads of their jackets. Nothing – but he hadn't really thought there would be. Next he swept up the eight Mauser cartridges. No point in leaving extra clues for the Austrian police, or whoever found the two men.

He listened carefully, but there was no sound of movement anywhere else in the house, nor from outside. He searched the chest of drawers, pulling out the bottom drawer first and working upwards, so that he didn't have to close the drawers each time. There was nothing but a hypodermic syringe and a phial of colourless liquid, in the top drawer. Again Carr listened, his senses made hyperacute by the adrenalin pumped into his system. There was a distant police siren. Carr froze for a moment as it approached, but the sound faded as the car moved away again. He went to the front door and pushed home the bolt. It would at least delay anyone trying to enter, give him a few extra seconds to get away if he had to make a break for it. He went to the back of the house and checked there was an escape route through the patch of garden.

Then he checked the other rooms, but they were all quite empty, and thickly covered with dust. Only the kitchen had been used.

Carr took another look in the first room, in case he had overlooked anything. He regarded coldly the stiffening figures of Capek and Berti. The latter had spoken only the one word 'Nothing' from the moment Carr had met him to the moment he died.

'I knew you'd unloaded my gun the moment I picked it up,' Carr informed the dead Capek. 'I could tell from the weight. I reloaded it in the bathroom when I went back for the watch I hadn't forgotten and the crap I didn't want.'

Capek's eyes were wide open, and a shadow concealed the two small holes in the front of his head. He seemed to look reproachfully at Carr.

'You tried to be too clever, Capek,' Carr said. 'A whack on my head and a laundry basket was all it needed, back at the hotel.'

There was nobody in the street when Carr drove away in the Volkswagen, but his pulse-beat wasn't back to anything like normal until he'd crossed the Danube Canal, with no sign of anyone following.

It was already much too late for a flight to London; the last one had left in the afternoon. If he pushed it, he could probably get the local SIS station to lay on an RAF aircraft to fly him out, but that would draw unwelcome attention to the fact that he was in Vienna. And was it even necessary? He could hire a car and put a lot of distance between himself and the city. Or maybe take a train.

But what was it Capek had said? *We'll all wait here, and tomorrow night* . . . That meant he had twenty-four hours, maybe more. There was no need to flap. It was enough if Mr Sam Connell checked out of his hotel and disappeared without trace, and Mr Geoffrey Chatfield, loss-adjuster on holiday, returned to the Spellbinder Tours' hotel near the Franz-Josefs Station.

He left the Volkswagen behind the Esterhazy Park, towards the tiny Vienna River, and walked the rest of the way to the hotel. He told the desk to prepare his bill and went up to his room, where he spent five minutes looking through the papers he'd taken from the dead men. Neither had been carrying a red KGB identity card. The documents seemed straightforward enough, but he'd give them to Hillier back at the SID for close examination. There was also a surprising amount of Austrian, Swiss and Italian money that looked genuine. Carr put it in his pocket.

In five minutes he'd packed his bag and was on his way out. He walked to the West Station, took a taxi and changed twice before finally getting out at the Franz-Josefs Station. From there he phoned Streeter in London. 'Hello, Mr Sidney. I'm sorry to call you so late. This is Geoffrey Chatfield.'

'Can you talk?'

'No, I can't talk. I'm in Franz-Josefs Station and Franz-Josef himself is in the box with me.'

'Any news?'

'Yes. Our local representative has retired, I'm afraid, because of health reasons. Permanently.'

'I see.'

'That new man won't be joining us. Another company got him instead.'

'Pity.'

'I have all the information. I'll give you a full report as soon as I get back.'

'Yes. Anything else?'

'A couple of our competitors were rather anxious to get me, too, as a matter of fact. They were very persistent.'

'And?' Streeter didn't waste words on the telephone.

'I made it quite clear to them my decision was final. I won't be hearing from them again.'

'Very well. When will you be returning?'

'As scheduled. I'd be glad if you'd have someone pick me up at the airport in case I have difficulty getting away.' Streeter knew what this meant: have someone there to make sure there'd be no trouble with Customs.

Carr left the phone-box and looked round. There were no familiar faces, no one in baggy trousers, and no one reading a newspaper held up in front of his face. His senses alert, he walked the five or six hundred metres to the hotel.

The reception clerk was surprised when Carr, carrying his suitcase, asked for his room key; but after a quick check of the register and a sidelong glance at the Spellbinder Tours label Carr had put back on his suitcase, he handed it over.

'I take it you will be leaving tomorrow with the rest of your party, sir?' he asked.

Carr looked at him blankly. He'd forgotten that the package tour ended tomorrow. At least something had worked out all right for him.

'Ooh, you're back!' came a voice from behind as Carr walked to the lift.

Daphne Brook was staring at him with an enormous water-melon smile.

'Yes. I didn't get on all that well with my friends, and so I decided to leave them.'

She came up to him and took his arm. 'I've missed you. I hoped you'd come back here. Honestly, there's *nobody* interesting on this tour. Nobody. I've been properly fed up.' As they walked to the lift she looked at the key in his hand. 'Number forty-seven. This time I'll come to your room. I'm not letting you get away from me again.' She squeezed his arm. Carr had the feeling that if he locked his door she'd only bang on it until he opened up. 'D'you think I'm awful?' she said.

'Anything but,' he said, and managed a smile that passed for sincere. 'Give me half an hour to get unpacked and have a shower.'

He didn't make the mistake of leaving his gun out of reach again. He put the Steyr under the pillow, and left the smaller Mauser in the bathroom, concealed in his toilet case. As soon as he'd showered he put on a dressing-gown without pyjamas, and lay on the bed, thinking. He mentally retraced the events of the past few days, and the last couple of hours in particular. As far as he could remember, he'd left no traces, no loose ends which could be followed back to him.

There was a movement in the corridor outside. In a moment he was off the bed and into the bathroom, where he snatched up the Mauser. Daphne entered quietly. Through the crack in the bathroom door he saw her bolt the bedroom door behind her. He hid the Mauser again and went back into the bedroom.

She was wearing a lime-green kimono which brought out unexpected reddish glints in her hair. Now that she was actually there with him, she had about her a hint of uncertainty, of hesitancy, even of modesty. Carr felt a surge of desire and, quite unexpectedly, of affection for her. He smiled at her, with real sincerity this time. She smiled back without affectation.

She stood, just inside the room, almost as if she was afraid to come further in. She seemed a totally different person from the slightly brassy woman on the aircraft. All at once he sensed what it was: her outspokenness was merely a cover for basic timidity. She talked provocatively about sex, but when it actually came to it, she was insecure.

'I know you'll think I'm just saying this,' she told him, 'but I don't just with anybody.'

'I didn't think you did.'

'I mean, I haven't at all while I've been here on my own, and I could have. There are three of them that have been giving me looks and making remarks.'

'I can believe you.'

'I just didn't fancy them.' She looked at him searchingly. 'But you . . . you're nice. Perhaps it's because deep down you look so . . . ' He wondered what she was going to say. It was the last thing he expected, and it threw him completely off balance. 'Deep down you look so . . . *sad.*'

'Well, I'm not really. Particularly not now.'

His own surprising uncertainty seemed to reassure her. She walked over to him, and keeping her arms at her sides, kissed him. Her mouth was soft and warm and tasted sweet. It was, at first, a tentative kiss; little more than friendly. He slipped the kimono down from her shoulders and kissed the hollow at the base of her neck. She sighed deeply. She took his face gently between her hands and kissed him on the lips again, but hungrily now, shifting her hands behind his head to press her open mouth harder on his.

She drew back a little so he could see and touch her. When he gently stroked her breasts, she looked down at her nipples swelling and hardening. She slipped a hand inside his dressing-gown, tracing the hard ridges of muscle on the diaphragm with the tip of her finger. Without speaking, they undressed and went to the bed, where they lay facing each other.

She was going to move the pillow. Afraid that she might see the Steyr beneath it, he held both her hands in his, kissed her on the palms, then on the mouth again, effectively pinning her motionless with his busy lips and tongue. She forgot all about the pillow.

Simply looking at her aroused him. Her eyes were half closed, the tip of her tongue just visible between her soft, moist lips. Her full, firm breasts were pushed together by her upper arms.

She stroked his chest again, progressively moving her

hand lower, so slowly and deliberately that he impatiently grabbed her hand and moved it down until she took hold of him.

In turn she took his hand and guided it between her legs. As he caressed her, she pressed against him with an unconscious, insistent drive.

Her voice was husky when at last she said urgently, 'Now, please, *now*,' turning on to her back.

When he moved on to her she gasped, but she quickly responded to the rhythm of his movements, clutching him to her with her arms and legs.

As he moved his hand, he accidentally touched the Steyr under the pillow. All at once his attention utterly left Daphne. His body automatically continued its activity, but his mind and thoughts left his straining body.

He remembered Anatoli Renkov, shot through the temple while sleeping with a Turkish whore; Sam Lewis, killed by the woman who had just seduced him, slaughtered like a fighting bull, with a broad knife between two cervical vertebrae . . .

Carr was aware of a prickling sensation between his shoulder-blades: the hairs on the back of his neck began to rise like a wary animal's. In his imagination he heard the door opening stealthily, felt the cold touch of a knife-point on the nape of his neck . . . heard the click of the trigger preceding the explosion . . .

Oh, not again, for Christ's sake! Every time I have a woman outside the safety of my own home I get these bloody paranoid fantasies. Soon the only thing I'll be good for is looking at dirty books.

Daphne gave a long drawn-out moan of pleasure. It shook Carr out of his morbid introspection, and he became aware that he was soaked with sweat – it was gathering in the hollow of his back and trickling down his ribs. She, too, was covered in sweat: her forehead, her upper lip, her shoulders and the deep valley between her breasts were running with a mixture of her sweat and his. A drop from his forehead fell on the corner of her half-open mouth. Her tongue moved out sensuously and licked it.

Carr looked down at her, really seeing her properly for the first time. He realised with a shock that she was quite beautiful: her eyes were brilliant and enormous, her face coloured by her passion and exertions. Her arms were stretched above her head as she gripped the headboard behind her – raising her naturally firm breasts with stiff, darkened nipples standing out tautly. Now fully aware of her again, his senses sharpened. He felt his desire quicken and harden.

She moaned again. 'Oh, God . . . Oh, God . . . ' she repeated over and over again.

He wondered how long he'd been making love to her like an automaton, his body with her but his mind elsewhere in its dark, private world. From the sweat and their heavy breathing it was obviously a long while.

Abruptly she stopped murmuring and took a great breath, arching her back and pressing up against him frantically. Her excitement increased his own and he pulled her tighter to him. He thought of nothing; he only felt.

Later she said, 'Oh, darling . . . ' The word fell uneasily on his ears. She shook her head in bewilderment. 'Darling, that was . . . I mean . . . God, I thought you were *never* going to stop. On and *on* . . . I've never, ever . . . '

When she went to the bathroom he took the Steyr from under the pillow, pulled the bottom sheet from the mattress and slipped the gun under it. It was fairly accessible there, and she wouldn't accidentally find it during the night. He realised that meant he didn't want her to leave him . . .

He awoke to sudden and total awareness. His heart beating furiously, he scrabbled under the pillow for his gun, remembered where he had put it, and felt under the mattress. Then he calmed down.

The other half of the bed was empty. He looked towards the door; it was no longer bolted, but the 'Do Not Disturb' sign had gone from inside.

The phone rang. 'Yes?' he answered it at last.

'Good morning, darling,' Daphne said. 'I thought I'd let you sleep for a while. You were so tired . . . And no wonder,' she added archly. Carr cringed. It was as cloying as hot fudge before breakfast. He said something suitable.

As Daphne continued, an unbidden thought nagged at him . . . There was something Capek had said which hadn't registered at the time, but Carr now felt was significant – if he could only put his finger on it. He searched for it, forcing himself to go over the previous night's scene of bloody murder, trying to remember every detail of what was done and said – while he carried on a shallow conversation with Daphne. That wasn't very demanding: he had only to say an occasional 'Yes' and murmur friendly noises.

'No, I'm sorry, darling,' he said at last. 'I have to see some people on business before we leave. I'll see you on the plane going home.'

As he hung up, he suddenly remembered what Capek had said.

We knew you were coming.

All at once he really did have some business to attend to. He looked at his watch. There was just time, if he hurried.

Carr still had an hour or more to spare by the time he reached the last of the dead-letter drops where he'd left the coded messages telling Ondrach where to find him. It was the underside of a shelf in a phone-box by the Stadthalle.

The note was still there, just as all the others had been. Not one of them had been picked up – not one. So Capek couldn't have discovered where to find him from the messages, and couldn't have known the rendezvous points.

Yet, Capek *did* know he was coming and what name he would be using, at which hotel he'd be staying.

How?

By the time he returned to the SID offices in Kensington, Carr had worked it out. Now all he had to do was prove it.

6

He'd done most of his thinking on the flight back to London. It made him a dull companion for Daphne; she was still swimming in the warm, euphoric after-glow of the previous night, and insisted on clutching on to him ostentatiously, like someone who had just won a prize. Finally, to explain his grumpy silence he borrowed the oldest of female excuses for opting out: a terrible headache.

Before they left the aircraft he gave her a beautiful handbag he'd bought on impulse in the Mariahilferstrasse. He also gave her his name and address. If she wrote to him there, her letter would be returned 'Gone away – no forwarding address', but he didn't think she would write. Or he didn't want to think so.

His last sight of Daphne was a hand waving to him from the airport bus as it pulled out of the terminal. He felt the whole scene was rather like a bad movie.

Back at the Kensington house, Carr went through all the routine as quickly as he could. He gave Hillier the papers taken from the two corpses, and handed the Steyr to David Nurse. He kept the money.

Nurse looked as if he'd discovered that Father Christmas lives after all. He began to explain how the Steyr automatic has an unusual loading system and one fault of construction – the barrel is thin and has a tendency to split at the muzzle end – but Carr didn't have the patience to humour him this time. When he returned the Mauser and the magazines Nurse counted the cartridges.

'Five used,' he said.

'Five used,' Carr said flatly, and left it at that.

Upstairs, he took out a number of operation files and

carried them into his office. He read solidly for two hours, making notes. When he had finished, his face was grim. He put his own notes into the document-shredder and returned the files. After that he typed out a carefully composed report on his run to Vienna, leaving out one or two important details. When the report was finished, he took it to Streeter.

Streeter read it without expression. Crossing to his computer terminal he punched up Capek's name.

Jiri Capek was an STB man with a particularly nasty record – especially during the Czech uprising against the Russians in 1968. Berti was just a muscular trigger-man.

Carr sent a signal to the Waterloo Birdcage, reporting the two men's 'change of status', and that was the paperwork done.

'Will you give me a drink before I go home?' he then asked Streeter. Streeter moved towards the drinks cupboard. 'Not here,' Carr said.

Streeter looked at him carefully. 'We'll go to the flat, then.'

On the 180-yard-wide Kutuzov Prospekt in Moscow, not far from the Hotel Ukraine and the all-glass, circular Borodino Panorama building with the triumphal arch commemorating Kutuzov's victory over Napoleon, is a handsome apartment block. In a sixth-floor flat secret agents were thoroughly prepared by KGB instructors for service in the decadent Western democracies. Access to the flat was from the floor below . . . through a cupboard in another flat and up a concealed staircase.

Carr was inevitably reminded of this when he stepped from Streeter's office into a cupboard with a false-back partition. Behind was a staircase leading to his flat on the floor below.

'Do you ever consider,' he asked Streeter, as they walked down the narrow spiral stairway, 'why we exist – all of us: KGB, CIA, SIS, SDECE, BND, and the rest? We're the perfect example of symbiosis. We're all parasites, having other parasites for hosts, while we're the hosts for the parasites we live off.'

'The staircase making you giddy?' Streeter asked.

'If the KGB packed up tomorrow, the rest of us would start to atrophy and finally disappear.'

'Interesting thought,' Streeter said, sounding bored.

The two men emerged from another cupboard into the main corridor of Streeter's flat. He carefully locked the steel-lined door behind him.

'Well, what is it you didn't put in the report?' he asked as soon as they were settled with drinks. He offered Carr a cigar, which was refused. He lit one himself.

'I've been thinking. Ondrach was blown, and they were waiting for me. Capek knew my cover name, and what hotel I was booked into. So there's a leak – here in the department.'

'But the Comenius group were all put in the bag, and they had nothing to do with our department. You can't blame us for them.'

'Ondrach and Zvalen were the links. The opposition bagged Ondrach, who led them to Zvalen. Through him they got to the Comenius people when they "debriefed" him.'

'Christ,' sputtered Streeter, 'I hope the lot down at the Birdcage don't connect the Comenius arrests with us. If by any chance you're right . . .'

'It all comes in a straight line back here. Somebody in SID tipped off Capek's lot.'

Streeter was silent for a long time. 'And?' he managed at last.

Carr ticked off the names on his fingers. 'The only people who knew either about Ondrach's operation or my run to Vienna were: you, of course; Norman Hillier, documents; Roger Chapman, communications; David Nurse, armaments; Boyd Gatward, travel. The only ones who knew about *both* were . . . you, and Chapman. That's one advantage of a small department: there can't be all that many suspects. Well, I've been through the operational files and duty sheets, and it all fits. Chapman's the leak.'

Streeter slowly shook his head. 'You're wrong.'

'I'm not. There's no possibility that –'

'I tell you: you're wrong. Chapman's completely reliable. Take my word for it.'

'Henry, you can't just say that. I've checked and re-checked. There have been other cock-ups recently. And they started happening after Chapman came into ops-communications.'

Streeter was quite adamant. 'You've made a mistake. It's not Chapman.'

Carr was badly thrown by Streeter's obduracy. Nevertheless he persisted. 'How the hell can you be so certain you're right?'

'You'll just have to accept that I am.'

'Jesus H. Christ, they nearly had me delivered to the KGB gift-wrapped. You don't think I imagined it all? *Somebody* betrayed me.'

'Maybe. But not Chapman. Richard, leave it to me. I'll take care of it.'

'But I'm –'

'I said *I'll* take care of it.'

Carr didn't like it, but had to accept it.

'There's a Foreign Office reception on Friday. I mean Foreign and Commonwealth Office. I still can't get used to these new names. Go and enjoy yourself. You'll probably meet some old friends.'

'And new enemies.'

'Do try to be a little more agreeable.'

'I'd like to see you being agreeable after you'd been stuck in a back room with a couple of goons who were going to put you through the wringer. And F.O. receptions aren't my idea of a wild swinging time, or a therapeutic one, either.'

'Go, anyway.' Streeter stood up, leaving his barely half-smoked cigar in the ashtray. He took Carr's now empty glass and put it on the sideboard. He looked at his Philippe Patek watch. 'I'll have to kick you out, I'm afraid. I have a dinner engagement.'

'Nice,' said Carr about the watch. 'New, isn't it?'

Streeter nodded. 'I don't like these modern quartz things.

They may be accurate, but there's no craftsmanship about them, no artistry. They're soulless.'

'Time's time,' Carr said. He moved towards the front door of the flat. Streeter touched his arm to check him.

'When you were with Capek did he say anything, make any reference at all, to PSI? Parapsychology, that sort of thing?'

Surprised, Carr said, 'No, I don't think so. No, he didn't.'

'You're sure? Not even indirectly?'

'No.' He paused. 'Except . . . No, it's too ridiculous.'

'Tell me anyway.'

'He said "We knew you were coming". At the time I thought he meant . . . ' Carr stopped. He remembered what Yelkov had said, and suddenly it didn't seem so ridiculous after all.

He felt cold fingers of fear lightly touch the back of his neck.

Carr leant against a Whitehall pillar, genuine marble, not a painted plaster one, a slimline tonic with ice and lemon in his hand, surveying the other guests at the Foreign and Commonwealth reception.

If a bomb fell on this place right now London would lose half its entire Intelligence community in one go, he thought. *And a bloody good thing too.*

As usual at this sort of function in England and all over the world, the career diplomats and Intelligence employees kept to their own kind. He knew that, for the most part, Intelligence personnel weren't very popular with members of the Diplomatic Service. They didn't fit into the strict hierarchical structure of the Service, and diplomats were frankly jealous of their Intelligence compatriots, whom they considered spoiled, overpaid and arrogant. (Russian diplomats, however, didn't make audible criticisms of the KGB.) In fact, 'regular' embassy and consular staff of mutually antagonistic countries frequently got on better with each other than with their own countries' Intelligence staff, and the same went for Intelligence personnel. So, at this typical reception, the guests were divided into two fairly well-defined groups.

Carr could see Paul Orlenko, the KGB *Rezident* in London, talking to a man from *Mukhabarat el-Aam*, the Egyptian Secret Service. His name escaped him for the moment. Also present was Jean-Paul Félix, an agent of SDECE – the French Intelligence organization: *Service de Documentation Extérieure et du Contre Espionage.* He was talking animatedly to a tall Scandinavian-looking girl who was stealing glances over his shoulder at a butch woman journalist.

There were East and West Germans – MfS and BND – Czechs, Poles . . . a full set of representatives of the major countries' Intelligence services. Carr's feelings that their principal function was to justify the existence of the opposition was stronger than ever.

Major Patterson of MI5, that master of the portentous look, walked by Carr, so studiously not recognising him that only a drunken cretin would believe that they didn't know each other. In any case, probably the only person in the place who didn't know that Patterson was MI5 was the doorman, who was new to the job anyway.

'Hello, Major,' Carr called out. 'How are things at the Playboy Club annexe?' MI5 is in an ugly, brick-faced building with no street-level windows in Curzon Street, not far from the Playboy Club. He winked. 'This is a bit better than the War House's parties, eh?'

Patterson looked at him as if he'd sold the Crown Jewels to the Russians and pissed on his host's carpet. Carr grinned back, but only briefly. Baiting Patterson was rather like shooting a sitting bird.

'Hi, Richard,' came a voice from behind him. Carr turned to see the sunburned face of Mark Westbrook. He and Carr were old friends, with a strong mutual respect that had been hard earned.

Lying naked on a beach by the Black Sea, Westbrook would still have been instantly recognisable as an American. There is a distinctive American baritone voice – Lawrence Tibbett had it, Sherrill Milnes has it. Mark Westbrook had a quite unmistakable American physiognomy: he looked as American as black-eye peas and blueberry pie. Wherever he was in the world, whatever the climate, he always wore a dark-grey suit, button-down shirt, plain tie and plain black shoes, and short hair. Clean-cut and crisp of manner, he was the archetypal popular conception of a CIA operative. So much so that everyone assumed he must be an accountant, insurance-salesman or undertaker trying to look like a CIA man. A real CIA agent would be much more inconspicuous.

In fact Mark Westbrook *was* CIA. In countries where every quiet American is suspected of being a CIA man, looking so obvious could be the best deception.

Despite his utter loyalty to his own country, Westbrook was an Anglophile, with a respect for tradition, and the more admirable English institutions, which bordered on idolatry.

'Where did you get that tan? Middle East?' Carr asked.

'Sun-lamp. It's a disguise. I've been checking the strategic importance of the railways in Iceland.'

'There aren't any railways in Iceland.'

'I know that *now*, but I don't want it to get out.'

Carr grinned. 'Give me a ring at home and we'll have a drink. Mark, d'you know who that is over there with Vernon Beech?'

'So that's Beech.' Westbrook's smile froze as he recognised the second man. 'The other guy's Tchalenko, Arcadius Tchalenko. He's KGB, Victor Section. I expect he's here as a trade-union observer or cultural adviser or something. If you have any unsolved murders in the next few days, I'll give you six to four on Tchalenko. I met him in Ankara once. He's not very nice.'

Carr studied Tchalenko covertly. He seemed quite good-looking until Carr noticed his eyes, which were as cold as a crocodile's. Despite his neat Italian clothes his light-heavyweight's body with its bull neck looked uncomfortably offensive.

'Shall we go over and say hello? I haven't actually met

Beech.' Westbrook had become so Anglicized he actually used the word 'actually'.

Carr shook his head. 'I'd rather not. If Tchalenko doesn't know me, I'd prefer to keep it that way as long as I can.'

'Okay, you can introduce me to Beech another time. I'd really like to meet him.'

Westbrook's interest was understandable. Vernon Beech was an extraordinary man, even in the bizarre world of Intelligence. He was very tall, thin-faced, clean-shaven, bald with a thin fringe of greying hair. He had the faintly preoccupied, superior air of a cardinal's confessor. He was immaculately dressed, but not in the same way as Streeter. No one could remember seeing him in anything less formal than a black jacket and striped trousers of the severest cut. It was generally believed that he had never owned a coloured shirt.

Beech towered over everyone, not only physically but morally and intellectually as well. He was the sort of man who could look down on de Gaulle, and sometimes had. However, even Homer nodded, and Beech had made one catastrophic mistake in his career.

He'd firmly believed in Philby's loyalty and had stood up to be counted as one of his friends. When Philby finally defected, Beech was shattered. He didn't run for cover and explain how he'd really suspected Philby all along but had been told to keep quiet by his superiors, which was a popular line that saved a lot of necks at the time. Beech was openly contemptuous of the people who pleaded that defence. He admitted that he'd been deceived, and resigned from his senior post in Intelligence because, he said, he clearly wasn't competent to hold it.

This puritanical *mea culpa* attitude was highly embarrassing to many of his colleagues, who wanted no martyrs erecting their own crosses and climbing up on them in case they were required to do the same.

Beech was made Senior Executive in charge of the 'Paper Clip Distribution Section', or some similar department where he'd have no access to anything classified higher than Confidential.

Paradoxically, Beech's stern devotion to his insignificant duties and the rigid honesty which brought him to this lowly estate meant that his eventual promotion was more rapid than it would have been if he'd stayed on the Civil Service escalator where everyone ascended gently at the same rate.

A new government was elected and the incoming Prime Minister was suspicious of many of the senior people in the executive. He made a major reshuffle of advisers and counsellers, and Beech was brought near the top of the pack. His return to favour was the one appointment that both the Cabinet and Shadow Cabinet agreed couldn't have been bettered.

Beech became Special Adviser to the Cabinet – which effectively meant the Prime Minister – for Support Services. It put him in a sort of Cardinal Richelieu situation, only with rather more security of tenure.

There was no doubt that the efficiency of the Intelligence services markedly improved after Beech's appointment. He strongly approved of the SID, and gave it his invaluable support, both official and unofficial.

Beech reported directly to the PM . . . when he believed that a politician could be trusted with the information. Without bothering his masters, Beech gave orders and made appointments he 'knew' the PM would have ordered himself – if he'd had time to study all the facts (and could understand them), as Beech himself had. Beech was very aware that prime ministers were temporary and concerned mostly with party advantage. His own single, unwavering loyalty was to the Crown, which was unelected and permanent. Like Beech himself, in fact.

Across the reception hall, Beech nodded at Tchalenko, effectively dismissing him. Carr moved round the pillar so the Russian wouldn't see him as he moved off – though he couldn't be sure whether Tchalenko had already noticed him earlier.

Ten minutes after the Russian left the reception, Carr decided he'd stayed long enough himself. In the entrance hall Eli Yelkov came up to him.

'I've been waiting for you. I've got something for you.'

His expression made it clear it was no birthday present. He held out a flat round tin. 'It's a film. The STB made it.' He anticipated Carr's question. 'It doesn't matter how we got hold of a print. I think you should see it.'

'Why me? Why not give it to Willie Parker, or Guy Adams at the Birdcage?'

Yelkov ignored the question. He slipped the tin into Carr's overcoat pocket. 'Pass it on to them afterwards, if you want to. You can tell them where you got it or not, as you like.' He took hold of Carr's arm and looked him directly in the eye. 'Richard, you'll need a strong stomach.'

He left while Carr was still wondering.

Carr ran the film at the Kensington office of the SID. Streeter watched it with him. It was an 8mm colour film of uneven quality, probably because the print had been made in a hurry, but it was clear enough.

Neither man spoke during the twenty minutes of the film. It was something neither of them had seen before, or wanted to see again. It left them both covered in sweat and feeling very sick.

When Josef Frolik defected from the Czech Secret Service in June 1969 he said that the STB made films to discourage agents from trying to come over to the West. They killed a would-be escaper slowly – very slowly – and filmed the process in colour. This was one of those films. The STB and their 'uncles' had made technical progress since their first productions: it had sound as well. The subject was Dr Zvalen.

The film was obviously for showing to other scientists who might be thinking of defecting.

It came to an end and the projector switched itself off. Neither man moved for a while, not even to turn on the light.

'You'd think they'd know better by now,' Streeter said at last. 'That might scare off some people, but it'll encourage a hell of a lot more to make a break for it when they realise what sort of animals are running their country.'

'Maybe,' said Carr.

'Why the hell did Yelkov give it to *you*?' Streeter asked.

'Why the hell *did* he give it to me?' Carr muttered, pondering. *Why did Yelkov want me to know about Zvalen? Or was he telling me he knew about our Czech operation? And if it was that, how did he find out?*

Carr got up from his seat, wound back the last few minutes of the film and started running it through again.

'For Christ's sake!' Streeter said, his voice hoarse. 'What the hell's got into you?'

Carr stopped the projector, leaving a still image on the screen. He went close to it. The face of the torturer who had butchered Zvalen was clearly visible. He was even smiling.

Carr studied him for a long time.

'Right. I'll recognise you if I ever meet you,' he said, unaware that he'd spoken out loud.

'Richard, that sort of feeling can get you into trouble,' Streeter warned.

'It'll get him into a lot of trouble if I come across him.'

'You're a professional. You should know better. Rule number one: don't get emotionally involved.'

'I'm not emotionally involved,' Carr said in a flat voice. 'If ever I see him, I'm simply going to rip his guts out and stuff them down his throat. Unemotionally.'

Streeter insisted that Carr take a week's leave, but it didn't straighten out his knotted nerves. He always suffered from delayed reaction when he killed someone, no matter how justifiable the circumstances. But the Vienna deaths weren't the only things making Carr uneasy. He kept thinking of what Yelkov and Streeter had said about parapsychology – PSI and ESP. He had a mental image of a secret army of faceless men sitting in some space-age laboratory, concentrating on getting inside people's minds to affect their thoughts and actions.

To feed his fears, it had been a terrible week for news.

A senior trade-union leader invited a Russian counterpart to visit Britain, and made a quite pathetic speech eulogising him and the trades unions in the Soviet Union. It seemed that almost everyone else in the Western world was well aware that this Russian was a senior KGB officer.

Then seven hospitals were closed by a strike of ancillary workers. Three men had been suspended on full pay after being caught in possession of expensive property stolen from the hospital they worked in. Although the men admitted stealing, the strikers wanted them reinstated – and an apology from the police. One or two politicians gave the men their support.

British Leyland received an order worth fifty million pounds from the Middle East, but strikes immediately stopped production nationally. 'Sincere' parliamentarians loudly denied any communist influence at shop-floor level in the car industry. There were the customary potty noises from the lunatic left and right respectively.

None of these incidents on its own was surprising, although for so much to happen all at once was fairly unusual. However, one incident badly rattled Carr and reminded him sharply of Streeter's words about political and diplomatic leaders acting out of character.

The Foreign Secretary, one of the country's more intelligent and responsible statesmen, was making a speech at a White House dinner, which was televised worldwide. It was supposed to be a tension-easing speech, because Anglo-American relations over certain Middle East problems were strained to breaking-point. He seemed quite sober and clear-tongued when he announced to the American President, the dinner guests and the TV cameras: '. . . *and, without going into details at this point, I want to make it quite clear that, with certain minor exceptions, Her Majesty's Government completely repudiate the recent declaration by the American Secretary of State on United States policy concerning Britain and the Middle East.*' There was a buzz from the other guests, which seemed to surprise him, while all over the world important blood-pressures shot up and phones started ringing.

The Foreign Secretary's subsequent excuse that it was a simple slip of the tongue – he had meant 'reciprocate' instead of 'repudiate' – all sounded very thin. After a stormy

Press conference there was an even stormier meeting with the Prime Minister, but the Foreign Secretary again insisted that it was a genuine involuntary mistake.

All these incidents increased Carr's unease. The pattern accorded with what Yelkov had said about Russian use of long-range guided PSI.

During his leave, Carr went running on the Embankment, visited the gymnasium for work-outs, and trained with Warrant Officer Perkins, the department's unarmed combat instructor. None of it made him feel any better; only tired.

For three nights Peg-the-Legs tried to make herself agreeable to Carr, but with little success, till her patience finally ran out as they lay in bed. Until now their relationship had been uninvolved but pleasant and mutually satisfying. Her talents were physical, not intellectual, and she could neither understand nor cope with his present mood.

'Ever since you came back you've been as much fun as an unkept grave. What happened while you were away?' she asked petulantly. 'Or have I got bad breath or something?' She hiccuped angrily, which made her spill some of her drink – Carr's usual champagne-brandy mixture. It quickly filled her navel, overflowed down the crease between her left leg and pubis, then trickled out of sight. She sat up with a sudden yelp, dabbing at herself, and spilling more. 'Christ, that *burns*!' she squeaked, opening her legs and fanning herself vigorously.

Carr burst into laughter for the first time in three days.

'I suppose you think that's funny!' she said furiously.

'Yes. Bloody funny.'

'Well, at least it's cheered you up, you sadistic bastard,' she said grudgingly. She continued to shift about uncomfortably.

'Come here and I'll kiss it better,' he offered. His gloominess had now gone, for a while at least; and Peg began to chuckle.

This time their lovemaking was frenetic and exhausting, as at last they released the frustrations and tensions accumulated over the past few days.

Peg the Legs had breakfasted and departed, bright and

vibrant as a new valve spring, when Carr's phone rang next morning.

It was Streeter. 'Get over here as soon as you can. Use your own car. It'll be quicker at this time.'

Near the Kensington office there were a number of parking spaces marked off with a cross and painted 'No Parking. Doctor's Car'. He pulled into one and stuck a printed 'BMA: DOCTOR' label inside the windscreen. The local residents would have been surprised to know how many owners of cars in doctors' parking spaces didn't know an aspirin from *spiritus sancti.*

Streeter was waiting in his office, smoking his second big cigar of the still-young day. Also in the room was a fresh-faced young man of about twenty-five. He looked like an ex-choir boy who'd just passed out from Sandhurst, or maybe a seminary.

'This is Geoffrey Haynes,' Streeter said. 'Richard Carr.'

'Hello, sir,' said Haynes, giving Carr a firm, dry handshake and looking him directly in the eye. 'I've heard a lot about you.'

'I sodding well hope not,' said Carr acidly, hoping to defizz the younger man a little. He turned to Streeter, who offered no explanation, but simply said, 'Sit down.'

'Have you heard of Dr Oleg Kolunin?' Streeter began. The other two shook their heads. 'He's one of the Soviet's leading experts on PSI, "guided telepathy" and the rest. He's been running the research station in Leningrad. He wants to come over.'

'How do we know? Is it a reliable source?' Carr said.

'It's solid.' Streeter didn't elaborate. 'And according to our source, Kolunin says he's got some very important information about techniques already being used against the West.' There was heavy silence for a moment. Carr felt his heart beating faster.

'Do we know *why* he wants to come?' Haynes asked.

'The best of reasons. Money and a better standard of living. Not ideology.'

'That's a relief,' Carr said. 'If it's greed, it means he won't change his mind.'

'He's still very much in his masters' favour, and he's been given permission to go to an ESP and Parapsychology Symposium in Vienna.'

'I thought the Russians were being completely secretive about their work on PSI,' Carr said.

'He's going to listen, not to talk.'

'Is it his first trip outside the Soviet Bloc?' Haynes asked.

'No. He's been out a dozen times.'

'So they won't be watching him all that closely now,' Haynes said.

'Don't bank on it,' said Carr. 'If losing someone you're supposed to be watching means you'll have your balls cut off with a rusty nail-file, you keep on your toes.' He knew he must sound aggressive to the younger man, but he couldn't help himself.

'When you've finished . . . ' Streeter said heavily. 'Kolunin is being very careful. There's only one man he trusts and will defect to. He's a Swiss scientific writer named Desvins who's met Kolunin a few times inside and outside Russia at scientific conferences, things like that.'

'*Inside* Russia?' Carr asked sharply.

Streeter nodded. 'The Russians think he's sympathetic and "enlightened", but actually he's very pro-West. He's helped us once or twice,' he added almost casually.

'So?' Carr asked.

'You'll go to Geneva, pick up Desvins and take him to Vienna. Then you'll make sure he gets Kolunin and hands him over to us – and not to the CIA, BND or anyone else.'

'Are the Birdcage people in on this?' said Carr.

'No! And practically nobody here knows about Kolunin either. Although Desvins is on our files, of course. It'll help our position when the departmental budget comes up for review, if we can get Kolunin, so we don't want to hang about until the Birdcage mob get wind of it and try to snatch him.' He grunted. 'There's that bloody air-controllers' strike, so all the flights are completely unpredictable. You'll have to drive to Geneva. You'll need a car anyway, to collect Kolunin. The conference starts on the twelfth, which means you have just three days to fetch Desvins, get installed in

Vienna, then bring Kolunin back to the British Embassy in Geneva. Oh, yes. Codename for this operation is Songbird. Desvins will be Boosey, and Kolunin will be Hawkes.'

'Desvins . . . Boozy. Boosey and Hawkes. Very good, sir,' Haynes said. He wasn't trying to arse-crawl.

Carr stood up. 'I'd better make a cross-Channel booking.'

'It's been done,' Streeter said. 'Everything's been fixed: reservation on the ferry, hotel, meeting with Desvins at his flat.'

'Oh? So what time do I leave?'

'You both leave on the 22.00 Dover-Dunkerque ferry. As soon as you've picked up your documents and studied the photographs and files, go home, pack a bag and get some rest. You'll be driving all night.'

'Yes, I see.' Carr said evenly. 'Meet you downstairs in the armoury in about five minutes,' he told Haynes.

The young man looked first at him, quickly at Streeter, and then back at Carr. 'Jolly good,' he replied brightly. He kept the smile going as he left Streeter's office.

'What the hell's the idea of sticking me with that Boy Scout?'

'I told you the other day. I'm training someone to replace you when you take a desk.'

'Him?'

'You're showing your age: you're underestimating him. He's one of the best men they've ever had through training. All he needs is experience.'

'I've just come back from Vienna where some people may still be pretty cross with me for leaving two corpses there. I don't want to have to hold somebody's hand while I'm looking over my shoulder *and* trying to bring a nervous Russian out of the country under the noses of the KGB's cowboys.'

'You'll manage.'

Carr glared at Streeter. He looked more like one of Modigliani's close-eyed models than ever.

'Richard, there was a time when this country turned out hundreds of young men like Haynes every year – for which we were profoundly grateful at the Battle of Britain. The

Hayneses of this country saved the civilised world. These days they're supposed to be anachronistic curiosities, the butt of snide remarks from jealous little pin-headed nonentities. We're lucky to get Haynes. He's raw, but all he needs is some field experience. So do what you can, Richard. We need him, and I don't just mean the department.'

'Stop waving flags at me,' Carr said, but most of his bad humour had evaporated – for the moment.

By the time he reached the basement Carr was beginning to feel prickly again. 'I'll have the 9mm Browning,' he said shortly as soon as Nurse let him into the armoury. 'Where's Haynes?'

'At the range,' David Nurse told him. 'He said he'd wait for me before firing, in case he had a query about his gun.'

Carr walked to the door that led to the shooting range, a steel-lined extension to the cellar armoury. Nurse followed him.

Haynes was at the firing line.

'What have you taken?' Carr asked him.

'He has a Colt I-3,' Nurse said.

The I-3, now called the New Police Python, is a break from the traditional Colt design. It has a ventilating rib along the top of the barrel, and the ejector rod is shrouded for its full length. It takes the formidable .357 Magnum cartridge.

'Fired one much?'

'Only on ranges, sir.'

'For Christ's sake call me Richard. You're making me feel like a museum piece.'

Haynes grinned. It made him look about sixteen years old. 'Okay.'

'Well, are you going to fire that thing, or stand there admiring it?'

Haynes put on ear-protectors; Carr and Nurse followed suit.

The young man raised the gun and fired at the fixed target six times, quickly enough to take Carr by surprise. The New Python is not a lady's gun. Haynes rapidly ejected the spent cartridges and reloaded, then fired at the irregularly-moving target almost as quickly. He emptied the gun and put it down with the cylinder out. It was all very smooth and deft.

They all took off their ear-protectors, and Nurse wound back the targets. The fixed one showed five bulls and one inner that was a hair from being a bull. The grouping was impressive. The moving target had three bulls and two close inners.

'Seems to be firing a fraction low and to the right,' Haynes said. 'I'll remember that.' Carr was silent. He couldn't have done better himself. Nurse looked at him with the faintest hint of a smile.

So you're pretty good on the range, Carr thought. *How good are you when the targets are shooting back?*

He was to find the answer quite soon.

7

'What did you expect in this business?' Carr said. 'A blood-red Ferrari, or maybe a white Porsche? Or a nice discreet orange BMW? Try following somebody in a car like that without being noticed.'

'Yes, of course,' Haynes said politely. Even so, he thought Carr would have driven a livelier car than a Saab 99. He put his case in the back, beside Carr's. Plainly in view were a straw hat, a pair of flippers, a mask and a snorkel tube.

'We're going as tourists. We don't want any fuss at frontiers.' He knew what was bothering the younger man. Haynes felt he was going on a crusade and ought to be in shining armour and riding a white horse, not in holiday gear in an unobtrusive black Swedish car.

The run to Dover was uneventful. Carr didn't drive more than 60 mph on the motorway, but they still arrived early at the docks. Haynes got out to stretch his legs; Carr tilted back his seat and prepared to cat-nap. He fell asleep quickly; and woke again as soon as the other waiting cars' engines started up.

'Coming to get some duty-free?' Carr asked when they were aboard. He was trying to establish some degree of informality, if not intimacy, but it wasn't easy.

'I don't drink, actually.'

'I wasn't planning to drink it myself. It's just that the natives expect something better than beads these days.'

Dunkerque isn't a serious rival to Venice or Athens in the daytime; late at night it's a foretaste of limbo. Despite misleading signs that seemed deliberately planned to divert motorists from the Calais road into Dunkerque Western Docks, the town is as active as an unhaunted cemetery. Its one great virtue is that it's on the motorway network that connects all Europe, and Carr didn't waste time getting on to that.

Although the distance to Geneva is about 510 miles, all but 90 of them by motorway, he intended to cover it in less than twelve hours – including stops to pay motorway tolls, eat, rest, and fill up with petrol.

He took the Saab up to about 85 mph unspectacularly, barely above the motorway speed limit of 82 mph, holding the car there on the practically deserted A1 motorway. They drove past route signs with names that instantly evoked the 1914–18 war: Ypres, Menin, Armentières, Douai, Cambrai, Amiens. And one great sign in French: 'Battlefield of the Somme.' The World War I soldiers who never left that soil have now become part of it, but bits of the metal that killed them are still turned up by ploughs, more than sixty years later.

There was a lot of traffic on the Paris *Boulevard Périphérique* – the ring-road – which is never quiet, but the latest link between the A1 motorway to the north and the A6 to the south is quite short. Carr stopped to refill the tank at the first petrol station on the A6, then he pulled into the parking area for ten minutes to drink some strong black coffee from his thermos, and walk around briskly for a moment, breathing deeply. He needed the break to keep him alert because the next section of the road, immediately south of Paris, would be the most boring part of the entire journey. He opened the sunshine roof to make sure there was plenty of fresh air in the car, even if it was a little chilly.

After what seemed an interminable night, a grey, reluctant dawn unkindly revealed the featureless character of the countryside, helping to kill conversation between the two men. The front-wheel-drive Saab practically drove itself along the motorway, holding the road so well that they were hardly aware of a strong, blustery side-wind until they got out at Tournus, some 200 miles from Paris, to fill up with petrol again.

Here they left the motorway, taking the D975 to Bourg-en-Bresse. This *route départmentale* is very good for what is technically a second-class road, and Carr was able to keep up a reasonable speed.

Near St Julien-en-Genèvois, France became Switzerland almost by stealth. Apart from an inconspicuous sign 'Frontière' and another warning of a customs-post on the road, the only indication was that each village name-post had a small white Swiss cross on a red background.

After a long silence Carr said, 'I didn't ask you. Have you ever been to Switzerland before?'

'Only on holidays. Not to Geneva.'

'Where then?'

Haynes hesitated. 'St Moritz, and Gstaad.'

'On *your* salary?'

'My father was quite well off, actually.' He sounded mildly embarrassed.

The customs-post resembled little more than a concrete tram shelter. The Swiss customs officer hardly gave them a glance as he waved them on through, past a great rash of cut-price petrol stations and roadside *bureaux de change*.

Carr turned left off the main road into Geneva, towards the suburb of Petit Lancy, where Desvins lived. They were booked into a hotel less than a mile from his flat.

Carr went straight to the public phone-box in the hotel

lobby and called the Kensington office. Tom Duffy, one of the communications/ops room staff, came on the line.

'Hello. This is Richard Carr. I'm calling from Geneva.'

'Did you have a good trip?' Duffy asked.

'Yes, thanks. Picturesque and stimulating.' It wasn't idle chat. 'Picturesque and stimulating' was the prearranged recognition check. 'Is Mr Sidney there?'

'He's out for the moment. The meeting with Mr Boosey has been arranged for four o'clock.'

'Thanks,' said Carr, and hung up, thinking that he needn't have hurried on the journey.

Now they had more than enough time to shower, change, and have lunch. Haynes knew better than to suggest they go early to the rendezvous. It was one of the first things an agent learned: you always keep exactly to times. Turning up early could be as fatal as turning up late.

They had the cheap set lunch, £11.00 a head, without wine, in the hotel dining-room.

'Well, so far so good,' Haynes said brightly, as they drank their coffee.

'That's just what I was thinking, and it worries me.'

'You're a pessimist.' Although Haynes didn't address Carr as 'Sir', he couldn't quite bring himself to call him 'Richard' yet.

'There are two kinds of people in this business. Live old pessimists and dead young optimists.'

Desvins lived in a small modern block of flats over a parade of shops. It could have been in Barnet except for the fact that the pavement and rear courtyard were cleaner than any street in London. Before they entered the block, Carr and Haynes wiped their feet carefully like a pair of henpecked husbands.

No one answered when they rang the doorbell. Long before they rang the third time, the short hairs were standing up on the back of Carr's neck. He had a sick feeling in his stomach because he knew that – once again – his pessimism was justified.

'Now what?' asked Haynes.

The door of the flat had an ordinary pull-shut Yale-type

lock and two lever locks which looked fairly complicated. Carr pushed the door gently a couple of times and listened carefully.

'It's not properly locked,' he said. 'There's only the Yale.' He took a bank credit card from his wallet and slipped it between the door and the framework. He felt for the tongue of the lock, and after a few moments there was a soft click as the lock gave.

Carr pulled his gun and signalled to Haynes, who nodded. He glanced up and down the corridor, and took out his own gun to cover Carr.

Carr took a deep breath, crashed open the unlatched door and dived in, low, his gun seeking a target.

The room was empty. Feeling rather foolish, he got to his feet, but without relaxing his vigilance. Almost at once Haynes came in through the door and stood balanced on the balls of his feet, his knees half bent, so that even if he was hit there was a chance he could fall to one knee and fire back.

Although they made a search of the apartment, they both realised it was pointless. Broken and overturned furniture testified to a fairly violent struggle.

'They've got him,' Carr said bitterly. 'We're too bloody late.' Haynes stayed silent. 'I'm going to phone the office. You look round here; see if you can find anything.'

'Why not phone from here?' asked Haynes. He was going to say something else, but Carr gestured to him to be quiet.

'Careful. They could have left a bug to see who was coming to meet him.'

When Carr returned Haynes was waiting for him outside the block of flats.

'What did Streeter say?' Haynes asked.

'He was rather annoyed. I'll tell you about it in a minute.'

'I've been talking to the neighbours,' Haynes reported. 'One of them, a woman, said Desvins left about an hour ago with two men. He didn't look well.'

'Probably knocked about and shit-scared.' They got into the car.

'Are London going to warn Kolunin?'

'Probably too late. If the opposition know about Desvins and they've lifted him, they almost certainly know about the defection. I expect Kolunin's already well on his way to Moscow Centre.'

'And the reason they've lifted Desvins, instead of killing him, is to pump him dry?'

'Exactly.'

'How the hell could they get on to Desvins?' Haynes said.

'I wonder,' Carr said grimly. But he knew all right.

'What do we do now?'

'Get all the help we can. The SIS people at the Geneva station, of course, though we'll need to think up a good story to explain why they weren't told we're here. But the police first.' Haynes looked at him in astonishment. 'Well, don't look so surprised. It's one of their nationals that's been abducted, they've got a lot more men to look for him, and they can warn the frontier posts – for what that's worth.' He didn't bother to tell Haynes yet that when he went to phone he had also called Mark Westbrook in London and invoked the Old Pals' Act to ask for local CIA help.

Chief Inspector Gallet of the Swiss police listened to Carr's story with a certain amount of scepticism. Carr explained that he and Haynes were British government employees investigating a serious fraud and embezzlement case – even producing official, but unspecific identity cards to establish their bona fides. 'Monsieur Desvins had promised to help us with our enquiries,' Carr said.

The Swiss try to stay aloof from other people's Intelligence activities. All they want is for it all to go away. But they consider fraud, embezzlement and breaches of banking confidentiality rather worse than regicide.

'You're sure Monsieur Desvins has been abducted?' Chief Inspector Gallet asked.

'What other explanation could there be?' Carr replied. 'He made an appointment with us, and it's our experience always that he is completely reliable. We arrive for the meeting, find signs of a struggle, and the front door open' – there was no point in complicating matters by admitting a technical trespass – 'and he left with two men, looking frightened. And then there is his . . . possible involvement in this embezzlement case. I'm afraid I can't give details at the moment. There is a question of confidentiality.' Carr had now used all the three key words: fraud, embezzlement and confidentiality.

'Very well,' the policeman said. 'But I'm sure you realise that there are many places where they could have driven out of the country in a foreign car without being checked.' Haynes, remembering the bored customs man at the frontier-post, believed him. 'It's a different matter if we're warned in time and if you have our official permission to carry out your investigation as our laws require . . . ' Carr accepted to implied reproof. Gallet rose to signal the end of the interview. 'If you'll return to your hotel I shall inform you as soon as there is . . . *if* there is any news.'

Stanley Wile, the SIS Geneva Station chief, regarded Carr and Haynes like two nineteenth-century poachers found nicking salmon from his estate. He had a large, old-fashioned RAF moustache and a face so stuffed with carbohydrates that his eyes bulged.

'It's an industrial-technical matter, really,' Carr said equably. 'That's why you weren't informed by Immediate signal, but I expect there's a message in the pipeline somewhere.'

'We'll do what we can, of course,' Wile assured him with all the sincerity of a patent-medicine advertisement. 'If only you'd told us earlier, we could have kept an eye on him for you.'

'We didn't know ourselves, earlier.'

There was nothing more for Carr to do except keep contact with London, the police and Wile – and speculate. Before they left, he asked, 'You do log staff movements in and out of the Russian Embassy?'

'Of course.' Wile picked up an internal phone and asked for the information. 'Three domestic staff – chauffeurs or gardeners or something – left in a car at 15.29 and set off in a hurry. One of them came back with the car at 16.58. But there's nothing unusual in that.'

'It fits, though,' said Carr. 'Any idea what happened to the other couple?'

'We can't follow *every* Russian from the Embassy,' Wile said heavily. 'Apart from anything else, they've got three times as many staff as we do.'

Carr and Haynes took tea at the hotel, but not because either of them really wanted it; it was just something to do. It was rather like performing a ritual of religion that neither of them believed in any more. There came one moment of hope with a phone-call asking if Carr was there, and ten minutes later a man arrived. It wasn't Desvins, but an American Carr had met once: Laurence Van Houten, who was now number two at the CIA station in Geneva. He'd responded to Mark Westbrook's call from London to help out if he could.

'No sign of your man – and none of our contacts has heard anything about him,' Van Houten said. 'There seems to be some extra Russian activity going on, but we haven't managed to pinpoint it yet. Sorry I can't be of more assistance. The truth is, we're pretty tied up trying to keep tabs on the Swiss terrorists who're supplying arms to some of the hard groups throughout Europe.'

For a while Carr sat in an armchair in the hotel lounge, watching the sun go down over a distant mountain. Abruptly he got up.

'Where are you going?' Haynes looked up from a German magazine.

'In the field, always eat and sleep when you can. You never know when you'll have to go short of either. I'm going to lie down. Unless you have a better idea?'

Haynes put down the magazine. 'I'll join you.'

Carr had the useful talent of being able to fall asleep like blowing out a lamp. In the other bed Haynes lay still, wide awake but not moving, so he wouldn't wake Carr. He needn't have bothered: Carr slept like a three-day-old-corpse. Yet his internal alarm clock woke him up two hours later.

The two men showered and had dinner. By the time they

had finished there was still no news from anyone in Geneva or London.

Just before ten o'clock Chief Inspector Gallet called on them in person.

'We're almost certain that your man Desvins left on the train to Marseille, accompanied by two men. They were seen by the booking-office clerk, and the identification was confirmed by a porter.'

'How strong was the identification?' Carr asked.

'The clerk remembered them particularly because they asked to book an entire first-class compartment, but were told it wasn't possible.'

'They could have got off before Marseille,' Haynes said. 'Where else does the train stop?'

'Culoz, Aix-les-Bains, Chambéry, Avignon.'

'No, it's a pre-war pound to a pfennig it's Marseille,' Carr said. 'They couldn't find a better town for doing something nasty.'

'Did you ask the porter or booking clerk if they carried any luggage with them?' Haynes said.

'I thought of that,' Gallet replied. 'But they had no bags.'

'So they must have had somewhere fixed up to go,' Haynes said.

Carr gave him an encouraging smile. *He's got a brain behind that baby face.* But there was another possible explanation for the lack of luggage – they were tipped off only at the last moment and didn't have time to make preparations. He thought he knew why.

'What train did they catch?' Carr asked.

'The 16.33,' Gallet told him.

'That's more than five hours ago!'

Gallet looked at Carr disapprovingly. 'We had quite a lot to do. The booking clerk on afternoon shift had gone off duty when we reached the station, and he wasn't at home when we checked there. It took some time to find him.'

'Yes, I'm sorry,' Carr said.

'What time does it get to Marseille?' asked Haynes.

'At 23.20.'

'And the next train?'

'Not until tomorrow. The last one went at 21.36,' Gallet told him.

'Thank you very much for your co-operation, Chief Inspector,' Carr said formally. 'I'll make sure my people let your superiors know how helpful you've been.' He started to turn away.

'One moment, please,' Gallet said. 'Have you any idea why Monsieur Devins has been abducted by these two men?'

'Why do you ask?' Carr said, to gain time.

'Because, as you pointed out, he is a Swiss national, and if he has been forcibly abducted, we should contact the French police, either through Interpol, which will take some time, or direct, which won't.'

'I rather suspect that he wouldn't make any charges against these two men. I think we'll find they're accomplices he's cheated,' Carr said with wide-eyed sincerity. 'He'll be more afraid of them than of you.'

'And of you?' asked Gallet.

Carr smiled at him. 'We'll have to see.'

As soon as Gallet had left them, Carr said, 'Quick, we're going out. We've got to phone London.'

'There's a phone-box in the hall.'

'If the Swiss police are half as good as I know they are, they've tapped that line, just for our benefit. That policeman wasn't fooled for a minute, and I don't want to give him our London number.'

There was a public telephone a hundred yards from the hotel. Carr was about to enter it, but changed his mind and continued on to the next. He caught Haynes's look of surprise. 'All right. Maybe this business does make you paranoid.'

Carr put in half a franc and dialled the SID Kensington office. 'This is Richard Carr,' he said, and gave the number of the call-box. 'Ask Mr Streeter to call me back.'

Streeter rang back within a minute. Carr quickly described what had happened, then said, 'The train gets in at 23.20.

If the Marseille SIS station get their finger out they can keep an eye open for Boosey and the heavies that have got hold of him. But for Christ's sake tell our men not to try to pick him up, otherwise those goons'll kill him on the spot – and anyone who happens to get in the way. You know what Marseille's like; the police'll just put it down to a *réglement de comptes*' – a gangsters' settling of accounts. Tell whoever it is that if they spot Boosey and the heavies they're just to follow them and find out where they go. We'll take it from there.'

'Wait,' said Streeter, and Carr heard him giving instructions to someone in the communications/ops room.

'We'll go straight to the Marseille consulate to see if they've found Boosey. I'll need to know what Soviet-bloc ships are already in port, and what ones are expected. If there are any docked at the moment, somebody'll have to keep watch on them to make sure they don't get our man aboard.' Streeter's voice squawked in the earpiece, and Haynes could guess what he was saying.

'Put pressure on them to *find* enough men until you can get some more troops down there. Getting Desvins back isn't exactly going to be like picking flowers.' Streeter's voice squawked again. 'I hope to Christ you'll make a bit more of an effort if ever they pick *me* up,' Carr said sourly. 'By the way, any news of Hawkes?'

Carr listened for a moment, looking puzzled, and then hung up.

'What's wrong?' Haynes asked.

'Kolunin is still at the Vienna conference. The Russians don't seem to be on to him.'

'So there could be a chance of getting him over after all?'

'*If* we can snatch Desvins back, and *if* they don't get him to talk before we manage it. That's an awful lot of ifs.'

'Only two.'

'In this situation, that is a hell of a lot.' He started to move away. 'Come on, Sancho Panza. Let's have a swing at the Marseille windmills.'

There was no great problem about the route to take for

Marseille. Carr drove south from Geneva down the N201, past some spectacular mountains rising to nearly 4,500 feet on his left, beyond the dark mass of the Bois de Pomier on the lower slopes.

They hadn't driven far before Haynes began to suspect that the car wasn't so ordinary after all. Certainly it was going round corners faster than he expected; his static reel belt bit into his chest as Carr threw the Saab into a succession of bends where the road finished its lazy sweep round the mountains at Cruseilles. Haynes barely had time to take this in before he had a bad fright. It happened where the road made a double turn as it crossed a stream and started to climb.

As Carr took the rise, they came on a large lorry, laden with vegetables, labouring up the incline. Carr pulled out to overtake, flicking his headlights as he did so. Without warning an approaching car, driving only on sidelights and so practically invisible, switched on badly adjusted headlights as it careered down the incline towards them. There wasn't room for the lorry and both cars, and the lorry was going too slowly for Carr to be able to drop back behind it again.

Haynes braced himself for the inevitable crash. Instinctively he knew that a driver of Carr's ability would at least avoid a head-on collision at all costs. Either he'd side-swipe the lorry, making a terrible mess of his own coachwork but cutting down the impact of the crash; or he'd spin the car, if he could, so that it would hit tail-first, the least dangerous angle of all.

But instead of braking, Carr stamped on the accelerator. Haynes's last thought was that it was a hell of a time and place to have a major crash. It was miles from a decent hospital. He'd probably die in the car, or beside the roadside, and he felt, quite unemotionally, that it was all such a stupid waste . . .

There was a sudden whine and the car leapt forward, surging past and round the lorry as if a giant hand had taken hold of it. The car was still gaining speed as it went into the nineties. The approaching car's horn blared, reflecting the other driver's panic, changing pitch as the two cars passed and then drew further away with more than enough time to spare.

'What the hell was *that*?' asked Haynes, doing a good job at keeping his voice steady.

'The turbo cutting in. You probably didn't realise that this is the turbo version because I took the car's "*Turbo*" plates off the sides and back. That's the turbo pressure gauge,' he added, pointing to a dial on the top of the dashboard. 'What did you think it was?'

'Oh, one of those fuel economy things to tell you when you're wasting petrol.' Carr looked at him sharply, but it was impossible to tell whether Haynes was joking.

The strongly fortified ancient town of Grenoble was the largest one on the entire run between Geneva and Marseille. As they came up to the junction with the *route nationale* a mile or so from the centre of the town, Carr said unexpectedly, 'Interested in modern art?' It was the first thing he'd said for some while and took Haynes by surprise.

'Some of it,' he answered cautiously.

'They've got a great collection in the museum. And the university has the best-looking women students in France.' He drove on in silence for another moment. 'There's a lot of heavy industry here, too, because of the hydroelectric power.' Another pause. 'And a nuclear centre.'

'Really,' said Haynes, trying to put some interest into his tone.

'One of these days I'm going to come back and take a real look at some of these places.' He sounded unexpectedly wistful.

Although Valence is to the south-west of Grenoble, the road first heads north-west to skirt the enormous Vercors Park. The Vercors region is a mixture of rugged and soft beauties; and it is bloodsoaked, too. In 1944, three and a half thousand *maquisards* – members of the *Maquis* Resistance – held out for two months against massive German attacks, Carr told Haynes.

He went on, 'It was a thorough balls-up. In the first place, London wouldn't send them heavy arms – artillery and anti-tank guns – because they said they weren't suitable for guerilla tactics. London just didn't seem to understand the importance of the area and what the local people were up against, and what they could do. The *maquisards* were brave as hell and the Germans had to hit them with everything. They even specially flew in some crack SS troops.' He fell silent, glancing out at the massive bulk of the mountains.

'You said "In the first place",' Haynes prompted him gently.

'The bloody Resistance stayed put and fought a pitched battle. They didn't withdraw until it was too late – five days too late. When the Hun overran the positions they acted worse than animals. They tortured, burned and killed as nastily as they could think up, which was pretty bloody nasty. There was one woman who was raped by seventeen brave soldiers in succession, while a German doctor held her pulse, so he could stop the soldiers before she fainted. Another woman was slashed open and died with her guts wound round her neck. Want to hear what they did to some children?'

At last Haynes asked superfluously, 'It was all a bit before your time, wasn't it?' He felt he had to say something.

'I have French friends who survived it. But you can find out for yourself. It's all in the records. You should read M.R.D. Foot's book *SOE Operations in France.*'

They stayed silent again as they drove on, nearly always within sight of the Isère.

Soon Bourg de Péage was behind them and they were on the last stretch of ordinary road that led into Valence, and on to the entry to the A7 motorway a mile to the south of the town.

Once on the straight three-lane southbound motorway Carr made the most of the Saab's top-gear performance and pushed the speed up to something between 100 and 110 mph. Some late-night drivers of BMWs and Porsches – the bane of the French motorways – gaped a bit when the ordinary-looking saloon overtook.

ordinary-looking saloon overtook them without strain.

Soon the speed became commonplace, the white dashes of the lane markings became hypnotic as they flicked under the wheels. Carr thought Haynes had fallen asleep when suddenly he said, 'Why the hell Marseille? Why did the Ivans get that particular train? And why a train anyway?' His mind was back on the present operation.

'They couldn't go by air because of the controllers' strike. They couldn't risk hanging about in the airport for hours.'

'A car, then.'

'They didn't want to involve a car that could be traced back to the Embassy or one of the employees, and they didn't have time to hire one.'

'Okay, train then,' Haynes conceded. 'But why Marseille?'

'First of all, the Marseille train goes through the nearest border to Geneva, so it gave the Swiss police the least possible chance to alert the frontier guards if anything did go wrong.' Carr expertly overtook two enormous lorries with trailers carrying glassware from Saint-Etienne before speaking again. 'Second, Marseille's a port with ships going all over the world, and with as many smugglers and hard-nosed criminals of every kind as you can find anywhere. Think of it this way. Supposing the KGB knew *when* we were supposed to call on Desvins. They could reckon on an hour for us to realise he'd been lifted and for us to get the wheels turning. By then their train would be past Avignon, running into Marseille.'

'Unless they bagged him the previous night,' Haynes suggested.

'No. They didn't even know that Desvins existed until this morning.'

'You don't *know* that.'

'Oh, yes I do,' Carr said. 'Oh, yes I bloody do, all right.'

8

It took Carr less than two hours to cover the hundred and forty miles from Valence to Marseille. Small queues at the motorway toll-gates and deliberately unhurried cashiers slowed him down, but his average speed for the motorway stretch was over 70 mph. Only people who do fast, long-distance driving would appreciate how he must have pushed the car along.

The bright lights of the Shell oil refinery and Marignan airport, reflected in the salt-water lake of the Etang de Berre away to their right, signalled they were only a few miles away from Marseille. Carr slowed down on this last part of the motorway into the city. He knew that it was never empty – not even at three o'clock in the morning – and was used by some of the most deliberately suicidal drivers outside Tokyo.

They came at last to the elevated section of the motorway, past the vast docks complex.

'It's a dinosaur,' Carr told Haynes. 'The city and the docks. Marseille's gradually running down. A lot of people think that Fos, further west along the coast, will take over from it in a few years. Its got deepwater berthing, it's on the Rhône waterway system connecting up with the rest of Europe, and there's an oil pipeline terminal there. All the ships will go there eventually. But Marseille's still a great old town. I spent eighteen months here a few years ago and had a marvellous time.'

The motorway ends near the main railway station, the Gare Saint-Charles. Carr crossed La Canebière, the famous boulevard leading down to the Old Port, and continued along the one-way rue Paradis. The British Consulate is in a small dead-end avenue leading off an attractive small square between the rue Paradis and the fashionable avenue du Prado.

The SIS head of station was named Graham Murray. He was a long-lapsed Scot who looked as British as Nelson's Column, and as flexible. He was sandy-haired and his skin had never learned to come to terms with the Marseille sun.

'We've got our hands full enough down here without your lot adding to our problems,' he grumbled.

'We're not doing it just to annoy you,' Carr replied with a smile as warm as a shark's. 'What's the situation?'

'You're lucky. There aren't any Soviet Bloc ships in port at the moment. There are two due tomorrow night: the *Novgorod II* and the *Vladimir Domski.* They're both freighters and they're expected to be here for three days.'

'Tomorrow night . . . We'll have some back-up from London by then,' Carr said. 'What about our man and the heavies with him? Did you see them at the station?'

'Oh, yes,' Murray said. 'And followed them. We know where they are all right.'

'Don't you think you might have mentioned that to begin with?' Haynes asked in a very superior Old Carthusian voice that made Murray smart. Obviously Haynes didn't think any more highly of the local man than Carr did.

'Where are they? And who's covering the place?' Carr asked sharply.

'A house in the Old Port area. I've got two local men keeping it under surveillance. They've got walkie-talkies and a radio in the car. We're in constant contact.'

'Any idea how many of their people in the house?'

Murray shrugged. 'Could be just those two, although I doubt that – or a dozen. And it's not the sort of place you could rush easily.'

'I wasn't planning on doing a Battle of Balaclava. Well, let's go and have a look.'

'What, now?' Murray asked. 'It's three o'clock in the bloody morning. Don't you want to eat, or rest, or have a bath or something first? I told you – they're being watched.

Anyway, they're probably all fast asleep in there.'

'I doubt it,' Carr said shortly. 'And I want to make sure everything's properly buttoned up.'

Murray rose from his chair. He looked very fed up; clearly he'd hoped to get to bed fairly soon. 'All right,' he said. 'I'll drive you.'

As they followed him, Carr glanced at Haynes and rested his hand on his jacket, over the Browning in its shoulder-holster. Haynes indicated his own shoulder-holster with an almost imperceptible gesture.

During the war the Germans blew up a great deal of the Old Port area, including the famous transporter bridge. It was a nest of Resistance workers, black-marketeers, crooks and deserters; but somehow the destruction of the buildings didn't manage to flush out many of them. Most of the area has been rebuilt, and instead of the transporter bridge there is a modern road tunnel.

In the south-east corner of the Old Port a few streets survived the German destruction, and that was where Murray was taking them in his Peugeot 505. They drove along the Quai de Rive Neuve, past all the moored fishing boats and pleasure craft, towards the Quai des Belges on the eastern limit of the Old Port. Then Murray took a right turn down a one-way street little better than an alley. Here the little knot of old streets are narrow, dirty, ill-lit and sinister. They're full of hotels that rent rooms by the hour and resent it if you stay even that long, and ricketty, pock-marked houses that appear about to collapse at any moment.

Refuse, some loosely wrapped in newspaper, some just deposited as in Elizabethan London, stirred strangely as bright-eyed brown rats scavenged for food. It was a tough district, and Carr knew it well enough to be wary. The people there who carried guns were professional criminals, but amateurs in their use of firearms, by Carr's standards. They would shoot for unreasoning motives: for revenge, for pleasure, a few for weird concepts of personal 'honour'.

Their unpredictability made thoughtful people very apprehensive. Murray found a place to leave the car where there was just enough room for other vehicles to pass.

'They're in No. 27,' Murray said. Carr looked at the building opposite: No. 39. He tried to count along the houses, but in the poor light he couldn't be quite sure which one was 27.

Murray got out of the car, holding the keys in his hand. 'That's ours,' he said shortly, pointing to a black Renault 14 ahead of them. Carr and Haynes followed him.

When Carr looked inside the Renault he felt an unpleasant shock. There were two men inside, and earlier Murray had said only two men were keeping surveillance.

'But who's watching the back?' he asked.

'There's no back way out,' Murray told him, with a faintly superior smile. 'There aren't any gardens here, you know. The houses are back to back with the ones in the next street, which is on a lower level anyway.'

'How long have you been in Marseille?' Carr asked violently.

'Two years.' Murray looked startled.

'Don't you know the buildings in these streets are all connected? You can go in the front door in this street and straight through out of the front door in the next! Didn't you know?'

Murray's silent, shocked face proclaimed that he didn't. Carr wondered about the reliability of the two men in the car – whether they didn't know this fact, or simply hadn't bothered to say.

At that moment the street erupted into silent activity. Three men – two bigger men forcing the smaller third one between them – came out of No. 27. The two bundled the other into the back of one of those corrugated-iron Citroën vans. One stayed in the back with the smaller man; the other slammed the doors on them and ran round to the driver's seat, to send the van lurching away from the kerb. A one-eared black cat, accustomed to noise and violence, decided the fracas was sufficiently far away not to be a threat and went on pawing at a package of refuse.

'Christ!' Murray said. 'We're in luck – we got here in time. Quick, follow them,' he ordered the men in the

Renault. Then he hesitated, undecided whether to get into their car or run back to his own.

Carr stared at the disappearing van, then snatched Murray's car keys from his hand.

'Come on,' he shouted to Haynes, ignoring Murray's startled protest. The two men in the Renault set off after the van, while Carr and Haynes sprinted to Murray's car.

To Haynes's astonishment Carr slammed the Peugeot into reverse, and zig-zagged backwards, the wrong way down the ill-lit one-way street, without switching on the lights. The Peugeot side-swiped a couple of parked vehicles as it careered down the street. No lights come on in the houses, no shutters opened. It was a street where noises – any kind of noises – were nothing to do with anyone indoors. There was a strong sense of self-protective incuriosity.

Murray stood stranded in the middle of the street as the two cars set off in opposite directions. He was so surprised by the rapidly-moving events that he didn't even shout a protest at the maltreatment to his car.

As they reached the main road behind them, Carr pulled into the kerb and braked violently. A matter of seconds later a big Mercedes nosed out of the next street – one-way, in the opposite direction to their own street – and moved quietly along the road.

'That's them,' Carr said with satisfaction. He backed into the main road and set off behind the Mercedes.

'How do you know?' Haynes asked. 'And there were only two people in the car. I didn't see Desvins.'

'That little act in front of No. 27 was a distraction, and they overplayed it. They wouldn't have taken him out *struggling*. They'd take him out walking normally, with a gun in his ribs, or in a sack with a bump on his head. He's in the back of the Merc, on the floor – or my name's Victor Sylvester.'

'Then Murray was right. We *were* lucky we got there in time.'

'We got there in time, but whether we were lucky . . .'

The Mercedes drove along the route Carr and Haynes had come, towards the south of the town. Carr was able to follow without getting too close, often keeping a car or two between them as they proceeded along the wide boulevard Michelet. He guessed they were making for the motorway, probably heading for Toulon.

'We should have asked about Soviet-bloc ships in Toulon,' Carr said, thinking out loud.

Unexpectedly, instead of turning left towards the motorway, the Mercedes kept straight on, south, until they were on the N559 road leading to the small resort of Cassis and, beyond that, the shipbuilding and ship-repairing port of La Ciotat. Then they turned off on to a minor road.

Carr did his best not to make it obvious to the men in the Mercedes that they were being followed. He periodically switched to different lights on the Peugeot: headlights, sidelights, foglamps; and on a couple of occasions he used the parking-light switch to show only one sidelight. He varied the distance between the two cars to the point of risking losing it.

When they were a few miles outside Marseille the clouds cleared; and the half-moon seemed to pale as approaching dawn began to lighten the sky. The almost unused road turned east and climbed into the bare, rock-strewn hills. Patches of green that looked black in the moonlight made camouflage patterns on the light stony surface of the countryside.

On the winding road Carr was forced to close the distance between the two cars in case the Mercedes took one of the small side-roads when out of sight round a bend. He became aware that the Mercedes had slowed down, keeping to a steady thirty-five miles an hour when it would have been quite safe to do sixty.

Carr began to feel uneasy. 'What the hell are they up to?'

On the highest and most deserted stretch of the road the Mercedes turned right down a narrow, dusty road leading towards the sea. Carr was puzzled because, as far as he could remember, there was no way down to the beach. The sheer cliffs fell two hundred feet or more straight to the sea. There was no question of transferring to a boat from there.

He switched off the Peugeot's lights, ready to follow down the side-road, which was almost white in the moonlight but little more than a track. When they were still some thirty to fifty yards from the turn-off a big American car, low on its springs, came up fast behind them from the direction of Marseille.

Carr was concentrating on the Mercedes, but suddenly he was aware that the American car was alongside, not overtaking, travelling at the same speed.

He turned his head, and looked straight down the barrel of a submachine-gun.

In one all-encompassing glance, like a landscape seen in a lightning flash, Carr registered the car with four men in it. Those in the back had automatics, and the man in the front passenger seat was pointing the machine-gun.

The window beside Carr shattered and simultaneously his head seemed to explode. His sudden thought was *I've been killed.*

Simultaneously the face behind the machine-gun disappeared behind a pink and red and black curtain that billowed and spread before it changed into a spray of blood and mucus. The weapon fell into the road with a skidding clatter, although Carr couldn't hear it. His ears were still ringing painfully when his mind began to function again. As the car slowed, Carr began to understand. Haynes, alert and incredibly fast, had drawn his gun and shot the other man, firing just behind Carr's head. It was marvellously quick thinking and a superb shot.

The American car now slewed round, blocking the road. Shots from it cracked sharply and more glass shattered somewhere in the Peugeot.

'Out, and make for cover when I say,' Carr ordered.

'Right,' Haynes unlatched the door on his side, holding it shut until he was ready to jump. With his right hand held across him Carr did the same. He quickly took in the terrain on either side of the road. Fortunately it provided plenty of protection behind rocks and in hollows.

Just before the car stopped he shouted, '*Now!*'

The front doors opened simultaneously and the two men

rolled into cover on either side. Heavy bullets chipped at the roadway inches behind them, and richochetted away with angry whining. The Peugeot ran off the road slowly, rolled up a slight slope and nudged gently against a rock, then rolled back again, out of the direct line between the two opposing groups.

Carr lay in a horseshoe-shaped hollow, sideways on to the road. He had a parapet-like spur of rock, which reached almost to the track, protecting him from the men in the other car. A sheer wall of rock, about twenty to fifty feet high, rose behind him. There was an overhang which meant that even if someone got above him, they couldn't take a direct shot at him.

He was safe as long as he stayed where he was, but the only way out of the hollow was on to the roadway, where he'd be completely exposed. Carr didn't care too much for his situation.

He glanced across the road. As far as he could make out, Haynes was slightly better off. He was sheltered from any fire from the American car, and he could also move backwards still under cover – but he could be attacked from the rear.

'You all right?' Carr called to Haynes who was only a few yards away across the track.

'Fine.'

'That was smart thinking and bloody good shooting. Thanks.'

Something hit Carr in the forehead. A millisecond later he heard the sound of the shot that had sent a chip of rock into his face, followed by the high-pitched, undulating howl of a bullet turning end over end as it ricochetted away.

'Bloody hell,' Carr said quietly to himself, wiping blood from the cut.

Lying flat he looked carefully round the edge of the rocky spur. He fired twice, quickly, at where the car's petrol tank ought to be. The car shook briefly, and the aerial waved gently, but that was all. A second later he shot at the front wheel, and the car sagged forward with an almost human sigh as the air rushed out of the tubeless tyre. Quickly he shot and holed the rear tyre as well. The dead man sitting in the front seat turned slowly as if to look at him, then sagged forward until checked by his seat-belt.

Carr pulled back behind the rock just as more shots hit the road beside him. He was glad the machine-gun lay behind them somewhere.

'Don't waste ammunition on the car,' Carr instructed Haynes in a normal voice. 'It's armour-plated.'

'It looks as if they bought it from Al Capone's executors,' Haynes replied. 'How the hell did they pick us up? I'm sure we weren't followed.'

'Must have been a radio in the Mercedes. When they spotted us they called in their Fifth Cavalry.'

There were six quick shots from the direction of the car – three at Carr's position, three at Haynes's. *Covering fire*, Carr thought. Keeping his head in shadow so it wouldn't present a silhouette, he risked a glimpse over the top of his natural parapet. He could just about make out the shape of a man, almost flat on his stomach, edging his way to the right to outflank Haynes. More shots hummed angrily close to Carr's head.

Carr fired three times, then once more, though he was sure he'd hit the man with the second shot. He ducked behind the parapet as a fusillade of bullets whistled above him and whacked into the rock.

'Got one?' Haynes asked.

'I think so. I mean, yes.'

'Great. That evens things up a bit.'

Carr ducked as more bullets thunked against the rock-wall behind him and screamed off into the air above. He liked his situation even less than before. The next one could just as well richochet downwards and put a big hole in him.

'At least this shooting's going to bring the police eventually,' Haynes said cheerfully. 'So time's on our side.'

'Don't count on it. The opposition could be sending up another of those armoured battle-wagons full of goons to take us from the other side. And don't forget they've gone off Christ knows where with Desvins.'

There was the unmistakable heavy roar of Haynes's Magnum as he fired twice, then an awful scream from one of the men by the car.

'*Arrêtez! Ne tirez pas!* Not firing!' a man shouted in a panicky voice with a pronounced Slavic accent. '*Mon ami est blessé au bras. Il perd beaucoup de sang.* My friend hurt in arm, much bleeding, very bad.'

If he had been hit with a Magnum bullet he'd be bleeding all right. He'd be lucky if his arm was still attached to the rest of his body. He certainly sounded bad by the sounds of whimpering and groaning.

'I coming out! *Ne tirez pas!*'

Carr risked a look over the top again. A man slowly stood up behind the bonnet of the car, his hands held high and open. He was big and muscular, light on his feet when he moved. As far as Carr could see in the half-light, he looked pretty scared.

'*Ne tirez pas!* Not firing, please!' he said again as he slowly moved towards them.

Carr kept him covered, occasionally sneaking a look in the direction of the car. Nothing stirred there. The injured man suddenly groaned again, more loudly, and the cry changed into a shriek. Carr guessed the initial numbness was beginning to wear off and the pain was getting to him.

'Help me, please! In God's name, help!' he cried in a voice that sounded half choked with blood. Carr felt very cold.

The injured man dragged himself up from behind the front of the car and sprawled across the bonnet, whimpering, 'Help me, help me, help me.' It was difficult to judge how badly he was wounded. The dead man without a face, leaning slightly forwards, seemed to be listening to him politely.

Haynes came out from behind his cover, his revolver in both hands aimed at the man coming towards them. The gun was steady on target.

Several things happened at once in a single violent moment.

Carr bellowed, 'Get down!' The first man leapt athletically to one side and rolled swiftly into cover. The 'injured' man brought up a gun he'd been concealing and fired four shots at the unprotected Haynes – before ducking down behind the car again. Haynes was already dead when the last two bullets tore into his body.

Carr sent a shot in the direction of the first man, but he was safely out of the field of fire. It would be pointless shooting again.

He looked across at Haynes.

The young man had paid a terrible price for only five seconds' thoughtlessness caused by a simple lack of experience. He lay on his back, one knee drawn up, a great dark stain still spreading on his chest, another in the roadway beside his head. One arm was twisted awkwardly under him, the other was flung up, pointing towards Carr, the revolver just out of reach of the half-closed hand.

Carr felt sick and numb at the awful, stupid waste of that young life. And for what?

A shot hit the rock protecting Carr, then another, sharply reminding him of his predicament. He was in a shelter that was also a trap, and outnumbered two to one by men who knew their business. He had to think of something, and quick.

The first man was wriggling his way back towards the protection of the car. Carr peered round the rock parapet in time to glimpse him get back to the vehicle and roll behind it.

Carr lay flat once more, took careful aim, and pulled the trigger of his automatic. There was a click, not loud, but it seemed to echo and re-echo in that tiny battlefield. The two men by the car heard the gun click again: the sound of the hammer falling on the firing-pin of an empty automatic.

'It's a trick,' the first man said at last.

There was a long, jagged silence while no one moved. Finally Carr stretched out his hand towards Haynes's revolver. A bullet kicked up dirt and stone splinters between Carr's fingers and the weapon.

A moment later he was half an inch from losing a finger

when three shots discouraged him from making a second try.

A minute later Carr's belt flicked out and tried to capture the revolver. On the second attempt, despite more shots, Carr actually managed to snag the trigger-guard with the belt buckle, but he was either too clumsy or too hasty in trying to pull the gun towards him. He was about to make a third try when a lucky shot sent the gun skidding completely out of reach.

'I still think it's a trick,' the first man said in his own language.

'He nearly had his hand shot off.'

'Could be worth it to him if it makes us fall for his trick.'

'Let's see if we can remember how many shots he's fired. We'll work it out separately,' the second man said. They both thought intently. 'Well?'

'Nine.'

'That's what I make it.'

'He could have changed the magazine.'

'We'd have heard him doing it. Heard him cocking the gun, anyway.'

The first man pondered for a while.

'We've got to take care of him, one way or the other. You know what we're supposed to do. Get one or both of them alive if we can, but nobody gets away. There's always the chance that some stupid peasant has heard the shooting and called the police,' the second man pointed out. 'It could make things difficult for us.'

'Well, there are two of us,' the first man said at last. 'Let's move.'

They quickly formulated a plan of attack and moved off in opposite directions, keeping low. There was no Haynes for them to worry about now, but the narrow entrance to Carr's horseshoe hollow meant that they couldn't be too far from each other over the last few yards.

Keeping in touch by signal, the two men crept from cover to cover, always getting closer to Carr's foxhole. He made no movement, no sound, but he felt they could hear him sweating.

Without warning he shouted out. His cracked voice betrayed his loss of self-control.

'All right! I'm unarmed! I'll come out. Just don't shoot!'

Slowly he rose from behind the protecting parapet, his hands clasped on his head.

The two men were far too experienced to make the same mistake as Haynes. They remained under cover, their 9mm Makarov pistols pointed unwaveringly at him. Carr's mouth felt dry as desert dust. Slowly he moved out into the roadway, feeling utterly naked. He walked awkwardly, gingerly, on the uneven surface.

'Throw down your gun,' the first man said.

'It's back there,' Carr said. He stopped in the middle of the road, his body stiff and tense. 'Don't shoot. We can work something out.' He gave a mirthless, frightened laugh that was meant to be ingratiating.

The two men relaxed just a fraction, but they still watched him carefully, and kept their guns trained as they came out into the open. Carr was jumpy and scared, there was no doubt about that. With his hands still clasped on his head, he shifted his position slightly, as if too nervous to stand still. From his new position the two men were relatively closer to each other.

Carr had never moved faster in his life as he now pulled out his gun. He'd pushed it down the back of his collar, and barely managed to keep it in place – which was why he'd moved so awkwardly.

He took the two men off balance by leaping and rolling over and over on his side towards them. Before he hit the ground he let off one shot. The 9mm Parabellum cartridge, although not as powerful as Haynes's .357 Magnum, had enough hitting force to smash the first man's right shoulder and knock him to the ground. Carr was just aware of a stinging pain in his left forearm as he squeezed the trigger again. His shot went through the man's heart – he lived just long enough to realise he had been right: it was all a trick.

Carr rolled over again to face the second man. He missed him entirely with his first shot, which meant he had just one cartridge left. If he missed with this one, he was as good as dead. Either dead here, or much later in Moscow Centre.

Carr and his adversary surveyed each other for what seemed an eternity before they brought their guns to bear. Oddly, the strain made Carr's hand steady. His last shot hit the man in the throat, before he could fire, smashing his spinal column on its way out.

The two men's arithmetic had been faultless: Carr had fired nine cartridges and he hadn't reloaded. Their mistake had been to overlook one fact – or maybe they weren't aware of it. He had a Browning Hi-Power – an unusual weapon. Unlike most other automatics, with magazines taking seven, eight or nine cartridges, the Browning's magazine takes thirteen.

Carr kicked the guns away from the bodies and quickly went through their pockets. Their papers revealed that they were Russians – as was the faceless man still sitting in the American car. Carr had to turn his head away while he searched that one.

The fourth man, who'd tried to outflank Haynes, was French. He carried an identity card which showed he was a member of the SDECE, the French equivalent of the British SIS. The SDECE had been the most insecure and most penetrated service in the West, riddled with KGB informants and agents up to the very highest level. Many people believed it still was, and the presence of this man with three Russian agents seemed to confirm it. When word of this man's involvement got back to London it wouldn't help SDECE's credibility much, either. Carr left the papers on the man's body, but carefully noted his name. Discreet enquiries about who his friends were might help finger some dubious characters in the SDECE.

Naturally, Desvins wasn't in the Mercedes. Carr had realised that long ago. Oh, he'd been smart in guessing that the little set-piece in front of No. 27 was a decoy, all right. But the opposition had been a bloody sight brighter. The big car coming out of the next street was just another distraction. If the first decoy didn't work the second one certainly would. Desvins was far away by now, and his captors were laughing. Carr felt almost suicidal at his own stupidity in falling for the double bluff and leading Haynes to his death.

He went over to the Peugeot. It looked pretty sick, with shattered windows, dented body, twisted bumpers and a slightly pushed-in radiator, but the engine started at first try, and the car responded to all the controls. He drove it up beside Haynes's body. As he turned the steering-wheel it slipped in his hand, and he saw blood on his fingers. One of the shots had scored his forearm deeply.

Carr slipped out of his jacket and wound a handkerchief round his arm to stop the bleeding. Pressure would do it eventually: tourniquets are rarely necessary and are frequently dangerous when applied by laymen.

He climbed out of the car wearily, like a man who knew he'd lived too long, and bent to pick up Haynes's body. He wasn't going to leave him there to be subjected to the interminable sarabands of French bureaucracy.

Despite the carnage all around, despite the sharp pain and dull ache in his arm, despite the shocking reality of Haynes lying dead before him, Carr still hadn't quite taken in the awfulness of it all. But as he looked down at the corpse, a single tiny detail suddenly switched on his sensibilities once more.

Haynes's eyes were wide open, and a fly was standing on his left pupil. With preternatural clarity Carr saw the fly performing the ritual of feeding: lowering its long proboscis, regurgitating a digestive liquid and treading it into the surface of the eye to liquify it before sucking up the mixture. That Haynes didn't blink made Carr's own eye itch intolerably. He angrily brushed the insect away.

The full force of reaction hit him now, and Carr trembled violently, uncontrollably. He sank to his knees, then pitched forward on to all fours. His stomach heaved.

A few timeless minutes later he recovered. Then he struggled Haynes's body into the back of the Peugeot, laying it on the floor between the seats. He put his gun in with him. When the police came on the scene it would take them some time to work out what had happened and how many people had been involved.

Carr pointed the Peugeot towards Marseille. The dawn seemed to be long in breaking. He glanced at the dashboard clock. It must have stopped: it showed only twenty minutes later than when the shooting began. He checked his watch and blinked at it in disbelief. It *had* been only twenty minutes.

He drove the car straight inside the central courtyard of the Consulate. Murray and his men rushed out as soon as he arrived. His mouth open in shock, Murray had the sense not to ask what had happened to his car.

Carr opened the back door so they could see Haynes.

'Get him home to England somehow. I don't care how, but do it.' He turned away from them, ignoring their questions.

9

As soon as he returned to England, Carr visited Geoffrey Haynes's family: his elder sister and his widowed mother. They lived in stockbroker Surrey, in an expensive house that somehow seemed to have avoided change since the mid-thirties. The drawing-room was full of photographs of Mrs Haynes and her husband. Their entire lives were revealed in silver frames: from the wedding group, all through his career in the Army – including one of him looking suitably modest against the railings of Buckingham Palace, with a case containing some decoration – to the studio portrait taken to mark his retirement. Many of the framed pictures stood on a mini-grand piano covered by a fringed silk shawl.

Mrs Haynes had faded blue eyes and the white-blonde hair of someone who had lived a long time under a hot sun. She'd already been informed that her son was dead, and she clearly knew what his job had been. Haynes's sister, a strange, reserved but quite beautiful young woman, wore a wedding ring, although nothing was said about her husband. Not even his name. She was introduced as 'My daughter Lorraine'.

They gave him a formal tea before they allowed him to tell them what he'd come to say. It was agonising.

When at last they were ready to listen to him, they sat facing him with hands folded in their laps.

'I know it's small comfort, but I wanted you to know that you can be very proud of Geoffrey.'

'We always have been,' his mother said gently.

Carr felt dreadful. 'Of course. I'm sorry, but I'm not very good at this. I meant to say that he saved my life.' He then used an archaic phrase that would normally provoke smiles, but it was the only one that fitted: 'He was a very gallant young man.'

Lorraine saw him out. At the door they shook hands, and she gave him a long, unfathomable look. Later he saw her again at the funeral, when she gave him the same look. Carr wasn't sure whether she was blaming him for her brother's death, or giving him some sort of invitation. He didn't want to find out. Not yet, anyway.

When Carr arrived back at the SID headquarters after that first visit, Streeter was waiting to see him.

'I've just had word,' Streeter informed him. 'They got Desvins out on an Air Alger flight to Algiers. He went first class with two "friends", on a Bulgarian passport.'

Carr knew that Algerian co-operation with Russia was total. As soon as he arrived in Algiers Desvins was virtually on the doorstep of No. 2 Dzerzhinsky Square, Moscow.

'What about Kolunin?'

'Three days after they got Desvins away, Kolunin disappeared from the conference. No one knows where he's gone.'

'I can guess.'

'Couldn't we have warned Kolunin?'

'Obviously not.'

'Yes . . . Well, at least Desvins held out for three days –

for all the good it did him. Once they got hold of him, it was only a matter of time. How much did he know about this department?'

'Almost nothing. Not even names. Everything was done through a cut-out. So nothing's been compromised.'

'Hooray. Then we only lost Kolunin. Not too bad after all,' Carr said sarcastically. After a moment he added, 'I'm sick of it. Every time I come back from a run these days I have to report another bloody awful disaster. What the hell's happened to this department?' It was a rhetorical question. 'They're rolling up our people overseas. They've killed Geoffrey Haynes. I've been shot at more on the last two operations than I have in five years.'

It was night and the office curtains were drawn. Only the desk-lamp was on. From his chest down, Streeter was brilliantly illuminated, revealing a spotless shirt and a new, uncreased suit. Above the cone of light his face was in deep shadow. Occasionally there was a red glow as he pulled on a cigar.

'I tell you,' Carr went on bitterly, 'we were blown again. They've been a jump ahead of us at every single turn lately.'

He stared at the dark silhouette of Streeter's head. He rose suddenly, went to the switch of the overhead light and flicked it on. On his way back to the desk he was shocked by Streeter's appearance. His narrow eyes had shrunk into his skull and he had the leaden smear of sickness on them. His hand trembled.

'You all right?' Carr asked.

'Yes. I haven't slept very well for a couple of nights.'

'You won't sleep very well tonight either when you hear what I've got to say. I've done another check. It's Chapman.'

'I told you before – '

'Listen. Snatching Desvins was obviously a rush job. Now, Chapman came on at 1400 that day. What's the first thing a man does when he comes on duty in the communications/ops room?'

'Reads the log and the operations-in-progress file,' Streeter said automatically.

'Right. That would be the first time Chapman could have known about Desvins. Twenty minutes after he came on duty he went out for about a quarter of an hour. Within an hour the KGB were round knocking at Desvins' door.'

Streeter sat up. 'How do you know?'

'Same as last time. I looked at the duty roster, and checked back on the times. There's something else. I went through the operational files and signals. Chapman knew about Desvins, but *not* about Kolunin. That's why Kolunin wasn't picked up right away.'

'I meant, how do you know when Chapman went out of the ops room?'

The question surprised Carr. It seemed to be the least important point. 'Tom Duffy mentioned it.'

'Yes – when you brought it up.' Streeter was unmistakably angry. 'This is a very informal section. I don't run it like the Army, or even the Birdcage. But there *is* a chain of command, and I won't have you interrogating other members of the department without my orders or permission.'

'I didn't interrogate – '

'Don't try to fog the situation with semantics!'

'All right. But I'm not a beginner. Duffy didn't realise what I was after.' Carr was suddenly aware of his defensive tone, and felt angry with himself. 'Wait a minute! What the hell am I apologising for? We're missing the point. The Department's been penetrated, and I've found out who it is.'

'No you haven't. Chapman isn't a double.' Streeter crushed out his cigar and addressed him by his surname, for the first time in more years than he could remember: 'Carr, I told you once before, and this is the last time. Chapman is loyal. You are to leave him *strictly* alone. Do you understand?' Carr nodded, but this didn't satisfy Streeter. 'Do you understand?' he repeated.

'Yes.'

Streeter softened his attitude – a fraction, no more. 'I know what I'm doing.'

Carr didn't doubt it. The question was exactly *what* it was that Streeter was doing.

For the next three days Carr went to the office and cleared up his backlog of routine paperwork. Streeter gave him nothing special to do, but whether he was disciplining him, or there genuinely wasn't anything for him, Carr didn't know. To keep himself occupied he read back numbers of Intelligence Digests. Perhaps he was seeking an excuse to hang around the building and keep an eye on Chapman, although this was obviously a futile exercise.

Unaccountably Carr remembered the checks on the Nazi war criminals he'd made for Eli Yelkov. On impulse he picked up the phone and invited Yelkov round for a drink.

'Have you found him yet? Your man Hoenigger, or whatever he calls himself?' Carr asked, handing Yelkov his usual bludgeoning shot of whisky.

'Maybe. But he's had nearly thirty-five years to hide. We have to be certain.'

Yelkov glanced sideways at Carr. 'I hear you had a tough time of it in Marseille. Glad you're all right.'

'Where did you hear that?'

Yelkov did his stage Jew act again. 'Such friends I've got. I try to be friendly and all I get is questions like from a forty-nine per cent partner. Listen, there's an old Yiddish saying: a fool is his own informer.'

'Do you ever give a straight answer to a straight question?'

'Ask me if I'd like another drink.' Carr poured him one, and Yelkov continued in his normal voice, 'I didn't hear the actual details. What happened?' Carr explained, and when he'd finished, Yelkov said, 'You were lucky they fell for your trick – particularly as they'd pulled one just like it five minutes earlier.'

'That's what I was counting on – that they'd be looking for something more original, even if I wasn't. And being two against one made them a fraction careless.'

'Have your people turned up anything new on PSI?'

Carr shrugged. 'Not that I know of. And you?'

'The Russians are increasing the scale of their research and experiments. They've got a budget the size of an IMF loan.' Carr looked sceptical. 'I told you before, Richard,' Yelkov went on, 'the whole concept terrifies me. Now more than ever, the things that are going on. If they make a breakthrough, it could be the end of us all.' He paused, then continued in a tone Carr had never heard before, 'If they haven't made it already.'

Carr stared at him. The physical activities and perils of Marseille and the shocking reality of Haynes's death had made him forget abstract dangers. He'd forgotten how intent Yelkov had been the last time he'd spoken of parapsychology, and infiltration of people's very thoughts.

He took a mouthful of Scotch, more than he'd intended, and coughed. It burned his mouth and warmed his stomach, but didn't touch the chill in his heart.

Quite softly Yelkov said, 'It's a tragedy Dr Kolunin didn't get out. I suppose you know he's been buried in Verkhoyansk?'

'What?'

'Not literally. He's too valuable to be eliminated. Verkhoyansk is three hundred miles from the Siberian Sea, and a thousand miles from the nearest frontier. He'll die there.'

Carr's expression didn't change. 'You're very well informed.' They were both aware of the heavy double meaning.

He got up and switched on the hi-fi. The BBC was offering a choice of modern jazz, a Wodehouse short story and harpsichord recital. Carr appeared to be listening intently to the harpsichord before he switched off the set. He didn't know what to say.

Yelkov broke the silence. 'Richard, there's a word going round that your people have been penetrated. You're not to be trusted.'

'What, all of us? All SIS?'

'No. Just your section.'

Carr was tempted to ask exactly *what* section he meant, but he was afraid that the answer might reveal Yelkov knew more about the SID than he should. Carr had enough to worry about already.

'Some of your allies – so-called allies – are being instructed not to let you have any sensitive intelligence,' Yelkov went on.

'And you?'

'I don't take instructions here. I give them.'

So you still trust me?'

'You personally, but that's all.'

'Jesus,' said Carr. 'If I'd known this was what you were going to tell me I wouldn't have invited you.'

'Funny you did,' Yelkov said. 'When you rang I was on the point of asking you over to my place. You've saved me some Scotch. My people'll be very pleased. They're having another economy drive.'

By coincidence Carr met Mark Westbrook in Piccadilly the following morning. He knew it was a coincidence, because his decision to go out was entirely spontaneous, and in the course of his outing he changed his mind twice about where he was going.

'Come and have a cup of coffee,' Westbrook said. 'I've just got time, and my grocer does a fair cup, for an Englishman.' His 'grocer' was Fortnum and Mason. Carr had never tried to make Westbrook understand that American coffee was almost universally awful. American coffee came third in the list of the nation's sacred institutions after motherhood and apple pie.

They found a quiet corner table behind a fleshy redoubt of bluehaired women who thought that eating three cream cakes instead of four was strict dieting.

Westbrook looked round the restaurant unenthusiastically as they sipped their coffee. He clearly had something to tell Carr, but didn't rush into it. Carr decided not to hurry him.

'Have you heard anything about PSI – long-range guided mental telepathy, mind-reading, that sort of thing?' Carr asked.

Westbrook looked at him sharply. 'You're into that as well, are you?'

'Not really. I've just heard whispers.'

'Eli Yelkov?'

Carr nodded. 'Among others. I'm not following it up myself. Do you think there's anything in it?'

'It would explain some crazy things that have been going

on.' He paused. 'I don't know. A lot of our people think there is.' Westbrook vigorously stirred his black coffee though it had no sugar. 'We've been ordered to steer clear of your people,' he said abruptly.

'Clear of who, exactly, and why?' Carr asked.

'Everybody at the Kensington house. Our people think you've been penetrated.'

'What do *you* think?'

'Maybe.'

'How do you know it's not me?'

'You've got to be able to trust somebody.'

'First rule in the book is you don't trust anybody.'

'Screw the book,' Westbrook said, a little too loudly. A woman nearby looked round at him, her dripping *chou à la crème* poised halfway to her mouth. 'You didn't go by the book with me in Latakia.'

Carr didn't reply. They had survived that Syrian incident only by keeping their heads, trusting each other implicitly, and being better shots than the opposition. It had been rather like the Marseille affair.

'Besides,' Westbrook went on, 'I'm not all that sure about . . . ' He hesitated.

'About what?'

'Some of our people back at Langley don't exactly have me brimming over with confidence.' He was referring to the CIA headquarters in Virginia.

'The world's a mess.'

'So what else is new?'

Ten minutes after they parted, Carr stopped dead in his tracks in Regent Street. A man behind bumped into him and said something angrily in a foreign language, but Carr was unaware of him. All at once he was almost sure he knew the leak in the Department; he wondered why he hadn't seen it before. Maybe because he hadn't wanted to.

10

Carr couldn't bring himself to the point of making a positive move about Streeter. He knew this was cowardice rather than lack of conviction. He needed to talk over the situation with someone without actually mentioning Streeter's name, but Westbrook was away on a run somewhere and Yelkov was unaccountably noncommital and unhelpful.

One day Streeter took Carr to lunch at his club, which was heavily populated by the Establishment armchair mafia. It was a depressing, suffocating experience.

The lunch was excellent, and probably disgustingly expensive. Carr couldn't be sure how expensive because he was given a menu with no prices marked on it. He found the genteel discretion deafening.

During the lunch he covertly studied Streeter. He had the uneasy feeling that Streeter was doing the same to him.

Maybe he's guessed I suspect him, Carr thought. On impulse he said, 'Anything new on Chapman?'

Streeter stared at him with that long Modigliani face, his eyes seeming to squint.

'How do you mean?'

'Are you still satisfied about his loyalty?'

'Yes.' The single syllable was as final as a slamming door.

A few days later Carr learned by chance that information coming regularly from an agent codenamed 'Speedboat' in East Berlin was suspect. Speedboat worked for the MfS (Ministry for State Security) and all the documents he sent were Xeroxed copies of apparently authentic MfS reports, marked with series classifications and numbers. Then Carr got sight of just three documents with the same series numbers from a second source – a 'walk-in' who turned up with a briefcase full of Xeroxed papers. Careful analysis of the walk-in's papers left Carr in no doubt that Speedboat was being fed with specially prepared documents in a disinformation exercise by the MfS and the KGB.

There was always the possibility, of course, that Speedboat had been turned by the East Germans, but Carr thought that very unlikely. Speedboat was an agent who worked for SID for personal reasons, not for money. He had a deep-seated, ineradicable hatred of the East German MfS and the KGB. Nor was it likely that he'd been forced against his will to turn against Britain. The safety checks in his messages were invariably correct.

No, Carr was as sure of Speedboat as anyone could be in this business. That meant he was known to the opposition, and by extension – given all the recent incidents involving the SID – probably someone in the Kensington house had blown him. Streeter and Carr were the only ones who knew Speedboat's real identity.

Carr made three decisions. First, he managed to keep from Streeter the walk-in's reports that proved Speedboat's material was doctored.

Second, he did nothing about warning Speedboat. If he advised him to get out, or even to stop sending documents, it would reveal the fact that the SID knew their man had been blown. Furthermore, it would be evident that the SID would be looking inside their own organisation to discover if the leak had come from there. Anyway, now that Carr knew the intelligence coming from the East Berlin source was tainted, he could act accordingly. Speedboat would be safe enough as long as the MfS thought he was being unwittingly useful to them. In any case, there was far more at stake than Speedboat's safety if warning him meant that the traitor in London would dive for cover.

Carr's final decision was that he could no longer avoid reporting his suspicions about Streeter to someone higher up in the chain of command.

And that meant only one man.

Although Vernon Beech's office was located in a modern

building and had conventional modern fittings like telephones, he'd managed to give it the air of a mid-nineteenth-century lawyer's chambers by adding pieces of his own.

Beech listened carefully to Carr's accounts of the Vienna and Marseille operations, and without interrupting. Then he got up and went to his window to look out across the Thames. With back still turned he said, 'In essence, it amounts to this. You believe the evidence indicates two possibilities. One, Roger Chapman is the leak in your department, and Streeter is deliberately protecting him for reasons of his own?'

Carr nodded. Beech seemed aware of the movement behind his back.

'Two, and more likely, Streeter himself has gone over to the opposition and is trying to inhibit you from continuing any further investigation because it would positively establish his own guilt?' Beech turned to look him directly in the face.

'That's about the size of it,' Carr said inadequately. He had the fleeting impression that Beech found his inelegant phrase almost as distasteful as the situation itself.

'It's extremely worrying,' Beech admitted to Carr. 'It's obviously a situation that must be rectified as soon as possible, but at the same time we must be absolutely sure that we get the right man. Otherwise the real traitor will escape.'

'And we won't have had a chance to find out about his contacts, methods of communication and the rest,' Carr said grimly. 'Not to mention how much he's managed to tell them.'

Beech looked at him for a moment before continuing. 'It will be almost impossible to carry out a normal surveillance on a man in Streeter's position without his becoming aware of it. I'm afraid you'll have to keep a watch on Streeter's activities yourself – and Chapman's, I suppose – and report to me. It's most distasteful but it's necessary.'

'Yes.' Carr was suddenly reminded of the famous dictum 'Espionage is too dirty a game for anyone but gentlemen.'

'You'd better not come to see me here again. Your brother-in-law will soon guess you're reporting to me.'

Carr was jolted off balance. This reference to his relationship to Streeter was an oddly distracting emphasis on an irrelevancy. This was one of Beech's standard tactics to give himself psychological advantage in any discussion – offering the other person an occasional unexpected verbal nudge to make him unsteady. Beech pulled out a pocket-watch as thin as a shilling and looked at it a fraction too long. It was a gesture of dismissal as final as a royal 'You are excused'.

On his way home Carr realised that Beech's unsettling tactics had made him forget to tell him something important. Well, it could wait for another time.

A fortnight passed in dull routine matters. Intelligence work wasn't one constant round of rushing about. Peg-the-Legs came to see him and stayed overnight, saying rather tartly the next morning that she already had one brother and didn't need another, thanks very much.

He socialised with Streeter rather more than usual. Once or twice, when he thought Streeter had drunk a little too much, Carr cautiously and very subtly sounded him out on the possibility of someone in Intelligence becoming disillusioned with the West and being tempted to turn . . . It took Carr a long time to get round to it but, drunk or sober, there was no reaction from Streeter. Not even a faintly hostile reaction. Nothing.

The only practical thing Carr achieved was to get a good look at Chapman's flat near Sloane Square one evening when they went off duty together. He offered Chapman a lift, then accepted his invitation in for coffee. As they chatted he wandered around the living-room, mentally valuing the contents like a bailiff with a distress warrant. There wasn't the slightest hint that Chapman was living above his income, and there were no heavily locked cupboards or desks.

He found no signs in the bathroom or in the adjoining bedroom of any unconventional sexual inclinations that might make Chapman vulnerable to blackmail – no obvious signs of transvestism or homosexuality. Not that he was expecting to find anything, but it increased his near certainty that Chapman was innocent. Anyway, it would have to be a pretty outré perversion to lay someone open to successful blackmail, Carr thought. These days no self-respecting autobiography with a hope of newspaper serialisation was without admissions of some homosexual adventures.

Eventually Beech called Carr on the secure internal phone circuit and said it was time for them to meet again.

'I don't have very much to report,' Carr apologised.

Beech ignored this and went on, 'Thursday would be convenient. I've arranged my appointments to have the afternoon free, so we should have time to get away from this part of London, where we might be recognised.'

'Shall we go in your car, or mine?' Carr asked.

'I do not own a motor-car,' Beech said precisely. 'I'm afraid I'm not very good with mechanical devices.' His tone put the entire technological world in the wrong.

'I know a place we could have lunch, if you don't mind going in a Mini.'

'A Mini.' Beech's voice was expressionless.

'I promised to pick up my friend's car from servicing. Nobody'll recognise us in that.'

'Indeed not.'

'Twelve-thirty in the Hyde Park underground car-park, Bay A19.'

'Very well.'

Carr picked up Peg-the-Legs's maroon Mini and drove to the car-park. He arrived at Bay A19 precisely on time. As he drew level with it, Beech came out from behind someone's Rover and got into the Mini without a word.

They were in that maze of narrow roads with a bad case of thrombosis caused by illegally parked cars between Sloane Street and Brompton Road before Beech asked, 'Where are we going?'

'To a place I know the other side of Kingston.'

Carr drove over the handsome Albert Bridge, which always made him think of an old sailing ship with its latticework of slender girders. The run through Wandsworth and on to the Kingston by-pass was uneventful and quite rapid, although Carr missed the power of his Saab Turbo. Near the Tolworth underpass he turned off to the left and drove through some suburban streets which suddenly gave way to tree-lined country roads.

The last of them was quite dangerous for an unwary driver. Trees met over the top of the road, which hardly ever seemed to dry off in winter. Mud sliding off the road-side banks when it rained kept the surface treacherous. The road fell abruptly and turned to the left, just as a minor road joined it on the right. Then it widened, levelled out, and at a crossroads stood a large hotel and restaurant.

Carr was concerned that he had not booked a table, but as they drove into the car-park, he was surprised to find it practically empty. Before it had always been crowded. Maybe Thursday was a slack day.

While Beech went to wash his hands, Carr ordered sherries and studied the menu. The sherry was barely above cooking standard, but the menu listed some ambitious and exciting dishes.

'Ambitious' was the word. Halfway through the first course Carr began to understand why the restaurant was half empty; two mouthfuls of the main dish and he was certain. In fact he wondered that the place was even quarter full. The food was awful. Beech ate with a politely un-critical air. It was a good act.

'This place must have changed hands since I was last here – a couple of years ago. I'm sorry,' Carr said, but Beech cut short his apologies. It was possible Beech was enjoying the situation. He didn't have to do anything to put Carr at a psychological disadvantage; he'd done it to him-self.

Over the dessert Carr began to talk business.

'Well?' Beech prompted him.

'I'm afraid it's a nil return,' Carr said. 'The department's been going through a fairly inactive spell. Both Streeter and Chapman have had practically nothing to do.'

'But you've spoken to them?'

Carr nodded. 'I've been to Streeter's flat and had a couple of drinking sessions with him.'

'Is he drinking heavily?'

Carr considered his answer. 'Not heavily, but perhaps a little more than usual. I gave him a chance to sound me out about defecting if he wanted to. But . . . ' He shook his head.

'Chapman?'

'I still don't think he's the leak. He invited me in one evening and there wasn't the least sign of anything suspicious.'

'I'd hardly expect there would be. In any case, I've had his place thoroughly searched, to the point of having the floorboards up.' Carr stared at him. Somehow he hadn't associated the ascetic Beech with that sort of direct action. 'But after all, what equipment would either of them need?' Beech went on. 'You know as well as I do how it's done. The opposition would simply give him a number to call – public telephone to public telephone, each time with a new number for the next contact. There'd be no need to hand over documents. A traitor has only to remember foreign agents' names, addresses . . . contact procedures . . . '

Carr nodded agreement. 'The opposition wouldn't have anyone that useful run unnecessary risks like taking out documents.'

'I'd like to go over everything again,' Beech said, 'starting with the disappearance of Ondrach and your Austrian run. There may be something we've overlooked.'

Carr thought that unlikely, but gave the full account once more.

Beech listened patiently, then said, 'Frankly, I could hardly hope for any explanation other than that there's a traitor in your Department. However, I did hope there was a possibility it wasn't Streeter. But . . . '

'Have you considered the possibility that *neither* Streeter nor Chapman is a traitor?'

Beech sat up with a jerk. 'But it was your own suggestion that Streeter had gone over to the other side. And everything you've told me only confirms it.'

Carr spoke with some care. 'You know the Russians and Americans are working on PSI?'

'I've seen the Intelligence Digests, of course.'

'My personal contacts believe that the Russians have

made a great deal of progress. Particularly in a sort of guided mental telepathy . . . . ' Beech said nothing, and all at once Carr felt rather foolish, but he continued, 'I was wondering . . . perhaps *nobody's* giving information to the opposition. Supposing they've found a way to read people's minds . . . '

Beech was shaking his head. 'I'm not sure whether I'd prefer to believe it or not, but the question is academic. It's not that.'

'My own contacts are very reliable,' Carr said defensively. 'It's not impossible.'

'I'm sure it's not. But there are other reasons why I believe there's an active traitor – who is almost certainly Streeter.'

'What reasons, exactly?'

'I want to be quite certain before I tell you.' He glanced at his thin watch again. 'I must be getting back.'

As Carr signed the credit-card slip, he said to the *maître d'hôtel*, 'My compliments to the chef.' The *maître d'hôtel* looked at him in astonishment. 'For his effrontery,' Carr added.

The Mini's engine was cold and didn't start easily, despite its recent service. Carr drove it out of the car-park slowly, giving it time to warm up. They returned by the same road, taking the steeply-rising country road, now curving to the right.

Halfway up the hill they came in sight of the minor road. From the corner of his eye Carr noticed a heavy American lorry with a great double-barred steel bumper coming down the lane towards the junction with the major road. For a moment he had the impression that the lorry had been stationary in the lane and had only started up as the Mini came into view, almost as if it had been waiting for them.

The lane joined the road at such an acute angle that the lorry was coming at them virtually head-on.

Again Carr felt the adrenalin flood into his system like a physical blow. Beech tensed in his seat, but stayed silent.

Instead of slowing, the lorry was gathering speed, heading straight for the Mini. It would crush it like a toy under a sledgehammer.

The next few seconds until the sudden end were a confused blur of strange, illogical, violent action.

Carr slammed the Mini into second gear and stamped the accelerator to the floorboards. The car lurched forward, painfully slowly it seemed, as the engine coughed, while the murderous lorry plunged straight towards them.

Carr spun the steering-wheel and braked hard with his left foot, taking off a little power but still keeping the accelerator well down. The back wheels locked and the car tucked in its nose with the tail sliding out. When the Mini had made an almost-90 degree turn, Carr took off the brake and stamped the accelerator to the floorboards again.

The wildly spinning front wheels with their barely adequate tyres scrabbled for a hold on the slippery surface, then gripped, stopping the Mini's turning motion.

Carr thought, *If anything comes down the other way, we're done for, one way or another.*

At that very moment Carr was aware that the lorry driver had changed direction *exactly at the same moment he had.*

If Carr had frozen up the second he first saw the lorry bearing down on them, it would have hit the Mini head-on, crushing it completely. Carr's almost instinctive reaction had taken the Mini out of immediate danger so the lorry could pass behind them; but the driver's uncanny prescience had instantaneously cancelled out the effect of Carr's avoiding action. *The lorry was again heading straight for the Mini.*

It was so close now that Carr could plainly see the maker's plaque on the massive radiator, which seemed to tower over the tiny car.

Carr's pumping adrenalin slowed right down so he was acutely aware of each tiny movement. His mind raced.

As he formulated the desperate thought to swing the wheel again and brake with his left foot once more, the lorry driver changed direction yet again *just as if he was directly reading Carr's mind and intentions.*

Carr checked his own move, and the lorry, heeling over to one side under the force of its last-second turn, thundered past them, rocking the Mini with its slipstream. The sidewall of the great double rear tyre touched the Mini's fragile back bumper as lightly as a bird's wing, but the mass and speed of the wheel was enough to shear off the over-rider like a dead leaf.

Carr glanced into the mirror. Just before the lorry screamed round the bend and out of sight he was able to see that the back number plate was encrusted with mud, although the rest of the vehicle was clean.

The Mini gently nudged into the bank on the right-hand side of the road, and stalled.

In a matter of seconds Carr had become drenched in icy sweat. His hand trembled as he reached out for the key to restart the engine. He missed the first attempt to put the car into reverse and get back to the correct side of the road.

Slowly he drove to the top of the rise, then pulled into the side where the road widened. Only then did he look at Beech.

The older man was a putty colour, his lips pale and pressed together tightly. After a moment he took a handkerchief from an inside pocket and dabbed at his face. It was a pretty courageous performance from a man whose only experience of danger was second-hand from the reports on his desk.

'That was deliberate,' Carr said superfluously, when he was sure he had control of his voice. 'He bloody tried to kill us.'

Beech shook his head. 'Not us. Me.' He managed something like a smile. 'That's not the first attempt that's been made recently. It all started after you came to see me. This is the third occasion.'

'But why *you*?'

Beech suddenly looked very old. 'Over the last couple of months I've been discussing my successor with the P.M.' He wiped his face again.

'I don't understand. Your successor?'

'My retirement isn't all that far off, you know.' His next attempt at a smile was no better than the first. 'If I live that long. You see, my successor-apparent is – '

Carr felt cold again. 'Streeter.'

Beech nodded. 'After these attempts on my life, you can see why I'm fairly certain our traitor is Streeter. And if he is, think what taking over from me would mean.'

Carr didn't have to: the answer was all too obvious. It would be worse than the Philby situation over again.

As Carr walked into his flat the phone was ringing. It was Tom Duffy in the ops room.

'I've been trying to get hold of you for the past hour. You didn't leave a number.'

'I'm off duty.'

'You should have left one anyway. You're the Number Two and Streeter's in Whitehall. Get round to Roger Chapman's place, *now*. You need a car?'

'I'll get a cab. What's up?' But Duffy had already hung up.

There were no signs of unusual activity at Chapman's place, although there were two black cars with R/T aerials double-parked almost outside. Each had an expressionless young driver with a short haircut sitting patiently behind the wheel. There were no parking tickets on the windscreens.

When Carr rang the bell the front door of the house was opened immediately by a man he recognised as one of the SIS security people from the Waterloo building. Carr had an awful feeling he knew what was wrong.

Just inside the flat's front door was a uniformed policeman, who was probably there to give the other residents the impression it was a straightforward police matter. With him was another Birdcage man, who nodded at Carr.

'In there,' he said, indicating the bedroom.

Chapman was lying on the bed in trousers and a shirt. His sleeves were rolled up. He looked as if he was asleep, except for the waxy pallor of long-established death. Beside the bed was a bulky man who looked like a younger but more disillusioned Lord Boothby. Carr knew him: Dr Leo Pattman, the SIS's senior medical adviser and general fixer. He was examining a pill bottle, some ampoules and a used hypodermic syringe on the bedside table without handling them.

'Hello,' he greeted Carr.

Next to Pattman was Arthur Ling, an SID officer from the Kensington H.Q. He was wearing a pair of surgical plastic throw-away gloves.

'What happened?' Carr asked.

'Roger was due back on duty today after a forty-eight hour stand-down. When he didn't turn up or answer the phone, I came round. And . . . ' He indicated the bed.

'He's been dead thirty-six to forty-eight hours, I'd say,' Pattman reported with as much emotion as if he was cancelling the milk. 'I'll know better when I've got him back to the lab.'

'What killed him?'

'Almost certainly a self-injected massive dose of insulin. The ampoules are there.' He indicated them. 'I suspect he took sleeping pills, then gave himself the injections. If the bottle was full of pills, they'd be enough to kill him on their own.'

'There's a suicide note,' Ling said. He produced the note, already in a protective plastic envelope. 'It's his writing, all right.'

Carr thought that an oddly unnecessary observation. 'What does it say?'

Ling passed him the envelope.

The letter was short, and written in a firm hand that certainly looked like Chapman's. Carr would have thought the writing of a man on the point of suicide would be a little jagged. The note declared that Chapman was ashamed of what he'd been doing and couldn't bear it on his conscience any longer. He asked his friends to forgive him and apologised for the trouble his suicide would cause them.

'Any idea where he got the drugs?' Carr asked Pattman as he gave back the letter.

'The sleeping-pill bottle has his name on it. I expect we'll find his GP prescribed them.'

'And the insulin?'

Pattman shrugged. 'He could have gone to another GP – said he was a diabetic who'd just moved in and needed a supply.'

'And a doctor would give him a prescription, just like that?'

'Some might. Anyway, I expect anybody in your department could easily get hold of one of the cards that diabetics carry. If he showed that to the doctor . . .'

Carr knew he was right.

Ling started carefully packing away the pill bottle and ampoules for fingerprinting and general examination. 'Pretty straightforward, I'm afraid,' he said.

'Yes. Heart attack,' Pattman observed. 'That's what I'll put on the death certificate.' As Carr looked up he added with a bland expression, 'He'd been consulting me privately about his heart.'

'And you've got a folder full of case notes.'

'Naturally. Complete with nasty-looking electrocardiograms.'

Carr knew that if he died inconveniently, there'd be a nice full folder proving that Pattman had been seeing him over a long period, and could legally sign the death certificate.

Chapman's death was going to be swept up neatly and tidily, with all the paperwork in order and no publicity. Suicides are so messy, and give rise to all sorts of awkward questions when they occur in Intelligence services.

There was a sound from outside. A moment later Streeter was standing in the doorway. He looked round the room, taking everything in before he stepped inside. The harsh centre light made him look even more narrow-faced, and put his heavy-lidded, half-closed eyes into deep shadow.

'What's happened?' he asked Carr.

'Roger Chapman's killed himself.'

Streeter stared at him.

'Funny things people do when they get to the suicide stage,' Pattman said quietly, breaking the spell. 'The poor kid was so wound up that he killed himself with a hypodermic. But when I gave him his TAB and anti-tetanus jabs last year he practically passed out. Said he couldn't stand the thought of injections.'

Carr and Streeter carefully avoided each other's eyes.

Carr hadn't spoken to William Parker since the urgent late-night conference at Waterloo when news broke of the capture of the Czech Comenius group. So Parker was surprised when his red-circuit phone rang, and Carr asked to see him privately.

'Where?' Parker asked. He didn't ask if it was important. Carr wouldn't have rung him otherwise.

'Your club? This evening?'

'Seven-thirty. I'll leave word and you'll be brought straight up.'

In fact Parker was a member of several clubs, most of them as cheerful as the inside of a Pyramid and nearly as old. His favourite was in Mayfair, not St James's. He preferred it because the membership was much more varied and represented most of the arts, though often with more enthusiasm than distinction.

An elderly club servant took Carr upstairs to a small, dark-panelled room with three or four deep armchairs that had cost the life of a small herd of cows. Parker was seated with a decanter and a couple of glasses. Parker poured out a neat whisky for Carr, and one for himself.

'Well?'

Carr's first remark to the senior SIS man was innocuous enough on the surface, but shattering in its implications.

'Sir, who's head of Section E these days?'

In its small way Section E was the equivalent of the KGB's V Section, and the dark corner of the CIA's blandly named Department of Plans. However, Section E was not supposed to exist now, and not many people would admit that it ever had. In this modern, civilised world British Intelligence agencies didn't go round killing the opposition. Not even its own people. At least, that's what it said in the book.

Parker was a very self-possessed man. 'That's an odd question. You surely can't expect me to answer it.'

He hadn't denied the existence of Section E, though.

'Let me put a hypothetical case. *If* we had a unit like Section E, who would have the authority to get it to dispose of somebody?'

'Well, *you* wouldn't for a start. And it depends who the subject was. If it was a head of state, for example – '

'Nothing as exalted as that. Somebody else in the Service, say.' Parker shrugged. 'Would the head of my department have the authority to get it done?' Carr pressed.

Parker gave him one of his famous skull-boring looks before he answered. 'I should think so.'

'I take it the Section E lot would still be expert in not raising suspicions.'

'They certainly wouldn't jab anybody with a poison dart in a bus queue.'

'An accident . . . suicide . . . natural death?' Carr asked. Parker nodded. 'How important a person could Section E deal with, without reference higher up, sir?'

'Foreign or domestic?'

'Domestic.'

'Then pretty damned important,' Parker said. 'I should think,' he added for form.

'And who would I – somebody – have to see to get it laid on?'

'If you had the authority, you'd know.' Carr downed his whisky in one ungracious gulp, and stood up. 'Do you want to tell me anything?' Parker asked.

'No. Except, thank you, sir.'

Carr left the club. He had no illusions about the dark waters he could be stirring up. Long before he'd gone to see Parker, he was fully alive to the possibility that, for all he knew, William Parker himself might be the operational head of Section E. Which could put Carr in danger for turning over too many stones.

11

Four days after the cremation on a damp morning in West London, Carr had just about got over his illogical sense of outrage that Chapman was quietly tidied away while the people who'd killed him were walking around scot-free. He was fully aware that it was illogical, because he'd personally killed people enough, albeit in self-defence. Well, most of them. Maybe that was it: he was trying to obliterate his own deep-seated guilt through anger against others.

His outrage had changed to frustration, made more corrosive by his lack of progress in finding concrete proof against Streeter. It seemed fairly clear that Streeter realised he was suspected, and was lying very low. These days he was looking ghastly, and he'd lost weight. Carr wondered whether he was ill.

He was in his office, studying an analysis of possible Russian progress with charged particle beams – the classic 'death ray' – when his direct-line phone rang. This was unusual, for it was normally only used for Carr's outgoing calls, and not many people knew the number.

As he picked up the receiver there was the rapid *pip-pip-pip* of a public callbox. The money went in and a familiar voice said, 'Hello, Richard. You recognise my voice?' It was Mark Westbrook.

'Yes.' Carr supposed Westbrook had said that as a warning not to repeat his name if anyone else was in the office.

'I'm just back from a run. Can we meet? Right now.'

'Of course. Where would you like?'

'You remember where we sat and talked about Christoff's *Boris Godunov*?'

Carr thought. 'Yes.'

'There, in forty minutes?'

'Right.'

'Richard: make sure you're not followed.' Westbrook sounded thoroughly serious – alarmed, almost.

Carr left the Kensington house by the garden gate in the side road and hurried to Barkers department store. It was the end of a sale, and Carr was able to lose any possible shadowers. Finally he darted out and caught a No. 31 bus as it was pulling away from the stop. No one got on the bus after him, and as far as he could see, no car deliberately followed the bus. He got out at Earls Court station and took a train to Hyde Park Corner. On impulse he left the train at South Kensington, walked halfway up the stairs, then returned to the platform for the next train, just to be *sure* that no one was following. As he entered the train Carr thought, *You're getting bloody paranoid again. It's time you were out of this business.* He vowed inwardly he'd resign from the service once this case was cleared up – but he knew he was trying to kid himself. He was a junkie promising himself he'd give up the stuff after this one fix.

Five minutes after leaving the train at Hyde Park Corner Carr was sitting on a bench in Constitution Hill. The sun was low in the sky, and strong. Carr took a large pair of sunglasses from his pocket, slipped them on, and pulled his hat lower over his eyes. *Jesus Christ. Next it'll be a false beard.*

Westbrook was a few minutes late. For all the apparent haste and mystery of the meeting, he was impeccably dressed in a London-cut, dark three-piece suit.

'You're looking good. I haven't seen you for a while,' Carr said.

'I got back from Algiers this morning.'

'Oh? Who's your C.O.S. there now? Do I know him?'

'I didn't see any of our people.'

This surprised Carr. An operation that took Westbrook out of Britain into a 'hard-target' country where he didn't contact the CIA Chief of Station was something very odd. Carr made no comment, though, knowing Westbrook would tell him in his own good time.

'How was the city?'

'Depressing. The place is crumbling, coming apart at the seams for want of proper maintenance and management. The finances and logistics of a big city are too much for them.'

'You could say as much about New York,' Carr said with a wry smile.

'It's not the same thing at all,' Westbrook said sharply, not realising that Carr was half joking. He lit a cigarette and puffed at it nervously. 'Sorry,' he said after a moment. 'I'm a bit jumpy. I think I've been followed since I got back.' He rubbed the back of his neck. 'I had a pretty hairy time of it, Richard.' He ground out the cigarette he'd just lit.

'This isn't the first time you've had people following you, for Christ's sake. It's not like you to get twitchy.'

'Algiers gave me the creeps. Maybe things'll change now Boumedienne's dead, but I doubt it. Somehow it was like a foretaste of the collapse of Western civilisation. But it wasn't only the place, it was the things I heard there. I'm telling you, it's scared the hell out of me. This parapsychology, PSI, mental telepathy . . . I think the Russians *have* made a breakthrough.' He looked up gloomily, screwing his eyes against the sun, and watched the streams of cars going up and down Constitution Hill, which isn't much of a hill, really.

It was a warm day, but Carr felt cold; something he couldn't put his finger on, nothing more than a feeling, but strong, for all that. He remembered, too, Yelkov's words and they made him feel worse. *'If they make a breakthrough, it could be the end of us all. If they haven't made it already.'*

Westbrook was looking into the far distance, seeing something Carr couldn't see. 'You know, Richard, they *do* need us.'

'I don't understand.'

'These days they've got gimmicks that out-do science fiction. You can be standing in the Indian jungle with a Captain Kirk radio in your hand and talk direct to Langley through a satellite on one of its thirteen hundred, scrambled, untappable communications channels. You can drop a specially-treated handkerchief in a factory and it'll pick up minute traces of gases that'll tell you practically everything about the manufacturing processes. Computer-enhanced satellite pictures can show badges of rank on an officer's shoulders from two hundred miles up. But in the final analysis, they need people like you and me on the ground, using God-given common-sense and experience, and screw all your micro-circuits. The Poor Bloody Infantry of Intelligence.'

There was a strange noise, rather like someone hitting a piece of wood with a hammer. Carr looked round. He thought a couple of cars had bumped into each other somewhere, but everything looked calm and ordinary. Westbrook had apparently noticed nothing.

'When I was there I overheard that "they" were going to . . . ' He paused and searched for words. 'It's difficult to translate exactly. They were going to *get inside the mind* of a member of the U.K. Government. Or maybe more than one.'

Carr was silent for a long time. 'No details?' he said at last.

'No. Only that it was a psychological operation. I couldn't hang around. I had to get out, and quick.'

'What do your own people say about it?'

'I haven't told them.'

'What?'

'I haven't reported in.'

'Why not?'

'It's not only your people that are suspect now. Richard, there's something weird going on in the Company. Whether it's just local or it comes from Langley I don't know. And until I find out I'm going to be goddamn careful who I talk to. There's all the signs of another Sapphire affair boiling up. Whether it's your lot, or mine, or maybe the West Germans . . . '

As Westbrook paused to light another cigarette, Carr reflected on 'Sapphire', the codename for a vast network of

KGB agents in France who had penetrated the SDECE and even the French cabinet. As a result, the KGB had a direct pipeline into all NATO secrets. The first information of this penetration came from a KGB defector in America. The French SDECE and DST did nothing about it; it was almost certain that De Gaulle, jealous of his own reputation, tried to keep the lid on the affair. He said the 'revelations' were a revenge campaign directed against him by the CIA.

Westbrook continued: 'There's something else. Something I picked up. And it leads right back to Europe.'

'Can you tell me what it is?'

'I'm going to do more than that. I want you to go to this place, follow through for me. I can't do it myself; they know me now. Besides, like I told you, I don't trust our own people.'

'What is this place? Where is it?'

'I've got some material on it back at my house, but I can tell you enough about it on the way.'

There was the sound of a hammer hitting wood again, but this time it was more hollow, and nearer. Much nearer. Carr was looking at Westbrook, and saw him jerk against the back of the bench. His eyes were wide open with shock as he stared down disbelievingly at a spreading stain just inside his jacket. His face turned grey as Carr looked at him.

Carr was instantly aware of two things. First, there was a big hole in Westbrook's chest, a very big one. Blood was pumping out of it, seeping into his waistcoat and jacket. Carr snatched his handkerchief from his top pocket and pressed it against the awful wound. It did nothing to staunch the murderous flow of blood, and was soaked through in seconds. He let the handkerchief fall.

The second thing Carr realised was that there had been no sound of a shot.

He looked up and down the roadway. The nearest pedestrians were at least fifty yards away, and there was nothing to make one car look more suspicious than another.

Westbrook was trying to speak. Both he and Carr knew he was dying. It was grotesque: a man had been shot, somehow without sound, in a public park in daylight. And only Carr was aware of it. He leaned close to Westbrook.

'My keys,' he said, barely audibly. 'Richard, you remember . . . ?' His eyes closed and Carr thought he'd lost consciousness, but Westbrook opened them briefly and said, very quietly but quite clearly. 'The clay door. The clay door.' His head fell forward.

There was nothing Carr could do. Westbrook was dead, and Carr had no idea who'd killed him: the KGB . . . CIA . . . or even Section E?

Yes, there *was* something he could do. Move quickly, and find out what he could. Westbrook had trusted him. Carr owed him something for that.

Quickly he went through Westbrook's pockets until he found his key wallet. He was about to stand up when he remembered something. He removed Westbrook's wallet and CIA card from his inside pocket. He didn't want him identified too quickly; that way he could be in and out of Westbrook's home before the police and the Americans swarmed all over it.

At last Carr rose, looked once again at Westbrook, then briskly walked away.

Westbrook, that determined Anglophile, lived in a small but genuine Georgian house on the riverside at Barnes, in West London, a middle-class cosmopolitan district which estate agents were trying to promote as a Little Chelsea. That was supposed to be a recommendation.

Knightsbridge was almost solid with traffic, and it was a fair bet that the jam extended the best part of the way to Hammersmith. The Underground would be the quickest way. Carr fought his way on to a train at Hyde Park Corner and stood sweatily sandwiched between blank-eyed commuters to Hammersmith.

He was totally unaware of the discomfort. He kept puzzling over 'the clay door', wondering what the hell it could be. A clay door? His preoccupation with the problem almost made him miss his station.

When he got into Butterwick, the inaptly-named bus station at Hammersmith, he was luckier than he knew: a rare No. 9 bus arrived within five minutes and he managed to get on it. Taxis were thin on the ground at that time of day.

He journeyed a couple of stops beyond Westbrook's house, looking carefully at the street from the bus as it rumbled past. Everything seemed normal then, and also when he walked back. He'd already sorted out the front-door key so he wouldn't fumble in the doorway, attracting attention to himself.

The front door gave on to a small living-room, which Carr had visited a few times before. He entered, and stopped dead just inside. The room was unrecognisable: it looked as if it had been hit by a hurricane. It had been searched, ruthlessly, by experts – probably several of them. Later he discovered they had broken in through the back, by way of the miniscule garden which gave on to a narrow alleyway.

Every drawer had been pulled out and its contents scattered on the floor for easy examination. Upholstery and cushions had been slashed, the fitted carpet pulled up round all the edges. The bedroom had been dealt with just as totally. In the bathroom the top was off the lavatory cistern, the panelling pulled away from the bath, and the bottles and jars from the medicine cabinet smashed in the wash-basin. The soap had been cut open.

In the kitchen the fridge had been emptied. Jars and packets from the shelves had been emptied out to make sure they contained nothing but food.

Corridors, cupboards, even pictures had been thoroughly searched. The linings of suitcases had been ripped away; all the books had been swept from the shelves and lay sprawled open after being rudely shaken.

It dawned on Carr that if the searchers had been looking for something specific they hadn't found it. The rape of the house would have stopped as soon as they found whatever they were seeking, but the search had continued until the house couldn't possibly hold any more secrets.

There was another possibility, that the intruders were simply carrying out a precautionary search to see what they could turn up. Again, the indications were that they had found nothing, since the search had proceeded until there was nothing left to search.

Or was there?

The clay door. Was Westbrook trying to give him a clue to a hiding place? But why be so oblique in the last seconds of his life? Why not tell him directly? Perhaps the dying man wasn't able to think clearly. Carr went through the house again, trying to see something that could possibly suggest a clay door.

He shook his head. Nothing.

The garden, which he studied carefully from behind the kitchen curtains, and then again from the back bedroom, was as unproductive as the house.

What else did Westbrook say? *Remember?*

Remember *what*?

Then the answer to the second question came to him. It was so simple that Carr could almost laugh at not having thought of it before. There was an occasion when he himself had shown Westbrook a hiding place...

He went to Westbrook's portable typewriter. It was on its side next to its open carrying-case. The lining had been ripped out of that, too.

Carr took hold of the two knobs at each end of the roller, then twisted them simultaneously as if he were screwing them together. He needed all his strength, but suddenly they gave and began to come apart, unscrewing on their left-hand threads.

At last the roller came out of the machine. Carr took out a penknife with a screwdriver attachment and unscrewed the three screws holding the metal plate in position at the end of the roller.

It was hollow. Inside was a printed brochure, rolled up tightly.

Carr took it out and carefully smoothed it flat.

The brochure was for a health institute in the Haute Savoie district of France. It was clear from the information in the prospectus that it was nothing like the usual 'health farm'. It was a very expensive health clinic.

This, then, was Westbrook's lead to the European

advance post in the PSI and parapsychological offensive against Western Intelligence.

The name of the clinic was *Clés d'Or*: Golden Keys. The French pronunciation of *Clés d'Or* is 'clay door'.

12

The Alps stood in massive white, blue and dark grey planes against the lighter grey of the sky as Richard Carr drove eastwards through Annemasse and the Col des Gets pass, skirting the Franco-Swiss frontier, and then north-east in the direction of Abondance in the French Haute Savoie. Shortly after he crossed the River Durance, Carr left the main road and took a minor, unmetalled road leading up into the mountains. Six miles further on – if he didn't get lost – he'd come to the *Clés d'Or* clinic.

Carr's visit to the clinic as a patient had been meticulously planned.

He was driving a BMW 2800, taxed and registered in the name of David Tranter. In Carr's pocket was a passport and traveller's cheques in the same name. There was a real David Tranter, a senior civil servant. His record was in the Government computer in case the opposition had access to it, which seemed likely enough. He was a considerable sailing enthusiast, and at this moment he was on leave, enjoying a solitary boating holiday in and around the Orkneys and Shetlands. He was hardly likely to pop up in Haute Savoie and embarrass Carr. Tranter also owned a BMW with the same registration number as on the one Carr was driving. Tranter's car was locked away in his garage while he was away sailing. So, for a fortnight anyway, Carr's cover should hold without strain.

As soon as Carr found the *Clés d'Or* brochure in Westbrook's house he'd gone to Beech, who had run checks on the place. The clinic catered for people who were overweight, overstressed, or both. It provided individual dietary regimes and exercise, with special beauty treatments for women who wanted them. From a newspaper-cuttings library had come a couple of articles which were very flattering; although they hinted obliquely that some of the younger women patients there were no better than they should be, and went to the *Clés d'Or* to keep themselves attractive to Europe's most powerful and money-laden men. Some of the women patients, however, were respectably married.

Apart from any moral considerations, the worst that could be said of the place was that the people who ran it didn't embarrass easily when it came to fixing their prices. Curiously, for such an expensive institution, there seemed to be no Arab clients.

The owners were two Zurich-Swiss doctors, father and son, Gerd and Franz Schaffhauser. All investigations showed them to be medically and personally irreproachable.

Beech made arrangements for Carr to go to the *Clés d'Or* with a speed and efficiency that astonished him. How all the documents and the rest were produced, he didn't ask, although he knew it couldn't have been done through a Birdcage department, for reasons of security.

The magazine articles made it possible for 'David Tranter' to explain where he'd heard of the clinic when he phoned asking whether there was a vacancy.

Three weeks' sick leave from the SID for Carr was the easiest thing to arrange. A medical certificate was produced to the effect that he was suffering from tension and strain. The experiences of his last couple of runs made this quite credible. Taking a leaf from the real Tranter's book, Carr told Streeter and the communications/ops room people that he was going sailing, so he couldn't leave a telephone number or address.

It was a new and rather disquieting experience for Carr. Normally when he went on a run he studied all the available background intelligence first, and his objective was clear-cut.

This time he set off not knowing what or who to look for: whether it was the clinic itself, or one of the staff, or even a patient. In fact, he began to have doubts about the whole thing. 'It's a bit like suspecting Harrods of being an IRA front,' he said to Beech.

'It would be a perfect one if it could be managed,' Beech replied. Carr didn't have an answer to that.

As Carr drove higher into the mountains, towards Entremeaux, there was more than physical distance between him and London. Although it was a matter of only a few days since he was sitting in Constitution Hill with Westbrook, already there was an almost dreamlike – no, nightmarish – unreality about it.

When Carr left Westbrook's house he had made an anonymous phone-call to the police about the identity of the dead man who'd been reported sitting on the bench in Constitution Hill. Except that no one had reported him yet. That's the trouble about big cities. Almost nobody notices anything, and the few that do just pass by.

The bullet that had killed Westbrook, and another in a tree-trunk near the bench, were highly unusual. They were of unjacketed lead and appeared to be hand-moulded. They were bigger and heavier than the largest revolver or rifle bullet manufactured, and smooth without rifling marks – and with *no* trace of any explosive charge on them.

When David Nurse, the SID armourer, learned about them he was able to say confidently that they had been fired by an airpump gun, a weapon invented in the last century and called euphemistically a 'Naturalist's gun'. In other words, a poacher's gun. It is pumped up with a foot-pump for each shot, and dismantles into what looks like a couple of pieces of very ordinary piping. It is virtually silent, and as it has no recoil it needs no butt. In experienced hands it is a perfect assassination weapon for certain circumstances.

Nobody knew Carr was with Westbrook when he was murdered, except the assassin and the driver of the car. It was doubtful whether they recognised him: he'd been sitting sideways on to the road wearing dark glasses and a hat.

One or two fringe magazines went in for some lurid fantasies about CIA operations, but that was all. The inquest was adjourned for three months 'for further enquiries to be made'. Everyone knew that it would come to nothing, but by then public interest would have evaporated.

The BMW took the rise beautifully, the engine and automatic transmission making little of the steepening climb, the suspension ironing out the bumps in the road. For all the spectacular scenery, the route was more than a little alarming. Sections of the road, which was little better than a track, were unmarked and unguarded at edges, with sheer drops of anything between a hundred and five hundred feet. Occasionally the car's wheels sent stones skidding over the edge. Night driving along it must have been hair-raising. Carr was grateful for the direct and accurate steering. He felt entirely at home in the sleek saloon.

Before setting out on the long drive he'd spent half a day driving in and around London to familiarise himself with it. He'd also put some things from his own car into the BMW to make it look as if he'd owned it for some time. After a lot of hesitation he'd finally transferred the gun he always kept in a special holder under the seat of his Saab into the BMW as well. True, he couldn't foresee any situation where it might be of any use to him. His room in the clinic would be well away from the garage, and it would be far too risky to try to keep the gun with him. Nevertheless, illogically he felt better for having it. And yet, at the same time he was worried that having a gun with him *did* make him feel more secure – he was afraid it meant he was losing confidence in himself. And not only in himself; he didn't know who he could trust any more. He'd even been guarded with Eli Yelkov when they had met soon after Westbrook's murder.

'God knows what he was on to, for them to kill him like that,' Yelkov said, adding with deceptive innocence, 'Do you have any idea?'

Carr shook his head and turned away. Later he said, 'I'm going on three weeks' sick leave on Friday.'

Yelkov looked up in surprise. 'You look as healthy as a circus flea. What's wrong?'

'Overwork. Things have been a bit rough lately.'

'Where are you going?'

'Sailing, on my own. It's supposed to be pretty restful.'

'That's not what I've been told.'

'Mentally restful.'

Yelkov wore an odd expression when he spoke again. 'I may not be here when you return. It's possible that I'll be going back to Israel.' He added quickly, 'That's between us.'

'It won't be the same here, without you and Mark Westbrook. Will it be permanent?'

'The only permanent posting is in the cemetery.' Yelkov shrugged. 'Who knows? You can always come to see me on leave.' He made an effort to slip into his stage-Jewish act again, but his heart wasn't in it. 'I'll get you a special price at the hotel, and all the oranges you want wholesale.' His mood changed abruptly, and he looked directly at Carr, his expression deadly serious. 'Richard, be careful.'

Carr was brooding on Eli's warning as he came to a small crossroads with a single signpost: 'Clés d'Or, 1 km.' The road climbed and twisted for another quarter of a mile before levelling out and widening. Soon a high wall with a pair of handsome iron gates came into view. On one of the gate pillars was a discreet plate *Clés d'Or*, with an odd triple-key motif.

Carr pulled up and sounded the BMW's imperative horn. A uniformed gateman came out of his lodge and waited inside the gates until Carr got out and walked over to him, producing the letter confirming his booking. Only then did the man open the gates.

In a small, bare upstairs room half a mile away a man put down his field-glasses and went to a Nikon 35mm camera set up on a solid tripod. Its lens was squat, but of a considerably greater diameter than a conventional lens, even a long-range one. It was a mirror telephoto lens, which cost something like four thousand pounds. This rather complex piece of glassware, which was aimed directly at the gates, had a focal length of 2,000mm. This meant that with this lens the gates seemed as close as they would have done to a camera with a normal 50mm lens that was only twenty yards away. The man looked through the viewfinder and pressed the trigger in short bursts like a machine-gunner. The power-wind sent the film racing through the camera at seven frames every two seconds. During the brief moments as Carr approached the gates, the camera took some thirty-odd excellent photographs of him.

The gates closed behind Carr with surprising quietness. He drove up the gravel driveway between handsome lawns and gardens as neat as a California cemetery. The château was concealed until the last moment by a curve in the driveway and tall shrubbery. It was worthy of the setting, and would have looked great on a travel poster.

Before Carr pulled up by the stone stairs at the entrance, two porters in striped waistcoats came out of the front door. One opened the driver's door for Carr; the other took the bags from the boot and carried them inside. The first man slipped behind the wheel and drove the BMW away towards the garages.

The entrance hall was quite splendid and had been beautifully restored. Near the front door was an unobtrusive reception desk with a young woman wearing a simple black dress that had been cut by a man who had sold his soul to the Devil for his talent and got the better of the bargain.

'Good afternoon, Mr Tranter,' she said. 'Welcome to Les Clés d'Or. We are expecting you, of course.' Her English was almost accentless. She turned to the porter: '*Chambre cent-dix.*' Then to Carr again: 'Dr Schaffhauser would like to see you in his office at five o'clock for your initial medical examination, Mr Tranter.' She had the American trick of repeating his name to imprint it on her memory. She flashed him an air-hostess smile and handed the porter a key. They moved off like three children playing trains – the woman leading and the porter taking up the rear like a baggage van – to the concealed lift at the back of the hall by the service stairs – well away from the magnificent main staircase. Carr applauded the design. Putting a lift in that hallway would have been like giving the Mona Lisa spectacles.

Carr's room and private bath could have been found in one of the pre-war five-star hotels like the Hôtel de Paris in Monte Carlo or Claridges in London. The whole ambience oozed opulence and relaxation. It was difficult to associate this discreetly luxurious background with attempted subversion and a whole succession of murders, but Carr couldn't forget the sight of Haynes lying dead on a dusty French roadway; nor the sight of Westbrook watching his own life drain away and his whispered last words *'Clés d'Or'*.

A valet entered, taking over from the porter. 'Shall I unpack for you, sir?' he asked. Obviously the service was up to the standard of décor.

'No, I'll bath and change first,' Carr told him. 'Come back in half an hour when I've gone to see Dr Schaffhauser.'

The valet bowed and glided out backwards as if on little wheels.

Before Carr got into the vast bath, big enough for a small private party, he took a box of saccharine tablets from his pocket and tipped them on to a piece of paper. He studied them carefully until he found one indistinguishable from the others except for a small nick in the circumference. He swallowed it with a drink of water. The tablet didn't taste at all sweet.

At five minutes to five, Carr left the room for his medical examination, and met the valet coming to unpack for him – and, Carr suspected, to examine everything minutely.

Downstairs the same soignée receptionist greeted him, 'If you'll come with me, Mr Tranter.' She gave him a wide smile full of the empty promise of a 'Fly Me' commercial and carefully escorted him all of ten yards to the anteroom to Dr Schaffhauser's office, where she handed him on to the nurse-secretary, like a relay baton.

The secretary led him inside the office and invited him to sit down. She assured him earnestly in a German accent that Dr Schaffhauser would be with him in a moment, before exiting smoothly.

The office was formerly the library. Carr guessed that a few of the shelves of old and expensive books were really disguised cupboards and filing cabinets – but only a few. The lights were on, although there was still plenty of daylight outside, because the high narrow windows had dark stained glass. Part of the room was divided off by screens to form an elaborately equipped consulting room. It looked like an illustration in the catalogue of an expensive surgical-supply house.

Dr Gerd Schaffhauser entered on the stroke of five with such precision that Carr suspected he'd been waiting behind the door for the exact second. At first sight he seemed about fifty to fifty-five years old. Later, when Carr was close enough to see the tiny lines and ruptured capillaries of Schaffhauser's face, he put him at sixty or just over. Nevertheless, the doctor was a good advertisement for his own clinic: clear-eyed, straight-backed but not rigid, neat and lithe in his movements. His voice was firm and inspired confidence. His English, like everyone else's so far at the clinic, was almost unaccented.

They went through the standard preliminaries: name, address, next of kin, have you ever had tuberculosis, VD, 'nervous' diseases, and the rest. After that Schaffhauser said, 'Please go behind the screen and take off your shirt.'

He looked at Carr's muscular torso in surprise. 'Do you take a lot of exercise, Mr Tranter?'

'Hardly any,' Carr lied cheerfully. 'I'm just lucky. I play a round of golf or two, and go for a walk now and then, but that's all. My father was much the same.'

'It happens,' Schaffhauser said. He took Carr's pulse, which was about 85, and his blood pressure 150 over 90. The pill that Carr had taken in his room was doing its work.

'Your blood pressure is a little high,' Schaffhauser said. 'What work do you do?'

'Oh, I'm only a desk-bound civil servant, I'm afraid.'

'With responsibilities?'

Carr shrugged. 'I make decisions.'

Schaffhauser pointed to a small footstool. 'Put your foot on that, and raise yourself up as if you were going up a stair.' It was the first fault in his English. 'Thirty times, please.'

This was the standard test to see how quickly the heartbeat returns to normal after exercise.

After a few lifts Carr deliberately began to breathe more quickly and deeply, like a fat man going upstairs. By the twelfth step he was breathing quite hard. He kept this up, which also helped maintain a more rapid heartbeat than normal. The pill he'd taken made him sweat a little as well.

'Uhuh. Now let me have a sample, please,' Schaffhauser said, holding out a specimen glass.

'Oh, sorry. I went just before I came down. Can I do it later?' Carr didn't want to run the risk of Schaffhauser finding traces of a drug in his urine.

'Very well. Mr Tranter, you're suffering from the modern disease, the fatal disease' – he smiled thinly to take the edge off the statement ' – fatal, if it is not dealt with. Stress.' He rolled the *r* and drew out the double-*ss*. Strrresssss. 'I'll draw up a diet for you, and arrange for you to have a programme of light exercise and massage. There's one formality first: to sign our standard agreement and indemnity. It's a legal necessity in this country, I'm afraid.' Carr knew this wasn't true, but he nodded cheerfully. He wasn't going to sign his own name anyway.

Schaffhauser passed over a form printed in four languages. Carr appeared barely to glance at it but he managed to take in quite a lot. As far as he could see, it practically gave the clinic the right to chain him up in the cellar, use him as a donor for a heart transplant and charge him the earth for the privilege. He signed it with a flourish.

'Now get dressed, please, Mr Tranter. My son will show you round the clinic before dinner, which is at seven o'clock. We dress with complete informality during the week. Sundays we are a little more . . . correct.'

He was a German Swiss all right.

Carr was conducted round the clinic, like a one-man tourist party 'doing' a stately home, by Franz Schaffhauser, Gerd's son. He was a thirty-five-year-old, rather flabbily chubby man. He tried to disguise this unfortunate fact with a slightly too large white coat.

It was a magnificent house, almost entirely unaltered

except for the enormous conservatory, which had been transformed into a gymnasium. This, too, had been equipped by someone with a very fat chequebook and a heavy hand. Apart from the standard gymnasium apparatus there was a fair amount of shiny, gimmicky equipment like rowing machines and stationary bicycles. Even the exercise weights were shiny.

A number of middle-aged and older men were working, not too strenuously, in one part of the gymnasium, some women of a wide range of ages and shapes in another.

The man in charge was a muscular Swede of about Carr's age whom Schaffhauser junior introduced as Tage Falkman. In tee-shirt and gymnast's trousers he looked as hard as two dozen oysters in a one-dozen bag. His hair was like white Brillo pads. A dark-haired girl, whose too-tight sweater was no accident, came over to join them. Her name was Joanna Wright, a qualified physiotherapist and masseuse, but not the kind to be found in a Euston sauna. She was English and originally came from Slough, which she left some years previously, as she told Carr.

'I don't blame you,' Carr observed.

'Mr Tranter will be starting with you tomorrow,' Schaffhauser told Falkman.

'I look forward to it,' said Falkman.

'You're very kind,' Carr said with a smile, but he knew Falkman didn't mean it like that. Falkman's English was so good that it made Carr feel inferior.

'Can we have a look round the grounds?' he asked Schaffhauser.

As they walked through them Carr became increasingly baffled by the finances of the clinic. The cost of maintaining the château and the grounds must have been enormous. Even with the clinic's shamelessly inflated prices it was difficult to see how the place paid its way.

As they came towards the rear of the building the young Schaffhauser turned back, but Carr had caught a glimpse of something else he particularly wanted to see. Behind a grey stone wall, which cut it off from the grounds and the front of the château proper, was the 'new' extension. There were a pair of wooden doors in the wall that could cause an old-fashioned siege-gun problems.

As far as Carr could make out, the extension was a rather featureless three-storey, brick-built structure with a tile roof. The walls were almost hidden under thick ivy and creepers. There was a covered bridge between the old building and the new one, at the top-floor level.

'What's that?' Carr asked.

'Oh, the South Wing. It's only an annexe that was put up in the 1914–18 war,' Schaffhauser explained. Carr thought he sounded uneasy. 'It's practically empty these days. It's not nearly as comfortable as the main château building. We use it mainly for storage, although some of the domestic workers have rooms there.' He'd said just a little too much. Schaffhauser took Carr's arm. 'Time to get back. It can become quite fresh when the sun goes down. We can't have you catching cold in a health clinic, can we?'

It was the nearest anyone had got to a joke since Carr had arrived at *Clés d'Or*.

At dinner Carr met the last of the senior staff, Dr Samuel Bigelow, an American. Carr was told that Bigelow's speciality was stress disorders, and the psychopathology of compulsive eating.

Bigelow was a thickset man of above average height, physically not unlike Eli Yelkov but with none of his dominating personality and latent animal strength. He had the hunched shoulders and pushed-forward head of the man who has spent a life crouched over books and laboratory benches. He refused to meet Carr's gaze when they were introduced, but it was nothing personal against Carr – he noticed during dinner that the American rarely, if ever, looked anyone directly in the eye. He hunched over his plate, ate rapidly and left the dining-room without ceremony.

At a quick count Carr reckoned there were seats for about sixty to seventy patients, though less than half of the places were occupied. Of the staff, only the doctors, Falkman and Joanna Wright, ate there. The other paramedical and physical training personnel presumably had their own eating facilities.

The clinic dining-room was up to the five-star standard of the rest of the château, but it differed from a hotel restaurant in two important respects. There was no choice of dishes. Smartly-dressed waitresses served patients with their diets, and not half a slice of toast more. And the dress, as Schaffhauser had said, was informal . . . but expensive. Very.

A young woman came to sit at Carr's table, which was quite reasonable as there were five empty places there; but she chose to sit directly opposite him. Her skin, free of any make-up, was superb, and glowed golden in the light of the table-lamp. Her dark hair was pulled back ruthlessly from her forehead and held in place by a headband, emphasising her marvellous bone structure. She was wearing a black, deeply-cut pullover and black ski trousers. A golden chain belt hung loosely round her waist. She as much needed to go on a diet as Audrey Hepburn.

She took a few elegant mouthfuls of consommé, then made a deliberately provocative remark.

'Pass the salt, please,' she said. Her accent was Austrian. The fact that she addressed him in English meant that she must have enquired about him before sitting down.

A couple of minutes later Carr said, 'You remind me of St Paul's Cathedral.' She reacted by raising one eyebrow. 'The architect, Sir Christopher Wren, learned that the dome of St Peter's in Rome needed a chain round the base to keep the whole thing together and prevent it collapsing. So, as a rather superior gesture he put a chain round his dome at St Paul's . . . loosely, hanging from hooks. Rather like your belt: decorative but not functional.'

She smiled, and long before they were served their decaffeinated coffee he learned that her name was Krysta Börne, she ran a beauty salon in Salzburg, liked Mozart, Klee and Liverpool Football Club, and her room was No. 214, near the lift.

It was to be the first of several passes that were made at Carr. The reason was simple, although it didn't occur to him at first. Apart from Tage Falkman, he was the only male under sixty who wasn't overweight. And he was adequately good-looking, although this wasn't an essential qualification. Some of the unsatisfied women would probably have found Oliver Cromwell madly sexy.

Carr was on a high-protein diet, which wasn't too vexing, and his exercise schedule was far from arduous, although he remembered to puff and make it look like hard work.

For the first two days he did little more than follow the routine of the clinic and keep his eyes open as he wandered about the château. As far as he could see, there was nothing suspicious or out of the ordinary in the house, but he hardly expected to find anything there. He was convinced that if there was something to find, it would be in the new extension; but getting into it in daylight was clearly impossible.

On the second night Carr was invited to have dinner at Gerd Schaffhauser's table. It was rather like dining with the captain on a cruise ship. Bigelow, the first officer, as it were, sat at the bottom of the table hunched over his meal, saying very little, but occasionally shooting covert glances at Schaffhauser over the top of his cheap-looking, old-fashioned dark-rimmed spectacles. The younger Schaffhauser rarely had dinner with the others. Probably his father instructed him to stay out of the dining-room so his overeating wouldn't set a bad example to the patients.

The conversation came round, as it always does among people with lots of money, to taxation. Schaffhauser's reaction was immediate and virulent.

In a quiet, controlled voice he fulminated against 'penal' taxation, 'so-called welfare states', and the evils of nationalised medicine. Carr, in the persona of the senior civil servant David Tranter, politely agreed with him. In his work he was only too aware of the enormous sums wasted on impracticable, lame-duck schemes. Governments too often encouraged indolent spongers who made a career of avoiding work and living on social security, he was sorry to say.

Schaffhauser enthusiastically took up the theme. Initiative was being discouraged, ambition mocked and material success despised.

'Who was it,' Carr said, 'who said "Those who don't learn the lessons of history are condemned to repeat them"?'

'Indeed,' Schaffhauser said. 'But I'm sure you know the other quotation "Peoples and governments never have learned anything from history or acted on principles deduced from it." Yet all the signs of the pattern repeating itself are plain for everyone to see.'

Carr looked at him. 'The pattern?'

'Of the collapse of civilisation. *Our* civilisation, this time. Corruption in high places – corruption of every kind – no respect for authority and no self-discipline; all interrelated, of course. Already crime, violence, and financial and moral bankruptcy are making life impossible in big cities. New York, London, Paris . . . Urban decay . . . You know, of course, that the big cities go first in the disintegration of what used to be called empires.'

Like hearing the echo of a distant chord, Schaffhauser's words reminded Carr of what Westbrook had said a few minutes before his murder. After a moment Carr said, 'Perhaps it's inevitable. After all, man carries the seeds of his own destruction within him. The survival of the unfittest because the unfittest procreate most.'

'Men are unimportant. What counts is who commands,' Schaffhauser said intently. Down the table Bigelow coughed. Schaffhauser paused before he spoke again. His voice was calmer, more controlled. 'You are correct, of course, in saying that man carries the seeds of his own destruction within him,' he said, as if he were acknowledging an original thought that had just been revealed to him. 'And there is the danger. It is not from our powerful enemies that comes the greatest threat –'

'Enemies, Dr Schaffhauser?'

'You are being deliberately ingenuous, Mr Tranter. Enemies to our civilised way of ordered life. Enemies in countries who are hostile to our system and wish to destroy it, because they fear it. No, the threat is not from them, but from our weak allies and our weaker selves. It is not from the strongest that harm comes to the strong, but from the weakest.'

'That's an interesting concept,' Carr said neutrally.

Schaffhauser nodded. 'You may not believe it, Mr Tranter, but we had here an executive from an English television company. It had suffered crippling strikes, all provoked by one malcontent. Members of other unions loathed the man because they were affected by his union's strikes. These workers were on the company's side, but the company was . . . ' He searched for a word. 'The company was *pusillanimous.* They backed away from every confrontation he engineered. Finally they gave him a long paid holiday, so he could go to Moscow for a course in political and industrial agitation! I should not be surprised to learn the Russians gave him a diploma in industrial sabotage.'

Schaffhauser cut a thin strip from his steak with a knife as sharp as a scalpel, and chewed the meat almost as if it was a religious rite.

'The West lacks leadership at all levels,' he went on. 'The old Anglo-Saxon virtues of courage and self-reliance are becoming atrophied by lack of external stimulus. But it is not too late. A few men of strength and vision . . . '

Bigelow coughed again.

Schaffhauser paused. Eventually he said, 'I'm sorry, Mr Tranter. You came here for relaxation and . . . ' Once again he cast around for the correct word. 'For reinvigoration, not to listen to my views. I apologise.'

'There's no need, I assure you, doctor. It was most interesting.'

It was a hell of a sight more than that. Carr was badly thrown. He would expect someone working for the Soviets against the West from the inside to take up a right-wing posture like Schaffhauser's as a cover. But he'd also expect someone as clever as Schaffhauser not to overdo it – which he most certainly had done if he was playing a role.

He'd quoted three men in his conversation with Carr. The first was Hegel, whose philosophy could be interpreted – with a little latitude – to support totalitarianism of the right or of the left; but Schaffhauser had also enthusiastically quoted Nietzche of the Superman theory, and that other self-effacing democrat General Charles de Gaulle. *Men don't matter. What counts is who commands.*

What really got at Carr was the ominous, unmistakable ring of sincerity in what Schaffhauser had said. He wasn't a Communist sympathiser and champion of the common man, working for the Communists against the West. So what was the connection between the *Clés d'Or* and the Soviets?

It meant rethinking everything from the very beginning.

13

Carr was fully alert within seconds of waking. He switched on the light and looked at his watch. Five minutes to midnight. As usual, he'd fallen asleep as soon as he'd lain down, and woken up when his internal alarm clock roused him. He'd never understood the mechanism of it, and didn't try to analyse it in case prodding at it made it go away.

He swung his legs off the bed and sat up. He was dressed in dark pyjamas and a short, dark dressing-gown. His slippers were tight-fitting.

The château had been quiet for some hours. Organised activities in the *Clés d'Or* finished at 10.30 p.m. There wasn't exactly an official 'lights out', but patients were encouraged to be in bed by eleven. Nearly all of them were, but not necessarily in their own beds. The wholesome food, fresh air, light exercise and assurances that they were looking much better did wonders for their libidos.

Carr turned out the bedside light and went to the door.

He opened it cautiously on to the deep-carpeted corridor running between the main staircase at the front of the château and the service stairs at the back. Smaller corridors led off from the principal one. In all of them small but adequate wall-lights were burning.

As he expected, the main corridor was deserted. The nightly excursions between bedrooms – like in a Spanish holiday camp – were over, and the weary drag back again was hours away. Carr had carefully considered the best time to start out: late enough to miss the traffic, but not too late to be a delayed reveller if anyone should see him moving about inside the château. If he encountered anyone, an embarrassed smile with a hint of a leer would explain what he was doing out of his room – he hoped.

Carr's objective was the new South Wing. He'd studied the topography of the château and the bridge to the extension from the outside, and he had a pretty good idea of how to get to the bridge from inside the building.

As he moved along the corridor he kept close to the wall to avoid making any loose floorboards creak, though it was unlikely that there would be any noise from under that thick carpet. He made for the back of the château.

Gently he opened the staircase door a few inches, and listened intently before risking opening it fully. There was no sound, so Carr moved softly on to the landing.

When the stairs were first built there was an open well from the ground floor to the attic level, and anyone on the staircase could be seen from floors above and below. But now the lift shaft filled the well and restricted the line of sight from one floor to another.

Carr started to climb the stairs, again keeping close to the wall. He stopped at each landing and listened carefully before proceeding. At the third floor he left the staircase and came out into the corridor, which was almost identical with the one on his own floor.

Carr stopped suddenly. He stood, absolutely motionless, trying to identify what had touched the edge of his senses. Just when he decided that over-taut nerves had made him imaginative, and he was about to move on, he heard a faint sound. It came from somewhere outside the château. Carr listened intently. The sound was repeated. It seemed to come from an animal, but he couldn't be sure what kind. A rabbit caught by a stoat, perhaps; or a bird trapped by a fox. Carr felt a cold film of perspiration on his forehead. He breathed deeply and moved on.

If the lay-out of this third floor was the same as the first, there should be another corridor off to the left, and at the end of that would be the entrance to the extension bridge.

His heart beating fast, Carr tiptoed away from the service stairs towards the front of the house.

He almost missed the corridor. It had been closed off with a door like those to the rooms. Instead of a number plate it had *Private* marked on it. Carr tried the door handle; to his surprise the door opened. Presumably the management thought that their class of trade would respect the notice.

He waited again, his mouth dry, his senses hyper-acute, so that he was aware of the tiniest draught, the minutest sound.

He went through the door and along the short corridor. At the end of it was a handsome tapestry, which hadn't been woven in a convent. It showed a shepherd and shepherdess who were giving each other a lot of attention, and none to their sheep. One end of the bar from which it was suspended was fixed to the wall on a swivel and the other end was free, so the tapestry could be pulled away like a door. As soon as Carr swung it aside, it was obvious to him why the door leading to the corridor was unlocked. Behind the tapestry was another door which looked as solid as Westminster Cathedral west door, and with a formidable lock. He wasn't going to get through here in a hurry, that was for certain. But at least it confirmed the importance of the new extension. This hidden door and its solid lock weren't to protect stores and a few domestic workers.

Carr returned to the service stairs. If he couldn't find a way into the South Wing at top-floor level, he'd have to try to find one on the ground.

The stairs led down to the working area at the back of the château. Carr moved through the spotlessly-kept kitchens and past the storerooms to the back door.

It had two heavy bolts – and a lock. The key wasn't in it.

Carr felt increasingly frustrated, and he consciously suppressed his anger before it pushed him into taking foolish chances. But there was no avoiding the fact that he would have to go outside, which increased the danger enormously. If he was seen, he would have no credible excuse for being there.

The front door was obviously out of the question, but there was still another possible route.

Again Carr was acutely aware of the small noises of an old building: unexpected creaks and knocks as joists and frames expanded and contracted; soft scratchings from small animals and birds seeking shelter and food. The corridors seemed longer than in the daytime, and occasionally he imagined he saw a door move as if a hidden observer were secretly watching him.

At last he came to the gymnasium. Moonlight was streaming through the windows and skylights, so the equipment threw camouflage-pattern shadows on the floors and walls. The pieces of apparatus looked strange and menacing in silhouette: the wall-weights frame took on the form of a guillotine.

Carr would never run any risk he didn't have to, even the most remote. He always tried to give himself the best possible odds. So, he didn't walk straight across the gymnasium to the outside door, because that movement would attract attention if anyone happened to be outside – unlikely as that seemed. He hugged the wall from the inside door round to the large steel and glass doors leading on to the grounds.

There were top and bottom bolts, as well as a lock. There was no key in it. Well, he'd have to see about that afterwards. Carr crouched down and eased up the bottom bolt, then rose a little to look through the lower windows into the grounds. He waited, but saw nothing. Quickly he straightened up to his full height and pulled down the top bolt with one hand, stopping it from banging with the other. Now all depended on whether the door had been locked with a key.

It was not locked.

It had taken Carr more than four minutes to cover the

short distance round the gymnasium to the outer doors and unbolt them, but again he suppressed the inclination to hurry. Steel doors are notoriously noisy, and he took infinite pains in opening this one. Fortunately it moved silently on well-oiled hinges. Slipping out he closed it behind him. If anyone should pass, an open door would demand investigation.

The night mountain air was fresh and clean. Carr took one cautious pace, keeping close to the wall, and remaining in the shadow cast by a tall pine tree. He froze at a strong smell of tobacco in the air. Smokers don't realise how persistent the smell of tobacco can be to non-smokers. It was unmistakable: someone had passed that way quite recently. He waited, motionless, for a full two minutes, but there was no sign of anyone in the grounds. As cautiously as a foraging fieldmouse he moved on towards the South Wing, following the black path of the tall tree's shadow until he reached the tree itself. The smell of tobacco was very strong now, but he still couldn't hear or see anyone. He was just about to take another step when someone coughed softly less than a yard from him.

There was a man on the other side of the tree.

It took all Carr's physical and mental self-control to keep his breathing shallow and silent so that it wouldn't betray him.

Suddenly the man emerged from behind the tree. In the crook of his right arm was a 12-bore repeating shotgun. He was heavily built, but ominously light on his feet. He made no sound as he walked on slowly. He was obviously some sort of guard: Carr could see the outline of a walkie-talkie in the patch pocket of his windbreaker.

Carr circled the tree as the man proceeded, keeping it between them. He waited until the guard was out of sight, then prepared to continue towards the South Wing. He was even more watchful than before; it was possible there were other guards about.

Carr studied the cover between him and the wall of the South Wing, planning a route that would take him into the open as little as possible. While doing so he heard the sound of car wheels on the gravel drive. A few moments later a private French ambulance, without lights – a typical converted white Citroën DS – rolled quietly past the château and on to the gates in the South Wing wall. They opened almost without sound, just before the car reached them. As it drove in, the guard Carr had seen earlier came into sight from behind a bend in the wall and followed.

The gates were up to the high standard of everything else in the clinic: they operated easily and silently.

As soon as the gates closed behind the ambulance, Carr hesitated no longer. He kept to his planned route, but moved swiftly from cover to cover without pausing. If there were any more guards about, the moment when their vigilance would be most relaxed was immediately after the distraction of the arriving ambulance.

He reached the stone wall and crouched low in the shadows. No one called out or challenged him; there were no approaching footsteps.

Carr jumped up and grabbed hold of the top of the wall. Slowly he pulled himself up, with a sureness that would have shaken Tage Falkman if the PT instructor had seen him. When Carr's eyes were level with the top of the wall he saw with a shock that his fingers were under a network of thin, unbarbed wires impossible to see from ground level. They ran along the top of the wall on insulated supports about three inches high. He was careful to make sure that his fingers touched none of them. If there had been any doubts about the importance of the South Wing, they were resolved now. Clearly the wires were an alarm system.

To stop people getting in . . . or getting out?

The ambulance had pulled up at the front entrance, which had a canopy with a light under it. The white-coated driver and an attendant were pulling out an American-type stretcher with legs that unfolded to form its own trolley. There was a man on the stretcher, and he seemed to be unconscious. The guard with the shotgun was nearby.

Two more white-coated attendants came out of the building. The ambulancemen set down the stretcher-trolley and chatted to them for a moment. The patient stirred, and tried to sit up, straining against the wide straps that held him in.

He mumbled something, then feebly started to cry out. Carr could barely hear and couldn't make out what he was trying to say, or even what language he was using.

The guard with the shotgun transferred it to his other arm and moved over to the stretcher, taking something from his pocket. Carr watched incredulously as he raised his arm and hit the patient on the temple with a short, flexible club. The man fell back without a further sound. Somebody laughed.

Then two attendants wheeled the motionless figure inside the South Wing. Soon afterwards they returned with the empty stretcher and loaded it on to the ambulance.

Carr's curiosity had made him oblivious to the ache in his arms and fingers, but now it grew insistent. He let himself down to the ground.

There was nothing more he could do that night. There was too much light and activity for him to risk any further reconnoitring. Besides, he'd have to think out a way of circumventing the alarm wires on top of the wall. It seemed very likely there were other alarm systems as well.

As Carr reached the gymnasium something happened that took him entirely off guard.

From the top floor of the South Wing came a muffled scream, dying away to silence. It couldn't have come from the newly-arrived patient; there hadn't been time for him to be taken up there. A window shone brightly as the light was switched on. The scream was repeated. This time it was cut off dead. The light went out again, but not before Carr noticed that the window was heavily barred.

He quickly slipped inside the gymnasium and bolted the doors.

He had barely dropped down behind the solid lower half of the doors when the wooden gates in the wall were opened to let the ambulance drive away. The shotgun guard followed it out.

There were more unpleasant surprises to come. Two more guards, also with shotguns, approached from different directions to join the first man. Carr hadn't had any idea they were there. While he was hurrying across open space to the wall, and clung to the top to look over, at least two other guards had been patrolling the grounds. He could so easily have been caught.

Carr had opened the door of his room no more than a few inches when it struck him that when he'd left the room he'd turned out the lights. Now the bedside lamp was on.

In the second it took to fully open the door, he'd prepared a story to explain his absence. When he saw who was sitting in the bedside chair he was taken aback.

It was Joanna Wright, the physiotherapist. She was wearing a blouse and long skirt, and was lightly but carefully made up.

'Hello. Where have you been? No, let me guess,' she said sarcastically. 'You couldn't sleep, so you went for a stroll to get some fresh air.'

Carr smiled, hoping it looked confident. 'If I'd known you were going to call, I'd have stayed in.'

She ignored this and went on, 'I can't imagine how you got out of the house, with all the doors locked.'

'I didn't go out.'

Joanna rose. 'You astonish me.'

'Must you go already? I'm sure we have a lot to talk about.'

'You don't really expect me to stay when you've just come back from . . . getting some fresh air?'

'I shouldn't blame you if you don't believe me, but I haven't been getting anything else.'

She looked at him intently, then said, 'Perhaps. But I don't think I'll stay, just the same. Another time, maybe.'

'I'll look forward to it.'

She nodded and went to the door. Carr thought he glimpsed a strange look on her face, one he couldn't understand. He closed the door behind her. She was a very attractive young woman, but he was still suffering too much from the earlier shocks and strains to feel any real regret at her departure. He was bushed, and didn't think to wonder how long she'd been waiting for him.

He stripped off his pyjamas and dressing-gown and took a quick shower before getting into bed.

As he turned off the light and settled down, two men in a bare room some distance away were listening to the sounds of the bedsprings, transmitted by the Japanese-made, battery-less bug, range one mile, that Joanna Wright had planted in his room.

Next day after his morning exercises Carr took a stroll in the grounds. Now he knew that the wall of the South Wing was protected by an alarm system, and that the windows were barred, he needed to take another look at the château exterior and the bridge leading to the South Wing. A plan began to formulate in his mind, and he turned purposely away from the South Wing so that he wouldn't appear to be taking an unnatural interest in it.

He walked on slowly, thinking hard. Almost before he was aware of it, he came to the clinic's solarium – really a sort of glorified home extension built out on to a terrace. He only half heard someone say, 'Hello, Mr Tranter.' Then, 'Hel*lo*, Mr Tranter.'

'Sorry. I was far away,' he apologised to Krysta Börne, who was stretched on a chaise-longue under the already warm morning sun. She was wearing a decorous one-piece bathing costume.

'You've been far away ever since you arrived,' she said without emphasis.

'I'm settling in now. I found things rather tiring at first.' He sat next to her.

She turned on her side to face him. Carr found her very attractive.

'Then perhaps we'll see more of you now,' she said.

Carr smiled at her. 'You know, you really don't need to come here for treatment,' he said. 'You look – ' He broke off, aware of how trite his remark could sound, but his obvious spontaneity softened any hint of banality.

'I come here to look nice so my clients will think it's the treatments and *maquillages* I sell in my salon.'

It took Carr a moment to remember that she ran a beauty salon in Salzburg.

A dozen yards away the portly younger Schaffhauser was heading in the direction of the garages.

'Excuse me,' Carr said to Krysta, rising. 'Dr Schaffhauser!' he called out.

Schaffhauser stopped and looked at him with the enthusiasm of a man buttonholed by a creditor. 'What is it, Mr . . . er Tranter?' he asked with minimum politeness. 'I'm in a hurry.'

'I couldn't sleep last night,' Carr began, 'so I got up, opened the window and did some deep breathing.'

'Very good. Quite right,' Schaffhauser said. 'Now I – '

'And I saw something I didn't quite understand,' Carr went on relentlessly.

Schaffhauser looked at him sharply. 'Yes?'

'I'm quite convinced there were a couple of men wandering round the grounds. *Armed* men. And I'm afraid that's not all. I heard a cry – a scream, coming from the back of the house.'

Schaffhauser's round face began to crumple like a collapsed soufflé, and his ruddy colour faded. 'Will you be good enough to come with me, Mr Tranter?' he said at last. His voice was unsteady. 'Please,' he repeated, his voice firmer now. Shrugging, Carr followed him into the château, straight to Dr Gerd Schaffhauser's office.

'Father,' he said, 'I'd like you to hear what Mr Tranter has just told me.'

Carr went through the story again, while Schaffhauser senior listened without interrupting. When Carr had finished he said, 'Please come and look out of this window, Mr Tranter.' Carr joined him there. 'Do you see that gardener working there? The one with the . . . *Schubkarren* . . . wheelbarrow?'

'Yes?'

'Concealed in the barrow is a shotgun. And that man there, down towards the garages. I hope that in the open boot of that car is another gun. And there are a number of other armed men, armed guards, in the grounds.'

‘Are they to stop us escaping to the village and ruining our diets by making pigs of ourselves?’ Carr asked in a fair imitation of someone trying, not very successfully, to be funny.

Gerd Schaffhauser answered him seriously. ‘No, Mr Tranter. They are there to guard you. At this moment we have among our patients a senior civil servant – yourself; the wife of a French cabinet minister, the head of a major American company in Milan, and a number of patients from quite wealthy families.’

Carr knew that when Zurich Swiss say ‘quite wealthy’ they don’t mean ‘comfortable’. They mean ‘filthy rich’ or ‘loaded’.

‘We are near enough to Italy’ – he said the name like a dirty word – ‘and some of the less disciplined parts of France for kidnapping to be a possibility we must consider. So, we do our best to assure our patients’ security, with alarm-systems and patrols.’ It all sounded very reasonable. ‘Most of the guards are ex-Foreign Legionnaires. The best of soldiers, highly disciplined.’

That word again.

Franz plucked up courage to add something. ‘Some of the women bring expensive jewellery. They feel undressed without it. They want to wear it even in the gymnasium. It is another responsibility.’

‘A minor one,’ the elder Schaffhauser said shortly. ‘Property can be insured. But if one of our patients were abducted . . .’

‘I understand, and I’m most reassured,’ Carr said. ‘And impressed.’ He waited, and when neither of them said anything further he added, ‘And the scream?’

The Schaffhausers exchanged glances. Gerd’s look at his son almost shouted: ‘Shut up and leave this to me.’

He turned to Carr. ‘I must ask you to treat this in confidence, Mr Tranter,’ Gerd said heavily. ‘*Total* confidence.’

‘Of course.’

Schaffhauser walked round the office delicately, choosing his steps as carefully as his words.

'There are a number of . . . special patients in the South Wing.'

'I thought you told me it was only used for storage?' Carr said to Franz.

'If you will bear with me,' Gerd Schaffhauser said sharply. 'These patients are victims of the stresses of modern society. They have turned for relief to alcohol, or drugs, or even a psychological retreat from reality. You understand me, Mr Tranter?'

'Yes, I think so.'

'Some of these patients come from our leading families, upon whom, after all, the responsibilities of leadership are fallen.' The rare flaw in Schaffhauser's English betrayed his tension. 'They come here for treatment in complete secrecy and confidence,' he concluded.

'I understand,' Carr said gravely. He thought it best not to ask if that confidential treatment included knocking the patient cold with a blackjack.

Once again Carr lay on his bed, wearing his short, dark dressing-gown and dark pyjamas – waiting until it would be late enough for him to make another trip to the South Wing. This time he was too keyed up to sleep.

He'd studied the exterior of the château and the South Wing again, and he'd managed to work out a strategy. As he lay there he went over the simple plan again in case he'd overlooked anything.

Finally he looked at his watch. No point in waiting any longer. He had to force himself to get up.

'I really *am* getting past it,' he told himself. 'I bloody well *will* quit when this operation's over.' He put on his close-fitting slippers and tightened the dressing-gown cord. After a moment's hesitation he took a fountain-pen torch from his bedside table and slipped it into his pocket. He smiled ruefully. One pen torch: he wasn't exactly over-equipped for a major sortie.

He took the service stairs again, but this time he went past the third floor and on to the fourth. This and the attic floor were where many of the staff had their quarters. The fourth floor was much more plainly decorated than the lower ones. The corridor had only a thin carpet runner and the wallpaper was quite ordinary, while the light fittings were little more than purely functional. Carr followed the same course as on the floor below: along the main corridor and then the first minor one to the left. This one wasn't blocked off by a door.

At the end of the corridor was a sash window. Carr raised it with teeth-gritting care because the standard of maintenance on this floor was nothing like on the lower ones. Despite the pains he took, the window squeaked during parts of its journey. Each time it made a noise Carr waited to ensure no one was coming to investigate.

When the window was opened enough for him to climb out, he leaned over the sill and looked down. From his reconnaissance that morning he knew the window wasn't directly above the connecting bridge. With some dismay he now saw that the bridge was much further over to one side and there was a bigger drop than appeared from ground level. He wouldn't be able to let himself down directly from the window on to the roof of the bridge, which was some eight or nine feet below. Nevertheless he could give himself enough of a sideways trajectory to land on it if he started to swing from side to side while hanging from the window-sill.

But how would he get back?

Carr carefully surveyed the side of the building below his window. Halfway down the wall he saw a ledge. If he could edge along it, and if it took his weight, he could get from the window to the roof of the bridge.

And back again . . . perhaps.

Gingerly he climbed out. A brisk wind plucked at him. Although it was chilly, he was in luck because it made the trees rustle and creak in the wind, helping to cover any small sounds he made. Low cloud, broken by the driving wind, threatened rain and made the moonlight unpredictably fitful.

Carr lowered himself from the window, holding on to the sill, his arms still taking his weight as his feet touched the ledge. He tested it gingerly. It felt solid enough. Gradually he allowed his full weight on to the ledge. It held. Carr pressed his arms flat against the wall, his arms outstretched on either side, searching for cracks and niches in the stonework with his fingertips. He felt terribly vulnerable.

He inched along the ledge, aware of every irregularity in it through the thin soles of his slippers. Fortunately, the ledge proved wider than he had thought.

At last he could see the roof of the bridge directly below, only four feet beneath him.

For the first time it occurred to him that the roof might be made of something no more substantial than covered asbestos sheeting. If that was the case, he'd go clean through it – which would certainly be one way of getting into the South Wing. Well, there was only one way to find out.

He jumped backwards from the ledge.

The fall to the roof was one of the longest half-seconds he'd ever lived through. As he landed he allowed his legs to flex to a full squat position, absorbing the noise and shock of the impact. He knew instantly that the roof was solid.

He waited for a moment to let his breathing and heartbeat return to normal. He glanced up at the sky. A cloud was about to obscure the moon. As it did so he scurried across the bridge towards the South Wing.

The windows there were quite out of reach, but Carr had no intention of trying to get to one; in any case, most of the top-floor windows were barred. Instead he clambered up on to the sloping tiled roof, keeping to the side that lay in shadow. Then he made for the far end of the roof where there was a plain brick chimney-stack for the central heating plant in the basement.

Breaking and entering is a required pass course for certain specialists in Intelligence work. Apart from conventional subjects like locks, their mechanism and how to pick them, burglar alarms, safes and the rest, Carr had learnt the important subject of unorthodox entry.

On the continent tiled roofs are all built the same way. Only every fourth, or sometimes sixth, row of tiles is nailed into place on the wooden supports. The others just rest against each other in an overlapping pattern. Carr worked at a tile, but it was a fixed one. He tried the next one below it, lifting upwards and pulling forwards. It came loose at once, like removing a book from near the top of a pile.

Tile by tile Carr painstakingly opened up a space large enough for him to squeeze through, piling the tiles carefully against the chimney-stack. As he worked he kept a careful look-out for a movement on the ground. Twice guards came into sight below him, then went into cover behind a tree to wait motionless for minutes before continuing the patrol. The men knew their business.

At last beneath Carr lay a square well of black emptiness. He stared into it, waiting for his eyes to become adjusted to the lack of light. He didn't want to use the torch, but the darkness became no less intense with waiting and he was forced to.

A two-second flash from his torch held at arm's length well within the hole, so that no light could be seen from outside the building, was enough for Carr to see that he was over an ordinary dusty attic with crossbeams. He swung down inside.

Now he could use his torch rather more freely and find the stairs down from the attic. They were quite dusty: no one had used them for some time. Carr found a piece of cloth that had once been part of a curtain and carefully erased his footsteps in the thin dust behind him. Just in case.

At the foot of the stairs was a door. He listened, his ear pressed against the woodwork to pick up the slightest sound. He couldn't hear anything moving, only a faint, high-pitched hum, probably from an air-conditioning system.

The door was unlocked, and opened inwards. That was a bonus.

Again with enormous patience he eased it open an inch. Through the crack at the hinge side he could see part of a plain white corridor with fluorescent lighting, and rather more of the rest of the corridor through the other side of the door.

Carr stepped out into the corridor. To his left it led to the covered bridge; at the far end was the heavy door he'd already seen from the other side inside the château itself. To his right was what looked like an ordinary swing door.

Carr walked towards it, his heart beating fast, his mouth dry. He expected to be frightened – only fools and corpses never know fear – but he felt something more than that. He was seized by an inexplicable, irrational dread.

For once Carr didn't pause at a door and listen. He went straight through.

Straight through, and into a nightmare world that left him standing stock-still, wondering whether he'd gone out of his mind.

14

Despite the fact that he was now in his sixties, Gerd Schaffhauser had heroes of his youth that he still admired to the point of adulation after nearly forty years. Two of the most famous – or infamous – he tried to emulate were well known for their habit of working late into the night and making up the lost sleep during the afternoon. This often made life very difficult for their more conventional subordinates.

Gerd Schaffhauser was one of those fortunate men who need only four hours' sleep or less a day. A high proportion of millionaires have this talent. And fanatics.

Although well after midnight, Schaffhauser was in his ground floor office in the château. With him were his son Franz and Dr Bigelow. The American kept fairly odd hours himself, but Franz was feeling short-tempered and fractious. Apart from anything else, he hadn't had a drink for a couple of hours and he'd had to cancel a visit to a small three-whore house in Entremeaux, which his father knew nothing about.

The three men had discussed the general running of the clinic – a 'discussion' which was little more than Gerd telling them what they had all decided – and then Gerd had reviewed the clinic's financial structure. He closed the thick account book on his desk, rose and went to the bookshelves near the fireplace. As Carr had guessed earlier, some of the shelves were really disguised doors with realistic-looking book-spines glued to them.

Schaffhauser pushed against a section of the shelving which slid open to reveal a solid cupboard door behind. Opening that, he put the ledger away and locked the inner door before sliding back the false bookshelves. Franz and Bigelow watched him silently.

'Well, father,' Franz began. 'How much, er . . . '

'Our deficit? A quarter of a million Swiss francs.'

'God,' said Franz. 'I didn't realise it was *that* much.'

'It's a quarter of a million up to the end of this month. We shall need half a million for operating expenses to the end of the year.'

'What're we going to do?' asked Bigelow.

' "We"? *I* shall get more money from our friend, of course,' Schaffhauser said coldly.

Bigelow looked away from him. He took off his old-fashioned cheap-looking spectacles and began to polish them. When he wasn't wearing these, Gerd Schaffhauser's face appeared to him as little more than a pink-grey blur. That way he was rather less frightening.

'Something wrong, doctor?' Gerd asked hastily.

'No. It's just . . . ' Bigelow paused, then said in a rush, 'Who exactly *is* he? Where does his money come from?'

'Why? If his sources don't meet with your approval, will you refuse to take his money? And in that case, will you find your own funds to continue your research here? Well?' The other man didn't answer, but Schaffhauser waited until Bigelow could stand the embarrassing silence no longer.

'I can't help wondering *why* he gives us money like this. What does he want from us? I'm waiting for this guy, whoever he is, to send in the bill.'

Schaffhauser didn't consider it worth telling Bigelow that the bill had come in a long time ago, and was being paid. The price might have upset him. 'You take care of your research and leave everything else to me,' he said authoritatively.

'He's one of us,' Franz told Bigelow. 'Otherwise why would he – they – give us the money?'

'Exactly,' Gerd said. He looked directly at his son. 'Franz is so perceptive – as usual.' The sarcasm in his voice was stinging. He turned back to Bigelow. 'You underestimate the strength of our support, doctor. We have many like-minded friends and allies: men of wealth and influence who are awake to the creeping sickness that threatens the world, and are determined to do something about it.'

'Well, as long as . . . ' Bigelow said. He didn't finish the sentence. 'I'd better go and check on one or two of my patients in the South Wing.'

'Wait till I'm finished here and we'll come with you,' Schaffhauser told him. 'I'd like to see for myself what progress you're making.'

'Do you need me?' Franz asked. 'There's something I want to do.'

'It can wait.'

Franz looked on the point of arguing but, as always, he took the easier alternative of obeying his father. He sat down sulkily while Gerd switched on his recorder and dictated some letters in English, French and German for his secretary the next morning.

Franz licked his lips. He badly wanted a drink. Bigelow sat staring shortsightedly into the distance, busily working on some problem of his own while he unnecessarily polished his glasses.

At last Gerd Schaffhauser switched off the recorder and stood up.

'I'm ready,' he said. The others rose obediently. He carefully secured all the cupboards and drawers, then locked the door of the office behind them.

The three men set off for the South Wing.

When Carr entered the corridor he had to stand for a moment and touch the doorframe. The corridor was crazy: there wasn't a single right-angle anywhere. Walls were slightly out of vertical and not parallel, the floor and ceiling were neither quite horizontal nor parallel with each other. In addition, the entire corridor had been given a false perspective by being subtly wider at one end than the other. It made it seem longer than it really was from one end, shorter from the other. The doors in the corridor were just as extraordinary: none of them was an exact rectangle.

Just looking along the corridor made Carr feel slightly giddy and disoriented. His eyes and the vestibular apparatus in his ears, which is concerned with the sense of balance, were sending contradictory messages to his brain about whether he was standing upright or not. The confusion made him uncertain on his feet. He turned back and pushed open the swing-door to inspect the corridor he'd just come down, to make sure he wasn't hallucinating. It looked reassuringly normal.

The weird corridor had another feature that Carr hadn't noticed at first sight. The light was indirect and uniform: no bulbs or tubes were visible. He supposed the lights were permanently on because there was no way for daylight to penetrate.

Carr started down the corridor.

The first three doors had small, assymetrical windows in them. They gave on to a couple of small stockrooms with conventional supplies like cleaning materials, bed linen, stationery, electrical fittings and basic medical stores; and a compact kitchen.

Each of the next few doors had a lock and a judas window – a small aperture with a flap over it like the inspection window in a cell door. Carr paused, fearful of what he might see. He swung the first flap aside.

The room was as stark as a monk's cell. It contained a

narrow bed, a straight-backed wooden chair, and a plain deal table. The floor was uncarpeted, the walls and ceiling were an unrelieved neutral grey throughout. It was a colour Carr was to see much of. There was no window. The room had a single, harsh light in the middle of the ceiling, well out of reach of anyone in the room, even if he put the chair on the table and tried to climb up. The light was covered with armoured glass. There was no switch inside the room.

On the bed – not in it – a man in pyjamas and dressing-gown lay motionless, staring unblinkingly at the ceiling. He had three or four days' growth of beard.

In two other rooms there were men in much the same catatonic state. One further room seemed to be a sort of day-room for staff. Unlike the others, it had no lock on the door.

Beyond, there were two lavatories and two bathrooms.

The last door on the right-hand side of the corridor gave on to an office much like Schaffhauser's back in the château – fitted out so that it could also be used as a medical consulting room. This one, however, had even more equipment. Half the room was taken up by a small, modern-looking combination safe and a bank of microfilming apparatus. Carr was familiar with most of it, and knew how it worked.

There was a Recordak Microfilmer about the size of a desk-top duplicator, a film-processing unit, Jacket-Reader Filler, a Printer and a Diazo Developer – which together can duplicate a hundred A4-sized documents within minutes and reduce them to microfilm.

There were two other pieces of equipment: a document shredder, and a small incinerator of the kind to be found in women's lavatories for the disposal of tampons. A small pilot-light showed it was switched on.

The medical part of the room was also full of electronic hardware. There was a polygraph (lie detector), enkephalograph (for measuring brain activity), electrocardiograph, steriliser, instruments cabinet and drugs cabinet. Carr recognised the names of some of the drugs – hyoscyamine, mescaline, trifluoperazine, haloperidol, tranylcypromine, phenelzine, isocarboxazid, methacholine, and atropine. Some had stimulating or depressive effects on the brain, some affected the autonomic nervous system and could, for example, cause a rapid heartbeat and excessive sweating, just for starters. Mescaline is a powerful hallucinogenic drug. There were other drugs Carr had never heard of, and there were a few ampoules with only handwritten numbers on plain labels.

Carr's understanding of what happened to patients in the South Wing was growing.

Giving off from the office was a small private bedroom. It contained a single, high, hospital-type bed standing on a clear area of polished floor. The bed was unmade, the sheets and blankets folded at the bottom with almost military neatness. Carr got the impression the room wasn't used much. There were also a wardrobe, a small chest of drawers, bedside table and lamp, and an armchair. In complete contrast to all the other rooms Carr had seen, it was attractively decorated and had short but cheerful curtains. He pulled these open an inch. There were bars on the window.

Carr went back into the vertigo-inducing corridor. Opposite the office there was just one more room, which he hadn't noticed before. The door had no lock. It was held close by the kind of simple lever bolt that is fitted to the heavy doors on refrigerated stores.

Carr lifted the handle and released the door. It was about a foot thick, but perfectly balanced; it opened smoothly with a soft whooshing sound. The room was soundproofed.

What with the distorted corridor, the catatonic patients, the sinister collection of drugs and apparatus, Carr thought he'd had all the surprises the South Wing had to offer. But this room was the weirdest, the most frightening he had seen yet.

In Kensington at that exact moment a man sat at his desk, going through Intelligence reports. His phone rang.

'Yes?' he said.

'We have a delivery from Nimrod Three.'

'Bring it up.'

A man, too well dressed and authoritative-looking to be

an ordinary messenger, came in with a sealed packet about twelve inches by nine and some six inches thick.

The man behind the desk took it, then asked, 'Who gave these operations the codename Nimrod?'

The other gave a *I don't know* shrug.

'Somebody doesn't know his history.'

'How's that?'

'Look up Nimrod in Genesis.'

'I'll do that,' the other said hypocritically.

The man at the desk took a knife from the top drawer to open the packet. It was a long, wicked-looking knife as inappropriate for letter opening as a blowtorch for lighting a cigarette.

Inside the packet was a pile of photographs. He went through them fairly quickly, slowing down at one or two, then hurrying on again. At one picture near the bottom of the pile he stopped dead, then carefully examined the next six or seven pictures of the same man.

'Now what the hell is *he* doing there?' he said, mainly to himself.

'Who?' asked the messenger.

'Richard Carr. What the hell is he doing at the *Clés d'Or*? How did he find out about it?'

Carr surveyed the strange room. The uniformly grey walls, ceiling and floor merged into each other in gentle curves; there were no visible angles or edges. The lighting was direct and even, coming from almost floor level. Because of this, the true dimensions of the room were difficult to gauge: there was no perspective, and no point of reference. It was like being in an Arctic white-out, or stepping out into space.

In the centre of the room was a heavily padded couch, suggestive of a super-comfortable operating table. On it, held down by broad, padded webbing straps, lay a man. His forearms were in large tubes, padded inside as far as Carr could see. There were earphones over his ears. His head was towards Carr, who couldn't see his face.

Leaving the door open, Carr moved into the room. He

took two paces and stopped, puzzled. He stamped on the floor, but there was almost no sound. He went to the side of the couch. The man had a couple of days' growth of beard, and like the 'patients' in the cubicles, his eyes were wide open, unseeingly. For a moment Carr didn't recognise him. Then he did, and it was the worst shock of all.

It was Peter Harris, alias 'Godfrey', and assistant to William Parker of the SIS. Harris had no executive authority in the SIS, but he was always at the side of Parker, a man who knew as much about SIS workings as any man in the organisation.

Now Carr knew for certain what was being done at the *Clés d'Or.*

The Western Intelligence agencies had got it all wrong. The attacks on the West were nothing to do with parapsychology and ESP. The operation was against highly-placed men of authority in politics, administration, defence, Intelligence . . . They were subjected to scientific psychological conditioning, sometimes called 'brainwashing' but better defined as brain-*reformation.* Carr had read enough to know that profound changes could be engineered in subjects' characters, attitudes and reasoning, and so their loyalties. He had always assumed it was a lengthy process, but now he wondered.

Harris's presence in the clinic added an element of extreme urgency to the situation. Carr couldn't afford to waste time now. There was no telling how soon Harris would start to give away all sorts of highly secret information about the SIS – if he hadn't started already. And once he was up and around again he could blow the whistle on Carr the moment he saw him.

Carr rapidly considered the situation. There was a new danger to him. If he was discovered he'd be taken prisoner and himself put through the 'processing' centre.

Of course, he could always expose the *Clés d'Or* for what it was, before he was found out. But what was it exactly? And even if he could put an end to the operation, it would only be for the moment. There was no direct evidence against Gerd Schaffhauser or any of his subordinates. Obviously none of the people who'd been through the South Wing would give evidence against them. The 'processing' must be totally effective, otherwise somebody would have reported the place already.

This gave him another line of thought. Who could he approach with information about the *Clés d'Or* and be sure it wasn't a South Wing 'graduate'? And Streeter – had he been through there? Was that why he'd turned 'double'? How many had been through the clinic's processing?

There was one inescapable conclusion. His first priority was to obtain the list of patients already treated in the South Wing.

Certainly the records would be on microfilm, in that modern safe. The always-on incinerator: that was in case of discovery. A mere handful of microfilm records would be equivalent to several bulging files of notes, and could be destroyed in a flash just by dropping them into the incinerator.

He looked at Harris again. His eyes were unblinking, fixed on some other private universe of his own where the values were all upside-down.

Carr left the room, pulling the heavy door shut behind him.

He'd taken a few paces towards the swing-door leading back to the normal corridor when he heard footsteps approaching.

The nearest door led into the office. He slipped silently inside. He closed the door half a second before Gerd Schaffhauser pushed open the swing-door and entered the distorted corridor – followed by Bigelow and a sulky Franz.

'I'll go and have a look at Harris,' Bigelow said. Gerd nodded and turned into the office. Franz hesitated for a moment, then followed his father.

From the darkened bedroom Carr watched them through the crack between the door and the frame.

Gerd toured the office, looking at papers and making sure that the drawers and cabinets were locked. Then he went to the safe. Carr's heart beat faster. With luck he might be able to see the combination as Gerd opened it.

His luck held. Gerd Schaffhauser bent down to turn the dial and Carr could just make out the numbers over his shoulder as he turned the dial.

First 8 . . . then left to 43 . . . left to 16 . . . right to 3.

Carr quickly made up a mnemonic to fix the combination in his memory. Eight-forty-three . . . Easy – that was the exchange number for his own telephone at home. Sixteen . . . three. That made 1603. From his schooldays a fragment of information that had been hammered into his unwilling memory came to the surface. 1603, death of Elizabeth I, accession of James I. Now left, left, right. 'Two wrongs don't make a right' – but two lefts do. 'Two lefts make a right.' He had it now.

8 . . . left 43 . . . left 16 . . . right 3.

'*Was zum Teufel ist das?*' demanded Schaffhauser. He took half a dozen sheets of paper from the safe and banged them on to the desk.

Franz looked disconcerted. At that moment Bigelow came into the office.

'What the devil is this?' Schaffhauser asked again, in English this time.

'They're my notes on Harris and Levallois.'

Levallois – the name was vaguely familiar to Carr. He was something in the French Government.

'You know my instructions,' Schaffhauser said. His German accent was markedly stronger than usual. 'No papers. Once you have made the notes, you microfilm them and destroy the papers at once.'

'Goddammit, what's the problem? I only wrote them up today, and they were secure enough in the safe,' Bigelow said. It would have been a fair show of resistance had it not been for the tremor in his voice.

Gerd Schaffhauser walked over and stared at him from no more than a yard. 'Papers take time to destroy. Microfilm them *at once*, always. Do it now, doctor.' His voice sounded like broken glass. Franz watched silently from one side of the room.

Bigelow microfilmed the documents. While the film was

going through the automatic developer he put the sheets of paper into the shredder. Next he went to the open safe and took out a small plastic box like a card-file. It contained, as far as Carr could see, something like twenty to thirty plastic envelopes with individual microfilms in them. Bigelow sorted out two of the envelopes, then cut up the strip of microfilm and put the reduced pages into the correct envelopes. Schaffhauser held out his hand for them.

Bigelow sat down, took off his glasses and felt in his pockets for a handkerchief to polish them. Schaffhauser put the microfilm into a viewer to study the notes. He read them at his own speed, moving on to the next page as it suited him, and ignoring the fact that his son was reading over his shoulder.

'Good . . . good . . . ' Gerd muttered as he read.

Bigelow got up and moved towards the bedroom.

'Where are you going?' Schaffhauser asked without turning his head.

'To get a handkerchief,' Bigelow said. 'If that's all right with you,' he added with as much sarcasm as he dared. Putting on his glasses he walked into the bedroom, switching on the light at the doorway.

The room was empty.

Bigelow went straight to the chest of drawers and took out a handkerchief. He was about to return when he checked.

The wardrobe door was slightly ajar.

Bigelow walked over and pushed it shut. It clicked, then creaked open again. He muttered, and pushed the door again, rather more forcibly. He was halfway back to the office when he heard the unlatched wardrobe door open.

Bigelow swore, and turned back once more. He took out his frustration on the wardrobe door. He slammed it shut, and banged the heel of his hand on it. It shut, and then clicked open yet again. Something was preventing it from closing fully.

Bigelow yanked the wardrobe door wide open.

15

Krysta Börne threw the magazine across the room. It was a fairly expressive gesture, as the magazine cost the equivalent of three pounds. She'd looked at the same page half a dozen times without assimilating a word. She'd been hoping for a gentle knock on the door for the past half an hour, but all she'd heard were soft footsteps as patients discreetly visited each other's bedrooms. She was badly piqued. On more than one occasion she'd made it quite clear to David Tranter that her door wouldn't be locked against him, and she found his failure to accept the invitation badly vexing, to say the least. Her pride was badly dented. More than that, Tranter's dereliction was incomprehensible to her. Men *never* treated her like that. Briefly Krysta wondered whether Tranter preferred men, but it was a thought she didn't entertain for long.

She was seated on the divan, with the standard lamp above and behind her to light her to the maximum effect. She took off the semi-transparent peignoir she wore over nothing but a few dabs of criminally expensive perfume, and put on a nightdress. This didn't have a St Michael label either.

When Bigelow yanked open the wardrobe door all he saw were his own clothes hanging there. The reason the door wouldn't shut properly was simple. A corner of a jacket sleeve was trapped between the door and the frame. Bigelow moved the jacket along the rail a few inches. This time the door closed and stayed closed. He went out, switching off the light.

Carr let out a long sigh of mental and physical relief. He

lowered his legs, which he'd drawn up into his stomach while he hung from a crossbeam in the window recess behind the half-length curtains. His entire body ached. The thought of the long journey back to his room thoroughly disheartened him.

He tiptoed to the door to listen to what was being said in the office.

'How much longer will you need with Harris?' Gerd Schaffhauser was asking.

'Four days, possibly a week,' Bigelow said.

'We have only eight days. His leave will finish then,' Gerd said.

'How do you know?' Franz asked. There was no reply, but Carr could guess the sort of look Gerd was giving his son for this superfluous question.

'Are you coming back with us, Dr Bigelow?' Franz asked eventually, his voice still reflecting embarrassment.

'No. I guess I'd better keep a pretty close watch on Harris – and put Levallois back on treatment tomorrow. I think I'll sleep here tonight.'

That badly jolted Carr. There was only one door, and the window was barred. He could feel the trap closing.

'We'll have a look at the patients on the second floor before we go,' Schaffhauser said. 'The Faber girl – that's the addict – and that Australian who's here to dry out again.' He mentioned a name that Carr didn't hear properly. 'You'd better come with us.' It was an order, not a suggestion.

With enormous relief Carr heard the outer door open and shut. He waited for a minute, no more.

The office was empty, and so was the distorted corridor. He raced down it silently, through the swing-door and along to the attic stairs. Not till he reached the attic itself did Carr relax, and then but briefly.

He climbed out on to the roof. The return to the château was going to be much more hazardous than the outward trip had been. The clouds had thinned, so the moonlight was much brighter, and only half the roof was shadowed now. The hole he'd made was barely inside the sharp edge of shadow. The wind stirred the trees enough to cover any slight sounds he might make, but it was the only thing in his favour.

Below him, staying near the cover of the bushes, two guards stood talking in whispers.

Carr waited, pondering whether to wait until they moved out of range before he started putting back the tiles, and so risk the moonlight showing up the hole in the roof; or to do it now in the shadow, and risk one of the guards glancing up and spotting him. Just then the guards resolved the problem by moving on.

Deftly he replaced the tiles, edged across the roof – making sure he wasn't silhouetted against the skyline – and on to the bridge back to the château. These next moments would be the most dangerous, when he was out in the open with no possibility of cover.

He lowered himself on to the bridge, moved across it fast, and took off in a running jump for the ledge. His jump forward was ill-judged: he thumped up against the wall of the château so hard he bounced back, teetering on the ledge and swaying dangerously. His arms thrashed the air. Somehow he managed to push himself forward again, and his fingers found just enough purchase in a crack in the stonework for him to preserve his balance. A moment to recover, then he was crabbing along the ledge until he was beneath the window.

Carr slowly heaved himself up, his toes scrabbling against the wall to take some of the weight from his arms. His right arm reached out, across the sill and inside the window. One strong pull, a push with the left, and he was back inside.

He gently closed the window.

There was no one in this small corridor, nor in the main one running from front to back of the château.

At last he was on the staircase. And there Carr's luck ran out.

One of the staff was coming upstairs – a big man in a dark suit.

Carr couldn't remember having seen him among the instructors or attendants. He looked vaguely like one of the guards Carr had noticed in the grounds the previous night.

In any case, this was no time or place for an encounter. Carr hardly resembled someone who'd just been visiting a ladyfriend; he was covered in dust from the South Wing attic and dirt from the outside walls.

He slipped through the door to the second floor, almost certain that the big man was heading up to the top floor, where many of the staff had rooms. Nevertheless, he took no chances and hurried along to the minor corridor on the left, just in case the man came in from the staircase. This smaller corridor contained only broom cupboards and linen stores.

Carr listened intently, but there was no sound of a door opening, or of footsteps along the corridor. So he left the side corridor and advanced along the main one. He was four or five paces from the staircase door when he heard someone coming *down* the stairs. The footsteps slowed as they approached the landing outside the door. All at once Carr wondered if the man was checking floor by floor, like a nightwatchman on his rounds.

He might appear at any moment, and there was no time for Carr to get back to the small corridor. If he came through the staircase door, Carr would be caught. Unless . . .

He glanced at the bedroom door numbers: 212 . . . 214 . . . He prayed the door wasn't locked.

He tried the handle. It opened and he slipped inside. The bedside light was on.

Outside in the corridor the stairway door opened and closed.

'I thought you weren't coming,' Krysta said calmly. 'Why are you so late? *Lieber Gott!* What have you been doing?'

'Somebody came along the corridor and I had to hide in a cupboard for a while. It was rather dusty, I'm afraid.'

'But why hide?' she asked in genuine mystification.

'To protect your reputation.' He tried to sound as if he was wearing his old school tie.

Krysta laughed like a set of chrome tubular bells. 'You're just a little late, my dear. Gallant, but a little late. And now you'd better take those things off and take a bath.'

She poured in some of her own bath essence, which made

him smell like a very expensive tart. After he'd soaked for a few minutes she pushed him forward and massaged his neck and shoulders with surprisingly strong and knowing fingers. 'You're so tense. You're like marble, there,' she said, skilfully unknotting his trapezius muscles. It was marvellously relaxing and completely unsexual.

Her hand slipped round to his chest and gently stroked it in a circular motion. Something pressed against his back. He half-turned and saw their reflections in the full length wall mirror. She was as naked as he was, and the warm, sort-hard pressure on his back came from her breasts.

Instantly he became excited.

'Goodness, what is that strange creature rising from the water?' she said in mock terror, pointing.

'Actually it's quite friendly,' he said. 'Although it can be a bit pushy sometimes.'

She took a large towel from the heated rail and held it up for him. As he stood up, she put it round him and started rubbing. After a while he said, 'That part's *quite* dry by now.'

She was very, very good. And she looked stupendous. Like the very best models, she was always graceful. Her limbs seemed incapable of assuming an ungainly posture. She was, he conceded, quite the most beautiful woman he'd ever gone to bed with, almost too perfect to be real, like a schoolboy's dream of illicit sex. Her skin and fingers were superb, and her suntan was total. Carr found with a slight shock that her body was completely without hair, but she was so beautifully formed that it made her even more erotic-looking.

Krysta's performance in bed equalled her appearance, with a Germanic thoroughness about her technique. Her body, her hands, her lips and her tongue were skilled, subtle and inventive. She was uninhibited about telling him what to do: *'There, like that . . . Oh, don't stop . . . harder . . . harder . . .'*

When they were lying quiet for a moment, he thought how spectacular she was. Again he wondered why she had come to the *Clés d'Or* for treatment, and he felt a sudden flash of realisation. She adored and worshipped her own body. It was a narcissism of monumental degree. No effort or expense was too much to ensure her body's constant perfection.

Carr felt that Krysta was taking a male attitude to their sexual exercises. It was part of her narcissism to want to be able to think *God, how I screwed that guy. I had him out of his mind a dozen times.*

A dozen? Well, three times anyway. He chuckled at his mental correction of the score.

'What is it?' Krysta said sharply. Sex was deadly serious for her.

'I was just thinking how lucky I am.'

She seemed satisfied.

To hell with it, he told himself, turned his mind off, and simply enjoyed his sensations.

A delicious warmth flooded his loins. He opened his eyes to see Krysta lying on his legs. She was pressing her perfectly shaped breasts against him, moving her shoulders and arms like a slow-motion go-go dancer so they massaged him gently. She looked at him, enjoying the pleasure on his face. She lowered her head and nipped the skin of his stomach between her even teeth.

Quickly and gracefully she slipped forward, and in a moment she was straddling him. She guided him inside her, then leaned back, resting her weight on her hands behind her. Her eyes were half-closed and her tongue was flicking over her lips.

'Oh, God,' he groaned. He had the insane feeling that he was going to burst out of his own skin.

She lifted herself up, waited, then thrust down hard on him. It was shattering in its intensity...

Next day Carr was as relaxed as a burst balloon, and he didn't even have to pretend that his exercises were tiring. It wasn't only the hours with Krysta but also the clambering about the roofs and the nervous tension that had left him limp. Tage Falkman looked at him sharply a couple of times and Carr wondered if he'd guessed about Krysta. He seemed rather more demanding of Carr than he had been on other days.

At lunch Carr was very reflective. By now he was suffering from guilt at having spent his night in sexual pleasure instead of concentrating on his vitally important job. He'd intended to make another assault on the South Wing tonight, but now he wondered if he shouldn't postpone it. His reactions could be that dangerous fraction slow. Perhaps it'd be better to wait twenty-four hours to recover.

Carr was worried by the possibility – probability now – that the guards actually patrolled the interior of the château as well as the grounds. The big man on the stairs was a look-out; he was pretty sure of that.

You've lost your bottle, Carr, he told himself, and all his reasoning that it was a moment for caution failed to sound convincing to him. *So I'm not the Gung-ho glory boy I was when I joined the service. I'm entitled to be scared after what I've been through in the past ten years. Some day my luck is going to run out. God knows how many times I've survived on the strength of it. Anyone who isn't scared most of the time doesn't have the brains to be in this business.*

Carr was still considering his next move, staring at his thin slice of lean beef and some green beans without really seeing them, when Krysta came into the dining-room. She never entered anywhere unnoticed.

She came straight towards his table. He said quietly, 'Hello, Krysta,' and started to get up.

She replied politely, but distantly, 'Good afternoon Mr Tranter,' and sailed straight on past him as if he'd been a green traffic signal. She sat down at another table.

Carr checked his rise in mid-move and sat down again abruptly. It was the first time that sort of thing had happened to him. Briefly he felt like an executive's secretary the morning after the office party.

He smiled wryly. *Well, that's one port I won't be able to go back to in a storm.*

Joanna Wright, the physiotherapist, who was sitting a couple of tables away, didn't bother to hide her big smile.

Carr ate slowly, chewing each mouthful twenty times, not because it was a house rule and supposed to be good for you, but because he felt less hungry that way.

He glanced out of the tall, handsome windows as a chauffeur-driven Mercedes pulled up at the front door.

When the passenger got out, Carr's heartbeat quickened, but outwardly he acted unconcerned. Although the man wasn't wearing baggy trousers, his clothes were just as much a uniform. He had the sort of short raincoat and tight hat that CIA men wore ten or more years ago, and was now affected by the 'modern' KGB agents.

Then the man turned round. Carr stopped eating altogether and his stomach knotted up. Carr had seen him before, at the Foreign Office reception in London.

It was the man from Viktor Section of the KGB: Arcadius Tchalenko.

Carr wasn't sure that Tchalenko would recognise him, but he couldn't be certain that he wouldn't. One thing was certain: Tchalenko was sharp and observant, with a developed peripheral vision. He was a senior man in Viktor Section, where promotion is strictly by merit and the ability to survive, not by influence, seniority or party-line toeing. They don't count for much up at the sharp end.

If Carr wasn't in a hurry before, he was now. He had to steal the records from the safe in the South Wing and get the hell out of the *Clés d'Or* while the going was good.

Even when ballet dancers are appearing on stage in the evenings, they still have to do some hour and a half's practice during the day. In their practice clothes the girls are unrecognisable as those delicate creatures who float across the stage representing doves, swans, fauns, fairies . . . sometimes people. In weird woollen leggings and nameless garments that look like Oxfam rejects, they are all muscle, ligaments and sweat. Lots of sweat. They sweat on stage too, of course, but under thick make-up it's much less obvious from a distance.

In a West London practice studio Peg-the-Legs was looking as if she'd done a good quarter of an hour's wrestling with the great Ed 'Strangler' Lewis when the ballet-master approached her with small stabbing steps, his lips pursed in disapproval. He informed her that someone wanted to see her – and now. No, he didn't know who he was. She picked up a towel to mop all areas of exposed skin, and went off to the director's office.

A hard-faced man of about forty with no expression was waiting there. He looked at her for a long, uncomfortable moment, making Peg painfully aware of her appearance and the strong odour of sweat.

'Miss Hughes?'

'Yes. I'm sorry, I –'

The man interrupted her. 'Superintendent Walker, Special Branch. You know a man named Richard Carr?'

'Yes. Has anything happened to him?'

'When did you see him last?'

'Er, last week. Monday. No . . . Tuesday.'

'Did he say if he was going anywhere?'

'Why, has something happened to him?'

The way the man ploughed straight on through everything she said gave Peg-the-Legs the strange, disembodied feeling you have in a dream when you shout and shout, but there's no sound. 'Did he tell you he was going on leave?' he asked.

'As a matter of fact, he did. Well, on holiday, to be precise.'

'Did he give you any hint of where he was going?'

'He didn't hint. He told me outright.' She stopped there, determined to make him ask where, but the man simply looked at her steadily, and despite herself she added, 'On a boating trip to the Scottish Isles. Look here, Inspector. What has Rich –'

'Superintendent. Did you see him pack?' She looked at him blankly. 'Did you see what sort of clothes he took? How many?'

'No. What's happened to him? What's he done?'

'What makes you think he's done something?'

'The fact that you're here asking questions,' Peg snapped. The history of Welsh reaction to assumed English superiority goes back to the days of woad. Peg was becoming annoyed.

'Have you heard from him? A phone-call? A card?'

'No – to all three.'

'You can't remember him mentioning anyone he was going to meet? Please think about it.'

'I *am* thinking about it – and no I can't. What *is* all this? Have you any proof you're who you say you are?'

'It's a little late, isn't it, miss?' Walker said. She couldn't tell whether he was being sarcastic or cautionary. He took out a warrant card and held it up for her inspection. It was a very good specimen, indistinguishable from a genuine one.

'Here! How do you know about Richard and me?' Peg asked.

'Thanks for your help, miss,' Walker said. There was no trace of irony in his voice, and his face was still as lively as an Easter Island statue. He turned and left Peg standing with her mouth open ready to say something crushing – if she could only think of it.

She stamped out of the office and back to the large practice studio. The ballet-master met her at the door.

'If you're *quite* finished, perhaps you can get on with some work. And don't bother to apologise, will you?'

Peg looked at him with contrition. She took his arm, gazed into his eyes and said softly, 'As we say in Welsh, *Get knotted, you great peroxided fairy.*' She went back to the bar with a lightened step.

Tchalenko left the same afternoon he arrived at the clinic. He went straight from the car to Schaffhauser's office, stayed there a couple of hours, then drove off again. What the KGB man's connection was with a far-out right-wing fanatic, Carr still couldn't imagine.

From his visit to the South Wing, Carr had come to the conclusion that there were no ancillary staff – paramedical personnel or guards – permanently stationed on the top floor. After all, the comatose subjects in the cubicles and treatment room weren't likely to stage a mass escape.

Nevertheless, timing of the break-in was crucial. He'd

been lucky that there was no one moving about on the top floor when he went there that first time, but it *was* luck and he had to be sure of where the Schaffhausers and Bigelow were before he set off. But how? The château was a big place.

The problem was solved for him by the clinic itself.

Carr received an engraved invitation card requesting the pleasure of Mr David Tranter's company at one of the regular Saturday after-dinner *réceptions.*

Joanna Wright told him the next time he went for massage that the parties were to congratulate the patients who were leaving, to encourage the ones who were halfway through their cure, and to greet the new ones who'd just arrived.

Almost everyone at the clinic was on the high-protein low-carbohydrate point-count diet. According to some Continental practitioners, dry white wine and champagne carry no points penalty, so they were served – liberally – at the parties. After a week or two of abstinence a couple of glasses of champagne made everything quite lively. Before long people started dancing, then sloped off in twos, trying to be discreet but being as obvious as animal pairs going into the Ark, and for basically the same reason.

'It can be quite fun. Everybody goes, of course.'

'Everybody? Even Bigelow and the rather forbidding Dr Schaffhauser?'

She nodded. 'All the senior staff have to attend.'

'Just like Butlin's.'

Joanna laughed. 'Not quite.'

'I suppose the doctors just put in an appearance, have a quick drink, then quietly drift away.'

'Oh, no. They always stay at least an hour. Dr Schaffhauser takes his obligations very seriously.'

'At his prices he ought to.'

So the decision was made for him by the party invitation. It meant delaying his attempt on the South Wing for two nights but the delay would be worth it.

The party was held in the handsome main hall, and was

much as Joanna had described it: the patients were like kids who'd been let out of school. The staff were a little more reserved, with the exception of Franz Schaffhauser, who avoided his father's eye and managed to put away as much free champagne as a woman gossip-columnist, and as quickly. Bigelow stood around awkwardly, trying to be sociable, but his thoughts were obviously miles away. Gerd Schaffhauser circulated with mathematical precision, doling out his time in carefully-measured equal portions to one patient after another.

Tage Falkman, wearing a superb dinner jacket, looked like a ski-instructor near a Swiss finishing school for young ladies. Carr grudgingly had to admit that the Swede was handsome, with his regular features, immaculately-parted flax-blond hair, aggressively healthy complexion, at least forty perfect teeth, and athletic body. Women swarmed round him like iron filings round a magnet, but he managed to stay aloofly polite.

He glanced across the hall and saw Joanna Wright watching him. She gave him a wry smile. Carr thought she looked good enough to make a eunuch remember.

Soon after Schaffhauser had given Carr his five minutes and moved on, someone started a tape-recorder and one or two couples started dancing. Nothing modern, with partners out of reach of each other, but old-fashioned stuff with the man and woman in close contact where it mattered and everywhere else they could manage.

Carr worked his way to the periphery of the group, then quietly slipped away through the back of the hall and up the service stairs to his own room. In a matter of moments he had changed into his dark pyjamas and short dressing-gown to maintain his flimsy cover story if he encountered anyone in the château.

Within minutes Carr had a feeling this was going to be one of his better operations. When he left his room he met no one on the service stairs, no one in the corridors. The window above the bridge opened smoothly and silently. There were no guards patrolling the grounds below him as he sprinted across the top of the bridge, and the South Wing roof by the chimney-stack was in deep shadow. Very faintly he could hear the music coming from the party in the château.

The tiles came out of the roof like cards from a new pack, and Carr piled them quickly by the chimney. He had just taken out the last tile when there was a quiet cough below him. Two guards had appeared noiselessly from the grounds, and were talking quietly together. Carr drew back to the chimney-stack again, crouching as he did so.

His elbow caught the edge of the brickwork, jarring the nerve. The tile slipped from his suddenly numbed fingers and started sliding down the sloping roof. It was already out of his reach before Carr could react. The guttering was narrow here, and the tile would shoot over it, down on to the flagstones below, not a dozen yards from where the guards were standing. In a matter of seconds he'd be discovered.

Carr shot out a foot like a desperate, off-balance goal-keeper and managed to trap the tile by pressing it against the surface of the roof with the side of his foot. For the moment he could do no more than stay motionless, concentrating on keeping the pressure on the slippery tile with his thin, patent-leather slipper. With his leg stretched to its utmost length, Carr had to lean back to preserve his uncertain balance, and he could no longer see the guards. He had no way of knowing whether they had moved away or were still there, but he was afraid that if he tried to adjust his position the tile would slip away from him.

Very soon the strain of maintaining the awkward posture made his muscles ache. First, the muscle on the inside of the groin, then the calf, and finally the big muscle at the back of the thigh. It began to throb and contract involuntarily; Carr knew that it would seize up with cramp at any moment and he'd no longer be able to keep his foot on the tile. Whether the guards were there or not, he'd have to make a sudden movement, perhaps a noisy one. And there wouldn't be a second chance. If he didn't manage to grab the tile, even if the guards had moved on, the sound of it crashing down would bring them back in a hurry.

Carr carefully thought out exactly what he was going to do, got the sequence thoroughly fixed in his mind . . . and acted.

He pressed down hard on the tile, then dragged his foot upwards before jack-knifing forward to lie flat and grab at the tile. His fingertips clutched the last inch of the tile . . . slipped . . . then held it.

Not until he'd lain still for a long moment, trying to get his breath back and quieten his heartbeat, did he dare look down to where he'd seen the guards.

There was no one. The men had gone.

At last Carr moved, getting to his knees, then to his feet, helping himself upright with his left hand, while the fingertips of his right hand kept hold of the slippery tile as if his life depended upon it – which it probably did. With exaggerated care he placed the tile on top of the others he'd removed.

As Carr let himself down into the attic he wondered briefly whether his luck was running out and the operation turning sour after all. Or was it that he'd been incredibly lucky in managing to catch the tile against all the odds?

Less than a minute after he'd got to the safe there was no longer any doubt how things were going.

The safe wouldn't open.

Carr thought hard. His telephone exchange: *843.* Death of Elizabeth I: *1603.* Two lefts make a right. So, *8 . . . left 43 . . . left 16 . . . right 3.*

He was sure that was right. So what had gone wrong? It was inconceivable that the combination had been changed, so he must have misread the dial when he watched from the next room while Schaffhauser opened the safe. Carr made a quick calculation. Assuming he'd made an error of one digit on any of the readings, it meant that each turn of the dial could be one of three numbers: the one Carr thought it was, or one less, or one more. So the correct combination could be one of a permutation of 3 x 3 x 3 x 3 or 81, possibilities.

There was no easy way. He simply had to start trying. Maybe he'd strike lucky and get it in the first three or four tries.

Maybe.

16

The party thinned out as couples paired off and went to their rooms, but there were still a number of patients dancing when Bigelow went up to Gerd Schaffhauser and said surlily, 'I'll be going now. I've got things to do.' He made it sound like a statement, but they both knew it was a request for permission. Making sure there was no one within earshot he added softly, 'I guess it's about time for you to start talking to the Englishman, Harris, again.'

Schaffhauser looked round the hall at the patients who were still there. For a variety of reasons he either despised or hated everyone who came to the *Clés d'Or*: the self-indulgence that had brought them there, their vanity and self-deception, their moral and physical weakness, their gullibility and their determination not to see the things they didn't want to see . . .

He collected his thoughts. He couldn't pick out anyone he hadn't spoken to that evening, so there was nothing to prevent him leaving right away, but he didn't want Bigelow to think he'd been taken in by his transparent device. Falkman was dancing with a middle-aged German woman with improbably copper-coloured hair, keeping just out of bodily contact with her. Schaffhauser caught his eye and Falkman nodded almost imperceptibly.

'In a minute, then,' Schaffhauser conceded to Bigelow. 'Is Harris still in the treatment room?'

Bigelow nodded. 'I was planning on moving him into a cubicle tonight and putting Levallois back there.'

At the next natural break in the mechanical music, the last few couples still dancing in a desperate attempt to find a partner for the rest of the night reluctantly peeled themselves apart. Of the members of the staff only Joanna Wright was left in the hall. Franz Schaffhauser had long since left on legs made unsteady by too much champagne.

At that moment Gerd Schaffhauser, Bigelow and Tage Falkman were standing motionless in the doorway of the South Wing office, part of a weird tableau. They were staring in massive disbelief at Carr – who was kneeling on the far side of the room, frozen in mid-action of taking the box of microfilmed records from the open safe.

The first person to move was Falkman. He closed the door behind them, locked it, and put the key into his pocket. He went directly to the adjoining bedroom and returned almost immediately with a small revolver. It looked like a German .32 Pickert, not a particularly classy weapon but more than good enough to kill Carr at short range, and Falkman seemed quite at home with a gun. Carr kept still. This positive act on Falkman's part was the first indication that he was something more than a hired PT instructor. He removed the box of microfilm from Carr's hand and passed it to Bigelow. 'Check this,' he said, then he frisked Carr quickly and efficiently. Bigelow carefully went through the packet of plastic envelopes. Then Falkman picked up the phone and dialled a number. 'Come over to the top floor and wait outside the office. Both of you.' He hung up.

Bigelow finished his checking. He nodded at Falkman, put the box back into the safe and locked it.

'It's a pity you found out,' Falkman calmly told Carr. 'It would have suited us much better if you'd gone back and reported that the place was harmless – nothing more than it seems.'

'However, it's nothing we cannot rectify,' Schaffhauser put in. He said it forcefully, as if to emphasise his own authority. 'I take it you understand what we do here?'

'Aren't you interested how I got in and opened the safe?' Carr asked.

'You'll tell us later,' Schaffhauser said with flat certainty. 'And everything else we want to know. Now, *do* you understand what we are doing?'

Carr nodded. There was no point in trying to dissimulate. 'Brainwashing,' Carr said, not choosing his words carefully. 'Brainwashing by using sensory deprivation and drugs.'

Bigelow, who hadn't spoken yet, burst in impatiently. 'Brain *reformation.* Brainwashing's a goddamn stupid expression. A man of your background should realise that. I first started working on S.D. and brain-reformation techniques more than twenty years ago, when I was specialising in schizophrenic disorders. I was one of the first Westerners in the field. I was into brain reformation long before the Chinese started it with POWs in Korea.'

'Why don't you use the water-tank technique for sensory deprivation?' Somehow Carr felt the more he kept them talking the better his chances would be. He couldn't quite see how, but they couldn't be any worse.

'What do you know about that?' Bigelow sounded surprised.

'I've seen it used in astronaut training,' Carr said. 'I'd have thought it would give a much more realistic sense of weightlessness and caused quicker total disorientation than your padded-table thing.'

'You've already seen the treatment room?' Now Schaffhauser sounded surprised. He recovered. 'Well, you'll soon see it again.'

'The water tank needs constant supervision and monitoring – water temperature, air supply to the subject, things like that – while the table doesn't,' Bigelow said. 'There's nothing to go wrong. The subject can be left alone and no harm can come to him.' Carr didn't think it worth questioning the semantics of this argument. 'Drugs – drugs you've never heard of – more than make up for the limitations of the table. Sound, light and radio transmissions of the same frequency as the subject's brainwave patterns, all help to accelerate and deepen the disorientation process. With my treatment the average subject becomes quite disoriented and starts hallucinating within twelve hours.'

'It will probably be sooner with you,' Schaffhauser said almost genially. 'That is why we are telling you everything. Now you know, your own imagination will work against you and help the breakdown.'

Carr tried to keep the discussion impersonal. 'And when the subject's disorientation is complete, you – what was your expression? – you *reform* their thinking,' Carr said.

'Indeed,' said Schaffhauser. 'The subject is brought to a childlike state of unformed opinion and beliefs. By using a simple punishment-and-reward technique, among others, and establishing a parent-child relationship, we can reform his character and beliefs exactly as we want them. It is like writing on a blank sheet of paper.

'What is it the Jesuits say?' Schaffhauser continued rhetorically. He was becoming slightly euphoric. *'Give us the child until he is seven, then he is ours forever?* Well, we need much less time. Much less.'

'I don't think that's quite the quotation, though that was the sense of it,' Carr agreed. 'But doesn't the effect wear off eventually?'

He sounded much more composed than he was feeling. His mouth was dry and he felt more than a little sick. Being killed was one thing – but his mind . . .

'That's the beauty of it,' Bigelow said enthusiastically. 'First, *any* fear subconsciously reinforces the subject's dependence on the reformer as the one person who has comforted and protected him. And when the effect begins to diminish, the subject has an irresistible compulsion to return to get his batteries charged, in a manner of speaking.'

Carr believed him.

'So you're going to give me the treatment.'

'The alternative is that we kill you, which could be inconvenient.'

'Especially for me,' Carr said, trying to sound nonchalant. He didn't say it too clearly, though – as his mouth was dry.

Falkman spoke unexpectedly. 'More important, it would be wasteful. It's obvious you will be useful to us.'

'Unfortunately it means that we shall have to get rid of one of our subjects to make room for you. Our resources are still rather limited, I'm afraid,' Schaffhauser explained.

'Get rid? How exactly?'

'An accident, a long way from here,' Falkman explained. He gave a careless gesture. 'Killed by muggers in the Paris Metro, or perhaps a heart attack at La Scala, or a bathing accident in the Adriatic . . . ' He spoke like an expert.

'I see,' Carr said. 'A couple of questions?'

Schaffhauser nodded. There was a tap at the door of the office. 'Wait,' Falkman called out. 'They're here,' he told Schaffhauser unnecessarily.

'Why?' asked Carr.

'Why what?' Schaffhauser was puzzled.

'Why are you doing it?'

Schaffhauser looked at him in genuine surprise. 'You can't be serious. Have you forgotten what we said the other day? Western civilisation is weak and degenerate. It's being corrupted from within; its racial strength and natural heritage of leadership threatened by inferior masses who breed indiscriminately like animals and threaten to overwhelm it by sheer weight of numbers, like jackals pulling down a lion.'

There was a sudden change in Schaffhauser. It was as if something had been switched on inside him: he almost glowed and sparked with a fervour that was escalating into fanaticism. Carr stole looks at the other two men. Bigelow's emotions were conflicting: enthusiasm but also embarrassment and something like fear. But Falkman . . . he was cold, unmoved . . . unless there was a merest hint of something very like contempt.

Schaffhauser was now in full flight. 'There are still large sections of the Nordic and Anglo-Saxon races where complete racial purity has been preserved, and it is with them that the only hope of a lasting White Aryan civilisation lies. We are taking over from within, replacing the corrupt elements among the leadership, replacing the incompetent and the impure with strong men of vision and purpose who will give the West back its self-respect through fearless leadership and self-discipline. At first we shall be the great bulwark against the menace of the Communist masses and the Asiatic hordes; then as we gather strength we shall go over to the offensive and either subjugate or destroy them.'

'A thousand million Chinese for starters? Don't you think that might be a fraction ambitious?'

Schaffhauser was unperturbed. 'In 1943 one single nation was within a hairsbreadth of conquering, thanks to that leadership and self-discipline, all Europe with seven hundred and fifty million people – a Continent that even then was more technologically advanced than China is now.'

'And America?' Carr asked. 'How long will that take you? I should allow at least a week for subjugating or destroying America.'

'Are you really that naïve?' Schaffhauser asked. 'White America, which will prevail, will be with us. At least the majority of important Americans are awake to the insidious spread of the Communist virus.' He paused and studied Carr for a moment before continuing. Bigelow and Falkman stood like Madame Tussaud exhibits. 'In our New World only the genetically pure will be allowed to reproduce, ridding mankind of its weak and worthless subhumans in two generations. I shall not live to see it –'

'You certainly won't.' Carr sounded more nonchalant than he felt.

'I shall not live to see it completed, but it will happen,' Schaffhauser continued evenly. 'Finally the Nordic and Anglo-Saxon Western civilisation will realise its destiny and lead the world –'

'Heil Hitler,' Carr said.

Schaffhauser stopped dead. Then, his voice still completely calm, he said, 'If he hadn't been betrayed by his own politicians and attacked by nations that were Germany's natural allies, the so-called free world wouldn't have the Communists at its throat. We shouldn't be on the brink of a holocaust.'

'That really is one word you shouldn't have used,' Carr told him. He wondered how a senior KGB man like Arcadius Tchalenko was mixed up with a mob of neo-Nazi anti-Communists.

But, with a smile that chilled Carr to the bone, Schaffhauser went on, 'You are very fortunate. You were born an Anglo-Saxon; you are intelligent, you have no genetic defects, and in your position you can be a great help to us. Otherwise . . . ' He shrugged dismissively.

'You may find it difficult to accept now, but before you leave here, you will come to understand the basic truths of what we stand for. In a matter of little more than days, your conversion will become almost total. Later, because you want to, *of your own free will*, you will return here to be instructed again.' He gave another of his terrifying smiles. 'You will be proud to be one of us, the dedicated builders of the New World. You will believe as fervently as all of us, to the point that if it is required of you, you will gladly give your life.'

That brand of madness stated with soft reasonableness and the utter conviction of Divine revelation made Carr's blood run cold. The most dangerous maniac isn't the one who shouts, but the one who speaks with patience and sympathy to the less fortunate creature he is going to help. Even if helping means slicing away part of the creature's brain in a pre-frontal leucotomy operation, or assaulting him with massive electric shocks.

What made the whole situation even more flesh-crawling was Carr's certainty that Schaffhauser could do everything he said he could. Lunatic-fringe religious groups manage it without any of the *Clés d'Or* expensive equipment. They just take a little longer.

Falkman opened the door. Two men were standing there. They wore white trousers and short-sleeved jackets that showed off muscular forearms and hands that could strangle a python.

Falkman nodded to them, and they advanced into the room.

Carr supposed that he had been asleep, because he knew now that he was awake and he didn't remember being awake a moment ago. And there was a gap since his last memory, of the two white-uniformed attendants moving towards him. He also knew where he was: on the table in the strange treatment room. He was surprised that his mind was so clear and working logically, despite what they were trying to do to him.

Then Carr asked himself *how* he knew where he was, because he could see nothing but grey wherever he turned his eyes, yet he *did* know. He wondered what he looked like on the table, so he rose up from his body and gently floated towards the ceiling, and remained there.

He stared down at himself. He was in a plain, pyjama-like garment, and had a couple of days' growth of beard. That shook him. He had no idea he'd been unconscious for so long. There were earphones over his head, and his arms were in the large padded tubes he'd seen when he first saw Peter Harris in the room.

There was something behind his head, at the top of the table. He came down a little to get a better look at it, and saw it was a transfusion bottle of colourless liquid. The tube from it led into the large cylinder round his left arm. There was another tube leading from inside his pyjama trousers to a bottle underneath the table. Obviously they were giving him intravenous feeding and catheterising him to draw off the urine, but he could feel nothing.

Odd that he could see the bottle *under* the table – and he could see it there – even though the Richard Carr lying beneath him was as solid as the table he was lying on. This didn't bother Carr, who was aware that his body lying there was looking up and seeing him, just as he was looking down at the Richard Carr who was looking up at the other Richard Carr, looking down at him . . .

He started to move round the room. It was simple. He just *thought* where he wanted to be, and he was there. The idea came to him that maybe he could move outside the room and go into the château, or even further . . . It was then that he noticed a thin, bright line, almost like a beam of light, curved by its own weight as if it had substance, joining the two Richard Carrs at somewhere near the navel. The light turned and twisted and stretched, became more intense and dimmed, as he changed position.

Carr shook with fright. Supposing that thin thread of light between him and him became stretched so far that it parted! What would happen? Would it kill them both, or one of them? A worse fear gripped him. If it did, perhaps they would be locked apart in separate worlds. As he formulated the thought he felt himself drifting into unconsciousness. He fought unavailingly against it as the terror swept over him.

Sensory deprivation (S.D.) has been used in deep interrogation techniques by practically every 'advanced' counter-intelligence group. It beats pulling out fingernails hollow.

S.D. can be effected in many ways, from a bag over the head in a quiet room, through being left alone for hours in a plain, featureless room to being suspended in body-temperature water with the eyes and ears covered. S.D. causes illogical fears, inability to judge time, confusion, more sorts of hallucination than a normal man could possibly imagine – and then a lot more.

Some reactions are common to practically every subject of S.D. Curiously, one of these is that he almost invariably sleeps for most of the first twenty-four hours in S.D. conditions, even if he has just enjoyed a full night's sleep.

Once awake, sooner or later the subject begins to panic, sometimes within a matter of a few hours. If he thinks that he is under some sort of surveillance he will not panic as quickly. It is when he thinks he is alone, abandoned and uncared for, alone . . . alone . . . alone in this awful limbo, that he breaks quickly. People who have been through S.D.

say that it can be the greatest fear the mind can know. Carr was only too aware that he was being left unattended, unwatched, and this knowledge gnawed at him, eroding his resistance and weakening his fragile hold on normality.

Sensory deprivation is easy enough to impose on a captive subject, but for anyone who wants to use it as a tool to form that subject's attitudes, the problem is how to take advantage of his fears to channel his confused, dissociated and hallucinating thinking in a particular direction. This is what Bigelow had been working on for years (as have other 'scientists' whose masters will never allow them to publish the results of their work even if they want to). Bigelow had brought his technique with drugs, subliminal sounds and images to a high degree of accuracy. When the subject was confused, terror-stricken or utterly depressed, the 'figure of authority' reassured or comforted him. There was nothing new about this basic principle of persuasion, but Bigelow's actual technique was exquisitely refined and precise. Schaffhausen, of course, was the omniscient and omnipotent 'figure of authority'.

In the South Wing of the *Clés d'Or* the brain reformation process continued outside the treatment room, in the isolation cubicles. Drugs like those Carr had seen in Bigelow's office, which could cause unreasoning anxiety, depression, and changes in body temperature, together with the disorienting effects of irregular meals and lights being turned on and off at unsystematic intervals, made the subject utterly vulnerable to suggestion.

Another technique known to people working in the field of S.D.-induced brain reformation is the exploitation of the subject's desperately monotonous existence in the isolation cubicle. Simple switches give him the choice of two tape-recording channels which he can turn on at will. The first channel has a recording of a talk which is in agreement with the subject's own philosophy. The second channel is devoted to talks – plural – on the new philosophy to be imposed on the subject.

Hearing the single talk time and again intensifies the subject's boredom. Soon, he switches to the second channel –

'Just for this once,' he tells himself. But because there is a whole range of talks on this second channel, the subject turns to them for variety. Then the first, boring tape is played over and over again to him without his switching it on. He becomes sick of it, resentful of it . . . and there is a very easy way of stopping it. By switching on the other channel.

The subject is conditioning *himself* by making a *voluntary* choice of listening to the arguments that the manipulators want him to accept.

Each of these techniques on its own may seem little enough to reshape a man's mind and turn his lifelong beliefs upside down. But although the camel's back breaks eventually, one last single straw hasn't done it alone; and the human mind is far more fragile, complex and brittle, so much more liable to give way.

Carr swam powerfully and easily. He'd always enjoyed swimming. He found it the nearest thing to unaided flight because he could move in three dimensions, unaffected by gravity. Most of all he enjoyed swimming in clear, calm deep waters where he could see the sea-floor far below him. It was almost like being a bird.

The water was warm and he swam without any sense of strain, swam towards –

Where?

Where was he going? Which way was safety? He rose up out of the water and looked round.

Nothing.

He'd been abandoned in an endless grey sea under a grey featureless sky. He shouted, but it was a thin shout that died on the wind inches from his lips. An overwhelming sense of desolation swept over him.

With a roaring sound like an express train, a gigantic killer whale rushed towards him, turning on its side as it passed him, revealing a cruel gash of a mouth with a score of great white sabres of triangular teeth. The whale snapped its jaws shut with a force that could have cut him in half.

Carr started swimming away in panic, knowing that he could never hope to escape from the beast.

Deep in its throat the whale gave an awesome rumbling sound that unbelievably climbed three octaves into a blood-curdling shriek, turned in the water with a massive grace, and set off for Carr again with a single lazy sweep of its tail, powerful enough to crush a motor-car.

It swam straight at him, then swerved at the last second, turning on its side and brandishing those monstrous teeth. It passed so close that he was thrown violently to one side by its wash, then dragged helplessly into its wake.

Twice more it feinted to make the killing run, almost thrusting against Carr in its charge, leaving him bobbing about in its wake like a cork in a whirlpool.

The third time it turned to face him again it remained stationary for a while, facing him from about thirty yards. It turned its head slightly to stare at him with one cold, unemotional, appraising eye, slowly opening and closing its brutal mouth, designed to rip, tear and kill.

This time, Carr thought. *This time* . . .

Almost as if it enjoyed tormenting him – like a cat with a mouse – the great whale inched forward at first, gradually accelerating into its final killing attack. Terror gripped Carr and squeezed him. His life could be measured in seconds.

'Don't worry, I'll take care of you,' came a firm voice he recognised. It seemed to surround him like the sea itself. Carr blinked disbelievingly as the killer whale turned and swam away rapidly, out of sight in seconds.

'You know you can always rely on me to take care of you.' Schaffhauser spoke quietly into a microphone connected to Carr's earphones as he lay on the table in the treatment room.

There were other, recurrent moments of inescapable terror for Carr. In one of them he was on the floor of a cellar, unable to move, while a horde of red-eyed rats almost as big as terriers gnawed at a wooden lattice-work to get at him; in another he fell endlessly, endlessly down a pit-shaft towards a rocky floor. And yet these were not the worst terrors – the sharks and the rats and the flesh-ripping spiders and armies of ants; the endless falls through icy space. There were the indefinable, nameless dreads that threatened his mind more than his body. Once he thought he'd fallen into a Black Hole, into a different universe where there was not only no way back, but no God. But always, when it seemed that he was about to die of terror or lose his reason, Gerd Schaffhauser would be there in voice or person to save and comfort him.

Then there were the moments of calm – almost transcendental tranquillity – at the opposite pole from the times of awful terror, and unutterable grateful relief at being saved from the mortal dangers. During these peaceful periods Schaffhauser spoke to him softly, persuasively, making as much effect on his mind by gentle insistence as by sheer relief from violence.

At last Carr had a moment of lucidity. He knew what had been done to him, and that he could stand very little more. His whole being was near the point of total exhaustion; he was almost completely drained by the continuous assaults on his mind. As he stared up at the grey ceiling, he was fully aware that he was only a hairsbreadth away from going out of his mind – or dying.

Franz Schaffhauser and Bigelow came into the treatment room, and Carr was aware of their presence, although he was too tired to make any acknowledgement of it.

They looked down at him. Schaffhauser wore a stethoscope round his neck. He put it into his ears and listened to Carr's chest, moving it from one point to another. He looked increasingly disturbed. Then he touched the side of Carr's neck.

'Father told you not to overdo it,' he said at last with a mixture of anger and fear. 'You've killed him.'

'No!' said Bigelow. 'It's not possible!'

Franz Schaffhauser held out his stethoscope, and Bigelow started to listen to Carr's chest for a heartbeat. He pressed the instrument so hard against the flesh that it was painful.

At last Carr's bemused mind reacted. He opened his mouth to complain about the way Bigelow was hurting him, and to tell them that he wasn't dead, for Christ's sake.

But his mouth wouldn't open. No sound came from his lips. He decided to look directly at Schaffhauser. The movement of his eyes would be enough to make the two men realise he wasn't dead.

His eyes wouldn't move, either.

He was aware of Schaffhauser and Bigelow moving around at the periphery of his vision without being able to look at them directly.

'It might be a catalepsy,' Bigelow said, without sounding very convincing. 'It's happened before.'

Schaffhauser leaned over Carr and studied him carefully. He reached out a finger and brought it down on to Carr's right eye, cutting out half his field of vision. Schaffhauser pressed on the eyeball, sending excruciating daggers of pain clean through to the back of his head.

'He's dead all right. God, you'll have to tell father,' Schaffhauser said. '*I* won't do it.'

Carr felt a tear welling from the eye Schaffhauser had pressed.

Look at this! How could my eye water if I was dead? he screamed silently. *Look! Look!!* But they both turned away as the tear trickled down his cheek and into his ear. By the time the two men had returned to his side, the tear had dried.

I'm not dead! Carr screamed over and over again, but the sounds stayed inside his head.

I'm breathing! Look at me, for God's sake! I can't be dead if I'm breathing! Surely you can see I'm breathing!

Later two men came and picked him up roughly from the table and put him unceremoniously into a plain wooden box that was little better than a crate.

Carr rose up out of his body, and looked at himself lying stiffly in his rudimentary coffin, his eyes wide open and staring. Wasn't the look of horror on his face enough to tell the men he wasn't really dead?

The two men fitted the lid – three planks nailed to a couple of battens – on to the box. The lid was badly jointed and Carr could see the light shining through the cracks. He could even make out the movements of the men as they heaved the box on to some sort of trolley. They wheeled him through corridors and down in what seemed to be a service lift.

As soon as I'm able to move again, I'll budge this lid, he told himself. *This is only temporary. It must be!*

But what if he wasn't able to move again – or only after he was securely under six feet of earth? His mind almost burst remembering those awful stories of coffins being exhumed with scratches and splinter marks on the inside of the lid, while the corpse, its face hideously contorted, had torn and bloody hands with broken nails.

He was left alone in a cold, damp room that smelt of earth and death. He lay there for hours as the light slowly faded, fighting against the iron-bandage paralysis that gripped him. By the time dark fell he was more exhausted than he ever was in his life – and without having moved the tiniest muscle.

About an hour after dark Carr heard a door open behind him. A few moments later he felt the trolley being moved, but this time only a few yards before the rough coffin was lifted off the trolley and carried out of the building. He realised he was outside because the air was cooler and fresher, with the faint odour of woodsmoke.

I can feel! I can smell! I . . . am . . . alive! he shouted silently again.

A metal door was opened – the coffin dropped on to a metal surface and pushed forward, the door slammed shut. An engine started up and the floor began to vibrate. He was in a van of some sort.

The vehicle moved off down the gravelled drive and into the road. Quite soon it bumped off the road and drove across rough ground for some distance in a low gear, twisting and turning before it grinded to a halt. The coffin was dragged out and allowed to crash to the ground. The whole of his body ached with the impact, but still he couldn't move. He knew he was in a forest: he could hear the sound of the wind in the trees; he could even smell the pines. He had never been more acutely aware of sounds and smells, and they were infinitely precious to him.

One end of the coffin was lifted and allowed to drop

again, then the same thing happened to the other. The reason became obvious when one man said impatiently, in German, 'Pass the bloody rope.'

The coffin was raised, and it swung gently as it was moved to one side. Carr knew this because he could see the stars through the cracks in the lid. His eyes were starting from his head: his throat was sore with the effort of trying to utter a sound, any sound.

For Christ's sake stop! Stop! I'm alive! Alive! Oh, dear God help me! he screamed with all his strength, but the sounds just echoed and re-echoed inside his skull.

The coffin was lowered carelessly into greater darkness. It seemed to be a shallow grave. A few stars were still visible through the cracks immediately above him – but they vanished simultaneously with the most ghastly sound he could ever hear: the sound of earth falling on to the lid of his own coffin.

The last of the starlight was extinguished and Carr was left in the only true total darkness and silence: the darkness and silence of the tomb.

17

Only one light burned in the Kensington office where the photographs of Carr arriving at the *Clés d'Or* had been delivered a fortnight earlier. It was on the large, scarred desk. The tall man behind it sat motionless, staring at papers on the surface without seeing them. One of the double-glazed windows was open, and from the distance came the sound of two late-night buses, a No. 9 and a No. 33, racing towards the Mortlake Garage like old-time milkmen's horses at the end of their round. The buses leapfrogged each other at request stops, competing to see how many would-be passengers they could dodge.

The phone rang. Before he answered it the man at the desk shut the window and pulled the curtain across, even though he couldn't be overlooked. 'Yes?'

'Nimrod Three again.'

'Bring it up.'

The same well-dressed messenger walked in and laid a small envelope on the desk. The senior man took out his dangerous-looking knife and opened it. As he did so, the messenger asked, 'Why don't they phone instead of sending signals?'

'In a small place like that they couldn't trust telephones, and radio might attract attention.' He read the brief note the envelope contained.

'Trouble?'

'Our agent inside the *Clés d'Or* says that Carr has been out of circulation for a while.'

'So?'

There was a long pause. 'I think I'll go there myself.'

'Why? Carr's not our problem.'

'But if they're working on him in some way, he just might blow everything he knows and send them scuttling for cover. I'm not going to risk the whole thing collapsing now, after all this time.'

'Okay. How will you go?'

'Get me on tomorrow's first flight to Berne.'

'Not Geneva?'

'Geneva's an hour nearer, but you never know who'll be watching the airport. Less chance of being noticed at Berne. Get on to our consul there and have them fix me a car. You know,' he added gloomily, 'I've got a horrible feeling it's all going wrong. Sodd's Law: *If it can go wrong, it will.* Let's just hope Carr can stick it out.'

'Maybe they've killed him.'

'If they have, pray it was before they got anything important out of him.'

Carr drifted in and out of consciousness – although in the stifling, absolute darkness it was difficult to be sure if he was conscious or hallucinating. Panic had utterly overwhelmed him, yet he still couldn't make the tiniest movement. It was as if he was set in concrete. His head was spinning, which added to the sense of total unreality.

Things like this just don't happen, he tried to tell himself, but even as he formulated the thought he knew that such things *did* happen, and have happened . . . His dizziness increased and his head ached abominably. He dimly supposed it was because the oxygen in the coffin was becoming exhausted.

And then . . . *he felt the power of movement returning.*

He could move his right foot, he was sure of it, and the fingers of his right hand. But it was too late . . . too late. He would suffocate long before he could make any effort to free himself from his tomb. Perhaps it was as well: it would spare him futile effort that could only make his death more agonising. He should try to accept it and die peacefully.

He sank slowly . . . slowly . . . into the pit of final oblivion.

He heard a voice. A familiar voice. His last conscious thought was that maybe there was life after death after all. The voice became louder, and then there was an unmistakable scuffling, scraping sound above him.

More hallucination, or reality?

Something touched his face, softly, and ran off it. He tried to shout, sure it was a tiny animal, but then he guessed it was a piece of earth which had fallen through the gap in the coffin lid.

They were digging him out!

And at last he recognised the voice that was urging on the diggers. Gerd Schaffhauser.

Gerd Schaffhauser had come to rescue him from the grave.

How long he'd been lying on his bed in the cubicle, Carr couldn't be sure.

After Shaffhauser's men had dug him out of his forest grave, they had taken him in what seemed to be the same truck back to the clinic. There they put him in a two-bed ward. On the journey back Schaffhauser had raged at his son and at Bigelow for their criminal stupidity in not properly examining the possibility of catalepsy – particularly as it had happened before with other patients.

But after a couple of days in the ward they had returned him to the treatment room and subjected him to more sensory deprivation. Now he was out again, back in the cubicle.

The return of some degree of objective perception made Carr more depressed instead of comforting him. It wasn't his poor co-ordination and physical weakness that worried him. When he fell twice trying to get off the bed, because when the sheer effort tired him, he had enough detachment to realise it was only a temporary condition. Bedridden patients lose co-ordination and strength quite quickly and need physiotherapy to help them regain normal fitness. In fact Carr was rather pleased with himself for even having made the effort to get off the bed. It was a good sign. He remembered seeing other patients simply lying on their beds helplessly, staring at the ceiling.

Carr's physical weakness disturbed him far less than his new feelings about Gerd Schaffhauser. Whenever he thought of him he had an instinctive, warm sense of gratitude, of admiration, friendship and complete trust. Schaffhauser now stood in the relationship of a super-father. But whenever Carr thought of returning to England, he suffered rising waves of resentment against the Establishment that employed him. He was filled with bitterness and hostility.

His objectivity and powers of logical thought were seriously reduced, yet at another level of consciousness he was aware that his objectivity was warped and diminished. He forced himself to think about the past few days, though his recent memory had worrying blanks.

Why had they put him in a box, instead of just wrapping him in a plastic sheet or tarpaulin? In fact, why put him in anything at all? If he hadn't been in a box, he would have died within a matter of minutes.

Why had Schaffhauser waited until he was actually buried before checking on him?

Would Franz Schaffhauser and Bigelow have dared to dispose of him thus without Gerd's permission?

At this level of awareness he knew that the whole thing had been a set-piece – all part of his processing. It may even have been an induced hallucination. Yet on the lower level of consciousness he still felt this almost overwhelming reliance on Schaffhauser. At this level he *knew* this instinctive reaction was the right one. He *knew* that Schaffhauser's ideas were correct: he was a clever man and Carr admired him enormously.

Then there were dreams when he was menaced by a cold, nameless dread. Not the crude horrors of the sharks and the red-eyed rats and the endless falls down dark shafts, not even the 'reality' of being buried alive, but intangible terrors that threatened his mind more than his body. The dreams ended with an unutterable relief as Gerd Schaffhauser told him not to worry: he was safe now.

So, from time to time Carr had moments of undistorted insight when he understood what was being done to him – but realising that only added to his fears. He asked himself how long it would be before the last degree of objective insight was destroyed and he became completely shaped by Schaffhauser's treatment.

In one of his lucid moments he pondered whether Schaffhauser had underestimated his powers of resistance, and had transferred him to the cubicle too soon. Carr knew only too well that in time he would yield to the processing. Of course, he was trained to resist a certain amount of mental pressure. Most agents of a certain level are practised in the basic techniques of cheating the polygraph, or lie-detector; there are self-hypnosis techniques which can help combat the effects of drugs. Not overcome them, but at least minimise them.

So perhaps Carr's mental defences were proving a little more effective than either he or Schaffhauser realised . . .

As Carr knew, the longer a man is a prisoner, the more his initiative and determination atrophy as he develops a submissive prisoner mentality. In his present case the situation was much more acute because of the deliberate mental onslaught. He could concentrate on escape only intermittently; and his head ached with the effort.

Escape . . . *Escape.*

It had to be soon, or never.

There was but one possible way out of the cubicle, and that was the door. So Carr painfully concentrated on that.

It was fastened only by a lock. Fortunately, he told himself. It could have been bolted on the outside.

As far as he could make out he was given three meals a day, but at irregular times to maintain the sense of disorientation. For the same reason the heating and the ceiling light were switched on and off apparently at random. There was one time, though, when Carr could be sure that the light would be on. In the meantime, he examined his cell minutely to see if there was anything he could use as a tool.

Homo habilans . . .Dexterous man who can use tools . . . But he's got to have tools to be dexterous with. Leg of the chair? Can't pick a lock with that . . .

Face it, there's nothing.

In bitter disappointment Carr collapsed back on his bed.

It made a faint twanging sound. For a moment that didn't register, then slowly an idea began to form in his mind. He struggled off the bed once more.

Carr was lying motionless on the bed the next time the attendant brought in some food – the usual bowl of thinnish soup. The man put the bowl on the table and helped Carr to the table.

Carr took hold of the spoon clumsily and studied the soup through sleepy, half-closed eyes, as if he'd never seen a bowl before. But he was really keyed up, and it seemed impossible to him that the attendant couldn't hear the sound of his racing heart.

The man moved away. As soon as he turned his back Carr opened his eyes and stared at the key in the other's left hand, trying to register some idea of its shape. It didn't look too complicated.

When he was sure the attendant had gone Carr half moved, half fell from his chair to the side of the bed. He was conscious that this might be the only chance to prepare for an escape; and despite the sedative drugs in his system his hand trembled.

The twanging sound from the bed had prompted Carr to study its construction. It was basic in its simplicity: a braced wooden frame with a black wire lattice-work of three-to-four-inch squares covered with a thin, firm mattress. The end of each wire was bent down at a right angle and driven into the wood, reinforced with a staple.

Using the handle of the spoon Carr laboriously tried to prise one wire loose from the frame. He jabbed at it, levering the wire up so that it dragged at the staple. Normally this would have taken him only a couple of minutes, but his co-ordination was poor and his heart still beat as if he'd just run a mile. He was terrified that the attendant would return and find him working at the wire. But he dared not leave the task half done. Next time he had possession of a spoon he might not have the strength enough to complete the work. It had to be now.

At last the staple loosened and fell to the floor. He scrabbled around for it, and hid it under the mattress.

Carr struggled back to the chair and sat down, laying his forearms on the table. His face and hands were running with sweat; he wiped his face with the sleeve of his pyjamas, and ran his hands up and down the front of his jacket. When his breath had returned to something like normal, he took a spoonful of the insipid soup, then sat motionless, the spoon in his hand resting on the table.

Almost immediately the key rattled in the door and the attendant came in. He muttered something to himself, took Carr's hand and helped him feed himself like a child. He was still surprisingly considerate and gave Carr time to eat without hurrying. When he'd finished, the attendant took him back to the bed and helped him lie down.

As soon as Carr was alone again he felt for the wire he'd loosened. He could reach it without getting out of bed, and by feel unthreaded about a foot of it from the lattice work. He pulled his pyjama sleeve down over his hand to protect it, and began bending the wire back and forth to break it off. The light went out, as usual without warning, but Carr didn't close his eyes and went on working – how long for he didn't know. But at last the wire parted.

As he withdrew the piece of wire from the frame Carr felt a surge of excitement. He was no longer a helpless, hopeless prisoner. He'd taken the first step towards escape; he'd acquired a tool.

Carr slipped the piece of wire between the bottom sheet and the mattress and closed his eyes to rest awhile. When he woke, the light had come on again, and he had no idea whether that had woken him. The room was cold, too, which equally may have roused him.

He felt a strange sense of expectancy – like he used to experience on waking to what he knew was going to be an exciting day, even though he couldn't quite remember what was special about it. It took him some while to realise what was causing this sense of excitement. The piece of wire.

His spirits surged – then with a shock like an icy shower he wondered if it was only another hallucination. He scrabbled under the sheet. Sickening disappointment swept over him as he failed to find the precious piece of wire. He was close to childish tears, knowing it had been only a dream after all.

Then he caught his breath. His fingers had closed on the wire. Clutching it tightly, he pulled himself off his bed and went uncertainly to the door.

Carr studied the keyhole and measured its length – a fraction over an inch – against the wire. He put the wire on the floor and placed a leg of the chair on it so he could bend the wire in a sharp right-angle. He bent the other end to make a sort of handle.

Now he possessed a rudimentary picklock.

Taking the pillow and sheets from the bed he rolled them into the rough shape of a sleeping man and covered them with a single blanket. He went to the door and sat down on the floor to work at the lock. If anyone looked through the judas window, Carr wouldn't be visible and the bed might pass a casual inspection.

To prevent himself becoming over-buoyant he forced himself to remember how much more there was to do, and how much luck he would need to escape. He needed to pick the lock successfully, slip into the corridor when no one was there, cross the bridge into the château, then get past the guards to the walls.

Furthermore his escape from this cubicle would have to go unnoticed for some time if he was to have any chance of getting clear away.

The lock was quite elementary, and proved easier than he'd hoped. Obviously Schaffhauser didn't consider there was any possibility of someone trying to pick it from the inside. When the lock clicked back, an iron band gripped his chest, making it difficult for him to breathe. After an agonising moment of self-control, his breathing eased.

He opened the door a crack and looked down the corridor. It was empty.

Carr stepped out of the cubicle to begin the longest hours he had ever experienced – hours so full of shocks that the unexpected would become the commonplace. People would die violently; individual attitudes would evolve with self-discovery, and relationships change dramatically.

He closed his cubicle door behind him, and on impulse tried to lock it from the outside with the picklock. He succeeded almost at once, and smiled at the thought of Schaffhauser and the others wondering how he'd managed to escape from a room that had apparently remained locked.

He'd forgotten how powerfully the corridor's assymetry induced vertigo. In his weakened and drugged state it was almost too much for him. He swayed, bounced off one wall and staggered drunkenly across to the other. It was nightmarish, like trying to stay upright on a swaying rope-bridge with nothing to hold on to. He pinched hard the inside of his arm, mercilessly twisting the flesh until he nearly yelled with pain; but it cleared his head a little. At last he managed to reach the door leading out to the other, normal corridor. He fell through it, crashing on to his hands and knees. It seemed easier to crawl to the bridge, but some innate sense of self-respect forced him to his feet again.

By now he was beyond worrying about being able to hide if he heard anyone coming; it was a chance he'd have to take. Simply moving forward took all his strength and concentration.

His memory wasn't at fault about the door into the château on the far side of the bridge. The lock was a standard continental model with a square knob that could be turned without a key from the inside, but needed a key to operate it from the outside. It was the sort of lock found on the front doors of a million continental apartments.

Carr turned the square knob and the bolt slid back. He pushed against the door. It didn't budge. He pushed again – with all the strength he could manage. Still the door wouldn't open.

He paused and took a deep breath, concentrating like a weightlifter 'psyching' himself into a supreme effort. The second before he was ready to push the door one last time, he checked.

Then he *pulled* at the door. It opened smoothly and silently.

He entered the short corridor which lay in the château itself – wondering what time of day or night it was. The wall lights were burning, but that gave no answer as the corridor had no windows. When at last he reached the main corridor he perceived it was half-light.

Early morning or late evening? If it was evening he could hide in the grounds until it was fully dark before trying to get out. He forgot for the moment that he was wearing only thin pyjamas and raffia slippers. But if it was early morning there was no time to waste. *Press on, press on!*

His luck held almost all the way down the service stairs: there was no one about. On the last flight Carr felt his knees go, and that iron band squeezed his chest again. Breathing became agony. He knew he was putting an almost intolerable strain on his heart, which had suffered such stress in the past few days. He clutched the handrail, resisting the temptation to sit on the stairs even for a moment.

The iron band relaxed its savage grip a little, and Carr managed a few deep, shuddering breaths. As he gradually recovered he considered the next stage of his escape. If it was early morning, perhaps he could reach the garages and steal a car, or a service van, or something. He could 'hotwire'

– bypass the ignition – and start a van more easily than his own BMW or one of the other expensive cars with steering locks; and a van might get straight through the gates without being checked. Whichever way he got out, once in nearby Entremeaux he'd call Beech in London, collect. There was no one else he could trust to send help quickly. The local police would return him to the clinic as an escaped nut.

He half walked, half fell down the last few stairs, and made for the door leading to the kitchen corridor.

The long corridor was deserted, but there was something even more important. Sunlight was streaming through the windows along one side. Carr forced himself to think. The kitchens were on the south of the house, and the light was coming from the right-hand side. The right . . . the west! *It was evening!* His chances of escaping were suddenly very much better.

Carr took a deep breath and started towards the kitchens. A second corridor joined the first halfway down its length. Just before he reached the junction, Joanna Wright, wearing her white coat and slacks, turned the corner and confronted him. He shambled to a halt. She stopped in mid-stride like a child playing Statues. Now that he had actually encountered someone, Carr's last strength drained from him. But Joanna Wright was English: the only other English person there. Perhaps . . .

'For God's sake help me,' he pleaded. His tongue felt enormous in his mouth and he had difficulty in pronouncing. He concentrated hard and spoke more slowly. 'I'm being held prisoner. Help me get away before anyone sees me.' She looked at him with blank astonishment. 'I'm a British agent,' he said, and even in his lightheaded state he knew how improbably theatrical it sounded.

Joanna continued to stare at him, then at last she turned her head and called out, 'Tage! Tage! Give me a hand. I think Mr Tranter's ill.'

Almost immediately Tage Falkman and one of the big male nurses appeared from the second corridor. At another time Carr would have found Falkman's expression of total surprise amusing. He hurried forward and took one of Carr's arms; the nurse took the other. He couldn't have been more securely held if he'd been put in a straitjacket.

'Now what on earth are you doing out of your room, Mr Tranter?' Falkman asked solicitously. 'We must get you back to bed right away.' He turned to Joanna and said quietly, 'Mr Tranter has had a breakdown. Delayed reaction from stress at work. He's been quite ill.' Carr was too crushed to argue.

'I'll come with you,' Joanna said.

'No need. We can manage,' Falkman replied quickly, showing his faultless teeth in a smile that never touched his eyes. 'Did he say anything to you?'

'He mumbled something, but I couldn't make it out.'

Falkman nodded, satisfied. 'Come along, Mr Tranter. I'm sure you'll feel a lot better after some rest.'

Carr looked at Joanna, but couldn't think of anything to say. She avoided his eye.

Half an hour later, Joanna, dressed in ordinary outdoor clothing, walked down the main stairs and through the hall towards the front door.

'Miss Wright.'

She turned. Gerd Schaffhauser stood by the door of his office. 'One moment, please.' He came over to her. 'Where are you going?'

'To the village. It's my evening off, Doctor.'

'I'd like you to stay on duty. Two of the nurses are sick with some sort of intestinal upset and we'll be short of night-staff. Would you mind?' The tone of the question gave Joanna no option.

'Well . . . '

'We'll make up your time off, of course. You weren't going anywhere important, were you?'

'Not really, Doctor. Just a meal with a woman friend,' Joanna said.

'Thank you, Miss Wright.' Schaffhauser made it sound as if he had done her a favour. 'Dr Bigelow will give you your instructions.' He turned and went into his office.

Joanna looked round the deserted hall, then went to the

telephone on the reception desk. 'Can I have a line please?' she asked the clinic's switchboard operator. 'Local call.'

'What number?'

'It's all right. I'll get it.'

There was a click, followed by the high-pitched steady note of the continental dialling tone. Joanna dialled three numbers. The phone at the other end rang once and was picked up. She looked round before she spoke. 'It's Joanna,' she said quietly.

'Yes?' came a gruff, subdued male voice.

'I can't get out this evening. He tried to escape but they caught him.'

There was a click on the line. 'Hello? Hello?' Joanna said. The phone was dead.

Joanna put the phone down very slowly. Before she took her hand away from the instrument two men were standing on either side of her, another in front of her. She looked up. Gerd Schaffhauser stared back at her.

'So,' he said. 'Not very professional of you, Miss Wright. That wasn't your friend you were speaking to. Now, come with me.'

'Jesus Christ!' said Bigelow. 'They're on to us, then! It's not just Tranter. There's somebody else! What the hell are we going to do? We've got to get away from here before – '

'Doctor.' Falkman's voice wasn't loud but it silenced Bigelow as effectively as a slap in the face. 'There's no need to panic. They know nothing yet. We have nothing to worry about. So, please, keep quiet.'

Both Schaffhausers were with them in the South Wing office-consulting room. For once Gerd was taking a very secondary part.

'But Goddamnit, they're on to us!' Bigelow said. It was almost a wail.

'*Who* is on to us? And on to *what*?' Falkman said.

'It's obvious they know. The Wright woman must have told her people everything.'

'She doesn't know anything, Bigelow. She's never been in the South Wing,' Gerd Schaffhauser said contemptuously.

'And even if they did know, they could never proving anything.' The rare grammatical mistake betrayed that Schaffhauser's self-composure was spread thin.

'What're you going to do with the pair of them?' Franz Schaffhauser asked nervously.

'What are *we* going to do with them?' Falkman said. 'I should have thought that was obvious.'

18

'They're going to kill us,' Joanna said flatly to Carr. 'They'll have to now.' They were locked in one of the treatment cubicles. Carr didn't react, even though his head was much clearer now. He was thoroughly suspicious of Joanna. 'Look,' she went on, 'I had to turn you in. I knew Falkman was coming down the corridor. I couldn't possibly have helped you then – it would only have blown my own cover.'

'Keeping it didn't seem to do you much good,' Carr said. 'And why should they kill both of us?'

'Because they found out I'd been reporting to my people. I was careless with a phone-call.'

Carr sat up. 'Who are your people?'

She shook her head. 'It doesn't matter.'

'So why not tell me?'

'Oh, "Need to know".'

'Christ, you've gone very professional all of a sudden. Either that, or it's another big con to get me to talk.'

'No, Mr Carr . . . or may I call you Richard?'

He stared at her. Before he could speak, the door banged open to reveal two of Schaffhauser's goons. Carr hadn't seen them before, as far as he could remember, although one of them seemed vaguely familiar. His memory was still unreliable.

The two were armed, which made Carr smile wryly. He couldn't have handled a play-school hit-man with a catapult. The first man – the one he thought he'd seen before – gestured with his gun for them to move out. Carr mentally christened him Goonybird.

Falkman and the others were still talking when Carr and Joanna were pushed into the office.

'I can soon find out who she's working for,' Bigelow was saying.

'There isn't time, and it's irrelevant,' Falkman said sharply. 'Tie her hands – carefully, so it doesn't leave any marks. Just in case.' Goonybird handed his gun to Falkman and took a roll of bandages from a cupboard.

'Not me?' Carr asked with as much bravado as he could manage.

'You later,' Falkman replied. Goonybird was about to pull Joanna from her chair so he could tie her hands behind her, but Falkman said, 'In front will do. Otherwise it will be difficult getting her into the car.' He turned to Franz Schaffhauser. 'Get me a bottle of whisky – or brandy will do. I'm sure you'll find something.' He didn't conceal his contempt. Franz moistened his dry lips, and left the room.

'Don't tell me we're going to have a drunken driving accident,' Carr said. 'That'd be a bit banal, wouldn't it? What happened to a mugging in the Paris Metro, or a swimming accident in the Adriatic?'

'There's no time for finesse,' Falkman said. 'With a car accident we can kill two birds with one stone, in a manner of speaking.' He seemed rather pleased with his grasp of a colloquialism.

'I thought I was going to be useful to you?'

'You would have been, but not now. I'm afraid you're too much of a risk. Your training has made you a particularly difficult subject, Dr Bigelow tells me, and we don't have time to finish your treatment.' He threw Carr's homemade picklock on to the desk. 'It's a pity. You're most resourceful.'

Carr looked at Bigelow. 'Do you go along with all this?'

'I only need a little longer with him,' Bigelow said desperately. 'Jesus, we don't have to . . . ' His voice trailed away.

'And you,' Carr said, turning to Schaffhauser. 'I thought you were the great bulwark against the tide of communism? So what're you doing working for the KGB?'

Falkman gave the faintest flicker of surprise, but he was far too intelligent and self-controlled to try silencing Carr.

Schaffhauser smiled thinly. 'It's really quite . . . ' He hesitated, momentarily lost for the English word. 'It is really too infantile to try to divide us like this.'

'That man in the chauffeur-driven Mercedes a fortnight ago. Short raincoat and tight hat. Who was he?'

Schaffhauser glanced at Falkman before answering. 'He represents a group of German and Swiss industrialists sympathetic to our aims.'

'He's Arcadius Tchalenko of the KGB's Viktor Section. Isn't that so, Falkman?'

Falkman shrugged. 'If you say so.' Goonybird had finished tying up Joanna and retrieved his gun from Falkman. Joanna said nothing, but watched and listened intently.

'And what about Falkman here? Does he run things – or do you?'

Falkman answered. 'Dr Schaffhauser is in charge here. I am from the central organisation of our movement,' he said smoothly.

Carr managed a smile. 'They've got you, Schaffhauser. The KGB have taken you over and you don't know it. I bet Tchalenko's your paymaster, isn't he?' Schaffhauser looked at Falkman again. There was the merest shadow of uncertainty in his expression, but Falkman was completely unruffled.

The door opened and Franz entered. He held a brandy bottle in his hand. It wasn't quite full, and the smell of brandy was heavy on his breath.

'Right,' said Falkman. 'Now get Helmut and Egon.' Franz stood awkwardly, then went out again. 'What's his car?' Falkman asked, indicating Carr.

'BMW 2800,' Gerd Schaffhauser told him.

'New?'

'About five years old.'

'And hers?'

'MGB. An open two-seater. Nine or ten years old.'

'Eight,' Joanna said, speaking for the first time since entering the room.

'Ideal,' said Falkman. 'A crash will be more believable if she's driving an old car. We can fix that.'

'You're Viktor Section, too, aren't you?' Carr said conversationally. 'You've had a lot of experience at this sort of thing. Class always shows.'

Falkman handed him the brandy. 'You can drink it – or we'll pour it down you. Half the bottle.'

Bigelow rose. He looked pale, and there was a thin film of perspiration on his upper lip.

'Where are you going?' Falkman demanded.

'You don't need me here.'

'The doctor has a sensitive stomach,' Carr said. 'It's okay deforming people's minds or driving them mad in the interests of pure science, but murder upsets him. Well, Doctor, as your countrymen say: this is the bottom line. Murder.'

'Drink the brandy and shut up. Or I'll have the girl gasping for breath for half an hour – then you'll have your turn,' Falkman warned him. Carr took the bottle. He felt the weight of it in his hand, then looked down the barrels of two large-calibre automatics pointing steadily at him. He didn't recognise the guns, but it was no time for detail. 'We'd prefer not to shoot, but if we have to . . . ' Falkman added. Carr took a mouthful of brandy, and coughed.

The door opened. Egon and Helmut entered – two men with large, round heads and flat Slavic faces. Carr vaguely remembered having seen them about the place. Franz followed them into the room. Even the hired help took precedence over him.

At a closer look the two men reminded Carr of Berti, the silent man who had driven the Volkswagen in Vienna. Somewhere the KGB must have a mould for stamping them out.

Deep in Carr's memory something was struggling to the

surface, but he couldn't make the connections to bridge the image into focus.

The two men positioned themselves on either side of the door like a pair of stone dogs. Franz Schaffhauser took a couple of hesitant paces. 'Falkman,' he began uneasily.

'Not now.' It was as unarguable as a slammed shut door.

While Carr and Joanna took alternate drinks from the bottle, Falkman began to organise the operation for disposing of them.

Three cars would set off from the *Clés d'Or*: Joanna's MG, Carr's BMW, and Schaffhauser's Mercedes. Goonybird – whose real name was Karel, as it transpired – would drive the MG; Helmut would drive the BMW with Carr beside him in the front seat, and Joanna in the back with Egon beside her. Falkman would drive the Mercedes himself, with the fourth heavy, Willi, accompanying him.

Falkman gave his orders in German. 'About six kilometres along the Col de la Pelle road is one of those panoramic viewing points for tourists, just after the Chemin des Pélerins turn-off.'

'I know it,' said Karel. His German was oddly accented. 'There's a sheer drop of about five hundred metres.' He turned and grinned at Carr, who didn't feel like grinning back.

'Stop there, and wait for the other cars to join you,' Falkman went on. 'We need to keep a minute or two between each vehicle just in case there's anybody about . . .' He glanced at his watch. 'Ten to one. Hardly likely at this time of night, but no need to draw attention to ourselves.'

The brandy was beginning to work on Carr. He had an insane desire to sing 'You take the high road . . .' He concentrated with difficulty on what Falkman was saying. When all the cars had reached the viewing point, Karel would take the BMW further along the mountain road, then stall it on a straight stretch so that it blocked both sides of the road. With the BMW's headlights and hazard warning lights on, he would have the bonnet up and be fiddling with the engine, to delay anyone coming along the road from the direction of the Col de la Pelle. Willi would take the

Mercedes back the way they had come and do the same thing to stop anyone coming the opposite way. Finally, Falkman, Egon and Helmut would put Joanna and Carr in the MG, and send them over the edge. When Willi heard the crash he would bring the Mercedes up to collect Falkman and the others. All very neat and tidy.

While Falkman was giving the operational orders none of the doctors said anything, but at last Gerd Schaffhauser made another effort to re-establish some sort of authority. 'Do we have to go through all this? Can't we deal with them here, and then – '

Falkman interrupted. 'You should know better than that, Doctor. The most inexperienced pathologist could tell that the injuries caused by tumbling over the cliff had been caused *after* death. And the post-mortems on two people of their importance will be most thorough.'

Hearing this discussion of his imminent post-mortem should have made Carr feel at least uneasy, but he couldn't bring himself to worry particularly. He gave a quiet burp that had a strong flavour of Rémy Martin, and tried to think of something clever to say.

Schaffhauser pre-empted him. 'I didn't mean that, of course.' Even Carr could tell he was lying. 'I meant that it might save trouble if they were unconscious before – '

'Would *you* like to carry them out to the car, then have to transfer them to the woman's car in a hurry?'

For the first time since he had met Schaffhauser, Carr saw him as a bad second in the pecking order. Falkman's command was absolute. Franz Schaffhauser and Bigelow kept quiet.

'But suppose I don't care to walk out to the car – and make a lot of noise about being taken?' Carr asked, articulating his words with great care.

'That would be foolish. If you make difficulties at any time, Egon will do some very, very unpleasant things to the woman.' Egon looked as if he would like the chance to prove it. 'As I said, we would prefer not to shoot you, but shall if we have to. Face it: you're going to die. Whether it's an easy death or a hard one is entirely up to you.' It wasn't much of a choice.

Falkman was thinking hard – trying to make sure he hadn't overlooked anything. Abruptly he turned to Karel. 'Get on the phone. Find out who's on the main gate tonight. We don't want anyone telling the police that the MG left with two other cars at one o'clock in the morning. If it's one of our people, warn him what's happening. If he's not, Dr Schaffhauser will arrange for him to be replaced. I'll tell him who to send up there.'

Gerd Schaffhauser swallowed, but said nothing. Drunk as Carr was, he received the clear impression that this was the first Dr Schaffhauser knew about 'our people' in the *Clés d'Or.* All at once, Schaffhauser was looking his age. Franz stared at his father as if he had never seen him before. Bigelow was seated, staring at the ceiling, isolated in a temporary world of his own.

'Now,' Falkman told Helmut, 'go to his room and bring a full set of clothing for him. Don't forget a handkerchief, money . . . anything personal he has.'

At last they were ready to set off, with Carr properly dressed and his wrists tied with bandages again. His head was hurting like hell, but the whisper of an idea was trying to make itself heard above the hammering in his skull.

Willi lit a cigarette, and Carr said, 'Can I have one?' Falkman looked at him in surprise. 'I thought you'd never smoked.'

'I was trying to give it up, but I don't think it's going to harm my health any more.'

Willi pulled one cigarette up from the pack, and held it out. Carr took the pack with his tied hands, slipped the end of a cigarette into his mouth and pulled the pack away from it. Then he put the packet in his top pocket. Willi looked as if he was going to say something, but changed his mind. He held out his own cigarette for Carr to light his. Carr tried not to cough as he puffed on his first cigarette since a childhood attempt had made him sick behind the school sports pavilion. He was fourteen at the time.

Franz Schaffhauser opened the big gates in front of the

South Wing. Dimly Carr guessed that the four men in the convoy, and another on the main gate, meant that Falkman was running short of 'our people' he could completely trust at the *Clés d'Or*.

Showing no lights, the cars rolled slowly past the dark, sleeping château. Carr looked up at the windows, but blindly they took no interest in the small procession. By the time the sound of the wheels on the gravel could wake anybody curious enough to look out, the cars would be well out of sight down the long curving driveway.

Ill as Carr had felt before, it wasn't nearly as bad as when the fresh air hit him. Falkman had to help him into the front of the BMW. Behind him Egon held the gun in his right hand, pointing it directly at Carr's back. His left arm was around Joanna's neck, with his forearm across her throat. The powerful forearm could throttle her unconscious in seconds; the banana-fingered hand could do all sorts of unpleasant things to her face.

Helmut steered the automatic-transmission BMW with his left hand. His right held a gun, which he rested on his thigh.

Carr was very aware of his Magnum .44 under Helmut's seat, but for all the good it could do him it might as well be in the boot, gift-wrapped.

When they neared the main gates, Carr moved to open his window.

'Don't!' snapped Egon, and Carr felt the gun pressing into the back of his neck. Joanna gave a half-strangled gurgle as Egon's forearm pressed into her throat. Helmut's gun was also now pointing directly at Carr.

'I was only going to throw out my cigarette end,' Carr said. His words were blurred.

'Put it in the ashtray. And don't try anything again . . . '

Joanna cried out sharply with pain as Egon underlined his words by squeezing her face cruelly. It was obvious he enjoyed it.

Carr seemed unaware of what was going on. 'Bloody hell. I feel awful,' he said, without exaggeration. 'My head's splitting.'

Egon was the conversationalist and humorist of the pair. In bad French he said, 'We'll soon put an end to that for you.' He chuckled.

Once outside the main gates, Helmut let the MG pull away from them up the winding road. It was soon out of direct sight, but its position was easy to judge by the reflection of its headlights on the tall pine trees, and occasionally the rear lights winked redly through the trees before disappearing again as the road took another turn. Falkman's Mercedes fell behind, its headlamps sending sudden shafts of light at them from time to time.

Carr was having a bad time trying to stay awake, let alone concentrate. The massive quantity of brandy taken on an empty stomach almost completely stifled even the fear of imminent death. Carr was only jabbed out of his semi-comatose state when Egon asked Helmut, *'Wie weit noch?'* 'How much further?'

'Etwa noch ein Kilometer. Wir sind bald fertig und dann können wir abhauen.' 'About a kilometre. We'll soon be finished and then we can push off home.'

Carr didn't have a great deal of enthusiasm for his half-plan – it was no more than that – but it was better than nothing. He breathed deeply, then took the first step.

'I'm going to have another cigarette,' he said, with the drunk's air of coming to a major decision. Slowly, very slowly he moved his tied hands to his top pocket and pulled out Willi's cigarettes. 'Do you want one?' he asked Helmut. The other man shook his head.

With great care Carr turned round in his seat to face Joanna. 'You'll have one, won't you?' he asked. She was almost asleep from the effect of the brandy. He guessed that the thought of a cigarette would be almost enough to make her throw up. Before she could refuse he added, '*Do* have one.'

For God's sake have one! he mentally screamed at her. He broke into a sudden cold sweat at the thought that his plan would be killed because she refused.

She looked at him dully, but something got through to

her because she said automatically, 'All right.' He held out the packet and she took one.

Carr turned to face forward again, saying, 'I'll give you a light.' He pushed the cigar-lighter in the dashboard into its socket, still moving with careful deliberation. The sweat was running down his face by the time the lighter popped out of its holder, ready for use.

He took hold of it, and turned back again. His mind was not on the lighter or the cigarette but on the next moves he had to make. As fast as his sluggish brain could manage he mentally rehearsed them over and over like a competition diver thinking about his next complicated dive.

Carr held out the lighter for Joanna, but before she took hold of it, he dropped it, and it fell into the well between the front and back seats.

Egon stiffened, and Carr was terrified that he might fire as a reflex action. But he was smart . . . *too damned smart for his own good.* 'If you think I'm going to bend down and pick that up . . . ' Egon said with a sneer.

Joanna looked at him, then at Carr. She guessed he was planning something, and hoped she was saying the right thing. 'I'll get it.' She bent down to find it.

Carr turned to face forward once more. He experienced a weird narcotised sensation, as if time had suddenly slipped a gear. Everything seemed to go into slow motion: his own movements and those of everyone else, as well as the car itself, seemed dream-like, as slow as if they were all moving under water. With his bound hands he grabbed hold of the seat-belt up by his left shoulder, at the same time sliding down in his seat. He put his left foot up against the dashboard. With his right he swung at the gear-lever.

And missed.

Helmut was turning to look at him . . . his right hand with the gun coming up an inch or two . . . when Carr jabbed at the gear-lever with his right foot again. With the strength of desperation he crunched it from Drive through Neutral and Reverse into Park.

The noise from the transmission and engine was quite

awful: the death scream of some metal monster. The car stopped as if it had run into train buffers. Although he was prepared for the shock, Carr's arms were nearly wrenched from their sockets by the BMW's shattering deceleration, and his left leg was bent double despite the strength he exerted to keep it straight. He felt Joanna thrust against the back of his seat as if she'd taken a running jump.

Beside him Helmut described a graceful trajectory from his seat to smash against the laminated windscreen. The movement seemed slow to Carr's distorted senses, but the force of it made the tough glass balloon out – Helmut's head was twisted at a freakish angle. On his upward journey his thighs caught under the dashboard and the two biggest bones in his body snapped like sticks of celery. He bounced back to his seat, his face mashed in a fraction of a second. Before Helmut could fall back into his seat, Egon – flying up and forward even faster than Helmut, because he had no steering-wheel to hold on to – smashed his face into a bloody pulp against the back of Helmut's head. This sickening collision was not enough to absorb all the momentum of Egon's forward movement. He cannoned off Helmut up to the roof of the car, sliding along it and down against the join between the roof and the windscreen. Once again the glass bulged out, briefly outlining the shape of Egon's head before its elasticity sent him crashing back to lie across Helmut's slack body.

Somehow Carr saw all this, or was aware of it in some extrasensory fashion, as he fought to keep himself in his seat. But no human muscles could overcome the enormous forces exerted on his body. He felt himself rising up out of his seat . . . then he knew no more.

The first thing Carr became conscious of was a strange, irregular bubbling sound like a distant motor-boat. He slowly determined that he was in the passenger seat of the BMW and that his forehead was hurting like hell. Beside him Egon still lay across Helmut, who was doubled forward over the steering-wheel. It was Helmut who was making the peculiar noise as blood bubbled in his throat from the shapeless mass that had been his nose.

Something ran into Carr's eye and caused it to smart. He tried to raise his right hand, but it wouldn't move, and he felt at the same time an agonising pain in his left shoulder. At last he remembered that his hands were bound together, and raised both to his eye and wiped it with the back of one hand. It came away bloody. He'd hit his head on something.

Carr was tempted to shake his head to get rid of the pain and muzziness. Instead he squeezed his eyes tight shut for a moment, then opened them wide and took a couple of deep breaths. It did nothing for the ache, but unaccountably he felt very much less drunk; his thought processes seemed much clearer.

Almost at once he remembered his gun under the driving seat, but the two unconscious men blocked his way to it from the passenger side. He fumbled open the door, and pain knifed his shoulder again. He clambered out and fell over, cutting his knee on a sharp stone. As he got up a light flashed briefly in his face. It was the headlights of a car coming towards him. Karel in the MG coming back to investigate, for a certainty.

Carr staggered round to the other side of the BMW. It had come to rest at an angle of about forty-five degrees to the road. On the right-hand side was the steep wall of the mountain, on the left an unpleasant drop on to rocks below. It wasn't as high as the panoramic viewing-point where the 'accident' was to be staged, but a fall from here would almost certainly be just as fatal.

From the way the lights flashed through the trees Carr could tell that the MG was coming down the winding road towards him at a hell of a speed. Trying to shake the sluggishness out of his limbs, he pulled open the BMW's door.

Helmut's legs, pressed against the front of the seat, blocked the way and there was no way of getting to the gun from the side of the seat. Carr vainly tugged at the man's feet with his bound hands. He was unaware that he was swearing loudly. He paused briefly to scrabble around on the car floor in case either of the men's guns was to be seen, but they had gone God knew where – perhaps out of the open windows. Carr almost cried with frustration.

A brilliant light dazzled him motionless. The MG had rounded the last bend and was heading straight for him. The engine note rose sharply when Karel spotted him and accelerated flat out.

Carr knew he meant to hit him: either crush him against the side of the BMW, or the mountain wall; or knock him off the edge of the road to the rocks below. His only chance was to get back to the other side of the BMW – by racing round it or by scrambling across the bonnet. Carr's brain flashed the message to his muscles: *move!* But before they could respond, something extraordinary happened. For no explicable reason, one infinitesimal charge of electricity leaped between two neurons of his brain and provided the last link in a complicated memory circuit. A series of images flashed into his mind, one of them painfully sharp.

Karel.

Now Carr knew why he looked familiar; where he had seen him before. Only the battering his mind had taken had prevented him from realising earlier.

Karel was the butcher who had slowly tortured Dr Zvalen to death on the film Eli Yelkov had given him.

A great anger swept over Carr – and literally made him shake with rage. It made him act contrary to every dictate of common sense. But Karel didn't have a flexible mind, and almost no imagination. Carr's unpredictable reaction was the first of a quick series of unexpected events which temporarily stunned him.

Instead of trying to move out of danger, which was what Karel expected of him, Carr turned back to the BMW. His fury gave him a surge of abnormal strength. He pulled Helmut's legs away from the front seat, and sent Egon rolling off Helmut on to the passenger seat.

Carr grabbed at the Magnum .44, ripping it from its securing clips. It was the model with the 8.3-inch barrel, the most powerful hand-gun in the world, taking a cartridge also fired from rifles. The gun weighs three and a quarter pounds – a positive advantage when firing the Magnum cartridge with its massive recoil.

It was a gun Carr would not normally attempt to fire one-handed, but having his wrists tied made holding it rather awkward. Still, he was sure he had enough control to fire accurately – and it would have to be accurate. Karel wouldn't be scared by near misses.

Carr cocked the gun as he dragged it clear and swung round to bring it to bear. Karel saw him aiming and crouched low, peering over the top of the bonnet.

When Carr got the sights lined up, the MG was much closer than he'd realised, bearing down on him with frightening speed. Its blazing headlights now made it impossible for him to see Karel.

He knew he'd left it too late. Even if he blew Karel's head off with the first shot, the odds were that the MG would continue straight on its course and squash him like a bug.

Carr aimed exactly midway between the headlights and fired twice.

The first bullet, weighing more than half an ounce, travelling at some 1500 feet per second – *well over 1,000 mph* – and accelerating away from the muzzle, went through the car's radiator as if it was polystyrene, and smashed into the cylinder block of the marvellously complex piece of machinery that is a car engine. The immensely strong but brittle balance of minutely-calculated mechanical thrust and counter-thrust was destroyed in a fraction of a second by a single bullet; and the force that was moving a car weighing nearly a ton at about 60 mph became suddenly a rending, destructive explosion. When the bullet smashed the cylinder block the controlled energy of compressed, burning gases that were driving pistons to send a crankshaft spinning at more than sixty revolutions a second were liberated in a chain-reaction of chaotic violence.

The MG's back wheels locked as the engine ripped itself to pieces, sending the car into a skid before Karel could think of declutching or slamming the gear-lever into neutral. Fortunately for Carr, the MG slid away from the

BMW and towards the sheer drop at the other side of the road. Steam and hot oil sprayed out from under the bonnet, covering the windscreen and temporarily blinding Karel as he sat helplessly while the car went out of control.

The car was already dead by the time the second bullet hammered into it. The bonnet lid came halfway up as the catch was sheared by a flying valve spring, and a series of minor disasters culminated in the oil-filter bursting through the side of the engine compartment like a small shell.

The vehicle came to a stop a couple of feet from the naked edge of the road – and only a few yards from Carr. He ran several staggering steps to it. Karel was sitting with catatonic rigidity, his eyes glazed. His hands were still holding the steering-wheel so hard that the knuckles shone white in the reflected light.

As Carr looked, Karel visibly began to regain physical and mental control. When he saw Carr, his hand moved towards the inside of his jacket. Carr shouted 'No!' and gestured with his gun. Karel stared into the awful muzzle of the Magnum, and froze.

In a strained voice he scarcely recognised as his own, Carr spoke in German: 'This is for Doctor Zvalen.' Karel's eyes widened with the realisation that Carr wasn't quite sane.

Then Carr did something he had never done in his life, something that would haunt him for years. He lowered the gun and shot Karel in the gut. The bullet passed clean through Karel, the seat, the floor of the car and went whining away into the distance.

Carr shot him again. He shot to hurt as well as to kill; he wanted Karel to know that he was dying – and painfully. And Karel did. The second shot was higher. It smashed a rib and the splintering bone did ghastly things to Karel's liver and spleen.

There were two gunshots from behind Carr. There was no whine of bullets, so he knew they had gone nowhere near him. He swung round towards the sound.

The light of the two cars' headlights, reflected by the trees and the mountain wall, distorted shapes and cast strange shadows, so he needed some moments to take in the scene. When at last he had sorted it out, he could hardly believe his eyes. Joanna was a dozen yards down the road, under cover of a tree, firing at a car moving up the road towards them.

He'd completely forgotten about them . . .

Joanna fired again, but the Mercedes came on. She looked unsteady on her feet and was probably missing the target widely. Carr's Magnum now felt as if it weighed a hundred-weight. The savage pain in his left shoulder made him cry out as he forced up the gun to fire.

Don't hit the engine! he told himself. *We need transport.*

Behind the brilliant square headlights, the chromium frame round the windows glinted in a stray beam of light. Carr carefully calculated where to aim for the driver, and fired.

At that moment the Mercedes swerved and Carr knew that he'd missed. He groaned with the agony of his shoulder as he fought to keep the revolver up.

The headlights dipped sharply as heavy braking forced down the car's nose. It squealed to a halt, then with a shriek of smoking tyres it accelerated away in reverse. Carr guessed that the heavy sound of the Magnum – and the fact that he was coming under fire from two sides – was making Falkman think again.

Carr had one cartridge left. He aimed carefully, and knew that this shot was good. The car swung wildly, but instead of crashing, it continued into a perfect 180-degree turn as Falkman slammed on the brakes, helping the nose to swing round, then changed from reverse to bottom gear and stamped on the accelerator, sending the vehicle back the way it had come with another scream of spinning tyres.

Carr stood uncomprehendingly. The car was under perfect control, and to underline the fact he heard Falkman change neatly into second gear. But Carr knew he must have hit Falkman, and hitting someone with a Magnum .44 bullet was an incapacitating shot at the very least. Always. Just before the car went out of sight round a bend,

Carr clearly saw the hole where his bullet had come out at the back of the car dead in line with the driver's seat, at about chest level. It was impossible that Falkman could have escaped being hit.

There was the lighter crack of Joanna's automatic and the Mercedes lurched. She had hit a tyre, but the car kept on down the road, back towards the *Clés d'Or*. Too late Carr understood. Because the Mercedes was a continental model it had the steering-wheel on the left – unlike his own BMW and Joanna's MG. In his dazed state he'd forgotten that. He'd hit Willi in the right-hand passenger seat, not Falkman.

Carr allowed himself to fall back against the BMW, then he sank slowly to the ground as his legs refused to hold him any longer. Black waves of depression flooded over him. He'd failed. Falkman had escaped and was on his way back to the South Wing, where all the vital records of the people who'd been processed could be spirited away or destroyed. Even though the operation was blown, and with it the Schaffhausers and Bigelow, the whole thing could be started up again somewhere else behind a different front.

Joanna was propped up against the tree that had given her cover. Like Carr, she was half sitting, half lying. He was so bone-weary he couldn't worry about her. His own sense of self-preservation began to give way to total apathy as consciousness began to slip away from him. He knew it, but didn't care. He was roused a little by the sound of a vehicle, its engine near maximum revolutions as it shot up the mountain road in low gear towards them.

God! What a stupid bloody mess! Carr thought.

The vehicle stopped by Joanna. Carr now saw that it was a small bus or coach, like a VW minibus but more powerful. Once again he wondered if he was hallucinating, because the man who got out the back seemed huge, the biggest man he'd ever seen. As far as Carr could judge, he was nearly seven feet tall, and broad. He bent over Joanna, then said something to the driver of the bus.

It surged forward to where Carr was sprawling. When it

pulled up, he knew for certain he was hallucinating, because out of the front passenger-seat stepped Eli Yelkov, the senior Mossad officer from London.

He whipped a Beretta automatic from inside his jacket, aimed at Carr and fired twice.

19

The big Mercedes swayed drunkenly down the road towards the *Clés d'Or*, the flat tyre rumbling and thumping on the stony surface of the road. Whenever the car took a bend, the other tyres moaned in sympathy for the one that was being ripped to shreds. It was doing less than 25 mph, but even that was extraordinary in the conditions.

Driving wasn't made any easier for Falkman by Willi's very messy, blood-soaked corpse lurching into him at every bend, despite having his seat-belt on. Falkman found his grisly companion almost more than his nerves could stand.

He tried to recall as much detail as possible of the incident on the road where he had come under fire. How the two prisoners could possibly have overcome experienced men like Karel, Helmut and Egon, killed Willi, and damn near killed Falkman himself, was completely beyond him and more than a little frightening. But his main concern now was to contain the damage.

As far as Falkman knew, the two cars behind him were still serviceable, and the English couple would give chase. Were they working for the same people? he wondered. Abruptly he remembered: when Joanna had phoned her people earlier that evening, it was a local call, which meant that she had contacts nearby. She might even be able to pick up help on her way back to the clinic.

Falkman's one clear idea was to get back before the

others. Once inside the main gate everything would be under control again. He could warn Stefan, the man on the gate, not to let anyone else through. That was his main fear: that the provincial oaf Stefan would open up without question for any familiar cars.

Falkman didn't have much confidence in Bigelow or the Schaffhausers. If only he could screw down the lid at the South Wing, the final damage would be minimal. For a start, the police wouldn't cause trouble at the clinic, with all its highly influential clients. And there was no documentary proof to tie in Helmut, Egon or Karel with the clinic. The English couple certainly wouldn't want to get involved with the police over the shooting – Intelligence people stay clear of the police as earnestly as professional criminals. The mayhem up there on the mountain road would be ascribed to another gangland killing, involving innocent bystanders.

Once safely inside he would go straight to the South Wing and destroy all the records. Without them there was no real proof of the operation, and the processed subjects in England, Germany, France would be quite safe. There were full copies of the records at the KGB's First Chief Directorate in Moscow – copies that Arcadius Tchalenko regularly collected from Franz Schaffhauser, without either of the other two doctors being aware.

Of course, it was a serious setback that the South Wing operation had been blown at last, but that was probably inevitable since the CIA man, Westbrook, had made the first breakthrough. All in all, it could be a lot worse . . . as long as he could get back and destroy the records.

Falkman sharply brought his mind back to his driving. He swore as the steering-wheel slipped through his fingers at a bend and the Mercedes nearly went off the road. It was Willi's blood on the rim of the wheel.

He glanced into the rear mirror again. Still nothing. He was going to make it! Ten minutes, that's all he needed. The only other vehicle he'd seen since was a minibus going in the opposite direction – probably night-shift workers. It had slowed briefly as it passed him, then picked up speed again. He was sure they didn't get a look at Willi; no doubt it was the way the car was swaying that had attracted their attention.

The thought had just come to Falkman that the minibus must have reached the scene of the shooting, when he heard the distant, unmistakable sound of two quick gunshots.

'What the hell was that for?' Carr asked when his ears had stopped ringing. The bullets had gone within inches of his head.

Yelkov gestured behind Carr with the muzzle of his gun. Carr turned. Egon was only inches away from him, a broad-bladed knife in his hand – the sort that is strapped to the forearm for a quick draw. He was glaring venomously at Carr, who drew back in alarm by reflex action. But Egon's fixed expression was the unfocused stare and frozen rictal snarl of death.

'He was going to stick that in your neck,' Yelkov said.

'Jesus. I thought he was dead. Thanks,' Carr added after a moment, knowing how inadequate it sounded. 'What are you doing here, for Christ's sake?' His head was beginning to spin. Yelkov didn't answer. Taking out a big pocket-knife he cut Carr's hands free. He didn't use Egon's knife, so as not to mess up the fingerprints, in case the French police bothered to check it later.

Yelkov produced a hip-flask. 'You want a drink? You look as if you could do with one.'

Carr made a noise something like a laugh. 'That's the last thing. You wouldn't have a cup of black coffee on you, I suppose?'

The enormous man came over to join them. From Carr's point of view, sitting in the roadway, he seemed even bigger than before. Reaction was getting at him, making him quite lightheaded. 'Where are Fay Wray and all the little aero-planes?'

Yelkov understood even if the big man didn't. 'Yes, Daniel?'

'Daniel?' Carr interrupted. 'Pity the poor bleeding lions.'

'Shut up,' Yelkov said without malice.

'Joanna's all right,' Daniel reported, 'but she seems to have been drinking.'

'They made us,' Carr explained. 'It was for a drunken-driving accident. Fatal. Please blow into this bag, sir.'

He pulled himself together, then sat up with a jerk. He tried to struggle to his feet. 'Quick!' he said in a voice that was nearly normal. 'We've got to stop him – Falkman. You must have seen him. He was driving the black Mercedes.'

Yelkov glanced at Daniel. 'You were right – it *was* him. We should have – '

'No. We had to see what had happened to Joanna.'

'Stop the chatter and let's get moving,' Carr said. 'I'll explain on the way. We've got to catch Falkman before he reaches the clinic.'

Yelkov took Carr's arm and helped him into the coach, while Daniel sprinted back to where Joanna sat. As Carr climbed in he noticed for the first time a number of men sitting quietly in the back of the minibus. They had Uzi machine-guns across their knees, weapons as efficient as they are stark and ugly. The men reminded him of the patient, expressionless policemen who wait in armoured coaches parked unobtrusively near anywhere riots threaten in any half-a-dozen countries.

When the minibus reached Daniel, he handed up Joanna as easily as if she was a packet of sandwiches. She was almost unconscious.

'Keep your lights out,' Yelkov instructed the driver as the coach plunged wildly down the mountain road in a hair-raising drive that made Carr suspect the man at the wheel was a Tel Aviv taxi-driver. Fighting back an almost overwhelming desire to be sick all the way, Carr proceeded to give a comprehensive, but badly disjointed account of the situation.

Yelkov listened in total silence, then merely said, 'Well, already.'

Falkman glanced in the mirror. He'd stopped wondering about the shots behind him. The main thing was that there were no headlights behind him . . . but something attracted his attention. He looked again. There was a short red glow . . . and again. It mystified him until he identified it as a car's brake lights coming on. So they *were* after him! Anyone following without lights was no simple tourist. He risked driving a little faster, just a very little, taking the car to the very edge of becoming uncontrollable.

He wished now that he'd brought a gun with him, but he was always very careful about carrying arms in a foreign country; and one hardly seemed necessary with four armed KGB employees in the party. There was always Willi's gun if he could face up to rummaging in the clothes of that gory body. On second thoughts he'd be better off concentrating on flight rather than on fighting a rearguard gun battle against heavy odds.

Carr realised now that Yelkov's stage Jewish act was usually put on to conceal a strong emotion but, before he could continue, the brackish-water taste in his mouth overwhelmed him and he was violently sick out of the window. Joanna was too ill to take any notice, but the others behaved as if it was the most natural thing in the world for someone to be sick out of the window while a minibus hurtled headlong down a mountain road without lights.

When the last misery of empty retching was over, Carr felt as weak as a newly-hatched sparrow. 'Now forget the chicken-soup dialogue and tell me what you're doing here,' he said bad-temperedly.

'We've had the *Clés d'Or* under observation for weeks, for reasons of our own, photographing everyone we could who came here. Unfortunately for us, some people were sneaked in pretty secretively at night. When you turned up we wondered what your involvement was.'

'Do any of my people in London know about this?'

'We hope nobody anywhere knows anything. As I was saying, when you turned up Joanna bugged your room, but then you disappeared. Tonight we heard Helmut and the other fellow – '

'Willi.'

'We heard them getting the clothes out of your room, and

talking about taking you both out to dispose of you. By the time we saw the cars leave the clinic, we were ready to follow. We knew you and Joanna were in the BMW – '

'How?'

'Elimination. One person in the MG, two men in the Mercedes. So we concentrated on the other car.'

'I think that's him up ahead,' the driver observed in Ukrainian-accented Russian.

'Can you catch him before he gets to the gates?'

'I doubt it, in this,' the driver told him. 'And those gates would stop a tank.'

'We've got to get him,' Yelkov said. Carr naturally assumed he meant Falkman, until Yelkov added, 'After all this has happened, if we don't take him tonight it'll all go wrong and we'll lose him again.' He was very worried.

And it dawned on Carr that he still didn't know what Yelkov and his gang were doing at the *Clés d'Or.*

The Mercedes careened up to the gates and came to a halt in a spray of gravel. Falkman pressed the horn urgently. Stefan emerged cautiously from the small lodge like a tortoise head out of its shell.

'Quick, you bloody idiot!' Falkman shouted. 'Open the gates!' Surprised and rather sleepy, Stefan fumbled with the key. Although he wasted only ten seconds, to Falkman each seemed a minute. So far his only thought had been to get back and destroy the records, but now he was beginning to be concerned about his own position and the inevitable enquiry at Dzerzhinsky Square – though 'enquiry' was hardly the word to describe the sort of post-mortem that would follow this shambles. The investigations at No. 2 were always conducted by stone-faced senior officers of unlimited patience who asked the same questions over and over again, then minutely scrutinised and compared all the answers. And then they started from the beginning again. It didn't help the witnesses' peace of mind to know that one didn't have to go out into the street to get to the Lubianka Prison. Those boards of enquiry could collar St Francis of Assisi on a cruelty-to-animals charge.

Stefan dragged open the gates.

'Phone the South Wing and tell them to open up for me,' Falkman said urgently. 'And let no one in here, you understand? No one.'

'But – '

'No one.'

When there was still a quarter of a mile to go, Yelkov's driver had finally decided they couldn't reach the clinic before Falkman was inside and the gates locked.

Yelkov ordered the driver to pull up close to the clinic wall, just out of sight of the entrance, round a slight bend. Daniel got out and climbed on to the roof of the vehicle.

'Can you see over?' Yelkov asked.

'He could see over the Great Wall of China,' Carr said. He was still feeling bad-tempered, which was about all he had the strength for.

'Yes. There's no one about.'

'I think I noticed tripwires about a foot high, near the wall,' Carr remembered.

'How far from the wall?'

'Three, four feet. I've heard dogs, too.'

'I see. Thanks.' Daniel sounded unimpressed.

'We'll drive up to the gates and make a fuss,' Yelkov said. 'That'll bring the guard out from the lodge. He probably has an alarm-bell or phone inside.' Daniel nodded, stepped smartly on to the top of the wall, then launched himself off in a flying leap that looked like a parachute-jump without a parachute. He landed very quietly.

Half a minute later the minibus drove the couple of hundred yards along to the front gate. The driver blew the horn, and Yelkov walked to the side of the gates nearest to where Daniel had gone over.

'Ouvrez!' he shouted. 'Open up!'

'Nous avons un blessé grave qui a besoin de soins urgents' 'We've a badly injured man who needs immediate treatment.'

Stefan straggled out of the lodge. He carried a shotgun

in the crook of his arm. Yelkov repeated the request to open up.

Stefan took a few paces towards the gate. 'No admittance,' he said flatly.

'What's that? This is a clinic, isn't it?' He paused. 'I can't hear you.'

Stefan took two more steps towards the gates, saying, 'You can't come – ' when he stopped in mid-sentence. One massive hand clamped round his throat from behind and lifted him a foot off the ground; the other hand took the shotgun from him with ridiculous ease before he was set on the ground again, still held as if set in concrete.

Stefan was brave, or stupid – the two are often indistinguishable. He fractionally shook his head and made a sort of gurgling negative sound. Daniel took his head between both hands, lifted him off the ground and shook him like a set of sleigh-bells. Stefan frantically pointed to his pocket.

'Christ,' Carr said to Yelkov. 'You got any more like him?'

'A few,' Yelkov said.

'I suppose you bring them out for special occasions – like the good tablecloth and silver.'

Daniel took the key and most of the pocket with it, put Stefan down, hit him on the side of the head, and caught him as his knees folded. As soon as Daniel opened the gate he put Stefan out of the way in the back of the coach where nobody could trip over him in the dark. The men in the bus laid the unconscious man on the floor between the seats, then put their feet on him so he wouldn't roll around and get bruised. Or something.

The driver was able to make good speed without lights because the expensive white gravel of the driveway stood out against the darker grass and trees lining it. When the minibus slid round the first bend, Yelkov said with rare excitement, 'There he is!'

Falkman, thinking himself safe once through the main gates, had let his speed drop and wasn't keeping a close watch in his mirror.

Franz Schaffhauser was standing by the open gate in the South Wing wall when the Mercedes and the rapidly overtaking minibus came into view. Franz gestured vigorously behind Falkman, who had no idea what he was trying to signal.

Then Franz did something totally unexpected, because it was completely out of character – he took the first of two vital initiatives he was to take that night. He left the gate and ran back to the South Wing, wheezing and coughing, his face suffused and his eyes bulging. If any of the legitimate patients had seen him they would have asked for their money back. Almost too late, Falkman suspected something and looked into his mirror. The Mercedes swayed into an incipient skid as he accelerated hard, and he had to take off some of the power. He cursed Franz at the top of his voice for typical lack of courage.

'You cowardly fat pig!' he screamed. 'You could have shut the gates on them!' He was being unfair: it would have been impossible.

Falkman was resourceful. He manoeuvred the Mercedes so that it skidded sideways across the entrance to the building, effectively blocking it. The car hit one of the door pillars with jolting force that made his neck ache.

The dead Willi rolled in his seat, and when the belt checked this movement, his arms swung out as if to grab Falkman.

Falkman panicked as he felt himself being held tight round the chest. He shouted as he tried to pull away from Willi's unremitting grip. Somehow he forced himself to look at the gruesome corpse that would not let him go. But now the remains of Willi were lying back in the seat, and Falkman could see that it was his own forgotten seat-belt that was holding him back. He released it, but now had the problem of getting out of the car, for the doors were jammed hard up against the building.

Falkman smashed the window to get out, careless of the glass. It was hard to tell which was his own blood, and which was Willi's.

When Franz Schaffhauser ran into the entrance hall, he

was already almost done for. He had just enough breath left to gasp with relief when he found the lift where he had left it – on the ground floor with the doors open. He half fell inside, and punched the top button. The steel doors slid together just as the blood-streaked Falkman burst into the hallway. Still uncomprehending of Franz's motives, he hammered on the doors in frustration before racing to the stairs.

The minibus came up behind the Mercedes and gave it a massive nudge with its powerful bumper, but this failed to dislodge it from the entrance. The car was not squarely alongside the building but inclined towards it with the near-side front wheel caught inside the door pillar. Pushing the car forward only jammed it tighter.

Removing Willi from the passenger seat and climbing through the driver's window one at a time would take far too long. Daniel ran to the front of the Mercedes and tried to push it back. His face slowly turned red, and veins stood out on his forehead like small ropes. Carr was afraid that something would burst.

The Mercedes gave a heave like a death throe, and moved back suddenly with a metallic screech. Daniel went round to the front wheel and dragged the car's nose sideways, clear of the wall, leaving two curved black scars of earth in the gravel.

The driver of the minibus was just about to send it forward to push the Mercedes free when Carr, trying to get out of his seat to help in some way, momentarily collapsed and fell half across him. The driver had to lift him, then prop him back up into his seat. Carr thickly murmured apologies.

Seconds later – precious, lost seconds – the minibus hit the Mercedes again to send it rolling forward, clear of the doorway.

Falkman was halfway up the stairs when Yelkov, with Daniel and two of the silent men from the back of the coach, hurtled into the building, followed more slowly by Carr. As

Yelkov looked at the strip indicator over the lift door, it flashed 1. He jabbed the call button twice with the muzzle of the Beretta in his hand, breaking it, but it didn't stop the lift. The indicator went on to 2, the last figure on the strip.

Carr was puzzled. He knew there were three floors. It took a moment for him to think of the SID's own headquarters in the Kensington house, and of the lift that stopped short of the top floor.

'Third floor!' he called out. 'There's another floor. End of the funny corridor, on the right.'

'Funny' would have to do. He was in no condition for pedantry. His head was swimming simply from the effort of running the few yards from the coach into the building.

Yelkov's men rushed for the stairs, Daniel in the lead. Running up three flights of stairs – even walking quickly – was out of the question for Carr. He looked at the broken lift button, and prodded into the hole with the end of a pencil. The lift whirred into life and started to descend.

On the stairs there developed a wild handicap race that would have been ludicrous had it not been in such deadly earnest, and the issues so enormous. In front Franz Schaffhauser was lumbering up the last flight, wheezing horribly and looking on the verge of a cardiac arrest. Behind him chased Falkman, strong and fit, spurred on by the thought of what would happen to him in Moscow if anyone else got hold of those records. At the head of the group of pursuers was the terrifying Daniel, whose speed up the stairs was unbelievable. Behind him raced the two silent men, and then Yelkov.

On the ground floor the lift doors opened and Carr entered. By the time he reached the second floor the surrealist chase had gone past him. He didn't give a fourpenny sod for who had won, but he was curious to discover what Yelkov was really up to.

At the second-floor landing a door was open on to the stairs going up. The snap-to lock had been practically ripped off, and the woodwork by the hasp had splintered. The door had a sign in three languages: 'No Entry. Staff Only'. Carr supposed it didn't have a language Daniel liked.

Before Carr took the stairs he pushed the splintered wood back into place and closed the door behind him. All the running about was bound to make someone curious eventually. There was no point in drawing attention to where the action was.

As Carr got to the top of the stairs at the third floor one of the quiet men suddenly appeared, covering him with his Uzi machine-gun. Yelkov, of course, had secured his rear and was letting no one in or out of the third floor he didn't want to. Carr smiled weakly as the man waved him on with a minimal jerk of the gun.

The corridor with the distorted perspective was deserted, but Carr could hear a buzz of conversation at the far end. It didn't sound very frantic. He was beset by strange memories of things half seen and half remembered. *It still affects me, after all this time,* he thought, then recalled that 'all this time' was only since earlier that evening.

Although a little while ago he had been desperate to secure the records, now he felt suddenly apathetic. He paused to get his breath back and let his heart quieten. Then he continued on to the office. Not only was the lock broken, but the door was torn off the top two hinges and tilted precariously into the room, held only by the bottom one.

He studied it, then said to Daniel, 'I bet you ate up all your spinach when you were a child.'

Daniel didn't bother to look at Carr, who had the feeling he didn't care much for his sense of humour.

Carr quickly absorbed the scene. Yelkov, Daniel and the other silent type stood on one side of the room, all holding guns and pointing them in the general direction of the Schaffhausers and Falkman who stood on the other side. Daniel's gun, also a 9 mm Beretta, looked ludicrously small in his gigantic hand, and much less dangerous than the hand itself.

The situation had an air of banality about it – much of life's high drama frequently does – yet beneath the surface there was a sense of change, of a shift of emphasis in relationships.

Franz still hadn't recovered his breath, but despite his blotchy face he looked unexpectedly composed and pleased with himself. No, more than that: he looked content. Gerd was seated, and although he wore his usual dominating expression, it lacked the former total authority. Falkman, the bounding, detergent-white, super-efficient, self-controlled operative was a mess. His clothes were dirty and torn, his face and hands grotesque with his own and Willi's blood through which rivulets of sweat had made pale streaks. He had the stricken look of an undefeated champion who'd just got up from the first knockdown in his career, and knew he was facing more. The events of the past hour had made Falkman painfully aware of limitations he hadn't known, and the awakening shocked him badly.

Yet there was something more to the strangeness of the atmosphere than that. Carr was sure he wasn't being fanciful: there was an unspoken, curious relationship between the two sides – an indescribable sort of common bond between these two most dissimilar and opposing groups, almost a complicity.

There was also something tangible in the atmosphere: the faint, acrid odour of burned plastic. He glanced at the incinerator. A trace of pale vapour still rose from the side of its closed lid. A couple of yards away the safe door was wide open.

'We were too late,' Yelkov said.

Carr took the news stoically. 'Have you looked in the safe?'

'Nothing. No names, no proof, nothing. They burned it all.'

Yelkov's admission of their failure recharged Gerd Schaffhauser's self-confidence.

In his best language-record English he said with almost total conviction, 'What is the meaning of this outrageous intrusion into a clinic where the sick are treated?'

Carr was forced to admit that theoretically Schaffhauser's position was unassailable.

To begin with, the *Clés d'Or* clinic would have some

powerful friends in the French Establishment, besides those who had been through the South Wing. More important, there was no evidence on which the French police would arrest Schaffhauser. In order to preserve their cover Carr and Joanna couldn't testify about the attempt to kill them. Both of them were Intelligence agents of foreign powers; and the reputable Doctors Schaffhauser and Bigelow would certify that Carr was being treated for incipient paranoid schizophrenia, while Joanna was under notice for heavy drinking or something. On the other hand, there would be a queue of the social, political and financial aristocracy jostling to get into the witness-box and give Schaffhauser a good character.

Even the DST – *Direction de la Surveillance du Territoire*, roughly the French anti-espionage service equivalent to MI5 – couldn't scrape up a case against Schaffhauser for any sort of Intelligence activity, anti-French or otherwise.

The shootings on the mountain road were nothing to do with anyone at the *Clés d'Or* – try to prove otherwise. It was a simple hold-up, and Falkman had escaped by the skin of his teeth.

In fact the ones most likely to wind up in a nasty French nick were Yelkov and his lot. Carr was feeling sick again. He sat heavily into an armchair and held his head in his hands. Unaccountably he slipped off his bracelet watch that Willi had put on his wrist and laid it on the desk.

Gerd Schaffhauser had brightened as rapidly as an addict with a fresh armful of high-grade stuff. 'I suggest you put down your guns,' he said, although he must have realised that was a little optimistic. 'Any moment now my guards will be here.'

The phone rang.

'Ah,' he said.

After Yelkov's small commando had rushed into the South Wing the two men left in the coach had quickly closed the nearby gates, shutting off any view of their vehicle. However, the main gates on to the road had been left open. One of the routine guards had found them unlocked, and immediately looked round for Stefan. When he could find no trace of him, the guard had called his two colleagues on their walkie-talkies.

Another guard reported seeing two cars heading into the South Wing area, but he hadn't taken much notice when he saw the gates were opened by Dr Franz Schaffhauser. He assumed the second vehicle was an ambulance. They were all used to ambulances arriving at strange times of the night; and there were still lights burning on the top floor of the Wing.

'Better make sure, though,' decided the first man. 'I'll ring the office there.'

'Answer it,' Yelkov said to Gerd Schaffhauser. 'Tell them everything's all right. If you give them the least indication anything's up, I'll blow your head off.'

Gone was all Yelkov's folksiness and stage Jewishness. Carr could see why this baldheaded old-age pensioner could command the respect and obedience of his commandos. He was as unemotional and professional a warrior as the gladiator who won his freedom from the arena and became a centurion. He scared the hell out of Carr.

The phone rang again.

Schaffhauser tried to bluff it out a moment longer. 'What good would it do?' he asked.

Yelkov answered him in German. '*Es würde mir das grösste Vergnügen machen und würde dem Staat die Unkosten eines öffentlichen Prozesses und dich am Leben erhalten ersparen*' (It would give me the greatest personal pleasure and save my country the expense of a public trial and keeping you alive afterwards.) Then he added, 'so you'd better answer it, Dr Erhardt Roeder.'

It took Carr a moment to place the name. *Roeder*! Of course! The doctor who'd been at Blestau Concentration Camp, and who Yelkov had asked him to look up in the SIS computer records. So this was Yelkov's operation: snatch Roeder – like Eichmann from Argentine – and take him to Israel to be tried for his war crimes.

The effect of the name on Schaffhauser was almost unbelievably dramatic. He was too shocked to deny it. In seconds his face lost its colour as rapidly as if he'd suffered a massive physical injury. His mouth opened and shut as he gasped for air like a stranded fish. *'Ich hab' nie was getan . . . Ich hab' nie was getan . . . Es wurde befehlt'* 'I never did anything . . . I never did anything . . . There were orders . . .'

Yelkov swore. He knew he'd made a bad mistake. Gerd Schaffhauser was incapable of answering the phone.

Falkman was unmoved by the revelation, and Carr felt fairly certain that he already knew that Schaffhauser was Roeder.

Franz, however, was staring at his father with an expression of disbelief, as if he had never seen him before. In a way it was true that he didn't really know him. Now fat, useless, apprehensive, indeterminate Franz looked at his father, and at last began to understand him – and to understand himself.

Thc phonc rang oncc morc.

'I'll answer it,' Franz said, sounding completely composed.

Yelkov studied him, staring at him as if he was trying to see inside his skull and examine his thoughts. Unexpectedly, it was Falkman who spoke.

'No!' he shouted.

Franz ignored him, and picked up the phone. Yelkov's gun was still at Gerd's head, but the threat was unnecessary.

'Dr Schaffhauser . . . Yes, Dr Schaffhauser Junior . . . Stefan is here with us. We had two special private patients come in this evening. They were a little troublesome and Stefan gave us a hand. The people who brought the patients will be leaving soon . . . No, you did quite right to telephone. Goodnight.' He hung up.

'You fool.' Falkman almost spat out the words. 'You cowardly, stupid fool.' Franz turned his back.

Falkman shrugged and turned to Yelkov. 'All right, but now what?' There was a faint but quite perceptive change in Falkman's attitude. The game was over. No more going through the motions, no more pretence: the professionals all recognised each other for what they were. 'You've got him,' Falkman said, indicating the silent Gerd Schaffhauser. 'But that's all you do have. No names of the people who have been through here. Nothing.'

'He'll tell us.'

Falkman shook his head. 'Could you trust him to tell you the truth? Besides, he wouldn't dare. He wouldn't be safe: not even in an Israeli jail.' At that Gerd looked up. 'And you can't do anything to him to make him talk if you're going to put him on public trial.' Falkman turned towards Franz. 'Him – he knows nothing. We didn't trust him with anything important.'

'There's you,' Yelkov said. 'You know all the names.'

Falkman was suddenly wary. 'You wouldn't get them out of me.'

'We could try.'

Falkman shook his head. 'You know it would cause too much trouble if you took me.'

They all knew this was true, that the relationship between Intelligence and counter-Intelligence services in foreign countries was a delicately balanced affair. Senior officers knew each other well, met officially and socially, enemies even co-operated in certain circumstances. If an agent was caught while getting or passing secret information, then he was declared *persona non grata* if he had diplomatic immunity, or arrested if he didn't. This was all well within the unwritten but universally accepted rules of the game. Kidnapping and taking an agent out of a third country for what is euphemistically called 'deep interrogation' would most definitely be a foul and cause instant reaction. The Mossad, with its tiny resources and manpower, couldn't take the risk.

'We're taking you along with us until he's safely out of the country,' Yelkov warned Falkman.

'Bigelow!' Carr said abruptly. In the excitement everyone had forgotten the nervous Dr Bigelow, or hadn't wanted to remember him. 'Where is he?' Carr asked Franz, who merely shrugged.

'He went out when Falkman arrived.' He added with new-found pride, 'He seemed rather frightened.'

Bigelow wouldn't have had time to get away from the top floor before Yelkov's men arrived, so he was still up there somewhere. Then, with terrifying certainty, Carr knew where they would find him, and how.

He signalled to Yelkov to follow and led him to the treatment room. Bigelow was there, on the table.

Of all the ghastly carnage of that night, for sheer Grand Guignol horror nothing compared with what lay on that treatment table.

20

Richard Carr pulled back the close-weave net curtains and looked out across the grey rooftops polished dark by rain. Directly in front of him in the middle distance were the tall pylons of a football ground's floodlights. Away to the right, further off, was a town hall's late Victorian red-brick tower with an imitation Houses of Parliament clockface. It was too far for him to see the time, but he didn't even care what day it was.

He turned back into the flat. For the most part, it was as functional and uninspiring a container for living as a jerry-can. The living-room and bedroom furniture was the bare minimum sub-G Plan. The only things that might be considered luxuries were a small black-and-white television set, a hi-fi system with a big rackful of tapes, and a powerful short-wave radio. It was the room of a man who didn't go out much.

The bed-linen and Carr's spare clothes were from Marks & Spencer, the kitchen utensils and crockery from Woolworth's. The kitchen cupboards contained a surprising amount of tinned and dried foods: enough to sustain a man for some months. The flat had no telephone.

Rates, electricity and service charges were all paid promptly in cash in the name of the registered lease-holder, Alan Ward. Behind the false back of a cupboard was a valid British passport in that name, and a Swiss one in the name of Alain Varenne. Both gave the bearer's profession as 'author', and both carried a photograph of Carr with receding fair hair and thick-rimmed glasses – looking startlingly different from his normal appearance. Also in the cache was a substantial amount of money in sterling, U.S. dollars, Swiss francs and German Deutschmarks. The last item was a plastic-wrapped package containing one of Carr's favourite guns, a Mauser HSc, and a couple of spare magazines.

Soon after he went into Intelligence he began to prepare his own safe house and escape route. None of Carr's colleagues or friends knew of this flat, and that was how he intended to keep it.

The few neighbours who were aware of Mr Ward's presence in the block of flats vaguely thought – when they bothered to think about him at all – that he was a Merchant Navy officer who was away for long periods, or maybe he worked on an oil-rig. Carr turned back into the flat and lay on the bed.

It was exactly a week since the night of his breakout from the *Clés d'Or.* He turned over the events of that night in his mind for the thousandth time.

Although it had seemed an age to the disoriented Carr, from the moment Yelkov and his men had arrived at the crashed cars on the mountain road until they burst into the South Wing, it was a matter of minutes, not of hours – not even half an hour.

Despite the frantic urgency of the car chase to the door of the South Wing, the only real noise of any importance had been the Mercedes' crunching into the wall by the door. Besides, the staff on the lower floors of the South Wing – the ones housing genuine patients, alcoholics and the rest – had always been strongly discouraged from being curious.

They had been warned that the patients on the top floor were often seriously disturbed, and therefore noisy. The guards in the grounds were still not suspicious; no one had called the police to the battlefield on the mountain road, so there had been no sirens or commotion.

The final stage of the South Wing operation had gone smoothly and efficiently. Gerd Schaffhauser, or Roeder, didn't resist when he was taken to the minibus. The change in him was staggering. Almost in a single moment he was transformed into an old man, frightened and anxious to please. His readiness to co-operate with Yelkov's men was almost sickening.

Falkman quietly succumbed to having his hands tied and his mouth gagged. He was a professional and didn't go in for gestures.

To Franz Schaffhauser, Yelkov said, 'You'll suffer no harm if you don't resist. But you'll have to come with us, too, until we're clear of the country. We'll release you then.'

'I shall stay with father, if you'll take me,' Franz said. 'He'll need someone.' Everyone stared at him. 'He *is* my father,' he added quietly. It sounded admirable, but Carr was as cynical as a divorce judge. He wondered if it was real compassion, or whether Franz was scenting revenge for years of studied humiliation. 'I'll stay with him to the end,' Franz said unctuously, and then everyone knew.

They prepared to leave, the gigantic Daniel a pace behind Falkman. His presence was more effective than the binding and the gag.

Halfway down the corridor Carr checked. 'Sod it,' he said, holding up his left wrist. 'I've forgotten my watch.' Before anyone could say anything, he turned and walked uncertainly but rapidly back to the office. He came out again almost immediately, strapping his watch on again. He looked a lot better.

In the minibus Carr quietly asked Yelkov, 'Where are you taking them?'

'To our place in the village, then to Paris by van, and then Israel by air.'

'Eli, will you give me time to get back to England before you release Falkman and make it public you've got Roeder?'

Yelkov turned to study him in the light from the dashboard instruments. He left all the obvious questions unasked and merely nodded.

Carr went straight through Customs and Immigration at Heathrow carrying a small overnight case Yelkov had given him so he wouldn't be conspicuous. Nobody seemed to be looking for him. Just the same, he took good care to see that he wasn't being followed. He walked quickly over to Terminal 3, caught the rail-link bus to Feltham, then took a train to Waterloo. From there he proceeded to Bank station down 'The Drain' – the Waterloo-City line – and took a ticket to Stratford. It was a little after rush-hour, but there was still a number of people about, making it easier for anyone to tail him. Carr still couldn't be sure that he wasn't being followed; he couldn't persuade himself that his uneasiness was just plain paranoia.

Before the train reached Mile End, crowds of youths and one or two older men sporting claret and pale-blue scarves and football shirts piled into the train. Some had badges with 'Super Hammers' on them; a few were more direct with simply 'West Ham'. It took no great detective powers to deduce that they were on their way to an evening match.

To be ultra-safe Carr changed on to the District Line with them at Mile End, and got out with the rest at Upton Park, successfully submerging himself in the crowd. The last time he had carried on like this was when he went to meet Mark Westbrook, Carr recalled. He hoped that wasn't an omen – then cursed himself for being superstitious. He had walked the rest of the way to his 'safe house'; and, as far as the SID, SIS and everyone else was concerned, Richard Carr disappeared from the face of the earth.

As Carr let himself into the flat, he was almost too tired, tired to the bone, to check that no one had intruded since his last call there. Almost, but not quite. The single hair was still in place between the top of the door and the door jamb, but any good break-and-enter operator would spot that and replace it on leaving. However, as Carr opened the door, he carefully studied the hinge side. The tiny length of black thread he'd put into the hinge bolt – impossible to see from the outside – fell out as he pulled back the door. The most careful burglar would miss it unless he was looking for it. The almost invisible seals on the windows were also intact.

Carr showered and found himself a pair of clean pyjamas. Before he got into bed he took a couple of Mogadon – he never, ever, took barbiturates – in case he was too exhausted to get to sleep.

When he woke again he couldn't believe his electronic watch, even though the seconds were ticking up regularly. It told him he'd been asleep for only two hours. Not until he rubbed his face and felt his growth of beard did he suspect the truth. When he pressed the date-button on his watch he discovered he'd been asleep for a full twenty-six hours. His pyjamas and bedclothes were soaked with sweat and he was thirsty as hell.

All at once the memories of his unspeakable, recurrent nightmares almost overwhelmed him.

Those same old H-certificate nightmares from the days in the South Wing: the killer whale, the rats, the falls down mineshafts . . . These were the least terrifying of them. The new ones were worse. In the first of them he kept reliving that last night when he entered the treatment room and found Bigelow on the table . . . Bigelow had committed suicide like the Swiss-born father of Jacobo Arbenz Guzman, Communist former president of Guatemala. He filled his mouth with water, put the muzzle of a .45 revolver into his pursed lips, and pulled the trigger. The shock waves of the bullet through the water blew his head off.

This is what Bigelow had done. The most unimaginative amateur psychiatrist couldn't miss the symbolism of his death. This man who had twisted and deformed men's minds had at last disintegrated his own brain on the table where his perverted techniques had been practised.

The sight that greeted Carr and Yelkov in the treatment room was foul beyond description. The walls and ceiling were splattered with blood and mucus, still trickling down the walls, leaving hardening trails on the matt grey paint.

And there was another nightmare. His murder of Karel. This time there had been little blood, no cries of agony. Yet experiencing it again in his dreams was almost unbearable.

It was during this nightmare that Carr first thought of the similarity between his own name and Karel's. In some inexplicable fashion his murder of Karel seemed to him a kind of suicide, a suicide of the spirit, because for the first time in his life he had killed not in the heat of battle, not for self-defence – he had killed for revenge, for satisfaction . . . for *pleasure.* The implications shook him beyond measure. Karel's fearful face, looking him directly in the eye, haunted him while he was awake and tortured him while he was asleep.

He couldn't accept a plea of diminished responsibility for his act. The only thing that separated him from the cold killers of Viktor Section was his present sense of guilt, but in time his capacity for remorse would atrophy if he stayed in his job. He knew that it was time for him to get out of Intelligence.

First, though, he must forget the past and work at solving the problem of who was the traitor in London. While he concentrated his mind on that, he daily put his body through punishing isometric exercises for hours on end, increasing his muscular fitness and recovery.

In the evenings he used headphones to listen to Bach on the hi-fi: the *Brandenburg Concertos, St Matthew Passion,* the *B minor Mass* and the *Art of the Fugue.* Bach's towering yet precise and mathematically pure genius helped give Carr a sense of proportion, of his own insignificance. It helped drive out some of his demons.

The key to his problem came in one great intuitive leap. From there the progression to complete understanding was logical and direct. Emotionally Carr tried to reject what he realised was the only answer – but it was inescapable.

So now he knew. Carr lay on his bed, staring at the ceiling. He felt sick to his soul because the traitor was a man that Carr admired and respected. The thought of his secret collusion with the enemy, at the cost of so many lives, made the sickness almost unbearable.

Why bother? he asked himself. *Why bloody bother? What difference will it make at the end of the day? After Philby comes Blake, after Blake comes another, and then another . . . And if it's not one of your own people's it's a friend or ally . . . So why bother?*

He pushed the question from his mind. He *had* to bother, whether he liked it or not; it was in his nature to bother; it was his raison d'être. Without that, his life was pointless and he was nothing.

So now he knew who the traitor was. But knowing was only part of it; the easiest part. The nasty part was yet to come.

A distant clock struck the hour. Carr switched on the short-wave radio. On the BBC World Service bulletin the lead story was a follow-up on the Roeder kidnapping and the forthcoming trial. Carr swung the dial and listened briefly to Moscow. There was no mention of it – nor was there on the Czech radio. There hadn't been since the story broke, days ago. As far as the Soviet-bloc countries were concerned, it might never had happened. The French were still investigating the mysterious shootings near the *Clés d'Or*. The popular theory was that it was something to do with drug smuggling. However, the police were also considering the involvement of an international gang of car thieves, because the BMW with two corpses had a false registration. Libyan radio ranted vituperously about 'Zionist gangsters', though whether this was anything to do with the Roeder business or was just the standard output, Carr couldn't tell.

He swung his legs off the bed, rubbed his face and prepared to leave the flat for the first time since he'd arrived there.

Before Carr left France, Yelkov had said to him quietly, 'You can keep in touch with me through the London office. Use the name . . . ' He thought for a moment, then with the ghost of a smile: 'Use the name Rudolf. Say you have a message for Zenda.'

The phone was answered on the first ring. Carr pushed a coin into the slot. 'This is Rudolf. Tell Zenda . . . ' He paused. 'Tell Zenda, I know who it is.'

He hung up. He had a lot to do.

21

Six weeks after Carr had been officially posted as Missing, and his personal file marked with a red tab, he walked into the entrance hall of a large Victorian block of mansion flats. It was dusk, five minutes before the main entrance would be locked and the residents had to press a button in their flats to release the remote-control lock to admit a visitor.

The flats had been built with painstaking care and some pride for solid upper-middle-class families by craftsmen who worked a twelve-hour day in constant terror of the foreman. They were designed to last as long as the British Empire, which they had already managed without difficulty, and still had more than enough life left to outlast the neighbouring concrete and plasterboard shoebox apartment buildings.

Throughout the block the rooms were large, with corniced ceilings high enough, some of the residents said, for clouds to form in winter. In truth the rooms were not ruinously expensive to heat because the solid walls returned the warmth, and kept out sound efficiently enough for anyone to practise the piano or trumpet without driving the neighbours mad. Most of the present residents were professional people, either middle-aged or retired. They all looked much alike, as did their flats, which were full of mahogany, leather, brown paintings and deep carpets.

The aged lift climbed slowly to the fourth floor, quietly

like a well-bred servant who knows better than to breathe heavily on the stairs. As soon as Carr got out, there was a soft click and the lift started discreetly down again.

He pressed the bellpush in a solid, dark door with a large polished brass knob in the middle. Above it at eye-level was an optical spyhole. Light from inside the flat flashed from it briefly as the shutter was lifted, then the tiny beam was cut off as an eye was put to the spyhole. Carr stared impassively at the tiny lens.

There came the sound of a key being turned, and the door was opened.

'Come in,' Vernon Beech said with complete composure. Carr felt he would have been equally unruffled if the man on his doorstep was a Caribbean voodoo-doctor in full ceremonials.

Though relaxing at home after a long day at the office, Beech was dressed as if he was about to leave for an audience at the Palace. Carr wondered if he was actually sewn into his immaculate white shirt and stiff collar each morning and cut out of them in the evening.

Beech led him along a sombre corridor into a living-room that could serve as an exhibit of gracious living at the Victoria and Albert Museum. Almost the only twentieth-century artefact in the room was the hi-fi system, but its slim elegance – with no vulgar brushed aluminium – blended inconspicuously with the other furnishings. The grilles over the speakers had been replaced with the same close golden lattice-work as on the corner cupboards.

Carr went straight over to one of the heavy-curtained bay windows and looked out cautiously, before sitting with his back to the exterior wall. It was no casual move: it had been carefully thought out.

'Please sit down,' Beech said a moment later, though he'd noticed Carr already was seated. In fact he was subtly underlining the point. Jolting people off-balance came to Beech as naturally as breathing, Carr knew, but he had learned a little of the technique himself. 'Can we have some music?' he asked. Beech studied him. 'Help cover our voices.

You never know who's listening,' Carr added, losing some of his advantage by explaining.

'These rooms are regularly examined by the DTMS, I assure you,' Beech said glacially. He was referring to the Diplomatic Telecommunications Maintenance Service, which checks Government offices and embassies for electronic eavesdropping devices or bugs.

'Inside *and* out?' Carr asked ingenuously.

'Oh, very well.' Beech shrugged. He sounded like someone making a concession to a retarded child.

'I don't suppose you have any brass band music? The Grimethorpe Colliery Band is very good.' Beech gave him a look that would have made a Pope feel sinful, but Carr had been through a great deal lately, and it had put protective callouses on his sensibilities. 'Act Two of *Aida* then? The Triumphal March is nice and rumpty-tumpty.'

Beech must have thought that Carr was slightly unbalanced, but after a long pause he put on the record. Carr had to admit that the equipment was superb.

'You realise, of course, that you've been posted Missing?'

'I should hope so. I'd hate to think that nobody noticed.' Carr had never spoken to Beech like this before. Probably no one had. Beech affected not to notice.

'Where have you been? What have you been doing since you left the *Clés d'Or*?'

'Hiding. Thinking. Working out who the traitor was. My problem was knowing exactly what to do, who to go to, in case I got it all wrong.'

Beech listened without interruption as Carr explained everything about the South Wing and what was done there, how he escaped and Yelkov's arrival on the scene.

'Yes, I know all about Roeder being taken,' Beech said thoughtfully. He got up and poured two glasses of a pale straw-coloured sherry that had the taste of hot sun and dry earth. He put one in front of Carr. It was an unheard-of gesture from him.

'It was a marvellous set-up, and perfectly situated,' Carr continued. 'The people who were processed in the South Wing were tricked or abducted and brought in from holidays in France, Germany, Switzerland and Italy. So, there was no suspicious pattern for a computer to pick up, of an unnaturally high proportion of VIPs going voluntarily to the *Clés d'Or*. When the subjects left, they were so "reformed" they kept quiet about it; some of them didn't even realise they had been there.'

Beech nodded. 'You said that all records of these people were destroyed before you could prevent it.

'Franz Schaffhauser incinerated them, yes.'

'Then there is still no way of telling who are the traitors amongst us,' Beech said regretfully.

'I didn't say that,' Carr said. He reached into his inside pocket and brought out a fat seven-by-five-inch envelope. He tipped the contents on to the coffee table: a pile of the plastic folders holding microfilmed records identical to the ones kept at the clinic.

The silence was deafening.

'What are *they*?' enquired Beech in a toneless voice.

'The full set of records from the South Wing.'

'Do not play games,' Beech said sharply. 'You told me that they were incinerated.'

'They were. These are copies I made the night of the party. When I was caught in front of the safe, they thought I was taking the records *out*, because that was the impression I tried to give.'

'When in fact you were putting them back after making copies.' As he spoke Beech looked like one of the carved heads on Mount Rushmore.

'Exactly. I'd already hidden this set behind the safe. In all the excitement nobody thought of looking there. On that last night, when Yelkov's little lot snatched Roeder, I went back to the office and picked them up.'

'How very resourceful of you.' By Beech's standards this was an extravagant compliment.

'As a matter of fact I delayed Yelkov's lot getting in – to give Franz a better chance to burn the originals. I know it was a risk, but I wanted us to be the only ones with a set. Of course, if they'd already found these . . .'

'Indeed.' After a pause Beech asked, 'Anyone we know among them?'

'You'll be surprised. A member of the Cabinet, a junior minister, some very heavy brass and a couple of people in the media, for a start. There's a file on Peter Harris, too, but they had to kill him to make room for me.' Carr moved the envelopes around like shuffling a pack of cards. 'There's a German cabinet minister, too, and a top-grade CIA man. No wonder Westbrook said he had doubts about some of the people at Langley. And as for *our* people . . .'

Beech had an expression of well-bred bewilderment on his face. 'Yelkov has no idea that you have these?'

Carr shook his head.

'Why not? Why didn't you tell him?'

'I'd begun to suspect that he was the traitor at this end.'

'But he's not SIS. He can't be *our* traitor.'

'He knows an awful lot of our people and our operations; even more of the Americans.'

Beech stood up and poured two more sherries with a rock-steady hand. At last he said, 'So Yelkov is the traitor.'

'Oh, no.'

'Then who is?'

'You are, Mr Beech.'

His strange, pale eyes unwavering, Beech contemplated Carr with a long stare that was hard to take. Finally he said, 'I suppose the most charitable interpretation I can make is that your recent unfortunate experiences have affected your reason. I hope that is only temporary.'

'Yes, it was "unfortunate" all right.' Carr had a bitter taste in his mouth, and he was aware that his heartbeat was quickening. 'But you can come down off that bloody great high horse, down here in the blood and shit in the gutter.' Carr felt his self-control slipping. 'And you can take that sodding superior expression off your face as well.'

'I think you had better leave,' Beech said quietly. 'I urge you to see your doctor as soon as possible. I shall pretend that this meeting never happened.' He rose.

'You'd like to pretend it hasn't happened, but you

can't. It's all over now. You're finished. *And sit down.*'

At last there was a hint of alarm on Beech's face; a hint, no more, but it was the first flicker of the needle on the seismograph. However, his voice was firm. 'I'm afraid that you'll be suspended with immediate effect. In view of your record I'll do my best to see that it is on medical grounds.'

Carr had no idea how he looked until Beech spoke again. It must have been fairly dramatic, because the imperturbable, glacial Beech said, almost conciliatorily, 'Oh, very well. If it will resolve this preposterous situation more quickly . . . ' His gaze dropped to the microfilm records on the table between them. 'You are not going to pretend that I am on that list? Because I am not.'

'How do you know? I told you: some people don't know they've been treated.'

Beech was equal to it. 'There haven't been three consecutive days in the past five years that I haven't had an official appointment or meeting. My diaries will confirm it.'

'Yes,' Carr said slowly. 'You're not a manufactured Judas made by the traitor machine, you're a natural-born one, like Philby, and Blake, and Blunt, though he was relatively a very small fish. Falkman was a bastard, but at least he was working for his own country.' The bitter taste was stronger in his mouth. 'It's odd, but Falkman was the one who blew you.' Beech stared at him. His mouth was a thin, bloodless line. Carr went on, 'When they caught me, Falkman said, "*It's a pity you found out. It would have suited us much better if you'd simply gone back and reported that the place was harmless.*" I was slow. It took a while for me to appreciate that you'd deliberately sent me there in the hope that I'd find nothing amiss. It would've been perfect if I'd come back and reported that Westbrook must have been mistaken, that the *Clés d'Or* was clean. And even if I did manage to dig up something, they could always put me through the South Wing.'

'And on the strength of that extraordinary flight of fantasy you suggest that I am disloyal?'

The King of Egypt burst into loud congratulations to

Radamès on his victory over the Ethiopians, on the hi-fi.

'Oh, there's a lot more to it than that.' He paused. 'It was weird. When they caught me they weren't at all surprised that it was *me* they caught. They were *expecting* me. And only you and I knew I was going there to investigate.'

'You are being paranoid. Or perhaps simply trying to find an excuse for your own clumsiness in being caught.'

Carr kept his temper. Having a handful of aces is a great help to equanimity. 'There's more to come. A lot more. That last night I asked Falkman for a cigarette.'

'What?'

'A cigarette. It was part of my escape plan. It surprised him – just as it surprised you then. He said, *"I thought you'd never smoked."* He was right, I hadn't. Not since school, anyway. But how the hell did he know? I'll tell you. He must have seen my personal file with *Lifetime non-smoker* on it, together with all the other little details like languages spoken and sexual preferences.'

'Perhaps.' Beech shrugged. 'But you're not thinking very clearly. It could be the KGB file on you which he'd seen. I'm sure it holds that information.'

'Now *you're* not thinking very clearly. KGB or SIS file, it doesn't matter. The point is, how did he know David Tranter was really Richard Carr? Only you and I knew that.'

Beech stirred in his chair, but said nothing.

'It gets more interesting as we go along,' Carr said. 'A long time ago . . . no, it wasn't all that long . . . Eli Yelkov asked me to check Dr Roeder in our computer. When I looked him up, I found someone had tried to fudge the records, to cover any possible trail that might lead to Dr Gerd Schaffhauser.'

Beech spoke at last. 'The computer always registers who it is who makes an entry or deletion, or retrieves any information.'

Carr nodded. 'You have to put in your personal authority code-number to operate it. The deletions to the Roeder records were made on Streeter's authority. My brother-in-law,' Carr added nastily, remembering how Beech had stuck this particular dart in when Carr originally reported his suspicions of Streeter.

'So?'

'The deletions were bodged, done by somebody who didn't know how to work the computer properly. Streeter is an expert, the best. Not like you. Somebody used Streeter's code to operate it – rather clumsily.'

'It could be anyone.'

'No. I shouldn't think there are four people apart from Streeter himself who know his code. And you're one of them.'

Beech had recovered much of his composure. 'I hope for your sake that you haven't told this ludicrously circumstantial story to anyone else.'

Carr wasn't going to be caught with that one. 'I haven't finished. And talking of Streeter, I was stupid to suspect him. When I was on the Vienna run, after the Comenius people were all blown, the man who pretended to be our contact there didn't know that I wasn't from the Birdcage. He thought I was regular SIS from Waterloo. So it couldn't possibly have been Streeter who tipped them off.'

'*I* know that you aren't regular SIS,' Beech said calmly.

'Yes. But I left London in a hurry. There wasn't time for you to contact the opposition by the time you'd learned that I'd gone. It was the same with the Kolunin operation Streeter sent us on. Although the opposition knew Geoffrey Haynes and I were going to meet Desvins in Geneva for something important, they didn't know what that important something was. They didn't know it was to go with him to bring out Dr Kolunin from Vienna. Kolunin wasn't picked up until much later, after they'd had time to work on Desvins. So that was the second leak that couldn't have been Streeter.'

'I really fail to see how you connect me with all this,' Beech said.

'I'm just about to do it,' Carr said coldly. The thought of young Haynes lying dead on that dry scrubland near Marseille made him angry again. 'Remember when I took you to lunch in the Mini?'

'I'm afraid I do. It wasn't the sort of lunch one would readily forget.' Beech's tongue hadn't lost its edge.

'And the lorry that tried to run us down?'

'Yes.'

'At the time we were into all that mental telepathy stuff, and I thought the driver was reading my mind as he tried to run us down. But it wasn't that at all. He was trying to *miss* us by inches. The trouble was I was too quick for him, and nearly got us killed by being so bloody clever. All he was trying to do was scare the shit out of us.' Carr looked at Beech with admiration. 'That was a great performance you gave. Even though it nearly went all wrong, you didn't forget your lines. I said *"He tried to kill us"*; and you said *"Not us. Me. That's not the first attempt. That's the third since you first came to see me."* That's right, isn't it?'

'Or words substantially to that effect, yes,' Beech agreed, using a lawyer's form of words. 'I don't necessarily agree that it wasn't an attempt to commit murder, but is it important whether the driver meant to kill or merely frighten us?'

'No. But what *is* important is how he knew we would be there, and in that particular car, and at that very moment? Because nobody but me knew where we were going when I picked you up at the Marble Arch garage.'

Beech looked suddenly wary. 'We could have been followed.'

'Not without my noticing it. I've been too long in the field. As soon as we got to the restaurant, you left me for a while. It was to telephone, wasn't it? To fix up the "murder attempt" that would convince me you were on our side.'

The record came to an end. In the unexpected silence the measured ticking of a grandfather clock somewhere sounded very loud.

'Nothing to say?' Carr said. He was suddenly very tired now that it was nearly all over.

'Not to you.'

For the first time Carr thought he detected a hint of respect in Beech's regard. That, and something else. 'I still haven't finished,' Carr said. 'It hasn't taken me all this time to work things out. I did that soon after I got back. Since then you've been watched very carefully – you, and all the people on these lists.' He touched the microfilmed records. 'It's been most instructive, and led us to some interesting contacts. Two of them have been turned and we're using them for disinformation. The others will be arrested or pushed out of the country as soon as they're no longer any use to us.'

There was no mistaking Beech's sense of strain now. Unaccountably Carr was almost sorry for Beech, and he was annoyed with himself for it, but the feeling soon passed.

With perceptible desperation Beech said, 'You forgot I have the Prime Minister's total confidence.'

'Not any longer. You haven't had it for weeks,' came a voice from behind Beech. He turned slowly: not the slowness of self-control and confidence. It was the sort of exhaustion that strikes footballers when they know the game is lost, and there is still five minutes to play; when the winner of the Marathon has crossed the line but the second man still has a lap of the stadium to cover.

Streeter stood in the doorway. He entered the room, followed by Dr Leo Pattman, the SIS medical adviser and fixer. There were a couple of large men who Carr recognised as SIS security officers, but he knew they would be unnecessary: Beech was not a physical man. It all reminded Carr of the day of Roger Chapman's 'suicide' at his home. There was a significant difference this time, though. William Parker, the senior SIS man Carr had consulted about Section E, was with the group. More than ever he looked like an undertaker who buried nothing less than Grand Dukes. To round off the group there was an SIS man dressed in a policeman's uniform to reassure any of the public who might see the strange gang.

'That's why I asked for some music,' Carr explained to Beech, indicating the arrivals. 'So you wouldn't hear them get in.'

'The P.M. has known about you for a long time now,' Streeter continued to Beech. 'Mind you, you'll be in the next

Honours List. We don't want anyone thinking our Intelligence people are unreliable. It'll be for your devoted service and the years of overwork which have caused your premature retirement on medical grounds.'

'A heart attack?' asked Beech.

'Oh good heavens no,' Parker said. 'That would be so obvious. No, your breakdown isn't physical. You're going to Grangewood.'

There was a heavy silence. Everyone in that room knew that Grangewood was a very special private mental hospital in the Lake District. It was comfortable to the point of luxury, and more secure than Alcatraz. The only trouble was it didn't have a very good record of cures. Nobody there had ever recovered and been discharged.

Dr Pattman said in a formal voice, 'I am here to certify the need for your emergency commital. It is for your own wellbeing and safety.'

'That is true enough,' Beech said with a ghost of a smile. In the face of inevitability he was recovering his style. 'May I pack a few bags?' he asked. Not one bag, but a few bags, Carr noted wryly. 'And I take it I shall have a private room.'

'Rely on it,' Parker said.

'And in that case you'll have no objection to my having some of my things' – he gestured to the furnishings – 'sent up.'

'Anything reasonable,' Streeter said.

'And at Government expense,' Parker added. 'Now, if you'd like to get on with your packing, some of us will give you a hand.'

Streeter stayed behind in the room with Carr. For once his eyes seemed wide apart in his narrow Modigliani face. He lit one of his large cigars and puffed on it with rare enjoyment.

Carr said, 'That's it. I've had it. I'm sending in my resignation. I'm quitting,' he added superfluously.

'You can't,' said Streeter imperturbably.

'Watch me.'

*

Carr glanced at the newspaper. Streeter had been as good as his word; or, more accurately, the Prime Minister had. Beech was in the Birthday Honours List. A couple of paragraphs in the accompanying background story paid tribute to his work for the Security Services.

The front page of the newspaper carried the headline 'Cabinet Re-Shuffle Shock'. A minister and a junior minister were resigning because of ill-health, the writer said, and asked the question, 'Do we ask too much of our MPs?' On the leader page the first editorial went on at great length about the strains of public life, without actually saying anything.

The phone rang. 'Answer that,' Carr said. Peg-the-Legs leant across him to reach for the phone on the other side of the bed, pressing her naked breast on his diaphragm.

'Hello,' she said. Then, 'It's for you.' This was hardly surprising, since it was Carr's flat. He took the phone. It was Streeter calling.

'Was that Elizabeth Hughes?' he asked.

'Yes.'

'I thought I recognised the voice. I met her at the practice studio. She may know me as Superintendent Walker of the Special Branch.'

'She wouldn't want to know you if you were really Santa Claus.'

'You sound sharp, Richard. Was my phone call *interruptus coitus*?'

'What do you want?'

'Ready to come back to work?'

'Get stuffed,' Carr said forcibly.

'Good idea,' Peg-the-Legs said. 'Now?'

'I've got Beech's old job,' Streeter said. 'I want you to take over from me at Kensington.'

Carr hesitated. At the other end Streeter registered the hesitation.

'Give me a ring when you've had a decent rest. You've earned it. We'll talk things over when you're ready.'

'No! I told you: I'm quitting.'

'Fair enough,' Streeter said mildly. 'Got anything fixed up? What are you going to do for a living?'

Carr didn't speak.

After a long silence Streeter put the phone down without saying any more. He was grinning.

FICTION

HORROR/OCCULT/NASTY

☐ The Howling	Gary Brandner	85p
☐ Return of the Howling	Gary Brandner	95p
☐ Dying Light	Evan Chandler	85p
☐ Curse	Daniel Farson	95p
☐ Trance	Joy Fielding	90p
☐ The Janissary	Alan Lloyd Gelb	95p
☐ Rattlers	Joseph L. Gilmore	85p
☐ Slither	John Halkin	95p
☐ Devil's Coach-Horse	Richard Lewis	85p
☐ Spiders	Richard Lewis	80p
☐ Poe Must Die	Marc Olden	£1.00
☐ The Spirit	Thomas Page	£1.00
☐ The Force	Alan Radnor	90p
☐ Bloodthirst	Mark Ronson	90p
☐ Ghoul	Mark Ronson	95p
☐ Ogre	Mark Ronson	80p
☐ Return of the Living Dead	John Russo	80p
☐ The Scourge	Nick Sharman	£1.00
☐ Deathbell	Guy N. Smith	95p
☐ The Specialist	Jasper Smith	85p

SCIENCE FICTION

☐ The Mind Thing	Fredric Brown	90p
☐ Strangers	Gardner Dozois	95p
☐ Project Barrier	Daniel F. Galouye	80p
☐ Beyond the Barrier	Damon Knight	80p
☐ Clash by Night	Henry Kuttner	95p
☐ Fury	Henry Kuttner	80p
☐ Mutant	Henry Kuttner	90p
☐ Drinking Sapphire Wine	Tanith Lee	£1.25
☐ Journey	Marta Randall	£1.00
☐ The Lion Game	James H. Schmitz	70p
☐ The Seed of Earth	Robert Silverberg	80p
☐ The Silent Invaders	Robert Silverberg	80p
☐ City of the Sun	Brian M. Stableford	85p
☐ Critical Threshold	Brian M. Stableford	75p
☐ The Florians	Brian M. Stableford	80p
☐ Wildeblood's Empire	Brian M. Stableford	80p
☐ A Touch of Strange	Theodore Sturgeon	85p

HAMLYN WHODUNNITS

☐ The Worm of Death	Nicholas Blake	95p
☐ The Judas Pair	Jonathan Gash	95p
☐ There Came Both Mist and Snow	Michael Innes	95p
☐ The Siamese Twin Mystery	Ellery Queen	95p

GENERAL

☐ Stand on It	Stroker Ace	95p
☐ Chains	Justin Adams	£1.25
☐ The Master Mechanic	I. G. Broat	£1.50
☐ Wyndward Passion	Norman Daniels	£1.35
☐ Abingdon's	Michael French	£1.25
☐ The Moviola Man	Bill and Colleen Mahan	£1.25
☐ Running Scared	Gregory Mcdonald	85p
☐ Gossip	Marc Olden	£1.25
☐ The Sounds of Silence	Judith Richards	£1.00
☐ Summer Lightning	Judith Richards	£1.00
☐ The Hamptons	Charles Rigdon	£1.35
☐ The Affair of Nina B.	Simmel	95p
☐ The Berlin Connection	Simmel	£1.50
☐ The Cain Conspiracy	Simmel	£1.20
☐ Double Agent—Triple Cross	Simmel	£1.35
☐ Celestial Navigation	Anne Tyler	£1.00
☐ Earthly Possessions	Anne Tyler	95p
☐ Searching for Caleb	Anne Tyler	£1.00

NON-FICTION

GENERAL

☐ Guide to the Channel Islands	J. Anderson & E. Swinglehurst	90p
☐ The Complete Traveller	Joan Bakewell	£1.95
☐ Time Out London Shopping Guide	Lindsey Bareham	£1.50
☐ World War 3	Edited by Shelford Bidwell	£1.25
☐ The Black Angels	Rupert Butler	£1.35
☐ Hand of Steel	Rupert Butler	£1.35
☐ A Walk Around the Lakes	Hunter Davies	£1.50
☐ Truly Murderous	John Dunning	95p
☐ In Praise of Younger Men	Sandy Fawkes	85p
☐ Hitler's Secret Life	Glenn B. Infield	£1.50
☐ Wing Leader	Johnnie Johnson	£1.25
☐ Me, to Name but a Few	Spike Mullins	£1.00
☐ Our Future: Dr. Magnus Pyke Predicts		95p
☐ The Devil's Bedside Book	Leonard Rossiter	85p
☐ Barbara Windsor's Book of Boobs	Barbara Windsor	£1.50

BIOGRAPHY/AUTOBIOGRAPHY

☐ Go-Boy	Roger Caron	£1.25
☐ The Queen Mother Herself	Helen Cathcart	£1.25
☐ George Stephenson	Hunter Davies	£1.50
☐ The Queen's Children	Donald Edgar	£1.25
☐ Prince Regent	Harry Edgington	95p
☐ All of Me	Rose Neighbour	£1.00
☐ Tell Me Who I Am Before I Die	C. Peters with T. Schwarz	£1.00
☐ Boney M	J. Shearlaw and D. Brown	90p
☐ Kiss	John Swenson	90p

HEALTH/SELF-HELP/POCKET HEALTH GUIDES

☐ Pulling Your Own Strings	Dr. Wayne W. Dyer	95p
☐ The Pick of Woman's Own Diets	Jo Foley	95p
☐ Woman X Two	Mary Kenny	90p
☐ Cystitis: A Complete Self-help Guide	Angela Kilmartin	£1.00
☐ The Stress Factor	Donald Norfolk	90p
☐ Fat is a Feminist Issue	Susie Orbach	85p
☐ Related to Sex	Claire Rayner	£1.25
☐ The Working Woman's Body Book	L. Rowen with B. Winkler	95p
☐ Woman's Own Birth Control	Dr. Michael Smith	£1.25
☐ Allergies	Robert Eagle	65p
☐ Arthritis and Rheumatism	Dr. Luke Fernandes	65p
☐ Back Pain	Dr. Paul Dudley	65p
☐ Pre-Menstrual Tension	June Clark	65p
☐ Migraine	Dr. Finlay Campbell	65p
☐ Skin Troubles	Deanna Wilson	65p

REFERENCE

☐ What's Wrong with your Pet?	Hugo Kerr	95p
☐ You *Can* Train Your Cat	Jo and Paul Loeb	£1.50
☐ Caring for Cats and Kittens	John Montgomery	95p
☐ The Oscar Movies from A-Z	Roy Pickard	£1.25
☐ Questions of Law	Bill Thomas	95p
☐ The Hamlyn Book of Amazing Information		80p
☐ The Hamlyn Family Medical Dictionary		£2.50

GAMES & PASTIMES

☐ The Hamlyn Book of Brainteasers and Mindbenders	Ben Hamilton	85p
☐ The Hamlyn Book of Crosswords Books 1, 2, 3, and 4		60p
☐ The Hamlyn Book of Crosswords 5		70p
☐ The Hamlyn Book of Wordways 1		75p
☐ The Hamlyn Family Quiz Book		85p

Also in Hamlyn Paperbacks

Gregory Mcdonald

FLYNN

A moonlight night – a sudden explosion – and burning people fall out of the sky.

Flynn is a highly unusual cop – smart and tough, but witty and gentle too – and he now has 118 murders to solve.

When the Boeing 707 explodes – and Flynn sees it drop into Boston harbour from his front window – he is called in to investigate.

Was it political sabotage (an Arab minister was on board), or mass murder (the Human Surplus League are pledged to solve over-population by wholesale slaughter), or just plain murder? There is no shortage of suspects: the judge with the new young wife who has taken out a huge life-insurance policy . . . the great English actor who has just stormed out of the first night of *Hamlet* . . . the young boxing champion with underworld connections . . .

It takes all Flynn's wit and brilliance to uncover the surprise solution. And he does it in a manner as stylish and outrageous as would do credit to his friend Fletch.

'Witty, intriguing and superb entertainment' – *Yorkshire Post*

'Flynn is one of the smartest, gentlest, most sarcastic cops you will ever meet' – *The New York Times*

UK 95p

0 600 33675 1